FALL FROM SNOWBIRD MOUNTAIN

C.S. Devereaux

Acknowledgments

Lynn Zeitouni, Jason Hyde's great granddaughter, asked me to write about her ancestors. I took on her project, and after years of research and conversations with his descendants in Robbinsville, North Carolina, Jason's story has been told.

Thank you to Jumpmaster Press, and their editors, for all you've done for me during this process. Thank you to my husband, Tom, for his patience, his encouragement, and for believing in me. I love you more than you can know. Thank you to the North Georgia Writers Group for their critiquing skills, Natalie Hanemann for her guidance during creative development, and to my beta readers for their feedback and honest evaluation.

A special thank you goes to Robbinsville residents, Leaudenia King, Edd Satterfield, Sheriff James Hyde, and Betty Hooper Carpenter for sharing their carefully compiled family research, and to Marshall McClung for meeting with me. Your contributions proved invaluable.

Historical documents and resources referenced as foundation material include *Snowbird Cherokees, People of Persistence*, Sharlotte Neely, *Storm in the Mountains: Thomas's Confederate Legion of Cherokee Indians and Mountaineers*, Vernon H. Crowe, *The Heart of Confederate Appalachia, Western North Carolina in the Civil War*, John C. Inscoe & Gordon B. McKinney, *Graham County Area History*, Tom Livingston, contributing writer, *The Graham Star* newspaper, *Mountain People, Mountain Places,* Marshall McClung, *A Counterfeiter's Glossary*, U.S. Secret Service, and *Catching Counterfeiters*, U.S. Marshall's Service.

FALL FROM SNOWBIRD MOUNTAIN is a work of historical fiction based on real and imagined events in the life of North Carolina native, Jason Hyde.

Lieutenant Jason Stephen Hyde 1829-1907

BOOK I

The War Years
1861 - 1865

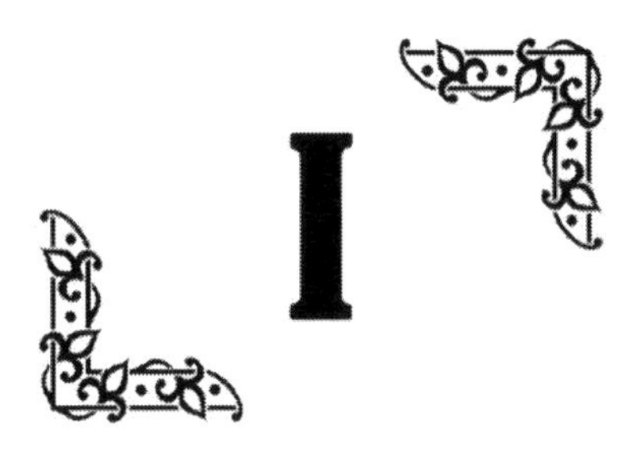

Buffalo Town, North Carolina
June 1829

Cornwoman, a *tsili*—apprentice medicine woman—performed her first birthing in a roughhewn Nantahala Forest cabin. That newborn child was Jason Hyde. Cornwoman's mother, Galila-hi, chief medicine woman to the Snowbird Indian tribe, opened the cabin door and her young apprentice stepped into the starry night, a tiny bundle swaddled in her arms. She held the infant aloft and sang:

Hear me, Orion, ghost of the shimmering summer dawn. Bless this child with health and strength. Sheath him in your protective mantle, O Mighty Hunter. And may the rainbow always touch his shoulder.

Orion smiled upon them and their spirits became forever connected.

Like everybody in the mountains, Jason grew up to be a farmer and family man. Unlike anybody else, he also became a teacher, a soldier, a lawman—and a criminal.

In time, Cornwoman's people bestowed upon her the name, Ama, beloved mother, a high honor. She healed them. They came to her in times of spiritual need. She knew their histories. But Jason's history perplexed her.

"Now, I am old," Cornwoman said. "I have seen all kinds of misery these many years. But nothing hurts like holding back an untold tale. Trouble is, you got to wait until the tale wants telling, and the world is ready to listen."

Jason Hyde's story is such a one.

1

Buncombe County Courthouse, Asheville North Carolina
November 1873

Jason Hyde followed the bailiff from the prisoners' hold, through the portico, up the stairs, and into the courtroom past the table bristling with counselors and their lackeys. Around him sat the spectators; a flurry of faces, their drone rising above the attorneys' murmurings. The hubbub hummed with the meanness of bees in honeysuckle. Heads turned, eyes censured.

Jason ducked his head and stared at his boots, counting steps to the defendant's box. He clasped his hands to stop their trembling. It seemed all of Asheville had turned out. Slagging criminals happened to be this town's favorite pastime.

How did it come to this? He dared to remember, a distraction more than last-gasp moralizing. *It began with the war—that damnable war—eleven, maybe twelve, years ago. Those days were hellacious. But I found a way through it. The only way.*

Heart thundering, he stole a peek at the courtroom—the portraits and pungent odor of nervous sweat, familiar. *The McNeil boy shot me in this room. I survived. Will I survive this?* He ventured a side-eyed scrutiny first of his defense lawyers, then the prosecutors.

Question is, how much do they know?

12 Years Earlier
East Buffalo, North Carolina
October 1861

At dawn, on a chill October morning, Jason leaned on the bedroom window frame of his homestead, slope-shouldered, forlorn, searching the sky for answers. A setting gibbous moon outlined the angles of his lean body, making him look taller than his six-foot stature. Finding no solutions in the stars, he dropped the worn curtain panel and it fell into place. Behind him, Nancy's even breathing hovered above the hush.

He pulled a pair of old dungarees over his patched long johns, slipped on a frayed, flannel shirt, and slid suspenders over his arms. Scooping a thin book and a metal box from the top of the chifforobe, he tucked them under his arm, and tiptoed down the steps to the gathering room.

He set the items on the pinewood dining table—rubbed smooth by thirty years of hot meals and family meetings—stoked the fire, put on a pot of what passed for coffee, and sat down. His accounting ledger open in front of him, he placed a sharpened pencil beside it, unlocked the safe-box, took out a small stack of bills and coins and set them aside. He labeled each of two envelopes in fine script, *Taxes* and *Food*, and arranged them on either side of the book. Finally, he removed yesterday's letter from its envelope, unfolded it, and held it closer to the flame, washing the creamy parchment with golden light. He read the words again:

PROPERTY TAX NOTICE. Delinquent 180 Days. Delinquent had been stamped in red, and 180 Days had been scribed in purple ink. The past due amount was irrelevant; he didn't have it, regardless.

Brows knit, he separated the coins from the bills, placing each denomination one next to the other in a neat row, and recorded the total in his ledger: Ten dollars short covering taxes. Two dollars for food, five pennies for a peppermint stick for each child.

He held a Confederate banknote to the firelight, and studied it. *Peterson's Brass Works* etched across the top, *Due to Bearer, One Dollar* under it. He chose another, *Greenville and Columbia Railroad Company*; and another, *Bank of Savannah, Georgia.* All odd denominations and distinct qualities of workmanship. "Look at me. I'm a stone-broke schoolteacher with no school and nobody to teach. If I had me a ream of paper, a bit of ink, and a whole lotta gumption, my troubles would be over—*Ha!*" He scoffed at the absurdity of the thought.

Behind him, a step screaked. He stuffed money into the respective envelopes and slipped them into his pocket.

Nancy crossed the room, pinning her dark brown locks into a twist at the back of her head. She kissed Jason's forehead, ran rough, work-worn fingers through his hair, and shuffled to the potbelly stove. "Frettin' again?"

"Nothing to concern yourself over."

Her brown eyes settled on him. "Wish you'd talk about it. Might help."

He responded with rocklike silence.

Nancy sighed. "You made coffee?"

"It's weak."

"It'll be fine." She poured herself a cup, took a sip, wrinkled her nose, and set the drink aside. Opening the grain bin, she frowned. "We need flour and cornmeal. Ain't enough to feed us another day."

His shoulders slumped lower. "I'll run into town after breakfast." He reached for the two packets, removed the bills from the *Tax* envelope, and stuffed them in the *Food* envelope.

His sons, Will, and Johnny, scampered down the steps. "Mornin', Daddy!"

"Morning. After you boys eat, how d'you all like to go with me into Fort Montgomery?" He'd ask his daughters next time.

"Would we ever!" Will exclaimed. He grabbed his threadbare jacket from the hook beside the front door, tossed the other to his younger brother, and they scurried outside. They completed their morning chores in record time.

Jason hitched the horses to the wagon, gazed skyward at the flat, gray overcast, and checked the woolen blankets and oil-cloth coverings he kept under the seat. Nancy had promised to pack a basket with day-old cornpone and leftover bacon slices. Once loaded for a journey that far, they wouldn't return before dark.

Fort Montgomery, North Carolina

At the door, Jason scanned Cooper's General Store. Stacked floor to ceiling with produce, dried meats, canned goods, sacks of grain, farming implements, and more. Almost empty of customers. He noted the omnipresent woodstove checkers-players were missing. Their absence eased his mind, allowing him to appreciate the warmth inside. He usually enjoyed the camaraderie of neighbors, but today he anticipated an unpleasant conversation with the store's owner, Tom Cooper.

"Sorry, Jace, can't extend your credit," Cooper said. "You owe too much. I'll sell you the sack of cornmeal, coffee, and penny candies. Newspaper's free. A week old, ain't worth nothing, anyway."

Mrs. Cooper finished showing a customer a bolt of fabric and joined them. "Come back for the flour when you got cash, Mr. Hyde—at least half what you owe." Ever the tough negotiator, today was no exception. "You're a respected man, but we got a business to run."

"Please, ma'am, my family's gotta eat," he said in a low voice. He stole a glance at his sons. They appeared absorbed with Cooper's selection of jackknives on the other side of the store.

An old floorboard creaked, and Joel Lovin, a friend and neighbor, stepped from behind a display and set his purchases on the counter next to Jason's.

"Give him a barrel of flour, Tom. I'll cover it."

Jason looked away, feeling heat rise to his face.

"Mr. Lovin, flour's a hundred and twenty dollars a barrel!" Mrs. Cooper exclaimed.

"I said I'll cover it." Joel opened his money purse and plunked down two fifties and a twenty. Jason noticed his pouch looked new, as did his leather jacket.

"And fifty cents," she added.

Lovin tossed a silver, half-dollar coin onto the counter. She snatched the lot of it and whisked it into the cash register.

"Joel, I–I can't let you do that. I can't repay you." Humiliated, Jason's cheeks flushed.

Lovin gripped him by the elbow and led him to a far corner, away from prying ears. "We been friends a long time, you and I. You need help. I'd like to offer it to you."

"Don't belittle me with handouts. I couldn't bear your pity."

"You'll pay me back."

Jason's shame deepened. "I told you, I'm not good for it."

"Listen to me and you will be. My money worries are behind me thanks to a certain enterprise I got into. My associates and I—you know 'em, Adam Cable and Jacob Rose—we'd welcome a right smart fella like you into our partnership."

Jason swallowed hard. "All I want is to pay my debts."

"Jace, I'm handing you a way to do that, and then some." Joel gazed over Jason's shoulder. "Think about your boys. How old are they now?"

"Eight and ten."

"And growing fast. You got a big family to feed and clothe."

"True enough."

"I'm offering you a chance to give 'em better'n what they got."

Jason studied him: his eyes, the set of his mouth, the furrows in his brow. A seed of hope sprouted. "Your, um, *enterprise* sounds fine as frog's hair. What's the catch?"

"No catch. And it's easy."

Johnny tugged on Jason's arm. "Come on, Daddy. We're loaded up and I'm dog-hungry."

"In a minute, Son, I'm finishing some business with Mr. Lovin." Jason hesitated, wanting to believe in Providence, yet unsure he trusted it. "Sure, I guess. Count me in."

"Good man." Joel lowered his voice. "Meet us Thursday night at Miz Penley's Boarding House, six o'clock sharp. The desk clerk will direct you from there."

"Daddy, it's cold!" Will called from the door.

Jason hurried to their wagon, his heart pounding. He already regretted his decision. However, by the time he rounded the last bend in the muddy road toward home, he had settled his inner turmoil. *Come on, Jace, take the bull by the horns. Least you can do is find out what this is about—right?*

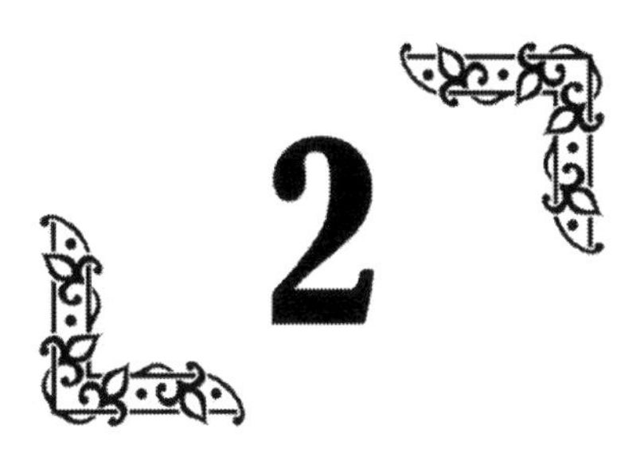

Inside the cabin, Nancy busied herself in a cozy corner of the gathering room that served as a kitchen while her two older daughters assisted with the evening meal. "Lord have mercy, what a dreary afternoon! I hope your daddy and the boys are all right. Rain like this can wash the roads out, quick."

Her middle daughter, Sarah, peered out the window. "Mama, there's five men headed to our gate. They got no horses." Old enough at twelve to be alert, she possessed a watchful curiosity.

Nancy glanced over her shoulder, then went back to cutting carrots for a pot of soup. "Come away from the window, Sarah. Them's most likely deserters. Outliers looking for a fire and a hot meal."

Mary took her younger sister's place behind the curtain. "They don't look like deserters. Plain clothes, full knapsacks slung about their shoulders. They're carrying a couple of guns apiece. Mama, they're standing at the gate like they're waiting for something."

"Well then, they ain't bushwhackers. Otherwise, they'd break down our door." Nancy lifted the rifle down from its rack over the door, loaded it, and handed it to Mary. "Use it if you have to. I'm gonna see what they want. Sarah, take Janie upstairs and stay there." She pulled on her yard boots, waited until Mary extinguished the lantern, closed the door behind her, and sloshed through the mud to the front gate.

She studied each stranger as she approached. They looked tired. Their clothing, soaked through but not tattered; their boots, not Army-issued. The rangiest, a broad-shouldered man, held a commanding air. He wore a stylish, black gambler's hat. A silk brocade vest visible under his greatcoat lent him the affectation of a gentleman. They lacked the haunted look common to shellshocked fighting men; their eyes were neither those of killers nor desperate men.

"Evening, ma'am." The tallest one tipped his hat, shedding a cascade of raindrops. "We need a place to settle back for the night."

"Y'all are welcome to warm yourselves by our fire. I'll give you some food, but you can't stay, we got no room. Good neighbors live up the road apiece. They might could accommodate you."

"Much obliged, ma'am." He opened the gate and pushed past her. The five men tromped to the cabin and stepped onto the porch, trailing muddy footprints across it.

"Wait —" A flutter of fear washed over her and she took off after them.

The tallest man scuffled through the door, trailed by his associates. From within the shadowy interior, a rifle cocked.

"Hold it right there, misters. One more step and I'll pump you full of shot."

Nancy heard the fire in Mary's voice through the open door and ran faster—*Oh my goodness, she ain't bluffing! That child is brave for fourteen.*

The tall man's companions backed onto the porch, hands raised.

"Put your weapons down, nice and easy, y'hear?"

"You ain't gonna let her talk to us like that, are you?" the man next to the tall one said.

"Do what she says and shut up," he replied. They laid down their guns but held their satchels tight.

Nancy caught up to them, and nudged them aside. "It's all right, Mary. I told 'em they could come in. You men take off them muddy boots. Put 'em on the porch—Go on, do as I say."

"That's not how I saw it, Mama. They shoved you out of their way."

"I said it's all right. Now lower the gun 'fore somebody gets hurt. Light a lantern and throw another log on the fire. These men'll join us for supper." Nancy tossed a quick glance at the leader then turned her attention back to Mary. "Your daddy'll be home soon. He'll sort out the rest. Till then, help me in the kitchen."

Despite trembling hands, she finished assembling the pot of carrot and potato soup and warmed up cornbread and milk while the strangers gathered round the big pine fire. Daylight faded into darkness, and they lit lanterns. An uncomfortable silence prevailed, broken only by the hissing and popping of burning logs, and the echo of rattling pots and pans.

Hearing Jason's wagon rattle up Hyde Road and halt at the front gate, Nancy threw on a shawl, opened the door of the cabin, and hurried toward him.

"We have unexpected guests," she whispered in a grim voice.

Jason thought of the chickens he'd stolen the week before; his stomach tightened. "Deputies?"

She tossed him a quizzical look. "They ain't dressed like lawmen. See for yourself."

He turned to his sons. "Boys, put up the horses and empty the wagon. Don't talk to those men when you come in. We dunno who they are."

Jason sat at the dinner table, watching the visitors scarf down their food. Will and Johnny—like their parents—never took their eyes off them. The girls concentrated on their meal and watched the guests through their eyelashes. The sound of tin utensils against crockery plates accented the tension.

"Where you fellas come from?" Jason asked.

The visitors exchanged glances, but remained silent.

"Not much of anywhere," the tall man finally said.

"Where you headed?"

"No place in particular," he said after a spoonful of soup.

"You got names?" Jason leaned on his elbows, feeling his impatience grow.

The man set his spoon on his plate, stuffed a bite of cornbread in his mouth and chewed, holding Jason's eyes with his own. He swallowed, then dabbed at his lips with his napkin. "None as you need to know. I hope that's all the grilling you plan on doing, brother, because that's all I plan on saying."

Jason narrowed his eyes. His dislike of these men grew with each word that passed between them.

After supper, while Nancy and Mary cleaned up the dishes, Jason instructed the younger children to make themselves scarce upstairs.

The visitors lounged around the fire. Jason kept an eye trained on his guests while he read the week-old *Western Democrat* newspaper. The snap and crackle of the flames and rhythmic tick-tock of the mantel clock harmonized with the crinkle of newsprint.

Jason broke the quiet. "Y'all seen much fighting where you come from?"

The tall man hesitated. "Some. South's outnumbered and outmatched. We win one, lose two. May I ask, why aren't you signed up? You look to be of conscription age."

"I got no stake in this fight. Don't affect me one way or t'other." He shook a crease from his paper and folded it.

"You mean, because you don't own slaves, there's no reason for you to risk your life for either their continued bondage or their freedom?"

The stranger's needling irritated him. "This mess took my livelihood away. I want no part of it."

"You may not have a choice but to become involved. I dare say, this war's going to affect every one of us before it's finished."

"This war!" The contempt in Jason's voice made his feelings clear. "I'm a thirty-two-year-old, able-bodied man who can't make a living cause of this war. The world's gone to hell and back."

The stranger dismissed Jason's reply with a wave of his hand, cast a fleeting glance at his sidekicks, and faced Jason again. "Sir, it's been a long day. We'd be much obliged if we could stretch out on the floor in here and you leave us be. We'll be on our way at sunup."

"I reckon we all ought to turn in. Nance, get these men some blankets."

After breakfast, the aroma of eggs and fatback permeated the house. The tall man soaked up the remaining redeye gravy with the final biscuit. "Oconoluftee River near here?" he asked, breaking the quiet.

"Oconoluftee's due east, but it's a far piece," Jason replied. "If that's where you're headed, don't. That river twists and turns through steep mountain country. Safest way outta here is to head northeast to Asheville."

The tall man chewed while he scrutinized his host, then swallowed. “Seems you know these parts pretty good. Supposing we wanted to go that way, I’m willing to bet you’d be the man to get us there.”

“I reckon.” *Where is he going with this?*

“How about you be our guide?”

“Your guide?” Jason flicked his eyes at his wife.

The tall one looked at her—jaws clinched; expression flat. “We won’t hurt you. You’ve been very accommodating.”

Jason drummed his fingers on the table. “I’ll draw you a map.”

“Take us. We’ll pay you well, cash money.”

Jason’s ears pricked up at the man’s last words. “I’ll take you to Stump Ford Trail.” Nancy abruptly stood and left the room. “You’re still gonna need a map. Mary, bring me paper and a pencil.” He looked at his guests. “Gotta say, you picked a hell of a place to tramp through.”

Jason drew directions from Stump Ford to the Tuckaseegee River, with further instructions to follow the vast network of creeks that flowed east. “Follow Scott Creek through Balsam Gap till you reach the Cherokee Broad River. Some call it French Broad. You’re within a few miles of Asheville when you get there. Folks in Charleston and Sylva are likely to help you—the Cherokee in Quallatown, too. They’re friendly, by the way—but lay low. There’s nowhere to go that y’all won’t stand out like a handful of sore thumbs. In Asheville, you can get food and shelter without drawing attention to yourselves. Horses, too, need be.

“Now listen to me. Stay off the main roads. There’s bushwhackers. Deserters desperate for a meal. Home Guard’s rounding up outliers. They won’t make no never mind about y’all. Any of ’em would kill you for whatever’s in those knapsacks of yours.”

They held their gear closer and grasped the butts of their revolvers. “How do you know we’re not outliers, or any of those others?” the leader asked.

Jason looked him square in the eyes. “I read people about as good as I read the sky, land, and any animal you’d care to name.”

One man half-pulled his gun from its holster. Their leader motioned for him to stand down. “That so? What do you think we’re about?”

"Never mind that. Since you picked my home to bed down, I'll help you get where you're going. Do what I say, you might reach Asheville alive."

"Fair enough." The tension eased. Three of the tall man's companions moved to the fireplace to warm their hands.

Jason spied Nancy skulking in the corner, arms folded, dark eyes narrowed. He rose from the table, crossed the room, and took her aside.

"What are you doing?" Nancy spat her words under her breath. "Those men could murder you and leave you for dead out there."

"They're not killers."

"What's come over you?" Nancy snapped. "Just give 'em the map and send 'em on."

"They found their way here, and I aim on helping 'em. Don't be mad. I'll be back 'fore you know it. I promise, I'll only take 'em as far as Stump Ford Trail." He bent to kiss her, but she turned her face.

Lips pressed to a thin line, she watched him remove his hat and coat from the hook next to the door.

"I'll saddle up horses." Jason gave her a reassuring look and sauntered outside.

The rain left behind a cleansed earth, ready to face a new day. Jason hoped he was ready, too, for whatever this day would bring. Their horses ambled down the trail while the fresh scent of evergreen filled the crisp morning air. No one spoke; not to Jason, not to each other.

The overhead tree canopy allowed little light to break through. Dawn became daylight. The woods brightened, illuminating wildflowers, ferns, mosses, and multi-hued lichen. Jason kept one eye on his charges, the other alert for broken limbs or partings in the understory and noted the animals that had passed through in the night by their tracks and their scat—deer, rabbit, racoon, fox. He listened to the birds awaken. The music of a woman's voice singing, delicate, beautiful—the lone sign of human existence beyond their own—floated through the air so far away as to obscure the words and any familiar melody.

The men dismounted at Stump Ford crossing and handed Jason the reins to the horses.

He tethered the animals together while he reiterated the directions. "Follow the creek east till it runs into the Tuckaseegee River. You'll know it cause it gets wide and flattens out. Take that north, then keep due east. The trails will guide you. I drew out two main ones and gave you markers. In a few days' time, you'll come to the French Broad and Asheville."

"Thanks, brother. You and your family's been more than kind."

Jason felt the morning's tension ease from between his shoulder blades.

The tall man's sidekicks stepped into the rippling water at the shallowest point and stopped, waiting for their leader. "Hey, LeFevre!" one man called to him. "Let's get a move on."

LeFevre cursed under his breath. "I told you, no names."

"Now remember this, I can't say it enough," Jason said. "Look out for bushwhackers, Union raiders, Home Guard. They'll kill you soon as look as you."

"Got it. If anyone should ask, you never saw us. Forget you ever heard my name."

"Sure. Good Luck." He extended his hand.

LeFevre reached inside his pack and pulled out a bundle of greenbacks. "Take this." He placed it in Jason's outstretched palm and followed his associates into the freezing water, then looked back. "What do they call you?"

"Hyde. Jason Hyde."

"Be well, Jason Hyde." Without another word, LeFevre accompanied his companions across the shallows. At a point where the creek bank sloped low, they ducked inside a cypress thicket and disappeared into the dense forest growth.

Jason counted the money—a small fortune. "Damnation!" He held the bills to the light and examined them. Federal greenbacks. "Union payroll?" He let out a belly-laugh that echoed through the trees. "You're good people, LeFevre."

Tom Cooper locked his store and took a couple of steps down the boardwalk.

Jason rode up next to him. “Hold on there, Coop. Got something for you.”

“Come back tomorrow. Store’s closed.”

“I reckon you’re gonna want this today.” He dismounted, unbuttoned his money pouch, and handed him what he owed.

“Well now, Jace.” Tom Cooper counted the bills, then stuffed them in his pocket. “Where’d you get this?”

He ignored the question. “Got time to sell me a paper?”

The shopkeeper hesitated, then unlocked the store and stepped inside. “Latest issue of the *Standard* was dropped off this afternoon. Come on in.”

The newspaper’s bold black headlines read:

NASHVILLE AND CHATTANOOGA RAILROAD HEIST

UNION WAR CHEST HIJACKED

Jason smirked when the description and number of robbers fit LeFevre and his men. Light on his feet and feeling an unaccustomed confidence, he tucked the paper under his arm and strolled down the walkway to Penley’s Boarding House.

“Why me?” Jason asked.

“Friends help friends,” Joel Lovin replied. “You’re smart. I gotta hunch you’d be an asset to us.”

"But—*counterfeit*?"

A small windowless supply room served as their meeting place. In it stood a card table, set with a half-eaten platter of sandwiches and a bottle of whiskey, partially drunk. Jason sat with three men: Adam Cable, a wealthy, gruff-looking rancher; Jacob Rose, a red-faced farmer and grain mill owner; and Joel Lovin, a balding middle-aged bookkeeper. Feeling apprehensive and a little frightened, he asked questions, of them and of himself. *What would happen if I said no to this venture? Would they trust me not to betray them? What if I said yes? What then?*

"Counterfeit is a big industry," Joel said. "It may not be legit, but around here, ain't nothing is." He seemed to be their leader.

"Teaching young'uns is legit," Jason said. "So's ranching and running a grist mill." He nodded to Cable and Rose.

"That working for any of you?" Joel retorted.

"Wouldn't be dealing in funny money if ranching was reliable," Cable said. "Cattle ain't a sure thing."

"Ain't nothing a sure thing," Rose said. "Except this."

Jason wished he had never kept this appointment. "Joel, you told me there wasn't a catch—passing fake scratch is a big one. You could all go to jail."

"Ain't gonna happen," Jacob Rose replied. "Half the greenbacks out there are counterfeit. Bet you didn't know that. Banks, legit and shady both, print money whether they got the funds to cover it or if they ain't. *Need cash?* they say. *Sure, gimme a minute. I'll make you some.* How is what we're doing different from that?"

"Anybody and everybody prints Confederate bills," Joel added. "You seen it; some of it's mighty sketchy."

Jason thought of the cash Joel bought groceries with a few days before. "No," he murmured, "oh, *no*." Louder, he asked, "Joel, did you give Tom Cooper fake money the other day?"

"Spends as good as it buys. It passes through Coop's hands when he uses it to buy more stock. He don't know the difference—and what he don't know won't hurt him."

"But you're cheating anyone who makes a living selling goods to the likes of you and me." Jason widened his eyes to drive his words.

"Listen, Jace. Federal government's printing these so-called greenbacks to finance the war," Joel said. "They's so many currencies floating around, who knows what's legal tender?"

Jason rubbed his chin, thoughts buzzing. *He has a good point. I know this, Cooper treated me with respect when I paid off my debt. I felt like a man again.*

"Jace." Joel's tone softened. "I helped you feed your family t'other day. I know you'd do the same. Folks here ain't got two plug nickels to rub together. By spreading this cash, we're helping our friends and neighbors."

A hundred thoughts for and against the insane idea tumbled through Jason's mind at once. He stalled for time. "How big is this operation? Do you print your own money?"

"If you want in, say so. No more questions till then," Cable groused.

Jason studied the three men and saw a self-assurance in their faces that he lacked and desperately wanted. His heart fluttered with indecision. The moral question pressed.

Thoughts of his children's five pairs of dark, expectant eyes squeezed his core. *So many mouths to feed! How many more chickens could I steal without getting caught? What happens to my family if the bank takes our land? Am I a fool to turn this down? What other choices do I have?*

He grimaced, then leapt from his chair and thumped the table with his fist. "I don't have to do this! I won't do it—I *won't*!" He flung open the door and slammed it shut, leaving three slack-jawed men behind him. He stormed down the hall and out of Penley's Boarding House.

With one foot in his horse's stirrup, he hesitated.

"No!"

He mounted his horse, steered the mare onto Main Street, and started for home. Thoughts of his family emerged once more—and taxes. *They'll be due again. Then what?—I'll think of something. The war'll be over soon—won't it? School will open. I'll go back to work—Maybe.*

"No, no, no! It's wrong." He urged his mare forward. *Think of yourself, your family.*

He eased back on the reins. *Joel means well, I believe that. Maybe I should do this, just till I'm back on my feet.* He angled his horse around. Thoughts of solvency removed the knot between his shoulder blades.

Ahead, he noticed Joel Lovin watching him from the front of the boarding house. Jason walked his mount to where he stood.

"Jace," Joel said, "money is money if everybody believes it."

"Belief is built on trust. Betray everybody's trust? Not sure I can live with that." Jason sighed. "On the other hand, I need this. I need it bad."

"You can quit when you want."

"I can?"

Joel stuffed his hands in his pockets, then nodded. "*I trust* you won't turn us in."

At length, Jason said, "Yeah." His heart hammered inside his chest. "Okay," he said louder, and with more conviction, "Count me in."

"Good man! Let's go inside."

Jason accompanied Joel back to their meeting chamber, feeling lighter with each step forward.

"Jacob, get the Bible. We have a new partner," Joel announced.

Adam Cable did the honors. "Jason Hyde, upon this Bible do you swear…" he began.

"I do." Jason swallowed hard, realizing the magnitude of his commitment and wondered if *till death do us part* applied to counterfeiting.

"Not even Nancy can know about your dealings," Joel said.

"I won't tell a soul."

"Jason Hyde, welcome to the Cheoah Valley Chapter of the Burchfield Counterfeiting Ring," Cable shook Jason's hand. "All right, to your questions." He rocked back in his chair, thumbs hooked under his suspenders. "We ain't but a twig on a mighty oak. Our money comes outta Ohio, but our members spread across the South. Texas through the Carolinas. The Gulf of Mexico to Lake Erie."

"Seeing the inside of a prison ain't much of a likelihood with an organization the size of ours," Joel said.

"The five of us make up the Cheoah Valley gang," Jabob Rose explained. "Dick Burchfield, over to Bryson City, he gives the orders. He got a bunch of boys over there."

"You said we got five in our group. I see four. Who's the fifth?"

"Miz Penley, of course," Rose said. "She's providing us with a safe place to meet."

A light rap at the door introduced the robust form of Louisa Penley. She entered the room carrying a leather valise. "Welcome to our little club, Mr. Hyde." She set the bag on the table and pushed a lock of graying brown hair from her brow. "Burchfield made the drop." She dumped bundle after bundle of newly minted bills before them—twenties, fifties, hundred-dollar bills, along with three bags of what appeared to be half-dollar coins. "Y'all ready to do business?"

Jason stared at the mound of cash. "Wh–when will I meet this Burchfield fella?"

"You won't," Cable said. "Secrecy maintains the success of our enterprise."

A shred of doubt clouded Jason's mind. *Too late now.* He drew a deep breath and forced a grin. "So, how does this thing work?"

It didn't take long for Jason's family to become comfortable, even as war ravaged the South. The plow got fixed. His children got new shoes. A dozen chickens scratched in the yard searching for grubs, and meat and biscuits always graced their table. He paid the delinquent tax bill. Nancy sometimes watched him with questions in her eyes but didn't ask where the ready money came from.

His debts paid, the load of worry lifted. However, his need for cash never ended. The more he had, the more he wanted. Counterfeiting became a way of life. Even so, his heart leapt with the fear of being found out every time he passed a bogus bill. The error of his pledge to these men plagued him.

Months went by. Nothing happened.

Still, his conscience nagged.

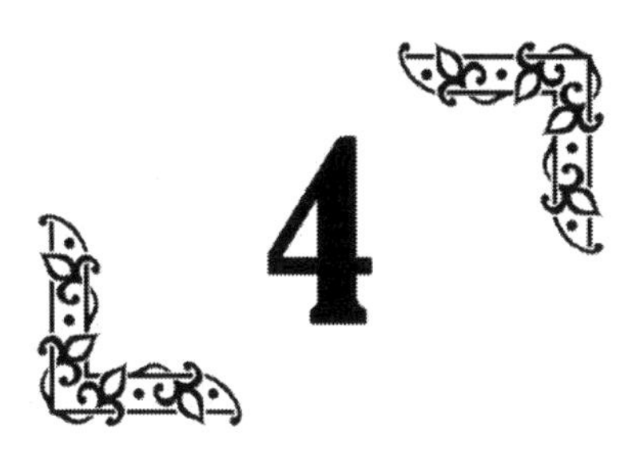

4

12 April 1862

Jason rose before daylight and prepared for a special journey. He tiptoed to the front door of his cabin and spied his flute laying on the mantel in the glow of the fireplace coals. He stuffed it into his pack along with a trowel, a leather pouch, and a fried fatback-and-hoe-cake sandwich wrapped in newspaper. He slung his canteen over his shoulder, grabbed his hat, donned a heavy jacket, and set out for a secluded Snowbird Mountain ridge. A location unknown even to Nancy, something all his own.

The crisp air heightened his senses. The moon had set, but the cold stars blazed and false dawn provided enough light to see the path in front of him. In his youth, the tribal elders had taught him the constellations, along with the trees, rocks, birds, and how to stalk any animal, four-footed or two. Now, he gazed skyward, seeking his celestial totem, *Konahalidohi*, in Cherokee: Orion, the night hunter. Cornwoman, the tribal medicine woman, explained to him when he was a boy, that Orion watched over him like a celestial father, and he often looked to him for guidance. This morning, his astral father's glittering belt shimmered in the darkness and he felt comfort in his presence.

Bound for his favorite destination, a mountaintop high above Nantahala Gorge, his go-to place for prayer and soul searching, he would arrive in time to witness the birth of a new day.

Sure-footed, he navigated the well-worn trail, keeping to the outer ridge. While he climbed, he thought about the ancient indigenous people who trod these mountain trails—the men and women whose moccasins carved out the very track he followed—and experienced a deep connection. Here, Cherokee traditions spoke to him in a clear voice, informing his Christian upbringing with ancient values. Man's rank on Earth became clear—equal to all creatures, an integral part of life which the Great Creator, in His infinite wisdom, placed on this planet.

He reached the mountain's crest as a dusky blue daybreak swept broad strokes of pink and orange that spanned the eastern horizon. Lavender wisps skimmed the ridgetops, each with an underpinning of fiery gold. The first shining rays of a brilliant sun pierced the sky and tipped the farthest peak with light. Morning, in all its glory, burst forth over the Nantahala while Venus sighed a last goodbye until night once again laid her velvety cloak upon the land.

He stood at the edge of a precipice and surveyed the pristine beauty that lay before him. Blue mountains pressed their craggy faces heavenward, rising from heavy white cloud swells nestled into valleys. Below him, a pair of eagles soared on airstreams.

Jason extended his arms high and shouted to the heavens, "O Lord, blessed be thy name!"

He pulled the small drum from his knapsack and beat a slow rhythm while he prayed to the seven directions—the four cardinal points of north, south, east, west, the sky, the earth, and the center—and then sang a prayer in Cherokee to the Holy Spirit:

"Lord, help me dispel any ill feelings separating me from my family, my friends, or you, my Creator. Help me live my life from a place of love. This is *Duyuktv, the Right Way*. The Cherokee way. Great Spirit, help me always whisper the truth, listen with an open mind when others speak, and remember the peace found in silence."

Deep within the Nantahala Forest, in Little Snowbird Creek, Cornwoman scooped her meager breakfast of egg, hominy, and reheated frybread into her mouth. The clay bowl and cooking pot washed, she threw her shawl across her shoulders, walked into the dawning day, and sniffed the brisk air, part of her morning ritual.

She wrinkled her nose. "I smell trouble. I will pray on it." Returning to the warmth of her hearth, she stoked the fire, lit her long-stemmed pipe, and settled down for morning prayers.

She puffed rings of tobacco smoke and relaxed into a state of meditation while she gazed around her two-room cabin. Overhead, bunches of dried herbs hung from low rafters and filled the cramped space with an earthy perfume. Colored stones glinted in the firelight while rows of dark blue tincture bottles and apothecary jars lined shelves over the sink, labeled by her careful hand. One wall boasted a shelf of old leather-bound volumes, used daily. In the middle of the room, the sacred fire burned without end in a fireplace with a swing-armed cauldron—The sacred fire ensured the continuance of the Snowbird tribe. It was her bound duty as medicine woman to maintain the flame and keep it alive—Wooden benches graced either side of the hearth, while a narrow table and chairs filled a corner. A small mirror anchored over the table was her one vain weakness. Cluttered but cozy, the place held an order that suited her.

The tobacco took effect and she set her pipe aside. She sang her opening prayer to the Great Spirit and heard a familiar voice join her chant.

"… whisper the truth, listen with an open mind, remember the peace found in silence." She focused on its owner.

Jason's image appeared within the dancing flames. He stood on a nearby mountaintop, a splendorous dawn emerging. She sensed his mood. *Distressed. He seeks forgiveness. What wrongdoing would a schoolteacher engage in?* Intrigued, she followed his maneuvering.

She watched him fill his lungs with pure mountain air. Sensed his niggling fears tugging. Puzzled, she listened to his thoughts*: What does the future hold? Prison? Humiliation for my family? Loss of respect?* His face hardened with resolve. He raised his arms heavenward once more.

"Lord, forgive me. I am a weak man and a sinner. My choices led me down a path of crime, yet honor lives in my heart."

Fixated by this turn of events for one of her most favored souls, she observed him scramble up the face of the bluff and walk along the crest to an ancient dogwood tree nestled among the boulders under an evergreen shelter. Next to the tree stood a small cairn of flat stones. He removed them, one by one, then scraped the soil with his trowel until it clinked against metal.

A red-tailed hawk glided overhead. With a screech, it landed on a gnarled branch and peered down at him with curiosity.

Cornwoman sensed an odd feeling creep into Jason's bones. *Why does it feel like I'm not alone?* His eyes darted one way, then the other.

He shrugged off the sensation. With the bird as his witness, he lifted an old, rusty box from the stony soil, opened it, and smiled, reassured at its constancy. Inside, cherished trifles from his youth beckoned: gold-flecked rocks that gleamed in the sun, old love letters from Nancy, a dried flower—relics from their days of courtship. The flower disintegrated at his touch.

"An omen!" Cornwoman exclaimed.

He removed a leather pouch from his backpack and revealed its contents—counterfeit greenbacks, genuine tender, and several Federal banknotes. Tightening the cords around his treasure, he laid it next to Nancy's letters.

Where would Jason Hyde get such money? Cornwoman wondered.

Digging a deeper hole, he reburied the box, smoothed the ground around it, and re-stacked the flat stones. His hand lingered on the topmost rock. "One day, I'll use this cash, tainted though it may be, for some kind of good." He brushed his hands on his pants and sat back on his heels. She sensed hiding the items here eased his fears.

At peace, he sat down cross-legged and drew a wooden flute from his satchel. The tranquil melody drifted across the miles as nimble fingers formed the notes, and man and measure became one. The hawk lifted on a breeze. His spirit flew with it, the moment a twinkle in time, soft as a breath exhaled then gone forever.

Stunned and concerned, Cornwoman delved farther, seeking what lay in his future.

A view into the Hyde's second-floor bedroom window materialized. She peered inside and witnessed him at Nancy's dressing table, counting money. A stranger appeared. He pounded on the Hydes' front door, calling for Jason.

Distressed, she ended her trance. It made no sense. *How, why?* Then, she remembered—In the white man's world, a war was in progress. It had the power to touch every life, even there in the mountains.

"I must speak with him, if he will listen!"

5

Jason kneaded the charley horse in his calf and adjusted his long, constricted legs inside the cramped knee cubby of Nancy's vanity; it, likewise, squeezed into the corner of their cramped farmhouse bedroom. He shifted his weight on the tiny wooden bench. It creaked in protest. However disagreeable his present workspace may be, privacy outweighed comfort.

He picked up a banknote, lifted it to the hazy afternoon light that filtered through shabby bedroom curtains, and inspected the inked paper with a careful eye. *Legal tender.* He laid it atop a stack of like currency.

Heavy boots stomped onto the front porch, breaking his studied concentration; a sharp rapping at the door followed. "Jason Hyde?" a stranger's voice called out.

Startled, he sprang to his feet and smacked his head against the low, rough-hewn ceiling rafter. The bench tipped; he caught it mid-topple. Two steps placed him at the window. He touched the rising knot on his forehead and winced, then focused his attention on the scene below, viewed between the curtain panels.

Mary and Sarah stopped hoeing the kitchen garden and stared at the visitor, hands shading their eyes from the sun. Will walked across the dusty yard with an armload of firewood for the cookstove.

"How-do, sonny. Your Pa around?"

Jason ran nervous fingers through shoulder-length hair. *Blast, it's the law.* He eyed the dressing table and the piles of money covering it.

"Don't reckon he is," the boy hedged. He'd been taught to be wary of strangers.

"How 'bout your Ma?"

Dammit! Jason retraced his steps, snatched his knapsack from the floor, shoved the bills to the edge of the vanity top, and into his pack.

He heard a loud clatter as Will's burden tumbled into the wood bin next to the front door. "What business you got with my mama and daddy, sir?"

The stranger thumped louder. "Miz Hyde—"

Heart pounding, Jason tossed two bundles of currency into a metal lock box and slid it into a hole under a floorboard.

Nancy hurried into the room. Winded, she skidded to a halt. Her eyes widened when she saw him stuffing clothing into his satchel. Their daughter Janie stood in the doorway, observing with a five-year-old's curiosity.

"What in tarnation—?" Nancy whispered between breaths.

"I dunno who's down there, but I'm not waiting around. Stonewall him as long as you can."

"I don't understand." Her dark eyes glittered.

He pressed the key to the strongbox into her shaking hand and closed her fingers around it. "Ready money's in our hidey-hole. It'll get you by for a long while."

"Long while! When're you coming back?" When he didn't answer, she clutched at his arm. "Don't go!"

"Got to." He pulled free of her grasp and kissed her goodbye. "Be back soon as I can. I'll write you." He dashed out the bedroom door, knocking into Janie, then sprinted down the short hallway to the back window.

Nancy charged after him. "Jace, no!"

Jason climbed out the window and dropped to the storeroom roof. Above him, he heard Janie bawling. His feet touched the soft earth behind their home, and he sneaked to the barn without making a sound.

Hidden from sight, he watched Nancy open the front door, raise a rifle, and hold it on the unwelcome visitor. His heart thudded in his ears, and he struggled to control his panting, so loud he worried they could hear it across the yard.

"My husband ain't here… Dunno… What d'ya want with him?"

Jason eased the bridle over his horse's muzzle. She whickered and side-stepped. "Shh, it's okay." He stroked her flank and led her to the hay door.

A shower of straw followed a thump overhead. Jason spun around and drew his sidearm. "Who's there?"

"Daddy," Johnny whispered from the loft. "What's goin' on?"

"Hush! Stay put until I'm well on my way."

Nancy set the rifle aside. "We'll wait for him together. Want some pie? It's fresh-made." She flashed a furtive glance over her shoulder and ushered the stranger inside. Will, Mary, and Sarah followed on her heels.

Jason swung one leg over the horse's back and climbed into his saddle. The old barn would soon be a memory and he stole a lingering last look. Livestock stalls, tools, yokes and bridles hanging on the walls. A few chickens clucked and scratched the dirt outside the barn door. He felt the cool barn air and inhaled its musty scents of hay and feed, tinged with dung.

"Where ya going?" Johnny whispered.

Jason recalled the words of his business partner, Adam Cable. *Will Thomas done put together a Confederate Army regiment. They made him a colonel for it. It's headquartered in Strawberry Plains, over to Tennessee. Might head that way, need be.*

"After that stranger clears out, tell your mama I'm headed to Tennessee. Make sure you don't say a word about it till then."

Johnny's lower lip trembled. "Okay, Daddy. When are ya coming home?"

Jason leaned alongside his horse's neck. "Gonna miss you, Son. Tell 'em I love 'em." He took a route through the trees to the road, then prodded his mare to a gallop.

On the Buffalo road, near the Tennessee border, Jason squinted at the figure ahead, sitting astride a white mare and flagging him down as if an urgent matter were at hand. Blue jay feathers in her silver hairpiece identified her esteemed status as the tribal medicine woman.

He reined his mare and addressed her, unable to hide his impatience. "Ama, what do you want?"

She regarded him through narrowed black eyes. "Where are you going in such a hurry, Jason Hyde?"

"If you don't know the answer to that, then you've lost your powers." His sharp tone betrayed his anxiety.

"I want you to tell me yourself."

"I'm off to war. Whatever you got to say about it won't change a thing."

"Why, a promise of regular pay? No. You got money."

How can she know? He gave her a piercing glare.

"You itching for a fight, like some hotheaded boy? Naw, you are too smart for that." She smacked her fist into her open hand. "You are making a mistake! Stay here."

"And hide like a coward? There's no honor in that."

"You are a fine one to speak of honor." She pointed toward Tennessee. "Go there and no good will come to you or your family. Stay. They need you."

"Can't help 'em inside a prison. Outside, maybe there's a chance." He spurred his horse and galloped across the state line, bound for Strawberry Plains, Tennessee, headquarters of the Thomas Legion of Cherokee Indians and Mountaineers.

Cherokee braves from Tennessee border towns joined Jason on his journey; their company renewed his sense of belonging, though they hardly spoke to each other. Observing them as they rode, he noticed the blackness of their hair and eyes; skin pigmentation—caramel to bronze—and variety of clothing. Riding with them recalled boyhood memories with Snowbird friends. Later—childhood nostalgia set aside—Jason reminded himself, *what awaits at the end of this trail is no game.* Every mile closer to his destination, the siren song of the unforeseeable future grew louder.

On the second day, he called out to his nearest traveling companion, "How much farther?"

"Just over the next hillock," a young man riding a dappled pony said.

The entourage crested the last rise, and Jason halted his mare to scan the vista. "Don't wait for me. I'll be along directly."

The pony rider signaled to the group, and whooping with anticipation, they descended into Colonel Thomas's headquarters.

The sight below unnerved him. Razed of every tree save those bordering the edge of the encampment, men had transformed a formerly lush valley into a ragged sea of canvas. Teepees dotted the space like cone-shaped islands, an impermanent contrast to the ordered ripples of eight-hundred bivouacs. Recruits clustered around scattered campfires marked by rising tails of smoke. Officers' tents amassed under budding shade trees. Centered amongst them, a simple log cabin provided the single fixed structure.

Will Thomas's quarters? he wondered.

The camp bustled with the energy of an interim village. From a central drilling field, the far-off commands of a sergeant exercising a company of soldiers-in-training floated over the air waves. Larger pavilions lined the opposite side of the field, one of which was a kitchen. The aroma of fatback and cornbread sifted across the distance. Jason's stomach growled, reminding him he had not eaten since the day before.

Last chance to turn back—Was Cornwoman right? Will I die out here? Not waiting for answers, he drove his mare down the hill, his heart filled with apprehension.

He signed his recruitment forms and picked up his kit: pants and an ill-fitting jacket. Uniform parts only. Enlisted men wore their own shirt and shoes, if they owned shoes. Canteen, a half-tent, other necessities of camp life. He nodded a greeting to familiar faces and hurried on. After locating a space to set up his tent within his assigned company quarters, he stowed his gear and unpacked a pair of shears, a razor, and a small mirror.

Settled on a tree stump, he gave himself a makeover: dark hair, shaved clean on the sides, spiked on top. A long scalp lock at the nape, held in place with a leather cord. The style of a Cherokee tribal warrior.

"Bear grease will keep your spikes straight." The speaker handed him a miniature container.

Jason turned his attention to the voice and saw a stocky warrior standing a few feet away, scrutinizing him through gentle, wide-set black eyes.

"I am Onacona." He cut a scrap from the back of a colorful cotton tunic and passed it to Jason. "For a headband. Tie it this way," he instructed, then stepped back to observe the results. "It is good." He next offered him his own bright calico sash. "Put it on."

"Thanks, friend, I couldn't."

"I have another. Take it." Onacona narrowed his eyes. "Gray eyes. Blackish hair, cut like mine. You look like a mix-blood now. Why you bothering? Lotta folks treat us no better'n livestock. You want that?"

Jason angled his head, one way, then another, and smiled at his reflected image in the hand mirror. "If I'm gonna fight with my Native brothers, I must become one of you."

Now I am a man with a blank slate, he thought to himself. *No longer a schoolteacher, nor a farmer. Today, Jason Hyde becomes a Cherokee soldier.*

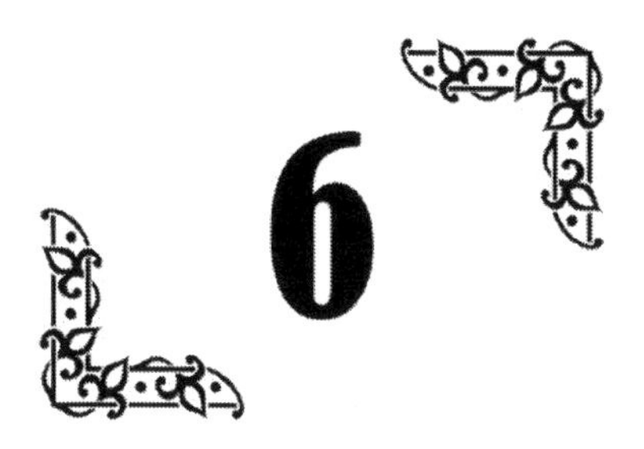

6

Stone's River, Murfreesboro, Tennessee
2 January 1863

The first day of the Murfreesboro battle lasted from first light to twilight, with men on both sides falling like raindrops from the sky. A ceasefire lasted from the New Year's dawn until half the next day. Jason and others who escaped injury collected bodies and carried them to freshly dug mass graves, and they transported anyone found breathing to makeshift hospitals. Jason knew that hope for the men's survival was slim.

He and three companions remained on the field—his cousin, Sam Leatherwood, Onacona, who he had learned was a Cherokee warrior from a village near Chilhowee, Tennessee, and Ira Lovin, his former student and Joel Lovin's nephew. Jason surveyed the bloodied and now-barren landscape, and noted with dismay that Union troops were lining cannons along the riverbank opposite them, preparing for another onslaught.

Sam, his brown slouch hat pushed back on his head, toyed with a rifle he'd garnered off a dead soldier. On a nearby hillock, the warrior culled through the post-battle detritus. Jason watched him pick up a wallet, flip through its contents, and stash a few bills inside his shirt.

The young man spied a pocket watch laying in the snowy slush, dyed brown with two-day-old blood. He wiped the case clean on his pants leg, examined it, then opened it. "Look, Mr. Hyde, it's real gold," he boasted. "Made in Zurich, Swit-zer-land." He sounded out the country name. "I remember, in geography class you showed us where

Zurich is, next to Germany. Imagine, this got all the way from there to this battlefield. And now, I'm holding it in my hands. Listen, it's ticking."

"It is! You were always an outstanding student, Ira. Wisdom tells us, *time waits for no man*."

Ira stuffed the timepiece in his pocket. "Time moves on, don't it? Uncle Joel said he'd send me to the Mars Hill Seminary if I wanna go. After the war, that's where I'm headed. You went there, didn't you?"

He put an arm around the boy's shoulder. "I did. My daddy wanted more for me than he had. Same as your uncle, I imagine. Education opens doors, and Mars Hill is a good opportunity-maker. Son, you'll be successful at whatever you choose to do."

"Thank you." He regarded Jason for a moment. "Wish I could get up like a warrior, same as you, Mr. Hyde, but my red hair would tell on me."

Sam and Onacona soon joined them. Sam held out his prize for approval, a Tarpley Carbine, breechloader. "Ain't she a beaut?"

"Better shoot it before the next battle," the Cherokee cautioned. "Coulda got bent. It will throw off your aim."

Jason took no notice of the rifle and instead motioned toward the river. "Over yonder, they're getting ready to have another go at us. I'll bet half our men are dead. Bragg aims to get us all killed before this battle's finished."

"You know he claimed victory for t'other days butchery," Sam said. "He sent them soldiers into sure death without a care for their lives. Ain't no honor in that."

That afternoon, the Confederates organized for the next attack. On command, four of Breckenridge's battalions, including Jason and the rest of the Thomas Legion battalion, ran up a forested hill east of Stone's River after the departing blue uniforms.

"Stay close, Ira," Jason warned.

The Yanks hightailed it down the other side, where a Federal brigade waited on the opposite riverbank with over fifty cannons pointed at the pursuing Rebels.

Jason crested the rise, and perceived the impending blitz of firepower. "Drop now!" He tugged Ira to the ground as he and others dove behind a stand of limestone boulders.

The Union fired the first blast. Soldiers in front of them perished. The forest to the back of them flattened.

Those who survived took shelter beside him and his compatriots, preparing to fire at the enemy. The thunder of cannons foreshadowed showers of rock and debris. To the right and left, men fell, screaming or dead.

Next to him, Sam opened the breech of his newly found rifle and filled it with ammo.

"Onacona warned you about shooting that," Jason said.

Sam regarded the gun with studied devotion. "Can't wait to fire it."

On the other side of him, the Cherokee took aim with his weapon, and downed a Federal soldier near the bottom of the hill. Jason and Ira followed his example.

Sam discharged his Tarpley. It misfired. He tried again. Nothing happened. He checked the breech. He locked it, aimed, and pulled the spark once more. A flash, and metal flew in every direction.

Bits of shrapnel embedded in the side of Jason's skull and a sharp-edged tintinnabulation in his ears replaced the din raging around him. The smothered rumble of cannon roar inside a roomful of cotton vibrated his body while the world pressed on in horrific slow motion. He ran his palm along his numb head and warm blood oozed between his fingers. Part of his ear was missing.

Next to him, Sam kneeled, staring at the smoking powder-burned right stump of his hand, his face blackened with gunpowder.

"Get down!" Jason reached for him.

"Look out!" Onacona leapt across Ira and Jason, pulling them both to the ground.

A cannonball sang through the air and soared over their boulder, landing behind them in a blast of mud and rock. It passed over the three companions, but severed Sam's head from his shoulders. Blood spewed from his torso, showering those around him; a bucket of warm red paint falling from the sky.

Jason propped himself upright and surveyed the scene. Sam, still grasping his stump, remained on his knees, motionless, before his lifeless frame fell backward. Ira and Onacona lay sprawled atop each other, unconscious. Jason collapsed against the limestone mass and the world went dark.

Jason woke to the growls and yaps of a pack of starving dogs fighting over a stiff body. Night blanketed the battlefield. The dog fight ended, leaving behind an eerie stillness in the aftermath of chaos. Slouched behind the boulder, he felt like a stick bobbing down the Little Tennessee River. Half frozen, his teeth chattered; he couldn't stop shaking. He staggered to his feet, teetered on wobbly legs, and gazed at the field before him.

There lay Armageddon.

In a sky swept cloudless by an icy north wind, the bright beacon of a full moon illumined the end of the world. The day's battle made stagnant blood-rivers through the mud and churned lingering snow into slush the color of crushed mulberries. Their aberrant composite, now hard frozen, glowed in the crisp night. The dead appeared as mangled specters with parts missing, limbs helter-skelter, each covered in cold-thickened lifeblood. The stench of war hung in the air.

Across the way, not one Confederate soldier reached the river that afternoon. Blue lay mixed with gray—The Yanks who led them to their death had sacrificed their own lives in the foray.

On the hillside, a few scorched tree trunks stood in testimony to the day's carnage, replacing the once lush evergreen forest. Fires burned here and there, crusty human silhouettes mingled amongst the char. A Bible verse filtered through Jason's mind. *And behold a pale horse. His name that sat on him was Death, and Hell followed with him.*

Scattered across the battleground, pickers searched for whatever they could find. A cigarette case. A ring. They dug gold teeth from gaping mouths of the dead. Stole boots for their own bare, cold-numbed feet. A firearm for a later battle. Medics looked for survivors amongst the fallen.

Three bloodied men lay nearby, one missing his head. In a flash, Jason remembered.

"Sam—Sam, dear God!" he gasped. Gunpowder-infused air blistered his lungs while shock and a deep, bone-rattling sob shook his body. He turned his gaze to the boy. “Ira!” To his relief, the young man was breathing.

He knelt by Onacona’s side and felt for a pulse, then willed his feet to support him. “Over here. Hurry!” he hollered to the medics in the field.

An intern rushed to his aid and checked the downed men’s vitals. “Survivors! Bring gurneys, quick!” he called to his comrades. “You’re one of them Injun soldiers, ain’t you?”

“Nuh—” Jason stopped mid-reply, then bobbed his head. He almost forgot his charade.

“Good Lord musta watched over you today. Hang on, Buddy, we’ll get you to a field hospital.” He offered Jason a sip of water from a canteen, then focused his attention on Onacona as two more medics arrived with a gurney.

Jason’s gaze shifted to his feet. Sam Leatherwood’s slouch hat, highlighted by the moon, lay tucked under a scrub bush. Somehow, his blood missed staining it. He leaned forward to pick it up. Suddenly dizzy, his knees crumpled beneath him.

Jason awoke screaming, stretched across a cot inside a hospital tent. Sam’s hat rested on his belly. In cots beside him, Onacona and Ira half-sat up, propped on their elbows, peering at him with concern.

Breckenridge’s adjutant flipped open the canvas flap, a sheaf of papers in hand. “Privates Hyde, Lovin, Onacona, your battalion is moving out.”

Strawberry Plains, Tennessee
Spring 1863

Returning from a patrol, Jason saw Onacona waiting near the camp entrance.

"Jace, Colonel Walker wants to see you."

Jason wove through the bustling encampment, and found Lieutenant Colonel Walker in front of his tent with Colonel Thomas and several other officers. He saluted his superiors. "Private Hyde reporting, sirs."

"At ease, soldier. We were discussing recruit reorganization. Now that you're here—"

Jason learned that large numbers of volunteers had enrolled in recent months, and the Thomas Legion now comprised two full battalions and half the alphabet in companies.

"We will divide the battalions between Lieutenant Colonel Love and myself. I will command the Cherokee companies—Hyde, I hereby promote you to Second Lieutenant, Company H, Walker's Battalion."

"Thank you, sir." *Walker's Battalion— 'H' is a Cherokee company. I'll fit right in.*

Colonel Thomas stood and moved to a table with a map spread across it. "Come look at this." With Jason at his side, he pointed to a railway running from the northern Tennessee line into Chattanooga, in the southeastern corner. "The Union is advancing troops through Virginia to Chattanooga, building their forces. They're moving along the East Tennessee, Virginia, and Georgia Railroad line, an important artery." He swept his hand from north to south through the state. "Along their route, they take turns destroying bridges and ripping out rails. At dawn, Company H and the rest of Walker's boys will decamp and march to Zollicoffer." He pointed to the town. "I assigned you and your boys to guard the railroad bridge. Advise your men, Lieutenant. Dismissed."

On a late summer afternoon, Jason paced the clearing on a bluff in a wooded range outside Zollicoffer, Tennessee, overlooking the Holston River. A rustle in the bushes caught his attention.

"Who's there?" He clutched his sidearm.

Joel Lovin, a leather satchel slung about his shoulders, stepped into one side of the open space. "It's me."

"What took you so long?" Jason grumbled.

"Don't be so all-fired huffy. I been tailing you for days. Dang boy, you're a lieutenant now—and you look like a native. Turkey feather in your hat band is just the thing."

"That's the idea. If the law's looking, they ain't gonna find me."

"They ain't after us, I'm telling you."

"So *you* say. Got what I sent for?"

"That's why I'm here." He let his satchel slide off his arm.

"I been thinking," Jason said. "The Yanks hit every burg, large or small, along this railroad line. Every time they blow up the rails and bridges, we come behind, fixing 'em. Up, down, and back, we stop everywhere on the way, and so do they. Gives me opportunity a-plenty for passing funny money. You know what that means. The more I exchange big bills for small items, the more of our counterfeit scratch gets into Union hands—Blue-bellies steal everything, especially money."

His friend stared at him. "Lemme get this straight. You go into these towns, buy stuff with big bills and make change just so the Yankees can rob 'em? There's a fifty-fifty chance the store owners' cash is as fake as your play money. What if they ain't got Federal greenbacks?"

"I'll take Confederate. Figure I still break even in the long run. I know legal tender when I see it. They can't dupe me. The point is to get bogus bucks in Yank hands and flood the Union with it. They make their way back up north, spread the stuff around, and sink their own economy—Damn Federals done destroyed everything we got. Why not give 'em tit for tat?"

Joel kicked the dirt under his feet, then shook his head. "It'll take time. War'll be over soon."

"Burchfield's gotta put more of us out here. From what you said when I signed on, there's konlackers in Rebel armies everywhere. If we work together, we can bust 'em from inside."

Joel paced the expanse, then stopped. Gazed out at the Zollicoffer Bridge. Rubbed the stubble on his chin. "Good point. Cable's out here now, and others from Burchfield's boys. And more enlisted across the South, you're right about that. If everybody worked undercover, passing out queer bills, we could do serious damage and no one'll be the wiser. Smart thinking." He regarded Jason a moment. "When you came on board, I never thought you'd take to this business. Now you're planning, and scheming, and making yourself rich. *The student surpasses the master*. Ain't that the way it goes? You done good, Jace. I'd join you, if I was younger."

"Consider yourself lucky, Joel. This war is hell."

"Of course, you're right again. How much you want today?"

"How much you got?"

"Plenty. Burchfield smuggled us a shipment a few days ago. He's selling at ten cents on the dollar. You can have it for a nickel if you buy enough."

"What denominations you got?"

"Bundles of twenties, tens, and threes. Got a couple bags of Mexican half-dollars, too. Folks like silver coins." Joel picked up his bag and reached inside. "Gotta crack artist up in Ohio. No one'll guess this ain't the real deal."

"Show me."

Joel handed him a packet. Jason flipped through the bundle and tossed it back.

"Dammit, Joel, it's printed on wallpaper. What do you mean, no one's gonna know?"

"Look closer. They're spot on copies of Federal greenbacks. Can't help the paper. It's scarce. Most folks don't care, anyway. Could be, the Union prints them on granny's wallcovering, too."

"I doubt that. If it's the best you can do—" Jason stuffed the fake bills into his pack and fished out two envelopes. "I got a letter for you from Ira. The other one is for my family."

Joel's face lit up. "Ira! How's he getting on?"

"Well as any of us. We've all suffered hard times. He'll pull through, he's strong—Ira's a good boy."

"I raised that young'un from the time he was a babe in arms. Worried me sick, him running off to fight like he did. Thank the Lord he's with you. Watch over him, won't you?"

"You know I will." Jason patted his satchel. "Gonna need more in a few months."

"Sure thing. I'll get this other letter to Nancy." Joel tipped his hat and trudged into the brush.

Dearest Nancy *2 September 1863*

Hope everybody is doing well. Mary and Sarah write often. Sometimes the boys do, too. Yet, nary a word from you. I wonder why? I ache for a kind word from you, Nance.

Bushwhacker attacks make post runs irregular. I send letters with Joel Lovin, with the assurance that he will look in on you from time to time.

Here, it's just hot, thankless work, following the path of Federal raids from one end of the state to the other. We guard tracks, carry out repairs, and repeat. While reports of Union vandalizing fill the newspapers, nobody writes of those who put the trains back to running troops and delivering supplies again. Meanwhile, I'm doing my part to put an end to this madness. Lord willing, this war won't last much longer.

Give our children each a kiss from me. I miss you more than you will ever know and long for the day we reunite. Please write. Keep safe.

Love Always,

Jace

Strawberry Plains, Tennessee
September 1863

At dawn on a late September morning, Colonel Walker mustered his men. After roll call, Jason stood at attention and waited for the man's instructions.

"Colonel Thomas has ordered us to decamp," Walker bellowed. "We're moving to Cherokee County, North Carolina. We'll regroup near Murphy.

"We'll have our hands full. Deserters hide in the forests. Bushwhackers, Union raiders, and bands of vigilantes infest the surrounding mountains. They rob the families who live there, burn their villages, steal their food and livestock. Some sink to murder. Our mission—protect the residents. Men, pack your gear and ready yourselves to march."

Onacona slung his backpack around his shoulders and evened its weight across his back. "Why so glum, Jace? We will be in our hunting grounds."

"Our families are in danger," Jason replied. "What if we're too late?" A half-truth. *Don't forget,* he scolded himself, *the law came for you. That's why you're here.*

Cherokee County, North Carolina
December 1863

On a frigid morning deep within the Nantahala Forest, Jason, Onacona, and Green Longfeather traipsed through the dense undergrowth, a scouting party of three. Overhead, snow threatened from a blustery, low-hanging, silver sky.

After searching a cave-pocked expanse known for harboring deserters, they forded frigid Slickrock Creek, a dangerous bit of whitewater bordered on one side by large boulders. On foot, they focused on not falling into the water.

A bullet zinged past Jason's shoulder as blasts rang out from behind the trees. Bushwhackers launched an assault.

"Snap to—we're under attack!" Jason yanked out his pistol and felled an assailant. Longfeather took out a second attacker while Onacona picked off a third. The rest of the outlaws jumped them from boulders, and they fought hand-to-hand in the freezing creek.

A burly fellow with a matted russet-colored thatch smacked Jason's weapon from his hands and grabbed him by his mullet, knocking his hat from his head. Mean, ice-colored eyes glared into his, filling him with the chill of judgment. "How 'bout that?" the ginger yawped in an outsider's accent. "They're stinkin' Injuns!"

The foul stench of the scoundrel's breath sharpened Jason's wits, and he caught him hard in the mouth with a right hook. His blow snapped the bushwhacker's neck backward.

Unfazed, the outlaw returned a roundhouse jab, splitting open Jason's cheekbone, then followed with an upper cut to his ribs.

Jason lost his foothold on the slippery rocks and stumbled into the numbing water. The raw shock jolted him. He sprang up and delivered a headbutt to the man's gut, knocking him back a few paces.

It seemed his assaulter would fall, but he regained his foothold and lunged with renewed vigor. He grabbed Jason by the throat, wrestled him to his knees, and held him underwater.

Jason sloshed and clutched, but could not get a grip on his assailant. The aggressor suddenly let go and Jason staggered to his feet, sputtering and hacking.

An arrow to the back had pierced his assailant's lung. A second shaft sliced through his attacker's neck and protruded from his throat. The bushwhacker splashed into the creek and his lifeless form drifted downstream, bobbling over frothy, reddened water and small rocks.

Jason spit, coughed, and gulped air, then swiped his hand across his lacerated cheek, smearing blood from one side of his face to the other. He looked for the marksman. High above the scuffle, he saw a golden-skinned young woman with long, jet-black braids and dressed in men's clothing, perched on a bluff. Even from where he stood, he could see her extraordinary green eyes gleaming in the wintery light as she concentrated on her next shot. Astonished, he watched her draw back her bowstring, aim, and let fly an arrow into a fifth robber, even larger than his attacker.

It lodged in the bushwhacker's shoulder as he turned to run from the scuffle. The injury slowed him long enough for Onacona to discharge a round at him. It hit him in the thigh. The outlaw bellowed and stumbled, dislodging his hat and revealing a scraggly mop, similar to Jason's assailant. On the second try, the Cherokee's pistol jammed. The archer's next arrow pierced the bushwhacker's knee, but he hobbled onward till his ginger-colored head disappeared amongst the trees.

"Ferries, don't leave me here with them Injuns!" the last bandit, hardly more than a lad, called to his buddy as he ran. "Ferries!" Longfeather knocked the fellow unconscious.

Panting, Jason arced his body toward the woman. Their eyes met and the corporeal intensity of her gaze shook him. She pivoted and vanished into the woodlands.

A vague memory tugged. He'd seen her before while exploring the Nantahala; she captivated him even then.

Chests heaving, the other two scouts scrambled out of the water while Jason retrieved his hat from amongst the reeds. On foot, wet, freezing, and in deep woods, they were several miles from camp with four dead bushwhackers and one unconscious.

"You men okay?" Jason asked in a raspy voice. He rubbed his bruised throat.

"Sure," Longfeather said.

"Everything we got on is soaked," Onacona grumbled.

"Which means we gotta keep moving," Jason said. "Otherwise, we'll catch our death. Round up these bounders, then we'll head back to camp. If we're lucky, it won't snow on us."

Longfeather motioned toward the bluff. "Who in Sam Hill was the gal with the bow and arrow?"

"I dunno," Jason said. "But she showed up right when we needed her."

"We're alive, thanks to her," Longfeather declared. "She can shoot, for certain."

Onacona stood over one of the dead assailants and nudged him with the toe of his wet boot. "Who were these boys?"

"Purty sure they're the Rebel bushwhackers we been hearing about," Jason replied. "They been robbing the locals for months. Hear tell, they got it in for Cherokees. Walker told me to keep an eye out for 'em—Seems they found us before we found them."

"Should we go after the one what got away?" Onacona suggested.

"Let him run. He's not coming back. Longfeather, secure the young bub before he comes to. We'll take him with us. He'll freeze to death if we leave him here. Onacona, hog-tie the others. If they aren't as gone as we think, they could crawl off."

"What about him?" Onacona motioned downstream at the body, caught in the limbs of a waterlogged tree. The markswoman's arrows pointed a warning to the gray sky.

"Put him with the others," Jason replied. "I'll help you,"

"You sure he's a goner?" Onacona squinted at the corpse bobbing amongst the branches.

"Quite. Nobody could survive an arrow through the lungs. He woulda drowned in his own blood if not in the water. We'll come back with pack mules and carry 'em to camp. They'll want their names, if they can find 'em."

The abandoned young bandit moaned and stirred.

"What happens to him?" Longfeather asked.

"He'll stand trial," Jason grumbled. "He's earned himself a trip to the gallows."

April 1864

The promise of spring kissed the air despite frosty gusts that bit noses and fingers. Trees alight with bright-green leaf buds contrasted against majestic evergreens. An endless, deep-blue sky seemed close enough to reach out and touch. Jason and Ira Lovin guided their horses through the dappled light of the radiant understory, on course to deliver a message to Colonel Walker, where he convalesced at home nearby. A planned meetup with Joel Lovin was to take place on the way. Jason intended to buy a few bundles of counterfeit scratch and drop off the last few months' profits, less his cut. The young man would spend an afternoon with his uncle.

They neared the agreed-upon location when an anguished voice cried out, followed by a blast of gunfire.

"Uncle Joel!" Ira spurred his horse to a gallop.

"Wait—" Jason hurried after him.

He caught up with the boy in a clearing, and saw Joel Lovin propped against a tree, bound, gagged, and bleeding, but conscious. His nephew hunched over him. The brush parted and a red-headed hulk of a man appeared, his movements awkward as if dealing with a physical affliction.

The attacker grabbed Ira's right arm. "Hand over your loot."

Before Ira could answer, the outlaw wrenched his arm. He howled.

Jason scrambled from his horse, unholstered his pistol, and ran toward them. "Unhand that boy and throw down your weapon!"

The giant flung Ira into a blackberry thicket, where he lay with a broken arm wedged at an odd angle. "I'll be goddamn, if it ain't the Injun what kilt my brother. You som'bitch!" He rushed at him, firing willy-nilly.

Jason opened fire; missed his target. He let loose a war cry and charged, shooting twice more, his aim wild.

Steady, dammit. He lunged behind a tree. His opponent matched his actions and the two men popped shots at each other. His weapon empty, Jason reached for his gun belt, then heard a round fired from another direction.

Right arm dangling at his side, his pistol in his left hand, Ira leaned from the backside of a sapling and aimed at his assailant. The enormous man stepped from his shelter, pointed his firearm at the boy, and pulled the trigger. The shot hit Ira in the shoulder. He staggered backward, and fell to his knees. "Mr. Hyde!"

With studied calm, the bandit limped to the boy's side. Ira shrieked.

Jason slipped two bullets into the gun's chamber. He fumbled three more, scattering them into the dirt. Cursing, he snapped the loading lever in place and cocked the hammer. Leaving the safety of cover behind him, he aimed at his target with forced concentration. "Over here!"

The outlaw turned and glared at him with pale mean-spirited eyes. A scar rippled from his nose to his temple across one. In them, a mountain of hatred, the vile nature of which Jason had not encountered on any battlefield. The sight made his blood run cold. The brute sneered and shifted his aim again to Ira.

Still on his knees, the boy uttered a barrage of unintelligible glossolalia.

"Shaddup!" A burst from the outlaw's gun ended Ira's wails. The young man toppled and lay lifeless, his unseeing gaze lifted to heaven.

Joel struggled against his restraints, and gave vent through his gag to muffled cries. The murderer swiveled, raised his weapon, and pointed it at the defenseless captive.

Jason's first bullet knocked the hulk's pistol from his hand. The brute bellowed and lurched at him. He dodged the tackle by mere inches and lobbed a second wild shot. It missed. The killer swung at him, connected with his cheekbone. The blow smacked him semiconscious.

The hulk bent awkwardly at the hip and yanked the pistol from his hand. Groaning, he straightened and sited the gun at Jason's forehead. He squeezed the trigger. The pistol clicked.

Woozy, Jason eyeballed him.

The murderer squeezed again. Again it ticked, empty of ammunition.

Shouts and the rumble of approaching horses from Colonel Walker's farm filled the air.

Jason's would-be assassin tossed the useless weapon and stormed toward Joel Lovin's horse with a cumbersome limp. He ransacked the saddlebags. Grabbing a burlap-wrapped bundle, he tore it open, flipped through the counterfeit greenbacks, then re-stuffed the bag and blanketed it over his shoulder. He hopped onto his own steed, spurred its flanks, and galloped into the woodland.

From a bluff hidden high amongst the tree branches, a mustachioed stranger observed in horror. Cold sweat dotted his brow and his arthritis-knotted hands shook while he scribbled as fast as he could into a pocket-sized log book:

17 April, 1864. Followed J. Lovin to meetup. Partner is an Indian! Boy rode with him, both in Rebel garb. Counterfeit exchange bungled by intruding thief. Lovin beaten, boy murdered. Indian risked life to save them. Who is he? On lookout for murderer.

9

May 1864

Jason had grown to love Ira like a son, felt responsible for his death, and grieved miserably over his murder. A week later, bushwhackers murdered Colonel Walker in his home. His murderers remained at large, as did Ira's. While his and Ira's senseless deaths hovered over the camp, Jason felt the pain of it more than most.

Pink clouds streaked a brilliant Tennessee sunrise while Lieutenant Colonel McKamy, who had replaced Walker, mustered the battalion for roll call. "Men, while we mourn the loss of our commander, the war remains to be won. Last night, I received new orders from Colonel Thomas. Tomorrow, Indian companies B and H will dispatch to Saltville. I'll go with you. There, we join Love's command and transfer to the Shenandoah Valley. We will support General William Jones as he battles the Union's Major General Hunter. The rest of you, under Thomas' leadership, will continue to offer much-needed protection to the local families here."

"Did you hear that?" Onacona clapped Jason on the back. "We are headed to Virginia!"

"Dammit," Jason growled, "Ira's murderer is *here*."

Dearest Nance, *28 May 1864*

I miss you and the children more than words can express. Mary tells me in her letters you are all well. For that, I am thankful.

It is with an anguished heart I relay this news. Tomorrow at first light I, with my company, am to begin the considerable journey to Piedmont, Virginia. They promised us we would serve only in this battle, then return. I must come home to you and our family!

One day, dear wife, I will embrace you with loving arms once again. Please write. I ache to hear from you.

Love Always,

Jace

The troop train lunged forward with a jerk, a clanking of metal on metal, a groan, a hiss of steam. It gained momentum as a light summer rain sizzled against the coal-fired engine. Two lengthy whistles and its mile-long string of soldier-filled flatbeds disappeared into the night. The chuga-chug of rotating wheels rattled over the rails—faster, faster—the fate of the men on board fixed by Providence.

Jason sat huddled in an open freight car, along with the other Thomas Legion soldiers. They protected each other from the wind and rain as they left Saltville, Virginia, bound for the Valley campaign. The train's endless movement whispered the words in Jason's mind: Shenandoah, Shenandoah, Shenandoah.

"We gonna lick 'em good," Onacona said, sitting next to Jason. "Justice for my people!"

On his other side, his boyhood friend, Standing Bear, cleared his throat, "Justice for wrongs committed against us all," he said in his quiet way. "Even better, the Lord tells me we will go home again."

Jason quivered with anticipation. He wanted to win this battle for another reason—Justice for Ira Lovin gave him a burning motivation to stay alive.

5 June 1864

Disaster claimed the day for the Confederates. Hunter's army outnumbered, outmaneuvered, and overran them. Union marksmen blitzed the Rebel commander, General Jones, then confiscated his bullet-riddled body. Afterward, chaos erupted among the Rebel's ranks. Hours later, when the smoke cleared, horses and men lay scattered over the field. Daylight faded, and the Battle of Piedmont ended. Bit by bit, an uneasy quiet, louder than a death knell, enveloped the battlefield.

Combat adrenalin worn off, a searing pain stabbed at Jason's ribs. Deep crimson spread from a mini-ball wound, soaking through his tattered garments. He cursed and put pressure on the hole in his side; it did little good.

Onacona ripped the sleeves from his own shirt and tied them around the injury to stop the sticky red flow. "You need help, my friend."

"It's not much." Jason gritted his teeth. "You took a bullet yourself. Better see to that."

Colonel McKamy strode over to the two friends. "You men need patching up." He craned his neck. "Quartermaster! Send litter bearers! Got wounded here!" He turned his attention back to them and pointed to a rise beyond the river. "Look there—"

Twilight cast its gentle glow upon a plantation, sitting on a knoll with a route to the water. While its prosperous days lay in the past, it was a vision to behold. Vegetable gardens lined the sides of the river pathway while at the end, a dock led to a boathouse. Cabins and outbuildings scattered the grounds. On the acres of surrounding land, young tobacco sprouts pushed tender leaves through the earth. That evening, lanterns dotted side lawns. It might have looked festive, were it not for the wounded soldiers littering the grass amongst the flickering lights.

"That place, yonder, is a makeshift hospital," McKamy explained. "They sent their wagons early. More are on the way—You there, over here!" he called to an approaching wagon. "Onacona, Hyde, climb aboard."

McKamy helped the driver and another boy riding with him assist the injured into the transport.

Jason clambered onto the front bench. "Where we headed?"

The caramel-colored coachman looked around sixteen. His light-hazel eyes appeared bright in the lowering daylight. The young man nodded toward the estate across the river. "Over dere, sah. Bagatelle Plantation."

Once on the road, Jason's curiosity overcame him. "Pardon me for asking, Son, but why are you here? Emancipation happened over a year ago."

The boy sized Jason up before replying. "Sah, dis my home. Anyways, me and my fambly doin' awright." He clucked to the horses. "After 'mancipation, man come tell us we can leave any time. What dat man didn't know was, we could go anytime we want. Some did. Dey come back 'less'n de Guard lynch 'em." He gave Jason a sideways glance. "No point in leavin'. Ain't no place for us out dere. 'Portant thang is, we free."

Jason liked his matter-of-fact way. "What's your name?"

"Akeem. My li'l broder, Zachariah, he in de back."

"A to Z, like the alphabet. They twenty-four more of you in between?"

Akeem laughed. "Naw, sah, but yo' on de right track. Dey's my twin sister, Akeela—we got A names cuz we de fus' ones. Din come Zach and his twin sister, Zylah. After two sets of twins, Mama say she ain't never havin' no more chil'run. She give 'em names start wif Z, markin' de enda dat bizness." He gave the team's reins a sharp snap, and the horses quickened their pace.

"My name's Lieutenant Jason Hyde. Nice to meet you, Akeem."

The wagon dipped and swayed over a pothole. Jason clutched at his side and sucked air as red fire shrilled through his ribs. The pain made his head swim.

"Pleasure be mine, sah." Akeem's cool hazels appraised him. "Yo' picked up a bullet, ain't ya? Must hurt powerful bad. I see it in yo' eyes. Hold on, we 'bout be home."

Home. The sound of it was music to Jason's ears. A few minutes later, they rolled through the gates of Bagatelle Plantation.

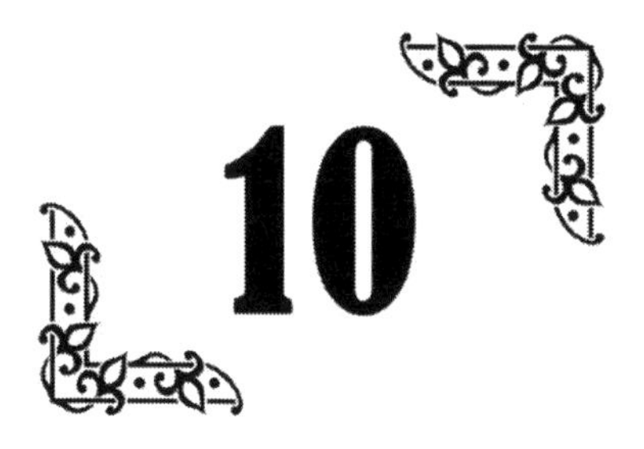

10

The acrid smell of gunpowder from the day's battle hung in the air while flaming torches lit their course along the tree-lined path to the main house. Moans of the wounded mingled with soft harmonica warbles drifting throughout. Scattered lanterns flickered, lighting the bodies of hundreds of injured soldiers sprawled across the grass. From beyond the river, Jason had seen more behind and to the sides of the mansion. S*o many. How can these folks help all of 'em?*

The path curved to circle a pond, its water glittering in the lamplight. Their wagon rounded the basin and a grand two-and-a-half-story residence loomed ahead. Its wide, multi-columned portico extended across the entire façade, and ballustered verandas projected from either side, creating a pleasing symmetry. Jason observed a tall, slender, middle-aged gentleman wearing a white shirt and dark trousers occupied one of them. He leaned on the railing and surveyed the scene, his stooped shoulders suggesting sadness at the sight before him. From every direction, bustling workers provided needed aid to the injured, and struggled to comfort them or save their lives.

Akeem's jerking halt redirected Jason's attention. "Whoa, boys!" Akeem hollered. "Easy now—We here, 'Tenant. Don't worry none. We take good care of y'all at Bagatelle."

A petite, auburn-haired woman with cinnamon-colored eyes hurried to their side in a flush of black skirts. She cradled a stack of folded sheets and blankets. "Akeem, sort out those Doc Pickering needs to look at first. Help Cassie bring them inside. Zachariah, show the rest 'round back. Make them as comfortable as possible."

"Yes, missus."

"Akeela and Zylah are passing out well-water. Ask Akeela to come find me when you see them. We must feed these men."

"Yes'm." Zach faced the soldiers in the wagon. "Y'all what kin walk, ain't got nothin' broke or ain't shot, follow me. Rest of ya, wait for Akeem or Cassie. Dey get ya to da doctor."

"Dis here's 'Tenant Hyde, missus." Akeem said. "He hurt real bad—took a dose o' lead in the belly and bleedin' hard. He need to see Doc, for sho'."

"Lieutenant Hyde? Well, now." Unsmiling, she studied Jason's face a moment. "Where are you from, sir?"

"North Carolina. Is it important?"

She briefly shook her head. "Cassie will show you to the ballroom. We're using it as the hospital. A nurse'll take over from there." She hurried off.

Cassie met Jason at the steps, and supporting him, she guided the motley assemblage across the porch, into the elegant great hall, and through wide pocket doors to a grand room. Onacona walked with them, a hand under Jason's elbow. Servants carried two others on make-shift stretchers.

Inside the ballroom a discord of misery engulfed them.

Candles sputtered within three polished brass chandeliers, shedding their soft glow on wounded lying shoulder to shoulder from one side of the floor to the other. Scores of inert bodies lay silent, while others moaned, groaned, or shuddered. A gilded folding screen, with hand-painted cherubs and a mirror insert, stood at the far end, ridiculously misplaced, and better suited for a ladies' boudoir. It partially shielded temporary operating tables where a trio of doctors tended patients. Women and boys tossed used, bloodied water out windows while girls replaced it with pans of fresh liquid. Assistants tore cloth into bandages and handed the physicians medical instruments. A rank combination of alcohol, ether, sweat, fear, and death assaulted Jason's senses. Overcome by the stench, he gagged.

Cassie led them through the throng. "Watch yo' step. Dese fellas done suffered 'nuff today." She sat her charges on a picnic bench placed against a wall. Close by, a medic sawed through a screaming man's leg just below the knee.

"Somebody bring me chloroform, *now*!" the doc bellowed. Two thickset men grasped the patient's upper body to hold him still.

Cassie crossed herself. "Have a seat. I'll tell Doc Pickerin' yo' here."

Jason took off his hat and passed his fingers around the brim, feeling alone and frightened in the bedlam while Cassie spoke to Pickering in a low voice and motioned toward him. Onacona slouched beside him, seemingly too weary for conversation.

A medic tossed the screaming man's bloody severed leg into a pile of disembodied limbs awaiting disposal under an open window. The man's cries ceased and he lay unconscious in a pool of blood. Another appeared to be cutting a bullet from a young man's hip. Jason knew from experience that if the soldier lived, he would never walk again.

A sour taste filled Jason's dry mouth; his stomach lurched, and he swallowed hard. Sweat beaded on his forehead. The sweltering room swam, and the surrounding ruckus undulated with his pulse. He clutched at desperate shreds of consciousness and scanned the room.

A youthful raven-haired woman who looked strangely like the markswoman at Slickrock Creek, kneeled at a shuddering man's side. She placed a hand on the soldier's forehead, the other on his heart. His shaking ceased. She met Jason's eyes with a licentiousness that challenged his sanity. *It's her! I can't get her outta my head.* Cassie passed between them on her way out; when his line of sight cleared, the vision had vanished.

"Wait, come back!" Jason's words a garbled muffle.

Onacona raised his head. "What?"

Jason hadn't the strength to reply. Onacona dropped his chin to his chest and resumed his exhausted trance.

Zachariah and a girl who looked like his female double entered, carrying a pan of water. The doctor set them to work binding wounds and filling hypodermic needles. "Twin sister," Jason muttered.

The tall gentleman sauntered through an enormous doorway, his spotless, starched shirt and pressed trousers discordant with the surroundings. Jason frowned at the sight of him—his manner of dress and wide grin were as unexpected as the gilt screen. *Doesn't he see the misery around him?*

"Lieutenant Jason Hyde! My wife alerted me to a patient with your name. I came to see for myself—I never thought we'd cross paths again. You look—different—from what I remember. Yet, here you are, sitting in my ballroom, such as it is. I'm honored to have you as my guest, though I wish the circumstances could be better."

Jason steadied himself on Onacona's knee and stared at the man. Feeling as if in a dream, he remembered his voice—rich, unforgettable. Befuddled, he reached for the man's outstretched hand and felt his body careen. The absurd scene before him faded to black.

Jason awoke to a warbler singing its cheerful song. Soft sunlight streamed between slits of heavy draperies adorning large windows. *Must be after noon*. He shifted his weight on the cotton-stuffed mattress and surveyed his bedroom: a carved dresser, writing table and chair, his bed—a walnut four-poster. Everything was spotless, smelled of lemon oil, and polished to a high luster. Beside him on a side table, a carafe of water, a bottle of quinine, and his hat, Sam's hat, bloodied and battered, a shot-hole in its brim.

He threw back the bedding, favoring his ribs, swung his legs off the edge of the bed, and gave a start—no clothes, other than a clean pair of drawers. He sighed, flipped the covers over himself, and pulled them to his chin.

Yesterday's events swamped his mind. The bloody battle, the mini-ball in his side. He ran his fingers over the bandage around his ribs. A memory engulfed him:

Strangers at the house. Lost. I helped them. One gave me money, lots of it. Jason searched his brain, battle-weary and foggy with fatigue. *Was that him last night? What was his name?*

A quick rap at the door startled him. "Come on in."

The woman from the day before swept into his room in a swish of crinoline under black-dyed cotton. He pulled his sheets higher. "Good afternoon, Lieutenant, I'm Hetty LeFevre. Welcome to my home."

Jason stared at her. *LeFevre—that's it!* He quickly composed himself. "Pleasure, ma'am. Miz LeFevre, why am I here? I should be with my men."

"Nonsense, Lieutenant. This is our way of thanking you for saving my husband's life." Her voice reminded him of warm honey. "If it weren't for you, he would have perished in the wilds of North Carolina. I know those mountains. I grew up in Raleigh."

He scrutinized her. A striking woman with determined features, the lines of her war-hardened brow softened by gentle, spice-gold eyes. Coils of fiery copper hair framed her face at the sides; the rest pulled into a chignon at the nape of her long, ivory neck, held in place by a simple tortoise-shell comb.

"I gave directions, is all. Your husband followed 'em."

"I beg to differ, Lieutenant. You offered him your much-needed assistance. It saved him. He didn't know how to survive the wilderness. I'll be forever grateful for your charity. Oh, how he went on over you and your lovely family after he came home!"

He blushed at the compliment. "I'm glad he got back safe. Never did I expect his home to be such as this." His sweeping gesture encompassed the bedroom.

Hetty's thin lips curved into a modest smile. "I'll make certain Mr. LeFevre soon comes by to visit. After that you'd better rest or Doc Pickering will scold us for bothering you."

"If you don't mind, I have one request. My friend is downstairs with a mini to his shoulder. Take good care of him and the others who rode in with me. "

"We shall treat your men as distinguished guests."

True to Hetty's words, LeFevre dropped in later. "Welcome to Bagatelle Plantation. Please accept my apologies for not introducing myself yesterday. Natchez Lefevre, at your service." He shook Jason's hand.

Jason swallowed his last bite of food with a cup of coffee. "Uh, a pleasure, sir."

LeFevre set his empty tray aside. "Your commander, Lieutenant Colonel McKamy, came by to check on his men. You were unconscious, so he left this note for you." He removed a folded paper from his vest pocket and placed it on the side table next to Jason's hat. "Nice hat—blood spatters, bullet hole, turkey feather, and all. Hang on to it."

"I will. It means a lot to me. McKamy brought my orders, I reckon. What's your part in the war?"

"I have various responsibilities. Last you and I met, I was delivering a cash deposit to the Confederate supply depot in Asheville."

"*You* robbed the payroll train!" Jason gaped at the man.

"A business deal gone wrong. My mission involved skullduggery of a different sort."

"Which was?"

"Confidential, I'm afraid."

"I see." Jason folded his arms over his chest, winced, and let them fall to his sides. "Afterward, you found your way to my cabin. And the men traveling with you?"

"I hired them to go with me. There's safety in numbers—and none of us worth a hill of beans for getting around in the mountains." LeFevre scratched his chin-stubble. "While I blame Jeff Davis's pridefulness for bringing this needless destruction upon us, I do what I can to aid the poor soldiers who fight for him. Unforeseen hazards come with the territory. In our case, fortuitous, as it led me to your acquaintance."

Jason sighed. "I agree with you, sir, our ruination didn't have to happen, not like this. All the same, it was coming. The rich built the Southern way of living on the backs of others. It couldn't last forever. I don't cotton to the practice of owning people, anyway."

"Nor do I."

Jason cocked an eyebrow.

"Don't get me started on the subject!" LeFevre pulled a slim cigar box from the inside of his vest, removed a cigar and lit it. After taking a few puffs, he reached for an ashtray. "Lieutenant, the South is akin to a charming belle whose billowing skirt conceals worn crinolines. Though her manner may be lovely, her ways are outdated. It's time for reform."

Jason pursed his lips. "Granted, but Yanks got no business wrecking our lives or spoiling our land. Land is sacred."

"My, my," LeFevre slowly said. "A hint of passion has replaced your apathetic outlook. What changed?"

"This godforsaken war is what. Once a man of letters, I taught school. Thinking myself a scholar, I have since learnt how little I knew of the world! Never have I met the unfounded hatred this war rubbed my nose in."

"Feeling judged, are we? Say hello to humankind's hypocrisy."

Jason frowned.

LeFevre returned a thin smile. "You're a teacher? You must love literature."

"I *was* a teacher. And I find scant opportunity for reading, except for newspapers."

"Then please enjoy my library while your wounds heal. Perhaps we'll have another opportunity to chat while you're here. I'm beyond curious, Lieutenant Hyde, why you arrived disguised as one of your Cherokee soldiers—when you are undoubtedly white."

11

Jason removed a volume from the library shelf and opened to the first pages. *"It was the best of times, it was the worst of times, it was the age of wisdom, it was the age of foolishness, it was the epoch of belief, it was the epoch of incredulity, it was the season of Light, it was the season of Darkness, it was the spring of hope, it was the winter of despair, we had everything before us, we had nothing before us, we were all going direct to Heaven, we were all going direct the other way... A Tale of Two Cities* by Charles Dickens. He could have written it today."

"So true, Lieutenant."

Jason slammed the book closed.

"Did I startle you? My apologies." LeFevre's voice emanated from the other side of a high-backed wing chair that faced the windows and gardens. The host lay his reading material aside and stood. "It's set in troubled times similar to ours. You should read it. Take it with you."

"I couldn't! Books are too precious—"

"I insist. Make yourself comfortable. I'll call for refreshments."

Jason sat, cradling the volume, and watched LeFevre stride to an embroidered tassel suspended from the ceiling. He pulled on the ring at the bottom, then seated himself near his guest. Moments later, a servant entered the room and he requested lemonade.

Jason looked on in amazement. "How did you summon her?"

"You've never seen one of these systems? The tassel connects to a spring bell in the butler's pantry. I'll show you how it works, if you wish, Lieutenant."

"Jace. That's what my friends call me."

"Then you must call me Nate." He studied him. "Your hair, your clothing. You pull off your deception well—Jace. But why masquerade as an Indian?"

Jason froze.

"All right, tell me this. Why are you *really* fighting in this abysmal war? Your allegiance doesn't fit your ethics."

"You get right to the point."

"I want to know my house guests. Don't misunderstand me, I like you, but in my line of work, I can't take chances."

Jason looked at him. "You're a spy."

LeFevre smiled. "Tobacco grower and courier are more correct. Here at Bagatelle Plantation, you and your injured men enjoy the advantages of quinine, chloroform, ether, and that rare commodity, morphine, thanks to my clandestine affairs. And for the record, I don't own the men and women who work here. Never did, never would."

"Is that so? We both got secrets, then." Jason rubbed his chin while he sized up his host. "If it's important, I'll tell you—I'm holed up."

LeFevre attempted to quash his astonishment. "On the battlefields? Aren't you worried about getting killed?"

"Sometimes."

"Why must a schoolteacher hide from the law? Were you teaching darkies to read and write?"

"I no longer claim to be an educator. I haven't the virtue for such an honorable profession. Since then, I've done things that require my prolonged absence from home."

LeFevre leaned forward. "What things?"

"I swore an oath not to speak a word of this business to anyone. I've kept it." His eyes drifted outside the library window to Onacona, strolling in the garden amongst the flowers, then turned back to his host. "However, my gut tells me I can trust you."

LeFevre nodded once, his expression serious.

"Where I come from, life is tough, and I got a family to feed. I owed money, money I didn't have. Then you came along—You saved me as much as I saved you."

The servant girl lightly rapped on the door. She entered with a pitcher of lemonade and two glasses on a tray.

"Thank you, Eliza. Set it down over here." LeFevre motioned to a small table. "That will be all." He poured two glasses and passed one to Jason. "Go on."

Jason sipped the cool, sweet-tart liquid. "I'm dealing in counterfeit. Shoving the queer, they call it."

"I'm familiar with the term."

"One day, a lawman came for me. I made a quick decision, signed up with the Thomas Legion. Figured to lie low awhile." He cast a wry smile. "So, here I am, a soldier in a Cherokee company of the Confederate Army—a lieutenant!—shaking off the law." He took another sip and set down his glass. "Then I hatched a plan, which I put into action."

LeFevre reached for a cigar box, selected a cigar, and offered one to his guest. "Try it. My best variety, a Queen of Babylon." Offer accepted, he lit both and relaxed into his armchair. "Tell me your plan."

Jason puffed his cigar. "Nice—So, this abysmal war destroyed our livelihoods. In return, I'm spreading fake currency in as many little hamlets and villages as I can, me and some of my buddies out here fighting with me. Yanks get hold of it, take it up North. We intend to bring down the Yankee economy from the inside. Not much chance of winning this war any other way."

"Pure folly. Union's too big, too strong, too organized. Your way will harm innocent people, and you're the one who profits. That what you're aiming for?"

Jason glowered.

"Mind if I have a look at one of your fake bills?"

Jason opened his money pouch and handed him a two-dollar bill.

LeFevre inspected it front and back, then compared it to genuine tender from his own pocket. "It's a good likeness, but they printed this stuff on wallpaper."

"Money is money if everybody believes it's money."

LeFevre flashed a glance at Jason and returned the note. "Interesting theory. How much have you learned about this venture of yours?"

"Some." He reiterated the basics of how counterfeiting operated.

"That's not the half of it," LeFevre said. "This country's so full of konlackers, it's hard to say who runs your operation. Could be the Sturdivants, but that's just a wild guess. Counterfeiting was their family business until the government ended it in the '20s. Ring leaders went to jail, the rest headed for Ontario. Could be Tom Ballard. He's in Canada, too. Is it possible your money's shipped by way of the Great Lakes?

Jason stared at him. "Maybe. Lake Erie laps at Ohio's shore. By what speculation would you target the Great Lakes an entry point?"

"I know people. If a waterway's involved, it's my job to learn how to get through and know what's routed across it. Furthermore, Union's blockaded the Southern ports. Best options are north." He grew serious. "You're looking at prison time if you're caught. Are you aware of that?"

"The prospect weighs on me, along with the guilt. Truly, I don't wanna hurt innocent folks. Especially not my family. When I started out, I thought I'd just do it until I got back on my feet. Didn't work out like that—the money's too easy." A few yards away, outside the window Onacona examined a rosemary shrub. "Yeah, I could go to prison. All the same, I need to get home. There's a wrong there that needs righting."

LeFevre raised an eyebrow. "What sort of wrong?"

"A boy died on my account. His killer is still out there thieving and murdering. I gotta stop him."

"Why do you say the boy's death was your fault?"

Jason explained, feeling as miserable as he did the day of Ira's death. "It shouldn't have happened, none of it. Not the ambush. Not the shootout. Not the killing." He slumped in his chair.

"Who attacked you?"

"Dunno, but he sure knew me. This fella got the devil in him. Saw it in his eyes. Ira was unarmed. The bastard drove a bullet into him out of pure meanness." His voice shook with emotion. He collected himself, then thumped his fist in the palm of his hand. "I *gotta* stop this animal."

"You say the law's looking for you—what about that?"

"It's a risk I have to take."

LeFevre regarded him for a long minute. "Want my advice? Don't lie to yourself. Just do what's right. Only you can say what that is."

Further conversations with LeFevre ensued, balanced by garden wanders with Onacona. Soon, the guests waved goodbye, gifted with a box of LeFevre's finest cigars, a bottle of Jake Beam bourbon, and quinine. Jason and his Cherokee friend took their first steps out the open gates of Bagatelle Plantation.

The cool morning air heightened Jason's anticipation of returning to his company. A light rain the night before dampened their route, preventing passing horses and wagons from creating the dust showers so familiar on most of their treks along the Virginia byways. Along the road, they encountered but a few travelers, and to those they tipped their hats and hollered a friendly hello. Virginia remained more congenial than Tennessee and North Carolina, states with divided sentiments regarding the war. Even so, Jason knew they must maintain vigilance for Union soldiers and sympathizers.

The landscape shifted as they walked, from the charred Piedmont hills, where they fought, to ravaged farmers' fields bordered by broken whitewashed horse fences in front and the Blue Ridge Mountains behind. All of it, a constant reminder of war. It mattered little to Jason. He cared about one thing—he was on his the way back to his troops, encamped at Rockfish Gap. Every step led him closer to the day he would go home. And closer to catching Ira's murderer.

12

Martinsburg, West Virginia
4 July 1864

My dear Nancy, now I write to you in my diary as intense fighting has ended mail service. The scratch of pencil marking paper serves as my refuge, and the only way my heart and mind may speak to you. If only my imperfect words could reach your ears instead.

After the Battle of Piedmont, my friend Onacona and I convalesced. At last, we reunited with our company. Our troops have since chased Hunter out of the Shenandoah Valley, clean into the new state of West Virginia. General Jubal Early is leading us now. Though foul-mouthed and tobacco-spitting, we respect him and will fight hard for him. But instead of marching home, Ol' Jube headed us north. We clash with the Yanks almost daily and under his leadership, we win more than we lose. Scuttlebutt is, he's moving us toward Washington City.

Washington
11 July 1864

As I write, dearest Nancy, the sun is lowering on a day that marks history. We arrived outside Washington early this morning and dug in at Fort Mansfield. Excited to be here, we chomp at our bits.

I may not write you again for a while. Until then, know that I love you. I will carry thoughts of you in my heart as we battle for victory—

"Come with me, Lieutenant." McKamy interrupted Jason's writing. "I need a word with you."

Jason approached his Cherokee companion outside his pup tent, where he cleaned his rifle. Onacona gave a start, and curiously eyed his friend's civilian costume.

"Where did you get them duds? You look like a dandy."

"McKamy. Saddle up, we got a mission." Jason briefly described their task as they rode out of camp while constantly alert for snipers. "Find out as much as you can. Meet me under the trees yonder in three hours." He showed their rendezvous site, and they separated.

Jason unbuckled the flap of his money pouch and flipped through its contents. "Should be plenty." He yanked at his waistcoat, buttoned his topcoat, and straightened his tie. Although McKamy's gentleman's suit fit him well, he'd never felt so gussied up. He cocked his hat at a confident slant and angled his horse toward Fort Stewart, the one open road into Washington.

Jason arrived at the toll gate, the sole rider entering amid a mass exodus.

"You'd be wise to turn around and go back where you came from," the sentry admonished him. "Everyone is leaving."

"I don't intend to stay, sir. My niece and her children live here. They're in danger."

"Then hurry. It's not safe."

Terrified residents departed on horseback and in heavily loaded wagons. Some fled to the docks. Others ran helter-skelter through the streets, arms laden with as many possessions as they could carry.

"Save yourself!" a passerby shouted.

"Get out while you can!" another called. "Gray-backs are coming!"

"Follow me, stay close!" mothers with crying children called to their families. Hooves and wheels clattered over cobblestones, horses whinnied in distress, all of it creating a raucous din. In the midst of the madness, war-seasoned troops in faded blue marched through the streets to the fortifications surrounding the capital.

Jason cantered to Seventh Street and guided his mount the few blocks to Pennsylvania Avenue, flanked at either end by the Capitol Building and the White House. He noted the reconstructed Capitol dome, completed a year earlier after the British destroyed it in 1814. Its grandeur took his breath away. At the opposite end of the broad boulevard, a flurry of activity flooded the White House lawn, where buggies darted in every direction along its perimeter. He watched in awe as a tall, thin, bearded man in a top hat sauntered from the side portico. He had a woman on his arm whose head, even with her bonnet on, hardly reached his shoulder. The lanky gentleman helped her into a waiting carriage and climbed in behind her. Their driver cracked his whip, and they sped toward Potomac harbor.

Two blocks from the White House, Jason stopped at a haberdashery to buy a suit of clothes. An hour later, with his saddlebags stuffed full and the latest edition of the city newspaper—still warm from the printing press—folded into his jacket, he hurried back toward his entry point.

"You there, halt!" a police officer demanded, motioning to him.

Jason swallowed hard and pulled up on the reins. "What is this about, officer?"

"Dismount. Now. Position yourself and your horse against the building."

He froze. *Should I make a run for it?*

"Dismount, I say, and be quick about it!"

No, I'll never make it. The instant he set his feet on the cobblestone street, the officer grabbed him and steered him and his mount to the sidewalk.

A battalion of soldiers rounded the block marching to Fort Stevens, their nearest column a mere arm's length away. The lanky, top-hatted gentleman he spotted exiting the President's mansion led them, now without his female companion.

"President Lincoln—but I–I just saw him leave," Jason stammered.

"Our President would never abandon us in the throes of an invasion," the officer replied, eyeing him. "You should know that."

"I don't live here. I'm from Delaware."

"Then I suggest you make haste to return."

Jason mounted, spurred his horse to a gallop. and reconnected with Onacona at their planned rendezvous point.

"My news is not good," Onacona said. "To dodge sniper fire I took a roundabout route. I saw Union armies entering Washington from all sides. General Seigel is dug in at our rear, near Harper's Ferry. Worse, I learnt that General Grant's army will be here by daylight."

"You're right. Troops are crawling all over the place. They've manned every fort. I even saw Abe Lincoln leading a company of Federals." Jason pulled the newspaper from his saddlebag. "Grabbed the latest daily, hot off the presses. So fresh you can smell the ink." He opened it to the front page. "Report is, Hunter's on an Ohio River steamer. My guess, he's headed to Harper's Ferry to join Seigel. Too bad we didn't hit 'em when we got here. Then, we had a chance. Follow me—we gotta find General Early's headquarters at Blair House. It's on the outskirts of the Union encampment— "

"So, it's agreed, we will attack at dawn," Early said as Jason entered the dining room. He found the general with a gathering of elites: Major General Rhodes and Generals Breckenridge, Ramsuer, and Gordon. Apparently they'd been conferring in a late night strategy meeting. The scents of fine brandy and cigar smoke permeated the place.

A wave of excitement flushed through Jason. He felt important for the first time since engaging in the conflict—and he liked it. He stood taller and made a crisp salute. "Excuse me, sirs, Lieutenant Hyde reporting. I bring information regarding our situation." He handed General Early the newspaper and gave his report to the seasoned war chiefs.

Their faces grew grim, then grimmer, as Jason spoke. Not wanting to leave them, he looked directly at Early. "Is there anything else I can do for you, sir?"

Early's concerned eyes settled on him. "No, thank you, Lieutenant," he answered after a brief moment. "You did well tonight."

The next day, Jason and all of Early's armies awaited the general's command to attack. None came. Tension mounted. Blistering heat rose with each passing hour.

"Pssst, Jace." Onacona wiped his brow, then handed him his spyglass. "Fort Stevens, up on the ramparts. That him?"

"That's him. When your young'uns ask what you did in the war, you tell 'em, you went to Washington City and saw the President."

General Early faced Jason and his other battle-weary fighters after the sun dipped low on the western horizon. "Brave soldiers, we are outmanned and outgunned. To attack would have been certain death, and I would not ask you to make that sacrifice. We'll pull out under cover of dark. But remember this, courageous warriors and gallant champions all, we didn't take Washington, but we scared Abe Lincoln like hell!"

White House, Office of the President
September 1864

Allan Pinkerton felt like a fixed installation in President Lincoln's stifling anteroom. He uncrossed and recrossed his legs and adjusted the collar of his dress shirt while he listened to the hustle and bustle of traffic on the cobblestones, sensing the world pass him by.

At last, the President's secretary, a harried, flint-faced man, glided into the waiting room. "The President will see you now, Mr. Pinkerton." He ushered him into Abraham Lincoln's private office.

Pinkerton observed his surroundings: A large square chamber paneled with mahogany wainscoting and decorated in green. Maps and strategic war plans lined the walls. A bad portrait of Andrew Jackson hung over the fireplace mantel. Lincoln sat behind a writing desk piled high with documents, pen in hand, studying the pages. Beyond two damask-draped windows, the broad expanse of the Potomac River coursed to Chesapeake Bay.

"How are you today, Allan?" The President looked up from his work. "Please, make yourself comfortable." His unhurried manner masked the fact that he had expressed extreme urgency in the matter at hand when he sent for Pinkerton.

Lincoln had demanded to meet with the head of the *exalted* Pinkertons National Detective Agency *sine mora.* Pinkerton smiled, relieved at the President's relaxed demeanor.

"I am well, Mr. President. I hope this day finds you the same." He settled in an upholstered chair facing his desk.

President Lincoln grimaced and shuffled through a mound of papers, mumbling to himself. "Where did I put that fool thing? This mess is impossible." He opened a drawer, grunted his satisfaction, and extracted an envelope. After setting aside the documents in front of him, he removed several greenbacks of varied denominations and spread them across the desk top.

"Tell me what you see." He sat back in his chair and steepled his fingers.

Pinkerton thumbed through the bills under the President's intense gaze. "They're counterfeit, sir. Looks like the same currency we've seen throughout the Southern states. Found some recently outside Philadelphia, in New York City, and a few other nearby cities and towns. Note the flowers." He pointed out a vague under-pattern behind the green-tinted etched images on the reverse side of each greenback. "Printed on wallpaper, same as the rest. Where did you get them?"

Lincoln shot him a withering glare and thumped his fist on the desk. Pinkerton flinched. "Vendors inside this city brought them to me. This city, the capital of these United States! Do you understand what that means? *Do* you?"

"Yes, I do." A flush crept up Pinkerton's neck and he tugged at his collar.

"The counterfeiters—the very ones I appointed you to capture—were, or are, here. Right here, outside the White House. This is unacceptable!" He rose and paced the room.

"Sir, it's possible that a *Union* soldier used them to purchase goods here. I expect that's how they spread."

"Just weeks ago," Lincoln ranted, "the Confederates intended to lay siege on our nation's capital. Thanks to our armies, they only got as far as our outer ring of forts."

"Yes, sir. Terrible thing. A foolhardy move." Pinkerton picked at a thread on his cuff.

"This currency came into Washington City the night Early's army camped on our doorstep." The President leveled angry eyes on him.

"How do you know, sir?"

"A local haberdasher, Grimley, owns a shop close by. He turned in several of these the day after Early broke camp. A gentleman calling himself Hiddenfield entered Grimley's establishment looking to buy a jacket and pants just as he locked his door to leave the city. While folks fled for their lives, this Hiddenfield fellow took time to buy a suit of clothing, but he was in too much of a rush to wait for a fitting. Odd, don't you think?"

"The name is almost worthy of a Dickens novel. Go on, sir."

"Seems the fellow chatted Grimley up right thoroughly. Asked a lot of questions, then paid for his purchases with these fake bills." Lincoln tapped the greenbacks. "I'm certain *Hiddenfield* was an agent for the Confederacy, hired to gather information and pass bogus currency. The nerve of these rebels, sending spies into our own backyard. They will stop at nothing!"

Lincoln moved to an open window and stared out at the Potomac. Distant blasts from passing steamships hung in the afternoon air.

Pinkerton shifted his weight in his chair and took a few deep breaths.

"Allan, you saved my life in Baltimore," the President said. "Had it not been for the Pinkertons, I may not have made it to my inauguration that February day. I will be forever grateful to you for that."

"I cannot take credit. Mrs. Warne saved your life. She is an invaluable asset."

"Ah, Mrs. Warne, my *sister* for one perilous night's journey. Is it true she remained awake all night, guarding me as I slept?"

"It is indeed. She inspired our new slogan, *we never sleep*. Catchy, eh?"

"Yes, quite. Mrs. Lincoln would approve of your decision to hire a female detective. However, I hired you to do a job. Catching counterfeiters is your specialty, yet I see no progress. Instead, the situation escalates."

Pinkerton ran a finger between his collar rim and sweating neck, and willed his jangled nerves to quiet. *How can I explain the counterfeit problem grew to outsize proportions long before I was commissioned to solve it?* "My agents and I work on it around the clock. The process takes time."

"We don't *have* time. This counterfeiting ring is of no small consequence. Its tentacles spread throughout the South. I'm sure they intend to infiltrate the entire country with bogus currency, flooding our economy with their so-called *queer money*. If you do not reel them in, they will cripple our nation."

Pinkerton cast a nervous glance at Lincoln's back. "We're trying our best, sir."

The President continued to gaze out the window. "You mentioned you found evidence of their counterfeit bills in our northern communities. What are you doing about it?"

"I'm unsure how it filters into our system. Our meeting today leads me to suspect this gang is more devious than we imagined. Mr. President, I have spies in every state south of the Mason Dixon Line rooting out their leaders and active conspirators."

Lincoln tossed an outraged glare in Pinkerton's direction but remained silent.

"In any case," Pinkerton went on, "these things take time. Our operatives must integrate themselves into the southern towns. They pretend to be friends, get them chatting. Gain their trust. Observe their comings and goings. Slow and easy, so as not to garner suspicion. One of my best men spent last year gathering evidence in the mountains of North Carolina, a ring stronghold. No simple task, mind you. Thanks to his work, we're closer to making arrests than we've ever been."

"Send your Mrs. Warne. She'll make them talk."

"Mrs. Warne is already on it, sir, along with three other very competent women. My newest lady detective, Mrs. Thorne, is, at this moment, traveling south with the agent I just spoke of."

"Good. Ladies can go places a man cannot." The President shifted from the window and gazed hard at Pinkerton, the gravity of his emotions etched into his lined features. "No more excuses, Allan. Hire more detectives and do it now. Find these sons of anarchy and bring them in!"

14

Fort Montgomery, North Carolina
October 1864

Her rifle at the ready, rookie detective Libby Thorne entered Fort Montgomery, North Carolina in the Bible-packed buckboard she and her partner, agent Coy Hawes, had driven from Chicago. Hawes reined in at Penley's Boarding House, a two-story structure of unpainted wood, distinguished by a second-floor balcony almost as wide as the porch below.

Libby's saucy grit had taken her far at Pinkerton's Detective Agency. However, on her first travel assignment, apprehension tugged at her in this strange town. All the same, a part of her felt right at home.

"You sure about this place?" Libby regarded Hawes, and waited for his answer. *Poor man, he is rather unappealing*, she thought, *save for an admirable black bush of a mustache. But those gnarled hands—* "Just because you spent a year in Bryson City doesn't mean you know it all. This little burg can't interest us." *Don't dismiss it, Libby. Remember why you took this post.*

Dusty and tired after weeks of hard traveling, she climbed down from the wagon, rubbed her aching back, and studied her surroundings, making a slow, full circle. She surveyed the two short blocks that comprised Main Street.

Hawes gave no answer. He loped up the three steps to the porch and opened the boarding house door. Libby made a face, then tucked a few chestnut curls into the bun at her nape and tightened the hat ribbon under her chin. After fluffing the dust off her skirt, she followed him inside.

Libby looked around the lobby, shadowy in the somber lighting. To her right, an intimate parlor, its faded damask upholstery worn but comfortable. Hawes stood at the simple oak wood registration desk on the left. The low-beamed ceiling and curtained windows gave the room a closed-in feeling, but it appeared clean and well-maintained.

"The missus and I would like rooms, please," Hawes said. "Overlooking the street, if you don't mind."

"The rate is one dollar per week," the receptionist replied.

Hawes dipped the fountain pen in the inkwell to sign the guest register, but the clerk slid the book aside. "We rarely get visitors in town. What's your business here?"

Libby moved to her companion's side. "The Good Book, sir," she stated in a practiced Southern drawl. "My husband and I are agents of the Lord. We sell the Scriptures and dispense prayers and healing words."

"Don't need no circuit riders. We got plenty of preachers."

"Sir, we trade in Bibles and offer spiritual aid." She curved her lips into a saintly smile. "So many of His sheep suffer these days."

"Bibles, you say." The man eyed them with suspicion. "How long you aim on staying?"

"I'd 'spec till spring, based on your winters," Hawes replied.

"What would you know of our winters?"

"I been peddling hereabouts for some time now. Folks been mighty hospitable. So much so, I fetched my missus, here, from back home. We're thinking on making a go of it 'round these parts."

"And where would *home* be?"

Before either could reply, a woman whisked to the welcome desk. Her rigid posture and no-nonsense demeanor befitted the proprietor of a respectable family business, and Libby assumed her to be that person.

"Good afternoon, folks—Is there a problem, Joe?"

"Couple of strangers in town, ma'am. Wanna rent rooms for the winter. The gent says he's a Bible salesman."

The woman brushed a graying lock from her forehead and gave them the once-over before answering. "We ought not question a Bible salesman's excellent character. Besides, we need paying guests. You can pay, can't you?" They nodded. "Half-board or full-board?"

Libby cocked her head and peered up at her. "Full-board. We'll give you the first month's rent in advance."

The woman's eyes gleamed. "Sign them in. Welcome to my establishment. I'm Miz Penley. If there's anything we can do to make your stay more comfortable"—She squinted at the roster as Hawes signed their names—"Mr. and Miz Hawes, just ask my receptionist. He'll be happy to accommodate you. *Won't* you?" she added.

Joe gave her a sideways glance.

"So," Mrs. Penley went on, "an upstairs front-facing parlor is available with a single bedroom, very nice indeed. On the opposite corner, a lovely suite with adjoining sleeping quarters. They belonged to my children. However, only one room faces the street."

"We'll take the adjoining rooms," Libby abruptly answered, then quickly added, "Children's bedrooms. They must be sweet."

"As you wish, Miz Hawes. You'll meet our other boarders at supper. Five o'clock sharp. I think you'll find everyone congenial." She picked up a bell—its pitted surface polished to a sheen—and gave it a quick tinkle, summoning a lad of about twelve years. "Our valet will help you with your luggage."

Hawes assisted the bellhop in lugging the couple's baggage up the narrow staircase opposite the reception desk.

Libby trailed behind them. She stopped a moment to take in her new lodgings and witnessed Mrs. Penley lean in toward the clerk's ear. Libby read the innkeeper's lips as she spoke and arched an eyebrow.

Keep an eye on 'em, Joe. There's rumors of suspicious persons of late, over Bryson City way. Not a couple, but one cannot be too careful.

After the boy situated the bags and exited the room, Libby locked the door and listened until she heard his footsteps on the stairs at the far end of the hallway. "The landlady suspects us," she said, checking the connecting room.

Hawes peered behind the window curtain. "Decent view, even with the darned balcony in the way. We can observe Main Street without being seen. What do you mean, she suspects us?"

"She told the clerk to watch us." Libby cracked open the window in the second bedroom. "Ugh, it's fusty in here."

"Then we'll all be watching each other, won't we?" Hawes let the curtain fall into place, removed his dusty brown plaid jacket and waistcoat, slung them over a chair, then plopped onto the child-sized settee to remove his boots. "You shoulda taken the other option. I woulda slept on the sofa."

"I like my privacy. Why did you pick this burg to hole up in, and not Bryson City, after spending so much time there?"

"Because, *Miz Thorne-in-my-side*, I learned all I could over there. What I learned led me here."

"Make fun of me again and I'll be a thorn in your *back*side." She shot him a look, that had it been a stone, could have put his eye out.

He smirked. "While the counterfeiters' ringleader may be in Bryson, the real action is here in Fort Montgomery. This outfit is small but crafty. These boys recruited at least one Injun into their little group. Only gang around done that. Saw him during an ambush near Murphy."

"What ambush?"

"More'n a year back, I followed one of the local counterfeiters to a rendezvous. Never guessed he'd be meeting an Injun and a young soldier. Both of 'em wore Confederate duds. They musta come from the Rebel camp nearby.

"An outlaw was bent on robbing 'em—a big fella with a limp and eyes that would make the bravest man's blood run cold. He surprised the counterfeiter and tied him to a tree. The ambush went sour when the graybacks arrived. The outlaw attacked the young Reb, then gunned him down. A cruel, vicious act. The native almost lost his life trying to save him."

"Why'd he kill a boy?"

"Easy pickings, I reckon, and mighty effective. The one bound up had a conniption fit and the Injun got so overwrought he could hardly shoot straight.

"Ought to help him at the trial. When we catch him, that is."

"Won't be a trial for the likes of him. He's an Injun, for Christ's sake."

"Well, that's a bad law." She chewed her lip for a moment. "What was his name?"

"Whose name?"

"The youngster. Surely you heard something. Everybody 'round here would know about it."

"Why do you care?"

"Because I do—"

Hawes stroked his mustache while he thought. "Biblical, maybe? Aaron? No, Ira—that's it, Ira. Last name, dunno. So many are alike down here."

"Did you say *Ira*?" Unsteady, she sat on the nearest chair.

"What's with you?"

"Nothing. It's nothing," Libby murmured.

"Humph, looks like you got no gumption for this business, after all."

She gulped. "Don't be so smug. It makes me smoking mad knowing there's a man out there with a heart so black he could gun down a child in cold blood."

Hawes grunted. "I said he was young, but he wasn't a *child*, for pity's sake."

"He was some mother's boy." Libby's voice shook with emotion. "Now he's dead. Murdered. If that beast had crossed my path, I would a shot first and asked questions later."

"Pshaw. You'd run like hell, if you're smart."

"Yeah? What did *you* do?"

"I did my job, then ran like hell—I got a theory on their operation. These sneaky counterfeiting rats use their army to spread their funny money around the South. Rebs pass it. Yanks pocket it and carry it North. Clever, eh? But, mark my words, Coy Hawes done found 'em out."

Warm Springs, North Carolina
Winter 1865

The last six months had been a living hell. For all the battles won on the way north, on the trek south, Early's armies lost men and morale. In late November the sixty-four homesick Thomas Legion soldiers—all that remained of the eight hundred high-spirited fighters who embarked with Jason for Shenandoah Valley—received long-awaited orders: Come home.

Relieved to be leaving Virginia, Jason shouldered his pack and boarded a train bound for Asheville, North Carolina. Twenty-five miles from the Carolina border, they disembarked. Federals had dynamited the tracks. Grumbling, Jason trudged southward with his small band of brothers-at-arms. At the border he fell to his knees and kissed the earth.

Near Asheville, the December temperature plummeted. Ghostly clouds roiled over mountain peaks, bringing bitter winds and a tornadic snowstorm that swallowed the horizon. Hungry and half-frozen, the soldiers struggled across a blinding white landscape blanketed in snow. Jason recalled tales of men lost in storms like this one—*Sometimes hunters found their frozen bodies miles off the main road. Sometimes the poor souls were never found at all.*

Shivering and frost-bitten, Jason and his comrades staggered into deserted Warm Springs, once known for its tourist resort and thermal pools. Snow pellets bit Jason's cheeks. Ice caked his lashes. Howling blasts of wind threatened to freeze his eyeballs. *Lord help me, I'm done for.*

Onacona grabbed Jason and shook him. "Look! Up ahead!" He pointed into the swirling white haze.

Squinting, Jason saw a sign. *Warm Springs Hotel.* The promise of life-saving warmth lit a fire inside him and he renewed his struggle.

The owners had boarded up the hotel before fleeing. "Kick in the door," Colonel Love commanded. He wheezed and clutched his rattling chest. Once inside, he divided responsibilities. "Hyde, inspect the cisterns. Break the ice, if you must, but make sure we got clean water." He stopped and took a breath. "You men, check out the wood stores. Light the first-floor fireplaces, then take a ration to each bedroom." A bout of coughing forced him to lower himself into a chair. "Cookie, get in the kitchen and find what there is to eat. Gather your helpers and fix us a hot meal." A lung-whistle accompanied each gasp for air. "The rest of you unroll the mattresses and set out linens. You boys will lie in warm beds tonight."

Sleep came with difficulty for Jason. He reflected on the miserable turn of events after General Early's failed raid on Washington. *After slinking outta there like tuck-tailed dogs, we lost our gumption to fight.* Jason sighed. *At least we're almost home.*

Home. A soft glow from the fire bathed the room with a shimmering golden hue, reminding him of a time before the war. He opened *A Tale of Two Cities*, read a few pages, and relaxed into a fitful rest.

A pitch black night roiled with fog and the ground shook. A horseman appeared, a dark creature with no face and no discernible uniform, neither blue nor gray. His horse galloped toward Jason, though, it seemed, at a turtle's pace, steam bursting forth from its muzzle in hot, slow-motion blasts while its flanks rippled and strained against its strappings. Heavy hooves pounded with a rhythm like cannon fire. He turned to flee. To his horror, roots sprouted from his feet, tying him to the earth as if he were in chains.

Jason awoke gasping, and sprawled on the floor. *Damn dream.* Outside, a horse's neigh prompted him to his feet. He threw open his shutter.

Below, Colonel Love stood amid a snow-driven whirlpool, hacking, his body shuddering with the effort. The mare next to him sidestepped while Love's adjutant pulled on her reins. The colonel glanced upward to the second-floor, and Jason saluted.

"Where y'all going at this hour?"

"Colonel Love's taken a turn for the worse," the aide-de-camp answered. "I'm taking him home to White Sulphur Springs."

"He coming back?"

"When he's suitable to travel. Lieutenant Colonel Smith is in charge till then. Go to bed. You'll wake the others." He helped Love mount his horse and passed him a woolen blanket for extra warmth over his hat and greatcoat. He then climbed onto his own pony's saddle.

Shivering, Jason watched as the company commander and his companion rode into the night, their horses' hooves muffled by drifting snow.

The hotel food supplies soon depleted. Jason and the other soldiers hunted squirrels and rabbits to forestall starvation. After their ammunition dwindled, they built traps, made blow pipes, and bows and arrows. They scavenged for acorns beneath the ever-deepening blanket of white crystalline powder, digging until their hands numbed. Month after month, day after day, to combat the tedium of the long winter, men played pinochle and poker, and checkers or chess on game boards found in the library. Those who could read, read every volume and dime novel available.

Jason grew ever more remote from his friends and distanced himself. In his mind, he envisioned their concerned eyes following him whenever he moved about the place. Fear battled his desires and he suffered from night terrors. He wrote of his obsessions in his diary: Relentless guilt over Ira Lovin's death. A venomous thirst for revenge. An irrepressible yearning for Snowbird Mountain. He worried about his family, and about the law coming after him. Vexed by his journaled ramblings, he ripped out the pages.

At dawn after a sleepless February night, Jason stood alone beside a steaming hot spring which overlooked the valley below. Relentless snowflakes cascaded from the sky and melted in the air around the pool, creating a swirling brume.

"Jace, we need to talk."

Startled, Jason swung around and faced Onacona. He peered into the Cherokee's serious black eyes and saw anger and concern.

Although he guessed at what he wanted to discuss, he wasn't sure how much he knew. "Listen, you're a good friend, but—"

"Friend? Unless you explain what you are hiding, I will not be your friend." He sliced the air with his hand. "No more."

Scowling, Jason turned away from him.

"Look at me!"

Jason felt at once confused, ashamed, and self-righteous. "I've done things," he blurted.

"What things?"

Jason gazed into the steamy haze and lowered his voice. "Swear you won't tell anyone."

The native raised his right hand. "By the spirits."

"Okay—I been running counterfeit." He rubbed his fingers over his forehead. "That's what you wanna know, isn't it?" He angled toward Onacona and back. "Figured as much. In the beginning, I needed to feed my family and pay my debts. I was desperate. A friend offered help, I took it. It came as dealing phony money. Greed got holt of me. I kept on and on. I told myself, the stuff is real to somebody—and it hurts the Yanks. That's good. Isn't it?" He stole another peek at his companion.

Onacona's blank expression answered his question.

Jason faced him. "You knew. All this time, *you knew.*"

Onacona held Jason's gaze.

"Blast! Then why put me through this? How long have you known?"

"Zollicoffer. On a scouting mission, a stranger caught my attention. I tracked him. I thought he might be a Yank. It was your friend. Come to meet up with you on that bluff overlooking the bridge. I shoulda left, but I stayed. I watched you take play money from him."

"Dammit." *I was right—he was judging me!*

Onacona's steely eyes cut through him. "What you do is wrong. It is hard to accept that a friend of mine would cheat people without remorse. I thought you were wise when I met you. I made a mistake. So did you. One day, you will get caught. You will go to the lock-up for a long time. Quit while you can and pray for forgiveness."

Jason gazed skyward. "I can't."

“Ah, Jace.” Onacona sighed. “Make amends with your Keeper. He will forgive you, even if I do not.” He turned and disappeared into the swirling mist.

Jason brooded a while longer, his mood plunging into melancholia. He shook a fist heavenward and cried, “O Lord, I love You well. Why have *You* forsaken me?”

East Buffalo Town, North Carolina

In Cornwoman’s secluded village outside Fort Montgomery, many people fell ill with scarlet fever that winter. Some died. Soon it spread to the neighboring community of East Buffalo. Cornwoman did her best to service them, as well, but heavy snow often rendered travel inaccessible other than by foot.

She and her mare struggled against the deep blanket of powder along Buffalo Road. Forced to dismount, she slogged the last quarter mile up Hyde Road, now a narrow snowbound path. The horse complained, snuffling and spewing steam from her nostrils.

A farmhouse stood at the top of the incline. Inside the fence, a white boy of about twelve years chopped firewood in the side yard. Snowflakes danced around him on drafts of air, a welcome pause in the heavy snowfall they had endured for three days. Behind him, Cornwoman saw a trail carved from the front porch to the woodpile, and another to the barn, with four-foot drifts piled on either side, but no pathway to the gate. No one had left the property since before the month-long series of blizzards cut them off from the outside world.

She neared the railing. “Ho there! Is this the Hyde farm?”

The boy gave a start mid-chop. “I’m *Will* Hyde.”

“My name is Cornwoman, healer from Buffalo Town. I heard you folks need my help.”

“Do we ever! We got the fever!” Will swung his axe into the chopping stump, grabbed a shovel and scooped snow away from the gate. Minutes later, he showed her to the cabin door.

Inside, four sick children stared at the medicine woman with dull, feverish orbs. The youngest, a girl seemingly around the age of two, lay gravely ill. The eldest child, another girl, appeared to be the strongest.

"Cornwoman!" Nancy Hyde clutched her breast. Dark circles ringed her eyes, her cheeks ruddy and sunken. She brushed a greasy string of hair from her weary face. "How did you know we needed help?"

"Word spreads fast, even in a winter storm."

"I tried the Fort Montgomery doctor, but he's busy. The local practitioner can't get up here, neither."

"You mean, Doc Hooper and Martha Taylor. Yes, this fever is everywhere. Many people in my village are ill. I try to keep up. We all do."

"The young'uns been sick for a week. Mary—that's my eldest there—and me made their beds downstairs so we could better tend to 'em, What else can I do? Little Lucy here can't hardly breathe." She stroked the youngest's feverish forehead.

"Do not worry, Miz Hyde. I will fix 'em up good."

After washing her hands, Cornwoman examined the children. "All show signs of the scarlet fever—They are lucky, it coulda been typhus."

"You sure it's *not* typhus?" Nancy asked.

"I am sure. Mary, I need you to prepare a bloodroot poultice, enough for each of them. Do you know how?"

"Yes, Ama. Right away."

She began her treatments, Lucy first. After lighting dried mullein leaves in a bowl next to the bed, she encouraged the leaves' aromatic in the toddler's direction with slow rhythmic motions and sang a prayer to the spirits.

Nancy stroked Lucy's damp hair while Will observed from the foot of the bed.

Mary brought the poultice and Cornwoman laid it across the child's back. "This will loosen the rattle in her lungs."

After looking over the five older children, she opened her medicine bag, extracted two small pouches of herbs, and explained their use. "Make a tea with the senna root and Christmas fern leaves. It will reduce their fever and heal the white spots in their throats." She handed Nancy the first one, then held up the second. "For their cough, black cherry bark. Steep this with honey and give them a teaspoon when they need it."

Nancy's eyes glazed over.

"I'll do it," Mary said. "Mama's tired." She took the herbs from her mother.

"Keep a careful eye on your littlest, here. Her swolled throat could cut off her air supply. If she cannot breathe, prop her up, and thump her back to loosen the *haktu*."

"Mommy, my t'roat hurts." Lucy forced a croupy cough and struggled to sob.

Nancy kissed her sweating brow. "Don't cry. She's doing all she can."

"Why did you not ask for me? I live nearby and coulda begun treatment before she got so far gone."

Nancy's cheeks flushed red. "Well, I thought—the white docs know—I mean—" She sighed and obviously gave up trying to cover her embarrassment. "Are you done here?"

"Oh, no." Cornwoman opened her bag and pulled out her medicine stick, a rattle, and a drum. "I am just getting started."

Cornwoman observed Nancy while she packed her things: massaging her temples, a rosy neck rash, over-tired. In the lantern light next to Lucy's bed, Nancy's cheeks glowed, but under her flush, she appeared pasty.

"Look at me, Miz Hyde." Cornwoman stood over her patient. "Open your mouth and stick out your tongue." She tilted Nancy's chin upward and scrutinized the inside. "White spots. As I expected."

"I can't get sick. I gotta take care of my babies."

"Mama," Mary said, "Will and I'll help you."

"Where is Mr. Hyde?"

Nancy pushed Cornwoman's hand away and snapped, "Off fightin' the war. He left us three years ago."

Nancy's words told her more than anger seethed beneath the surface. Troubled, Cornwoman gazed into the light of the pinewood fire and saw Jason's image. She felt his distress and longing for his family. "He is alive and misses you. He will be home soon."

"Don't gimme that claptrap. He come poking around here, I'll – I'll —"

"Meantime," Cornwoman interrupted, "you gotta care of yourself." She held her hand over the sweat beads on Nancy's forehead, its cast-off heat above normal. "Fever's got holt of you. Will, I need your help."

He leapt to attention. "Yes'm?"

"Go find me some mistletoe. Lots of it."

"Sure! I know where there's a big clump." He grabbed his jacket and shotgun and ran outside.

"Miz Hyde, you must rest. How will you tend your children if you run yourself into the ground? Mary, get the mortar and pestle and keep the kettle hot. I will show you what to do when Will gets back."

Wet flakes poured from the heavens once more, adding another layer to the powder, and making it tough going to the main road. Cornwoman rounded the bend and saw the tail end of a horse standing in the middle of the path. Its rider—a small adult or grown child by the size and bundled in a heavy blanket layered with snow—slumped over the animal's back, unmoving.

"Ho, there!" At the sound of Cornwoman's voice, the horse craned its head in her direction. No answer or movement from the rider. She hurried to the horseman's side.

"You all right?"

A slender young woman, about nineteen or twenty, lay astride her mount, long black hair shielding her identity. One hand limp at her side, ice cold. She brushed the woman's locks from her flushed, unconscious face. "Aramarinda!"

Unfocused, the girl sat up and slid partway off her filly. "It's Mama—"

The Snowbird leader, Dickageeska, and others had arrived at Aramarinda's tiny cabin ahead of Cornwoman and Aramarinda. "This is a sad day," Dickageeska said after greeting them. "Aramarinda, your mama now walks with the Great Spirit."

Cornwoman and Aramarinda watched them wrap the older woman's body in ceremonial robes. After a prayer ritual for the deceased, the villagers added it to the funeral pyre for all who died in the past three days. Soon, fire licked at her mother's shroud, then engulfed her frame. Aramarinda collapsed in Cornwoman's arms.

After the ceremony, Cornwoman took her home and while the snows of winter embraced the earth, she nursed her to good health. A quiet girl of few words, she hardly noticed her patient's coming and going. By spring, she decided her guest should remain with her.

"I will make you a deal," Cornwoman said. "You are a great huntress."

Aramarinda smiled. "Mama often said so."

"I sometimes go hungry, especially in cold months. You may live with me if you provide us with food. Would you do that?" Aramarinda hugged her neck, and Cornwoman took that as a *yes*. "I heard you once used your great hunting skill to save Green Longfeather's life."

"Mama gossiped too much," Aramarinda said, blushing. "But it is true. Some time ago, I came upon a scouting party in the Nantahala—Longfeather and two other warrior-soldiers I did not know."

"What happened?"

The young woman's eyes widened. "It was terrifying! Bushwhackers attacked them at Slickrock Creek. They outnumbered them and woulda killed our warriors had I not helped them—One, a mix-breed, like me, had light eyes. I saved him, too." A shy, half-smile lit her face. "He was tall, handsome. I think of him often."

Cornwoman recalled her youthful pledge to marry a well-favored young warrior, Uku. *I swore to love him forever. Government soldiers captured Uku and took him away. He died on the way to Oklahoma Territory—on the Trail of Tears.* Even now, her heart ached for him.

Her young guest remained with her throughout the winter. Cornwoman taught her to read and write; Aramarinda provided plenty of food. They often ate squirrel stew and turtle soup that season. Soon it seemed as if they had always been together.

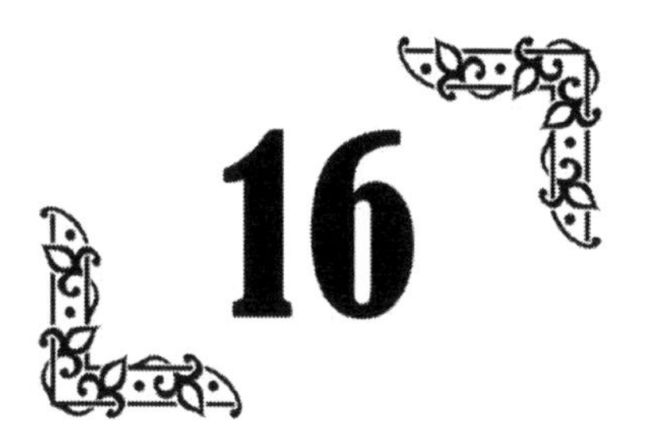

The Last Months of the War
Fort Montgomery, North Carolina
April 1865

Coy Hawes visited pastors and knocked on doors until deep snow made roads impassable. He engaged residents in a few minutes of friendly conversation designed to provide information about the counterfeiters. Meanwhile, Libby acquainted herself with everyone worth knowing and employed her charm to learn where and when the ring members met. Within a few months, she earned their wives' trust—all except one.

On a bright spring morning, she and Hawes stood outside Penley's Boarding House. He tightened the straps on his horse's saddle and checked his bedroll and saddlebags. He secured a stack of Bibles to the rear for appearance's sake.

Libby breathed in the mountain air. "Fort Montgomery couldn't be more different from Chicago. It smells so green here." She handed him a small bundle wrapped in waxed paper and tied with string. "Take this for later. Grit cakes and fried ham from breakfast. Cracklings, too."

Across the road, Caroline Cable exited Cooper's General Store with a bulky package under one arm, the other entwined with Evie Lovin's. "Morning, Miz Hawes," they called.

Libby waved hello, and pulled her shawl tighter against the light chill.

"My place for tea this afternoon?" Caroline asked. "I gotta a bolt of fabric for a new dress I wanna show you. *The Ladies' Companion* is just in." She waved a magazine. "It's got the latest fashion plates."

She shouldn't flash her money like that. "Sure, Miz Cable. I'd love a good chin wag."

"Don't waste your time with those biddies." Hawes made a final adjustment to his horse's bridle.

"Hush your mouth. Those *biddies* are a font of information—and they are gracious ladies. I'll thank you not to speak of them that way. Especially with Miz Lovin in mourning dress."

"Who's she grieving?"

"Her nephew. Some say bushwhackers attacked his scouting party a while back. I don't know her well enough to ask. It wouldn't be polite to pry."

"Not important. So, tell me again why you're so sure our counterfeiters holed up at Warm Springs."

"There's scuttlebutt around town about a faction of the Thomas Legion stationed at the hotel there," she said softly. "The ones that went to the Shenandoah Valley. Miz Lovin says Jason Hyde was amongst 'em. We still can't account for him or the Indian you saw at Murphy. If they're alive, that's where they'll be. Once you find 'em and learn their habits, then we can lay a trap."

"You better be right."

She squinted up at him, shading her eyes from the sun. "Be careful. The welcome at Warm Springs Hotel may not be so warm. Learn the name of that Indian fella at the ambush, if you can. I admire his bravery."

"Don't get carried away, Thorne. He's going to jail after we catch him. Remember, Injuns got no rights."

Libby looked daggers at him. "If women were in charge, we'd change that."

"Well, they ain't. Can you handle being on your own?"

"Don't worry about me, Coy Hawes. While you're gone, I'll work on smoothing Miz Hyde's bristles. Seems she's taken a dislike to me. Maybe I should get to know her daughters first. From a distance, Mary and Sarah seem amiable enough." A curtain flutter in Libby's second-floor bedroom window caught her eye. "Miz Penley's snooping again," she whispered.

"If we could stay somewhere else, we would." Hawes swung a leg over his saddle and guided his horse out of town.

Libby observed Nancy Hyde scurrying out of Cooper's store. She looked straight ahead and hastened down the walkway bordering the storefronts.

"Wait up a second, Miz Hyde." Libby dashed across the roadway, dodging wagons and riders, and hustled after her. "Howdy. Fine day, ain't it?" She sidled into lockstep next to her.

Nancy faced her, gaunt and pale. "Leave me be, Miz Hawes," she barked. "How many times I gotta tell you, I got no truck with outsiders."

"You look a little peaked. You feeling all right?"

Nancy cast a sharp glare. "Keep away from me."

"Good day, then, Miz Hyde," Libby said to her departing back. She spun on her heel and slammed headlong into Nancy's oldest daughter.

The girl's armload of bundles scattered over the walkway.

"Oh, my goodness!" Libby exclaimed. "I'm so sorry. Here, let me help you." They gathered the fallen parcels.

"It's my fault, ma'am. I ought not to run with my arms full."

Libby handed her a twine-wrapped brown paper package and faced the far end of the boardwalk where Nancy stood with her back to them and looked one side to the other as if searching for someone.

"Your mother's waiting for you." Libby turned to the younger woman, shifted her bundles to one arm and offered her hand. "I don't believe we've met. I'm Libby Hawes."

"Pleased to meet you. I'm Mary Hyde." She clasped the ends of Libby's fingers in an awkward handshake.

"We're new in town. Since last fall, anyway. We sell Bibles door to door."

"Yes, I heard about that. Thank you for your help. Mama paid for our groceries and forgot to take them with her. I almost worried she'd forget me, too." She giggled, then gazed at her mother. "One minute, she's fine," she said in a lowered voice. "The next she gets all huffy. I wish this war would end. Everybody's edgy these days."

"Why not send her to the doc?"

"We don't set store with doctoring 'less it's dire. Ready money is dear."

Evie Lovin drove by in her wagon and waved. "Good day, Miss Mary. See you later, Miz Hawes."

"You know the Lovin's?" Mary asked. "Mr. Lovin's been very kind. He encourages us to have faith in our father's safe return."

"Mr. Lovin seems like a nice man. He looks in on y'all?"

"Sometimes. When the mail stopped running, he brought us Daddy's letters and took packages to him in Strawberry Plains. Later on, Daddy was stationed near here—I wish we coulda seen him but men can go where ladies and children can't."

"Mr. Lovin's a regular carrier pigeon, it seems."

Mary looked away. "In Daddy's last letter, he said he had to go fight in Virginia. We've heard nothing from him since. I fear the worst with each passing day."

Libby's heart ached for her. "I can't imagine your suffering. Let's pray this war is over soon."

"We're blessed to have food to eat, which is more'n a lotta people can say."

Libby looked up and down the street. "True enough. I'll walk you to your wagon—Where is it?"

"My brothers took it 'round to the smithy to get a wheel fixed. Here they come now."

A rickety old buckboard rattled around the corner from the far end of Main Street and approached them.

"Over here, Will," Mary called, waving her free arm. He pulled to a halt in front of them. "Not a minute too soon. Mama's having one of her spells," she whispered.

She gestured to Libby. "This is Miz Hawes." Her brothers tipped their hats and mumbled hello. "Johnny, run inside and grab the sack of cornmeal Mr. Cooper's holding for us. Be quick about it." She gazed over Libby's shoulder. "Watch out, here she comes." Fretful, she set her bundles in the back of the wagon and fussed over their arrangement.

Nancy scuttled up the boardwalk, scowling, then flew into a fury. "What took you boys so long?" She waved her arms at Libby. "Get away from my daughter!" she shrieked. "And take your hands off our goods before I call you out for a thief!"

"Mama!" Mary's cheeks splotched with embarrassment. "Miz Hawes helped me. I needed it after you marched off and left our groceries on Mr. Cooper's counter, again." She took Libby's armload of packages and placed them with the others. "I apologize for my mother," she said in a small voice. "Thank you, Miz Hawes."

"Call me Libby." She took Mary's hands in both of hers. "Happy to help. And, Mary, don't be ashamed of what you cannot control. I'll pray for your mama's improved health."

Mary smiled and gratefully nodded.

Libby turned and headed toward the general store. *What luck meeting Mary! I couldn't have planned it better if I tried.* Smiling to herself, she held the door for Johnny as he exited, tugging on the sack. *Seems Hyde's providing for his family well enough.*

She entered the cozy store and absorbed its quaintness. The mingled aromas evoked memories of her childhood. Fresh cheese, pickles, kerosene, chicken feed, cured meats, and the vast array of products stacked floor to ceiling and everywhere in between.

She chose a shopping basket, then browsed the dry goods while mulling over her conclusions. *Does Nancy Hyde know her husband's involved in the ring? Maybe that's why she avoids me. Hawes tracked Joel Lovin carrying phony money to Murphy, and Mary revealed he took packages to Hyde in Tennessee. Running counterfeit is the most likely explanation for that—there's ample opportunity to spread a net wherever their troops move.*

Adam Cable enlisted a while back. He could also be a recipient. Amongst others. So, we know Lovin's the runner, but where does he get the cash? They're not printing it here, or Bryson City. Hawes confirmed that much. Pinkerton reported that counterfeit's expanded well into the North, even to Washington City. That's bad news but not unexpected. My question is, who raised the stakes? Jacob Rose isn't clever enough to hatch a scheme like that. Lovin's their leader, but not a schemer. I doubt Burchfield thought of it. She fingered a bolt of blue-and-white-striped cotton. *Cable could be behind it.* Sniffed a bar of lavender-scented soap, nodded, and placed it in her shopping basket. *Could be Hyde.* She curved her cupid bow lips into a cunning smile. *Where does the Indian fit in?*

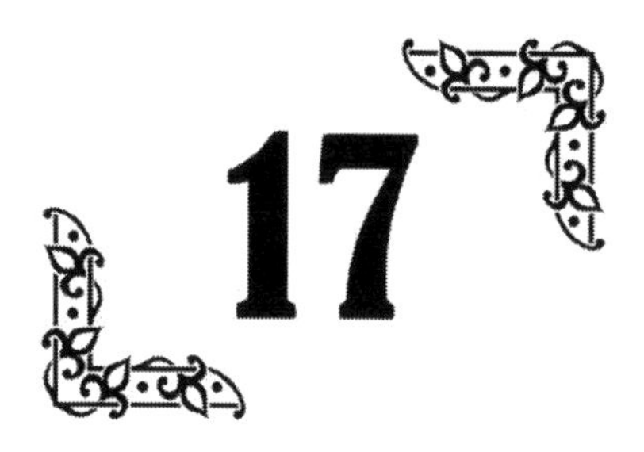

17

Warm Springs, North Carolina
1 May 1865

After a long hiatus, Colonel Love returned to his troops. Upon his arrival, Lieutenant Colonel Smith mustered his men in the hotel courtyard. Jason fell in line with the rest of his company, snapped to attention, and saluted his commanding officer.

"Welcome back Colonel, I trust you recovered well from your illness," Smith said.

"Yes, thank you, Colonel." Love made a visual assessment. "It appears our troop numbers grew since my December departure."

"Without a doubt, sir. Once word got out that we're stationed here, soldiers joined our ranks by the dozens."

"Beg pardon, sir," a private called out, "but our commissions passed their end a while ago. When we goin' home?"

Love pressed his lips to a thin line and surveyed the troops. "I'll remind Colonel Thomas that your conscriptions expired. Now, listen up. General James Martin, our new commander, is encamped at Balsam Gap. Our orders are to join them right away. Pack your gear. We're headed to the Gap, boys."

Coy Hawes arrived in Warm Springs at a deserted hotel. A search of the buildings and surrounding area disclosed evidence of at least one counterfeiter's recent residence. Stripping the mattress from the bed in an upstairs bedroom revealed most of a counterfeit bill caught between a slat and the rope that held it in place. He found a partway burned sheaf of paper in the fireplace.

By the scribblings, the writer appears to be half-mad. Hawes flipped through the pages, stopping to read snippets here and there. *Same family names as Hyde's: a wife named Nancy, a daughter, Mary, a son, Will. A partial, just legible, and more I can't make out. Whoever the author is, he's a pathetic man plagued by dreams of demons. If this is Hyde's doing, ain't no way he's a key operative of the Burchfield ring.*

He folded the journal pages in half, stuffed them into a pouch for safekeeping and left with no clue who the Indian counterfeiter might be. *For once in your life, Miz Thorne-in-my side, you are mistaken. Nothing to do but press on.*

Love's unit arrived at the Gap and reunited with companies previously scattered about the region. Together they boosted Martin's troops to a regiment of a thousand strong. After they settled in and pitched their tents, General Martin assembled them.

"Welcome to your new command post—Since many of those who returned from the Valley campaign are without horses, I encourage you to select a reliable steed from amongst the ones in the paddock. The corporal here will show you the way. Report back in one hour. There is much work to do. Dismissed."

A stallion, pure white, with eyes dark as strong coffee, hesitated near a stand of trees at the edge of the corral. Tentatively, the animal moved into the open, bobbed his head, whickered, and ambled over to Jason, nudging him in greeting.

"Now, if that don't beat all." Jason ran his fingers over the horse's velvety muzzle, then looked him over as he stroked his flanks.

"He looks like a Nantahala haint," Onacona said.

"He does. Think I'll call him Ghost."

White Sulphur Springs, North Carolina

Four days later, Colonel Thomas joined General Martin, Colonel Love, and the Thomas Legion outside White Sulphur Springs, a scenic but vulnerable hamlet rimmed on every side by lofty mountains. At dusk, one thousand soldiers led their horses to the summit overlooking it, careful to remain undetected. That evening, Jason watched the colonel pace the west rim. He seemed to be sizing up their intended target. Soon after, Thomas gathered the men.

"Colonel Bartlett has taken White Sulphur. Tomorrow, we're taking it back," Thomas announced. "At full dark, ring the cliffs with campfires—make 'em big! Prepare for battle! Paint your faces, tie feathers in your hair. Fire your rifles into the sky! Musicians, pound your drums! Let those Union bastards know what's in store!" Speech finished, he grabbed his chest, wheezing hard.

Outside his pup tent, with a small mirror in hand and pots of war paint, Jason painted a red mask on the upper half of his face and added blue pigment to the lower portion. A slash of black temple to temple, and narrow stripes down each cheek. One stripe down the bridge of his nose completed the look. He smeared his torso with red, drew symbols of protection over it, and regarded his handiwork. His image reminded him of the last time he and his brothers did a war dance, three years ago, the night before the battle at Murfreesboro.

We danced the te-yo-hi stripped to the waist. We circled the campfire, whooping and whirling, and hopping to the beat of a drum. One hand pointed to the fire. With the other, we waved our rifles high. He smiled at the recollection. *At the end, we wished each other well, went to our pallets, and lay down to sleep in the frozen mud.*

'Bout then, the bands struck up their tunes. Ours played "Dixie" and "Bonnie Blue Flag". The Yanks replied with "Yankee Doodle" and "Hail, Columbia," both sides playing against t'other. We fell into "Home Sweet Home." Yanks joined in, and Blue and Gray alike, they performed together.

'Be it ever so humble, there's no place like home... Home, home, sweet, sweet home,'

We were, all of us, of a mind in those brief moments, not a nation divided. What innocent babes we were, only just weaned from mother's milk! Oh, how we've changed.

At risk of becoming besotted with melancholy, he put down the mirror and left his tent to join the others around the fires. Along the way, he crossed paths with Colonel Thomas.

"Evening, Colonel." Jason saluted.

"Lieutenant." Thomas succumbed to a bout of coughing. "You look impressive. Tomorrow, let your hair go free. Wear that slouch hat of yours with the turkey feather in the band." Thomas squinted to visualize the total effect. "That will just do the trick. Ride up front with us. It'll help set the tone."

"Yes, sir. Thank you, sir."

Thomas coughed again. Before he stuffed his handkerchief into his pocket, Jason spotted blood. "After the war, I'd like it if we can go back to calling each other by our given names. No more formalities amongst friends. After all, I am godfather to your firstborn son."

"Yes, sir. I mean, sure, Will. That would be grand." He hesitated. "Sir, are you well?"

"Well enough, well enough. Now get yourself to the bonfires. Have some fun."

Soon, the throbbing rhythm of hundreds of drums pulsed through the darkness. Cherokee victory songs rose on the air. The Indian war party whooped and blasted rifles well into the wee hours. The message they delivered to Colonel Bartlett and his men was eerie and unmistakable, as the echoes bounced off the ring of cliffs.

Hawes made camp for the night. The nearby commotion alerted him, and he climbed a tall tree and focused his spyglass.

"Judas Priest, a war party! I wonder which one of those Cherokees over there is our Murphy ambush Indian?"

After steadying himself on the branch, he leaned against the trunk and observed their dancing. He listened to their songs of protection. Their cries for victory. He was at once awed and unnerved by the primal beauty of the scene. “Back East, they call this place the first Wild West. This is why.”

Later, before succumbing to sleep, he rubbed his eyes and mumbled, “I know you’re out there, counterfeiters. Tomorrow I will find you.”

18

White Sulphur Springs
6 May 1865

Adrenaline-spiked from war dancing and pre-battle entreaties for victory, Jason lay on a pallet outside his tent staring at a canopy of stars, feeling as if tomorrow's fight would prove more significant than any other before it. *Orion, my protector, watch over us tomorrow. Something tells me it will be a day to remember.*

He woke at the break of dawn, the camp already bustling with activity.

Thomas readied his soldiers. "I want faces painted and chests bared. Let's give 'em a show they won't soon forget. If you men see deviltry out of a blueshirt, shoot him. Prepare to mount up. We're heading out at six o'clock sharp."

Jason descended the mountain next to Colonel Thomas, the sonorous clop and scrap of one thousand horses' hooves announcing their approach. Near the village, people stopped their morning chores to watch the procession. Jason enjoyed the appearance of import it lent him but reminded himself it would be brief. Thomas was right—close to the town center, he and the other soldiers dodged Union sniper fire and fired back.

Inside White Sulphur Springs, it ceased. General Martin ordered the troops to disperse throughout the dusty streets and encircle the area, but Thomas kept Jason by his side. "Lieutenant, today you are my shadow."

Colonel Bartlett waited for them on the portico of his headquarters, The Springs Hotel, surrounded by his men. They stood at uneasy attention to the colonel's left and right, their anxious eyes darting from Indians to Confederate commanders and back again.

Martin and his retinue came to a halt in front of the colonel. "Colonel Bartlett, g'morning to you," he said casually, and tipped his hat. "You should know," he continued, less insouciant, "you're surrounded. My soldiers are aching for a crack at you, so best watch yourselves."

"Listen to the general," Colonel Thomas added. "Try any funny business and my Indians will scalp you and every one of your boys."

Jason folded his arms across his chest and pulled his six-foot frame tall in his saddle, certain his face paint reinforced the scowl he leveled on Bartlett. He caught the eye of the colonel's adjutant and held it until he looked away.

"Hold on now," Bartlett cautioned, putting up his hands. "No need for violence. There's been enough, wouldn't you say? I came into this town peaceable. I aim to leave it the same way." A slight tremor in his voice betrayed him. "Let's discuss terms. General, may I offer you a cup of coffee? Not the best, but it's fresh."

The Confederate commanders dismounted and went inside. Thomas motioned to three of his Cherokee bodyguards and to Jason. "Y'all come with us. The rest of you, guard the street." Jason followed the others through the lobby into the hotel dining room, their meeting place.

Bartlett frowned and gestured with his chin. "What do you need them for?"

"Insurance," Thomas replied.

Officers for North and South sat on either side of a long table. Negotiations progressed well, with Bartlett agreeing to Martin's terms. They had reached to shake hands when two of Thomas's soldiers kicked open the dining room door and dragged a Union courier into the room.

"General Martin, sir," the messenger said. "I bear an important dispatch from General Tillson for Colonel Bartlett."

"Release him," Martin ordered. The rattled envoy straightened his uniform jacket, saluted, and handed a paper to Bartlett.

The Federal colonel unfolded the message. A shadow of a smile twitched at the corners of his mouth. "This will interest you, General." He passed it to Martin. "From Washington."

A mix of emotions crossed the general's face as he studied the telegram. He dropped the notice, and with a bowed head, slid it across the table.

Bartlett pushed back his chair and rose to his feet. "It's over, gentlemen. The South lost the war." His expression solemn, he glanced at each man's reaction.

Stunned, Jason caught his breath. His mind reeled. *The South lost the war!* He sensed the weight those five words held for the nation. *How many died—How many more suffered for this war? And for what? For what?* He wrestled with rising emotions. *Finally, I'm going home!*

"Well, well. Our present situation reverses course." Bartlett brimmed with a newfound sense of superiority. "It says here," he waved the telegram, "General Lee capitulated to Grant almost a month ago. The report spread quickly, and your other generals followed his example."

Martin laid his palms flat on the table and raised his head. Bartlett met his somber gaze.

"General Martin, it is my duty to request your surrender. Therefore, I hereby place you and your fellow officers under arrest."

"What will you do with us?" Martin asked.

"An authority higher than mine decides the fate of traitors." Bartlett motioned to his guards, and they assisted Martin, Love, and Thomas to their feet. "Soldiers, hand over your weapons."

"Colonel," Thomas interrupted, "begging your pardon, but the Confederacy never issued arms to my legion. Their firearms belong to them. They'll need them to defend themselves against the miscreants who plague our area. Bushwhackers abound in these mountains. My soldiers' horses are personal property, as well. Furthermore, my bodyguards are my private employees, not enlisted men. They must go free, regardless."

"General Martin," Bartlett continued, "deliver the news to your troops. After they sign their paroles, they may leave."

"Colonel Bartlett, *please*," Thomas urged.

Bartlett glanced at Colonel Thomas. "They may keep their arms and horses."

"Thank you, Colonel." Thomas flashed his eyes at General Martin and back to Bartlett. "I'll take responsibility for informing them. These men report directly to me."

Bartlett nodded once. "Granted. Corporal, accompany him to the portico."

"Excuse me, sir, one more message." The courier handed Bartlett a second letter, worn from folding, opening, and refolding.

Bartlett opened it and the color drained from his face. "Dear God!" The paper rattled in his hand as he extended it to Martin. "You'll want to see this, too, General."

Frowning, the general studied the dispatch, his lips drawn into a tight, flat line. He passed the note to Colonel Love. Love scanned it, brows knit. Grave concern registered in both men's eyes. He handed it to Colonel Thomas. His shoulders slumped as he read. He sighed, and leaned his head against his palm, seemingly overwhelmed. The room filled with somber apprehension.

What could be worse than losing the war? Jason thought.

"Accompany me, Lieutenant Hyde." Thomas met Colonel Bartlett's objection before he voiced it. "I need your help." Colonel Thomas clutched both dispatches, steadied himself on Jason's arm, and walked with dignity through the hotel lobby into the morning sun to face his army for the last time.

Jason closed the door behind them, trembling with foreboding, and gazed at his Cherokee brothers. Thomas released Jason's arm as soon as they stepped outside. The troops snapped to attention.

"Men, we received an important announcement from Washington." Thomas held the first telegram aloft, then read them its details: "*General Lee succumbed to Grant at Appomattox on April 9th. Next, Colonel Mosby disbanded his Rangers. General Johnston yielded to Sherman on April 26th…* And thus, the list goes on." He refolded the paper. "They licked us. We're done. The South lost."

Uneasy murmurs filtered through the troops, their emotions as palpable as their war paint, then fused into a collective response. Gloom. Despondence. Joy. The news blazed through the ranks of the guarded Union soldiers and a cheer rose amongst them. Jason stepped away from the door, and placing himself at Thomas's side, positioned his rifle for defense, and glared at them.

"Come to order!" Colonel Thomas raised his voice as loud as his frail lungs would allow. "Men, there is a second, most unsettling message from the Federal War Department." He coughed into his handkerchief. "The *United States* War Department, that is." He cleared his throat. "*President Abraham Lincoln assassinated, bullet to the head, April 15th…*"

For a long, onerous moment, time froze.

"*Murdered by John Wilkes Booth from Maryland. Booth escaped. Tracked to Virginia.*" Thomas placed one hand on the porch column to steady himself. "*Lincoln's assassin dead. Vice President Andrew Johnson sworn in as President on April 15th.*" Thomas allowed his words to register. "Let us pray for President Lincoln." The colonel bowed his head.

Jason's emotions reeled. He stared at Thomas, unsure he heard him correctly. *The President dead? How can that be? What does that mean for the Federals? For us? But we're one, again. Lord, help us all!*

The shock of the moment touched Jason's senses. A spring morning in a dusty mountain town. Before him, a thousand bowed heads, many wanting a wash. A breeze prickled against his skin while the combined sounds of shuffling feet, horse whickers, and the creak of a solitary rocking, rusty hinge synthesized into a single note. All of it registered in Jason's memory, forever marking the end of an era.

He caught Onacona's eye, where he stood beside Standing Bear, and slightly nodded. He yearned to tell him, "We been to hell and back, my friend. Now, we go home."

"Men," Thomas said with genuine affection, "I will always be grateful to every one of you for your bravery, your loyalty, and your dedication. I sincerely thank you for that. You fought hard. You defended your land, valiant warriors, all. In the end—" Thomas's voice cracked. His eyes glistened. "It wasn't enough."

He gestured to the Union officers standing near him. "These gentlemen will issue your paroles and take your oath of allegiance to the United States of America. After that, go home to your families." The colonel attempted a thin smile. "Obey the laws. Preserve your honor."

Thomas trudged across the portico to turn himself in. Jason held the hotel door for him, closing it behind him so gently, it made no sound at all. A silent closure on a terrible chapter in the life of every man present, it set the stage for what was to come.

BOOK II

Aftermath
1865-1867

19

East Buffalo Town, North Carolina
8 May 1865

Nancy shucked peas in the crisp evening air on the front porch of their old homestead, and watched her youngest daughters giggle, laugh, and chase lightning bugs around the yard. Mary sat next to her, peeling potatoes. She admired her daughter's quiet grace and long dark hair with a certain sadness: Tomorrow, Mary would turn seventeen.

Were it not for the war, she would be engaged to a fitting suitor and preparing to begin a family of her own. Still, anticipation of a small birthday celebration lifted Nancy's mood. A smile flickered at the sound of young peepers serenading them from the nearby creek, now flush with icy mountain water from merciless winter snows. In a few weeks, cricket and cicada songs would signal summer.

More work with no man around to help out. Damn his eyes for leaving us. She darkened at the thought.

Hyde Road, a narrow wagon path, lent a scant view from their farmhouse to the Buffalo Road. All day, clusters of horses, followed by wagons, and more wagons, traveled the quiet crossroad bound for the village, a sign something was afoot. Now, the sounds of revelry echoed through the trees and mountain passes while the smell of gunpowder from celebratory shots drifted through the air.

Nancy rubbed her temples against a throbbing headache and called to her sons. "Will! Johnny! Mount up and find out what all the fuss is about up yonder. Keep an eye out for your daddy. Don't you boys dilly dally none. Have a look-see and get right home."

"Yes, ma'am!" They hopped on the old mule and hurried off, no doubt, eager to join the excitement.

"Let's all go," Mary said.

Nancy shook her head. "If this is what I think, I wanna be here when he walks through that gate."

"Mama, you never wrote Daddy once this whole time. Why not?"

"Honey, I begun a hundred letters, then burned 'em. What I got to say to him needs said to his face."

"But he had to go. You know that."

"He ran off. Can't forgive him for that. And with Lucy on the way, too."

"Did he know about Lucy before he left?"

"No. Don't matter, he done us wrong." She pressed her thumbs to either side of her forehead.

"Got another headache, Mama? Cornwoman could fix 'em. Her mistletoe cure helped you. You oughta give her another chance."

"She ain't nothin' more'n a *wise woman.* Birthing babies, poultices, magic charms. She ain't bonafide."

"She saved Lucy's life last winter. She even sent Two Feathers to bring us food."

"All the same, I'd druther stick with my own kind."

"Martha Taylor, then. They say she's the best lay healer around."

"I'll be all right. Put some water to boil, would you? A cup of my special brew will help."

Mary sighed and set her potato peeling chore to the side. "Yes'm."

In the moonlight, Nancy surveyed the scene in front of her. Sarah, her middle daughter, sat on the fence that marked the front yard boundary. She had said she wanted to be the first to hear news from town. Beyond her, Nancy watched a lone horseman turn right at Hyde Road. The clopping of his horse echoed off the trees lining the pathway.

"Granddaddy!" Sarah cried out. She hopped to the ground and sprinted in his direction, tailed by her little sisters.

John Aaron Hyde grinned at his approaching granddaughter. "Still a tomboy, I see. When you gonna trade them britches for a dress? Reckon you're climbing trees and swinging on ropes with your brothers, too."

"Course I am. It's fun."

"John Aaron, I declare!" Nancy set her bowl of shucked peas on the porch floor. "What brings you this way on a fine spring night?" She stepped into the yard, taking long strides to the gate.

Mary came outside, all smiles, and followed her mother. "Been a while, Granddaddy."

His grin spread wider. "War's over! Jace rode in yet?"

Nancy furrowed her brows. "No, he ain't. Explains the racket over yonder. Drums a-beating, whooping and hollering, and firing off shots for hours. Never heard such noise. I sent the boys to learn what's going on. Sarah, help your granddaddy off his horse."

She took the horse's reins and steadied it. Her grandfather hopped down. gave her a hug, and patted the little one's head. "Just came from the village. Didn't see Will and Johnny, but that ain't surprising. They's a mess of people in Buffalo." He pulled a bottle of moonshine from his saddlebag and ambled toward the house.

"Did a lot of soldiers come home?" Mary asked.

"Bunch of 'em trailed in this morning. They been trickling all day since. Jiminy Cricket, don't they got some tales, especially about what just went down over in White Sulphur. Hear tell, Jace rode frontline wearing war paint, hair a-flying, and all. Everybody's buzzing about it."

"So, he is alive," Nancy said. "White Sulphur Springs is only a couple day's ride. Say hi'dy to the young'uns real quick, then they're off to bed. Sarah, take Granddaddy's horse to the barn. Set a feed bag on him and water him, then help Mary tuck in the little 'uns."

John Aaron removed his gun belt and hung it on a hook next to the door while Nancy shoved a stack of Mary's textbooks to one side and pulled out a chair at the old wooden dining table. "Sit. Tell me the news."

He sipped his whiskey, and waited until Sarah passed them, heading upstairs. "The South lost the war, Nance. Lincoln's dead. Murdered by some fella name of Booth—John Wilkes Booth."

Nancy took a sip of tea. "Federal president, murdered? Makes no never mind to us—So, we lost. Lotta hoopla, starving, and killing for nothing. Humph."

While they chatted, the music from town ceased but celebratory pistol-cracks morphed into a barrage of gunfire. Peals of revelry cascaded into screams of terror.

Nancy set down her mug. "Listen—something ain't right."

John Aaron buckled on his gun belt, and they hurried to the front porch.

"Do you smell smoke? Laws a' mercy, where're the boys?" She wrung her hands and scanned the darkness, eyes wide.

"Shh, no peepers," John Aaron whispered. "No night critters a'tall, except the horses acting up over in the barn. Maybe got us a thief." He unholstered his weapon and took off across the yard.

"Be careful," she hissed under her breath. She grabbed the rifle from the house and dashed back to the porch.

Squeals and snorts from the horses filled the air moments before the barn burst into flames. Released from their stalls, the animals ran into the night.

John Aaron bounded toward the burning building, waving his arms. "Whoa there, whoa!"

Against the blaze, the black silhouette of an enormous man limped from the stable, his movements unhurried and confident. Standing near the entrance, the dark form raised his rifle and aimed. A shot rang out. John Aaron staggered and fell to the ground.

White-hooded riders bombarded from the surrounding woods, yowling as they bolted from the darkness. They blasted the air with bullets. Flaming torches illuminated the night. The first rider spurred his horse over the fence and knocked it down; more followed him. Those at the rear flung their firebrands onto the roof and the farmhouse's old shingles ignited like kindling.

Nancy returned to the house, shouting, "Mary, get your sisters out of here! Run for the woods back of the house." She sprinted across the yard and fired into the mass of hooded men. "Cowards! Take off them white caps and lemme see your faces."

She stumbled over John Aaron lying on the ground in a pool of blood. She reloaded and blasted again, wounding one of the night raiders. "Murderers! Don't y'all know the war is over?"

A rider, his face covered by a white bag with eyeholes cut out, rode over to her and growled, "The hell you say. War ain't over for us so long as a Yank, N– – – – –, or Injun is alive in these parts."

"We ain't none of them!"

"That a fact? Best heed our message, Miz Hyde—Get out." He slammed her in the head with his rifle butt.

Nancy crumpled into the trampled dirt, unconscious.

Mary and her three sisters ran out the back door for the safety of the trees, then Mary skidded to a stop. "My books! I can't leave my books! Sarah, take Janie and Lucy to the caves. Be quiet as mice and don't come out. I'll be there directly."

She dashed into the burning cabin. Through the smoke, she spied the stack on the dining table. She scooped them into her arms and raced for the door. A portion of the second floor collapsed as she leapt across the threshold.

From beyond the entrance, an enormous hooded figure reached out and clutched at her, ripping her sleeve. "Not so fast, Mary Hyde. I got business with you."

She shrieked and slipped from his grasp. The man overtook her with two awkward, gimping steps, then wrapped a hand around her loose hair and dragged her kicking and screaming into the smokehouse.

"Mama, Mama!" she cried.

No one came.

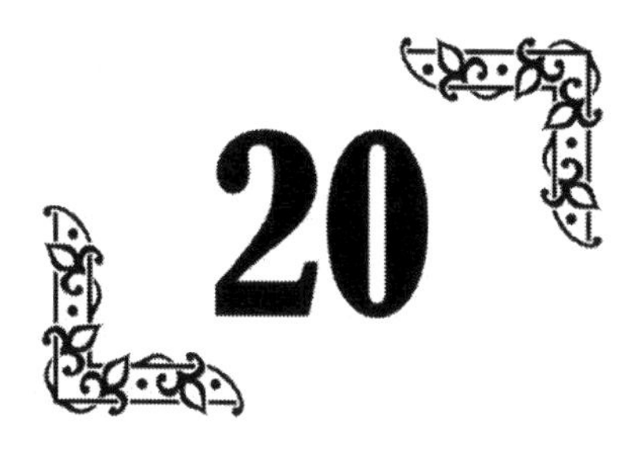

20

White Sulphur Springs

Jason sat on the floor of a jail cell in White Sulphur Springs burdened by the sudden turn of events. The symbols on his bare chest had blurred, and, he was sure, his face paint had smudged, making him look as miserable as he felt. The place smelled of urine and dank mold. He hugged his shivering, shirtless body while he listened to the muffled voices of Colonel Thomas, Lieutenant Colonel Love and General Martin as they conversed across their adjacent cells.

Colonel Thomas's labored breathing and cough grew worse in the damp chill of the jail and each morning the jailer removed blood-soaked rags from Thomas's holding tank. The day before, Colonel Love called him to send for a doctor. None came.

The war finished and for thirty days troops fought, unaware. Men died for nothing. That fact alone stymied Jason. *Damn that Jeff Davis—he did this to us. For what?*

On the second day, he worried they had issued a warrant for his arrest; his anxiety mounted. *Taxes owed, shoving counterfeit. Settle down, they got bigger fish to fry.*

Late on the third day, a young sheriff's deputy, short, scrawny, and wearing a battered tin star on a faded blue Union uniform, entered the back room housing the lockup and opened the door of Jason's cell. Anticipating what may come next, Jason grabbed his hat.

"On your feet, Injun!"

Jason stood, and the lackey shoved him toward the front office, a dim, barren place, with dust motes floating in air tainted by stale cigarettes, burnt coffee, and mold. A single desk stood in the middle of the room, and against one wall, a gun cabinet.

"Sign this." The deputy-soldier shunted a pen across the desktop and pointed to a document. "You can write your name, can't you?"

"I can," Jason said, then hesitated. "What am I signing?"

"This is your parole. It says you pledge loyalty and allegiance to the United States of America and swear not to take up arms against her no more."

Jason glanced over the paperwork; it looked like what the man said. He signed two copies.

The deputy retrieved Jason's belongings from the cabinet and tossed them on the desktop. "These yours?"

"I reckon." Jason put on his gun belt. "Colonel Thomas coming with me?"

"Not my decision," the soldier said, and handed him one of the parole copies. "Take this and don't lose it. And stop asking questions."

"But the colonel, he's bad sick. He could die." Jason opened his money pouch—cash intact—then buttoned it onto his belt. "Come on, Deputy, let him go. Thomas is a good man."

"Get the hell outta here before I throw you back in the clink. I'm taking a dislike to you, Injun."

Jason took a fifty dollar note from his bag and slid it across the desk. "Could you find it in you to help out a sick man? It would mean a lot."

"You're bribing me?" He wadded the phony bill without looking at it and flung it back at Jason. "Get lost, rotter."

Jason retrieved the crumpled bill from the floor, smoothed the wrinkles, and stuffed it into his pouch. "I'll be on my way then." He tipped his hat and left.

Outside, the last shafts of sunlight pierced the tree line of the westernmost mountains. He inhaled a deep breath of fresh air and rubbed the back of his neck.

"About time." Onacona stepped from the shadows, leading two horses, Jason's stallion, Ghost, and his own pinto.

"Dang, you waited for me. Mighty grateful."

"Three days, my friend." He shook three fingers at him. "Where is the colonel?"

"They're not cutting him loose yet. I tried—nothing I could do."

"Not good. He's bad sick." He handed Jason his haversack. "Might wanna scrub off that war paint and put on a shirt. You look a sight. There's water around back. Follow me."

"I'm chilled to the bone from sitting inside that stinking hole."

They strolled to a well behind the boarding house. After getting himself a dipperful of water and filling his canteen, Jason filled the trough with fresh water from the pump. Ghost and the pinto drank while he washed off his paint.

Onacona splashed water on his face, wet his gullet, then reached into his knapsack and handed his companion a few sticks of beef jerky and a dry wedge of army cornbread. "T'ain't much. Maybe we can get us a handout up the road a piece."

The jerky tasted ambrosial after three days of jail food. Jason gobbled it in two bites, then broke off a piece of stale bread for Ghost and dropped the remaining portion into his shirt pocket. "It'll be dark soon. Let's go."

The two companions, brought together in war and tied to one another by mutual experience, mounted their horses and rode west.

Before them, the sun slipped behind indigo mountains. "Hold up, Jace. Look." In the next moment, the sky burst forth in regal splendor, awash with brilliant orange, gold, and shades of blue. Cottony color-streaked puffs drifted across it, lit pink from below.

The scene filled Jason's heart with optimism. "It's been years since I saw the end of a day without a war attached to it."

His past nipped at his heels as his unknown future loomed ahead, and a wave of melancholy washed over him, flushing hope aside. He swiveled in the saddle to gaze at the backside of White Sulphur Springs, the remaining vestige of a three-year journey.

The last of the sun's rays melted into the mountains and the cool evening mist lifted from the verdant earth. An owl echoed its lonely chant from the top of a balsam before departing to seek its prey, perpetual life and death in the earth's cycle.

Onacona pulled his jacket tighter around him. "The killing. Wasting the land. The horror. What was it for?"

The dark silhouette of an eagle gliding across a waxing moon captured Jason's attention before it disappeared into a passing billow, and for a moment, he perceived the world with clear eyes.

"Our petty differences, our vainglorious endeavors, our wanton destruction of God's creation—Nothing more than symbols of man's arrogance. What *was* it for? A reminder, my friend, that our existence is fleeting. Mankind may destroy itself, but the earth will endure despite us."

East Buffalo Town, North Carolina
10 May 1865

The pall of wood smoke hung in the air as Jason and Onacona neared home late the next day. A haze tinted the sky a dull gray, blotting the sun and fading the vivid colors around them. A lone catbird called its mate in an unnatural quiet.

"You smell that?" The Cherokee frowned and pointed west. "Smoke."

"Maybe a back-burning got out of hand," Jason said.

"Not this time of year—it is coming from Raven Town!" Onacona spurred his horse to a full gallop and headed home.

Jason hurried to Hyde Road, a sick feeling in his gut, and as he approached his turnoff the smell grew stronger.

Before long, the clop of Ghost's hooves on the dry dirt road married with the rumble of rushing hoofbeats, and Dan Taylor appeared out of the cheerless afternoon.

"What're you doing here?" Jason asked.

"Onacona told me where to find you. Something bad's happened, Jace. I ain't letting you go to your place alone."

Minutes later, Jason sat astride Ghost and stared at the scene before him. A chimney stood amidst a pile of smoking embers. Every outbuilding was charred, save the smokehouse. The last broken splinter of its door hung from a hinge.

"Jace..." Dan whispered.

Jason signaled for silence, then dismounted and crept toward the devastation. Dan followed. He stepped through the debris and, with trembling hands, poked at the dirt with a stick, looking for clues. "Blood!"

"Here, too!" Dan called from the other side of the yard.

Mary's scattered school books behind the remains of their burnt-out homestead revealed signs of a struggle and led him to the smokehouse. Inside, he found further evidence. Scattered across the ash-strewn floor, he saw strings of dried fish and sausage that once hung from the rafters. A bloody rope knotted onto the meat hook. An enormous handprint on blood-splattered walls. A shattered bucket, its dipper crushed. The place stunk of sweat and urine.

"Looks like a battle happened in here," Dan whispered.

"For all the bloodshed and horror I seen in the last three years, this is the worst—This time it's *my* family's blood." Jason shuddered and wiped away tears with his sleeve. "By God, I'm gonna find the devils who did this. When I do, those sons of bitches will pay—with their lives." He brushed past him, hunched at the side of the structure, and vomited.

Dan wandered back to the remains of the Hyde homestead.

"What do you know about this business?" Jason said, walking up behind him.

"They're calling 'em whitecaps. A bunch of 'em razed Buffalo a couple of nights ago, then went after your place. They hit Onacona's village last night—I'm sorry, I let you down." Leader of Taylor's Raiders, throughout the war, Dan's rogue band defended local citizens from bushwhackers and Union renegades. Now they protected them from white-capped night raiders.

Jason glanced at his pained face. "Whitecaps?"

"Cowards that wear flour sacks on their heads to hide their identity. They're like bushwhackers, near as I can figure, but more organized. Nobody is safe who ain't white."

"Why'd they hit *my* place?"

"Maybe they think you're a Snowbird."

Jason scowled. "Hell, now the hate mongers been let loose, there ain't no stopping 'em. I'm afraid to ask—anybody killed?"

"Some," Dan replied, his tone quiet. "After the attack, the Snowbirds scattered about the countryside. Torn apart, again."

"Where's my family?"

"Can't say, for sure."

Jason whistled for his horse. Ghost trotted to his side, and he hoisted himself into the saddle.

"I'm coming with you," Dan said. "Where you headed?"

"Town. I gotta find Nancy and the young'uns."

Equally burnt, deserted, and devastated, a shroud of smoke hung in Buffalo Town's atmosphere. Slaughtered cows and pigs lay rotting, stinking in the sun; their dry, brown blood mingled with that of former owners. Shops had been gutted and villagers' dwellings had been reduced to rubble. A celebration had been interrupted, with tables upended, pottery broken, and bits of fly-covered food on the ground. In the middle of the square stood the charred effigy of a cross.

"Looks like the work of bushwhackers—or Yanks—except for this burnt cross," Jason murmured. "What does it mean?" His eyes leveled on a sign nailed to the remains of the council house. It read, *Old Mother*. "They're at the church! Come on."

22

Jason and Dan rode into the churchyard as a fading sun caressed the treetops and peepers chirped alongside a nearby creek. Wagons and horses tied to trees and hitching posts dotted the yard. They passed the remains of what must have been a picnic lunch held earlier in the day. Peaceful though it first appeared, on the hillside behind the Old Mother Church, freshly turned Appalachian earth marked multiple graves of the deceased, lining even rows across the grass. All-too-familiar wailing drifted from inside the church walls, combined with the hopeful strains of a Baptist gospel. A simple drumbeat and shiver of a tambourine kept time.

It's me, it's me, oh Lord. Standing in the need of prayer…

Jason and Dan tied their horses, and with grave faces, trudged up the steps and threw open the doors. Inside, lanterns flickered throughout the sanctuary. Prayer candles winked along the perimeter of the dais, adding to the heat of a room filled with mourners.

Reverend Old Tassel, a short Snowbird Indian with a thatch of white hair, round face, and rotund belly, led a mix of devout Christian Cherokees and highlanders in song. He stopped and stared at them. Jason did not recognize the lean young man wearing an ecclesiastic collar who towered behind the pastor.

The churchgoers one by one followed their pastor's gaze, their tune's words fragmenting into snippets of sound. Wails morphed into whispers while Jason scanned the crowd for his family.

After some initial bewilderment, an assembly of battered and bruised relatives and friends surrounded Jason, clapped him on his back or shook his hand. Oft-repeated phrases floated around him on a murmuring cloud.

"Almost didn't recognize you."

"We thought you was dead."

"Daddy, Daddy!" Two familiar voices called from within the mass of people. Will and Johnny climbed over the pews to the aisle, pushing and shoving in boyish zeal to reach their father.

"Let the children pass," voices said, and the throng parted. By the time Johnny reached Jason's open arms, his tears streamed. Will squeezed his eyes shut against his own welling emotions and grabbed onto his daddy, too.

"Thank God, you're safe." Jason sobbed with happiness. "How I missed you! Just look at you, so strong and tall."

"Daddy, why you dressed like an Indian?" Johnny asked, fingering his father's Cherokee sash.

Jason had forgotten about his warrior's uniform. "It's a long story, Son."

He looked up and saw Sarah—pinched and pale, and wearing Mary's faded hand-me-down dress. She moved into the aisle from the middle of a front pew leading little Janie and a much younger girl. He assumed she must be Lucy, his baby daughter, born after his departure three years before, whom he knew of from his children's letters. The crowd parted once more, allowing them to pass.

Jason's heart nearly leapt from his chest and he felt as if he may faint from joy! Laughing and crying at the same time, he hugged Sarah first, then Janie, then hugged them again and kissed their cheeks. His words caught in his throat.

He knelt in front of the baby. "You must be Lucy. I'm your daddy," he said softy. Lucy screwed up her face and he feared she would cry. "It's okay, little one. You got plenty a'time to get used to me." He patted her and stood up. "Sarah, Janie, my goodness, you're all grown up. And so beautiful."

Sarah brushed joyful tears from her cheeks. "I'll be fifteen my next birthday." She turned and looked toward the sanctuary.

Jason followed her gaze. Near the pulpit, a lone figure looked lost and helpless. Nancy. His wife's head was bandaged, both eyes blackened. She scrubbed her hands together in measured rhythm, as if to cleanse them of the horror she had undoubtedly experienced. Old

Tassel stepped to her side and, with a hand on her shoulder, he spoke a few quiet words, gesturing toward Jason.

"No." Nancy mouthed the word.

The congregation looked on in silence as Jason took tentative steps down the aisle to his wife. She stood fast and would not look at him.

"Nancy, it's me, Jace. I'm home. Home for good. I missed you so much!" He wrapped his arms around her. She stiffened.

"Talk to me, Nance. Wh–where's Mary?" He could barely voice the question and feared the answer. She didn't reply. He asked her again. "Where's Mary?"

Nancy whimpered.

Turning to the crowd, he called to them, "Dang it! W*here is Mary*?" Anguished faces stared back at him.

The new pastor took a few steps toward him, but Reverend Old Tassel held up his hand. "Preacher, wait. Josh, meet Jason Hyde, Nancy's husband. Please bid our parishioners good day while I speak with him."

"As you wish." The clergyman moved to the edge of the platform and opened his arms as if gathering his flock to him. "Thanks to each of you for coming today…"

Old Tassel embraced Jason. "Welcome home."

Jason narrowed his eyes. "Not too welcoming so far." He nodded in the new minister's direction. "Who's he?"

"I'll explain everything. Come sit. I need to talk to you. Nancy, I'd like you to join us." The reverend ushered her toward the tiny room where he wrote his sermons.

Trembling, Jason yelled at his back, "Somebody tell me, *is Mary alive*?"

"Yes, Mary is alive," Old Tassel replied.

"Sir, this is the Lord's house," the new preacher admonished. Jason's glare cut him short.

"Jace, this is Joshua Edwards. We call him *Preacher*. Josh, this is Jason Hyde. Jace just came back from the war."

Preacher Edwards held out his palm. "Mr. Hyde, I wish the circumstances were less grim."

"*Lieutenant* Hyde," Jason grumbled, refusing the preacher's hand. "Why is he here?" he asked the reverend.

Old Tassel offered a weak smile. "I'm getting old, Jace. The stress done wore me down. Josh came here last year from Tennessee. He will take over for me in time, but for now we share the responsibilities of our church." He gazed at Jason with sympathetic eyes. "Please come with me to my chambers."

Jason helped Nancy into a chair; she batted his hand away. He took a seat in another, and stared at the elderly preacher, lips pressed and eyes intense.

Old Tassel half-sat on the edge of his small desk, a chubby leg draped over the corner. "I'll be as delicate as I can. One of those hellions beat Mary to within an inch of her life—and worse. She's in Martha Taylor's competent hands and the Lord's mercy is with her."

Jason's head spun, one of his worst fears realized. He mouthed a "No," though no sound emerged.

"Nancy received a serious concussion. Your daddy got shot during the attack, but he's doing well."

Jason gripped Nancy's hand and cried like a child who'd lost its mother. She gave him a long look, her eyes filled with sadness and pain, and withdrew her hand from his grasp. She moaned and rocked back and forth, wringing her hands together in slow motion.

Jason cleared his throat. "I'm gonna find the bastards who did this—sorry, Reverend."

"Been three long years, Jace. You must understand what your family and friends went through. I will not equate their strife with the unimaginable horrors of war, but believe me, they endured trials of their own. From starvation and disease to raids by bandits and bushwhackers. This last attack on our village near broke 'em."

"Whitecaps, Dan said. What can you tell me about 'em?"

"In short, they are a small-minded faction of white men. After two centuries of fighting to keep our rightful place on this earth, these lowlifes use the basest means to push us off it. They brutalized white families who live side by side with us, as well. Some had enough. They packed up and left."

Jason squeezed tears from his eyes with his fingers. "When I was a boy, the Federal government imprisoned most of the Cherokees in these mountains. Forced 'em to leave their ancestral homelands to move a thousand miles to uncharted territory. Thousands perished along the way. Some of the Snowbird tribe escaped and hid in mountain caverns—They lived through the Trail of Tears but lost family members and friends. Did you forget those dark times?"

The minister pressed his lips together. "Of course not. I was in those caves, guiding my brothers and sisters through life's darkness."

"Then you know, it didn't break you or them. Reverend, we just fought a war against that same government. We lost again, but they did not whip us, and will not break us. Never. This is just another brand of civil war. Those whitecaps, they're nothing but a bunch of hooligans. When I find 'em, I swear, I'll put a stop to 'em."

"More bloodshed won't bring those who died back to life. It will not reunite our tribe or rebuild our homes. Solidarity, not discord, is what our people need most."

"Begging your pardon, Reverend, but we need both." Jason rubbed his temples, feeling overwhelmed. "What happened to my other children?"

Old Tassel stared at the floor, arms crossed over his belly. "Nancy sent Will and Johnny to the village to look for you. Soon as that band of devils rode in, the boys spurred their horses into the forest and kept outta sight. From there, they watched 'em beat and murder their friends."

Jason's jaw clenched as he fought to control his emotions.

"Sarah told me she and her sisters escaped into the woods behind your home but got lost in the smoke. She said Little People guided them to a cave, where they hid till morning." The reverend looked at him with a thin smile. "You know how youngsters imagine things."

Jason flicked his eyes at Old Tassel. "Sarah's level-headed. If she says she saw Little People—" Pained, he took Nancy's hand; she pulled it away again. "Will Nancy be all right?"

Old Tassel observed her for a moment. "You gotta talk to Doc Martha about that. She patched her up. Dug the bullet outta your daddy, too. I called on John Aaron this morning. Your father's a tough ol' bird. Not much stops him."

The pastor hesitated. "Jace, these whitecap fellas know our names."

An icy shiver raced up Jason's spine. "Locals. We got rats in the hen house—That true, Nance?"

She looked at Jason for the first time, her expression filled with rage. "Don't y'all talk about me like I ain't in the room," she mumbled in a dull voice.

"Then join the conversation!" his tone sharper than intended.

Nancy threw him a withering look. "The one that hit me—he called me Miz Hyde. Just before he whacked me, he said we better get out of here or else." She looked away. "Where were you?"

He slumped against his chair back. "Sitting in the White Sulphur jail. I'm sorry I got locked up, but nothing will change that. Nancy—" He reached out to her.

She leapt to her feet and backed up to the wall, pointing at him. "Don't! Don't come near me!" Her eyes focused on him, cold and hard, then she looked away again.

Stunned, Jason lowered his hand. He sighed, then glanced from Nancy to the minister. "We should be going, Reverend. Gotta find my young'uns. "

"They're in the sanctuary. Preacher Edwards is keeping an eye on 'em."

Jason opened the door from Old Tassel's study. Johnny sprang from his seat on the pew and hurried to his side, his siblings on his heels. Preacher Edwards stood when Jason and Nancy entered the chapel, now empty of worshipers.

"Daddy, can we go home?" Johnny asked. The rest of the Hyde clan echoed his pleas.

Jason turned to Nancy. "Where *is* home these days?"

"Granddaddy's," Will responded.

Home. The familiar longing welled up inside Jason's heart. He gazed at his waiting children's expectant faces. They reminded him of his missing daughter. *Should I take 'em to Daddy's place or—?* "When can I see Mary?" he asked, turning to Old Tassel.

"Talk to Martha. But don't go with small children. It would be traumatic for them. Take your family home. Visit Mary in the morning."

The creaking wagon jounced to nature's evening chorus and swayed up the narrow, rutted trail to Jason's father's mountain cabin.

Lanterns left and right of the old buckboard frame barely lit the way. He snapped the reins, encouraging the mules to walk a little faster.

"I grew up with these people, Nance," Jason said. "Hell, they're as much a part of me as my own skin. The army destroyed their homes and marched 'em off to Oklahoma. Did they quit? No. And the rest of us stood by those who escaped and hid 'em from the government till Will Thomas could get 'em pardoned up in Richmond. Since then we've, all of us, scraped by, like poor folk do. Got through hard winters. Together. This time's no different."

Ghost trotted alongside with Will and Johnny on his back. Nancy sat on the bench next to Jason while Sarah held Lucy, and she and Janie jostled on the seat behind them, holding onto the sides of the wagon so as not to bounce out.

"Hey-ah!" Jason shouted to the mules, shaking the reins once more. "I been waiting too long to come home. Now I'm here, I'm sifting through the pieces of what used to be our lives. I won't let go of what we had together."

"Our lives left us when you walked out that door three years ago," Nancy fumed.

"Things around here would be the same if I'd fought in that dang war or if I didn't. Nothing's like it was."

"Did you do any good being out there? *No.*" Nancy spat her words at him.

"Christ Almighty, Nancy. One man doesn't win or lose a war. It's over and done with. Help me build our family a new life."

"You thought the law come for you that day. Why?"

"I stole food so we wouldn't starve. Remember those days?"

"That ain't all the stealing you been up to, you and I both know it—You ain't gonna tell me true, are you?"

Jason felt his daughters' huge brown eyes bore into his back, and as a result, the knot in his belly pulled tighter. "It's not about you and me. We have children to take care of. Nancy, we owe it to ourselves, to all of 'em, to make the best of what we got." He waited for a reply, but none came. "Dang it!" He took a frustrated breath. "Let's not talk about this any more for now. We're almost to Daddy's place."

"Don't cuss in front of the young'uns," Nancy muttered.

Around the next curve, the cabin came into view. The boys urged Ghost ahead as their granddaddy hobbled with a walking stick out to the porch to greet them. Despite his bandaged upper body and right arm, he grinned ear to ear. "Gol durn, Son, it's good to see ya!"

Jason guided the wagon into his father's yard. "Daddy, you shouldn't be out of bed."

"A team of wild horses couldn't keep me down now you're here. I reckon if'n I made it this far, I'll get on long enough to say hi'dy to ya."

"Well, you done what you wanted. Now sit yourself down." Jason raised his chin toward the old rocking chairs lining the porch.

He pulled the wagon to a halt, and Nancy climbed down off the bench. His eyes followed her as she walked to the cabin and fumbled with the few objects inside the cloth bag hanging over her arm. She took out a brown medicine bottle. Removing the cap, she downed a hefty dose.

"That's the elixir Doc Martha gave her," Sarah explained. "Soon she'll be out cold and sleep till morning. Her head must hurt bad cause normally she'd make herself a pot of her special brew."

"Special brew?" Jason asked.

"Cornwoman told Mama to drink mistletoe tea for her headaches. She adds herbs and other things, too, calls it her special brew. She was hurting long before she got hit." She gave him a concerned glance, then hopped from the wagon. After helping Janie and Lucy down, they headed for the front door. "Come on, y'all help me make supper."

"Boys, put up the wagon and mules," Jason instructed. "Leave Ghost be, I'm gonna ride back to town and check on Mary."

"Jace, it's almost dark." His father shook his head. "You ain't gonna change nothing by traipsing down there this evening. Doc Martha might not even let you in. Come on, let it wait til tomorrow. We ain't seen each other in years."

"Granddaddy's right," Will added. "And, anyways, the reverend told you not to go. Stay with us, *please*?"

Johnny echoed his grandfather's and brother's protestations.

Jason looked at their faces and sighed. "Oh, all right. Will, brush Ghost real good and then feed and water him." Will led the horses to the barn, and Jason sat next to his father. He reached into his pack and closed his fingers around the almost-finished *A Tale of Two Cities* volume from Nate LeFevre. Briefly he reflected on his arrival at Bagatelle Plantation. His carefree spirit the day of his departure. The dreadful inhumanity that preceded—and followed—his brief respite. Already, it seemed a lifetime ago.

He placed the book aside along with thoughts of the past, grabbed the bottle of Jake Beam, and plastered a smile across his face. "How you feeling, Daddy?" He coated his voice in a cheerfulness he didn't feel and patted his father's knee.

"Don't know why everybody's making such a fuss. Ain't the first time I took a bullet."

After lubricating his daddy's whistle with bourbon and catching up on three years of events, Jason asked the inevitable. "Tell me what you remember about the other night. What you saw. What you heard. Don't leave out a thing."

Bathed, shaved, hair trimmed, and dressed in clean clothes, Jason felt eager to hold Mary in his protective arms, though he dreaded this visit. Worried, he guided his horse along the last stretch of road to Martha Taylor's home. A catbird called from the branch of a nearby tree; its cry echoed Jason's fears.

"Wish I knew what to say."

A gust of wind rustled the surrounding evergreens, its message whispered amongst swooping branches: *Tell Mary you love her. She's not to blame.*

After tying Ghost to the hitching post in Martha's front yard, he trudged to the house, his mind and heart heavy despite his confidence in *Doc* Martha Taylor to care for his daughter.

Martha Taylor was Dan's cousin and a rare mixed-race female healer. While neither a designated Cherokee medicine woman nor a licensed physician, she learned natural healing from her Snowbird mother and gained the respect of both the tribe and whites alike. Regardless, Jason's fears were not eased.

She opened her front door as soon as he dismounted. "Jace, good to see you." She showed him into her parlor.

"How's she doing?" He removed his hat and smoothed his hair.

"Resilient young lady, your Mary. She's beat up bad, but she'll make it."

"She's more'n beat up. Don't sugarcoat it, Doc. Tell me the truth."

"The truth?" Martha replied, solemn and steady, her arms crossed. "Mary's in a lot of pain, physical and emotional. She may never conceive after what that animal did to her."

Jason's stomach twisted.

"But," Martha added, "she'll get through this. Her spirit is strong."

"Did she tell you what happened?"

"Not in so many words. You'd do well not to press her. The night she arrived, she slipped in and out of consciousness. The times she came around, she rambled on near hysterics until she passed out again. She's in a delicate place. Mary will talk when she's ready."

"May I see her?"

"I'll ask her if she's up for visitors." Her expression serious, she moved to a door with a sign that read *Sickroom* and rapped twice. She entered and closed it behind her.

Jason paced outside until it opened again. Mary clung to its frame with Martha's support.

"Daddy. You're home." Mary spoke in a hoarse voice. She wore a clean, white dressing gown, her tall, slender figure stooped, protecting her mid-section. One arm in a sling, her fingers clutched a patterned quilt pulled tight around her. A bandage covered the bridge of her nose. Her face was swollen; her lower lip, split and puffy. A bruise extended from cheek to jaw.

Shocked at the sight, Jason gripped the back of the closest chair.

Mary released the door frame and reached out to him while tears washed her battered cheeks. Martha held her upright as, haltingly, Mary limped, sobbing, into his waiting arms.

He clutched her to him, his heart bursting. "Shh, shh. You're safe now, Mary-Fairybell. Nobody gonna hurt you."

Martha left the room, leaving them alone.

Jason remembered the moment he enfolded his first-born and clutched her to his chest. *When did my tiny babe grow into a young woman? How could anyone treat an innocent child with such vicious contempt?* "I'll always love you, Mary, no matter what," Jason softly said.

"I love you, too, Daddy," she murmured. Though nestled against his heart, her weak body sagged in his arms.

"You wanna sit?"

"I want to stand."

He took a deep, stuttering breath as he stroked her lustrous, dark hair and savored their moment together. "Mary, honey—"

She peered up at him and blinked an eye, the other blackened and swollen shut.

"Sometimes—sometimes bad things happen. It's Satan's way of reminding us of his presence. There's plenty good in the world, but sin exists right alongside it. Through no fault of your own, the devil visited pure evil on you." He spoke gently, making sure she absorbed every word.

Mary rested her head on his chest once more.

"Listen to me, now. Don't blame yourself for the terrible acts born upon you. You did nothing wrong."

Her breathing remained even and controlled.

"The guilt belongs," Jason searched for the words to describe the man who hurt her, "to the shameful creature that did this crime."

Rhythmic measures of the mantel clock counted leaden minutes while quiet sobs racked Mary's frail body.

"I play it in my mind," she said in a voice so soft as to be almost inaudible, "over, and over, and over. I see him hovering above me when I shut my eyes. A horrible sight. If I hadn't gone back for my books—" Mary shuddered. "Worse, had I stayed with my sisters, would this beast have visited his horror on all of us? I'll never know. But if that were the case, I'm glad to have suffered it in order to spare them the torture I endured."

In that moment, Mary's words amplified his vow of retribution on the creature who committed this atrocity against her. "Shush, child. You mustn't tax yourself with such thoughts."

"This won't go away just because we want it to. I never wanted this to happen to me." Mary raised her head, and he saw her determination. "But it did. Nothing will change that."

Anger cloaked him, its mantle woven with threads of pride for his daughter's resilience. "This devil will pay for his sins." Jason's voice shook as he spoke. He held Mary at arm's length and gazed at her—Her inner strength sparkled through her pain.

"I'm so tired. I need to lie down. Please come see me again soon, Daddy. You won't forget, will you?"

"Of course not, Fairybell. Let me help you back to bed."

Inside the whitewashed infirmary, the other five beds were empty. Glad she had it to herself, he tucked her in the way he did when she was little.

Mary squeezed his hand. "Thank you, Daddy." Her eyelids closed and, an instant later, she slept.

Jason blinked hard and tip-toed to the door. Martha waited in the parlor at a small tea table, set with coffee for two. The sight of her reassured him.

"Mary insisted on greeting you standing up. She didn't want to look vulnerable and downtrodden." Martha poured him a cup of steaming umber liquid from a blue and white china pitcher. "Her way of showing resolve. I think she's as stubborn as her daddy," she added with a half-smile.

Jason picked up his beverage, but his hands trembled, and he replaced it in its saucer. The lump in his throat made it difficult to speak. "She's stronger than I'll ever be."

Martha looked at him over wire-rimmed spectacles. "I beg to differ. You told Mary just what she needed to hear."

Jason stared back at her. "You listened to our conversation?"

"Forgive me for eavesdropping—it was rude, but my patient's wellbeing comes first. After I patched Nancy's wounds the night of the attack, I put her in the sickroom with the other patients, including Mary. The next morning, when Nancy saw her, she became hysterical. It's understandable. But she so upset the child—and the others—that I asked her to stay away while Mary heals."

"Oh. Nancy's going through a rough patch." Jason scrubbed his face.

"She blames herself for not coming to Mary's rescue," Martha said. "You might speak to her with the same understanding you showed Mary."

Jason observed Martha for a moment. "It's like I don't know her anymore."

"Nancy may feel the same way. Try talking to her."

"She wants nothing to do with me." Jason grabbed a sip of coffee and chose to change the subject. *That* topic was for another time. "Doc, what happened that night?"

Martha laid her hands on her lap, lips flattened. "Everybody had a story."

Jason clenched and unclenched his fists, trying to calm himself.

"John Aaron said, a raider set the barn on fire and let the horses out while his buddy made off with them. Nancy added that a band of horsemen in white head coverings stormed the place, then set it to burning."

"They're calling 'em whitecaps."

Martha nodded. "One came from behind the house, dragging Mary with him. She fought like the dickens but couldn't get free. He shut the both of them inside a shack—"

"Not a shack. The smokehouse." Jason grew irritated.

"I'm repeating what I heard," Martha replied, then lowered her eyes. "The one that hurt Mary, he—" She swallowed. Her usually pragmatic voice quivered. "He beat her senseless. That animal almost killed her." She stared at her hands. "Without a doubt, he did unspeakable things to her. My examination revealed that." Martha searched Jason's face over her coffee cup, then set it down. "Despicable," she hissed.

Jason's jaw twitched; his cheeks burned. His heart thundered in his ears. He felt as if he'd swallowed a mouthful of cotton. Fury surged, and he slammed his fist to the table, sloshing hot liquid from cups. Martha flinched and looked up at him.

"Who told you this?" He spoke low and slow, his words halting, fists clenched.

Martha pushed her glasses higher on the bridge of her nose. "Olly Oliver. He brought Mary in that night."

Jason narrowed his eyes. Oliver, a white neighbor and a trapper with a homestead a few miles from Hyde Road, lived alone and kept to himself, with no bad blood between them. "What in tarnation was Olly Oliver doing at my house?"

24

Dazed from his visit and not caring where his steed took him, Jason pointed Ghost toward home and allowed him to walk unguided. He came around in front of the Old Mother Church, dismounted, and climbed the steps. Once inside, he trudged up the center aisle, then knocked on Old Tassel's chamber door.

"Reverend, I'm sorry to bother you but I gotta speak with you."

"Not at all, my son. Please come in." The pastor rose from behind his desk and sat next to him. "How can I help?"

Jason unloaded his burdens, and the serious nature of their conversation drifted to tribal matters.

"Sadly, too many homeless Snowbirds packed their few remaining belongings and headed for Oklahoma Indian Territory. Family and friends took in some who stayed; others camped here, in our sanctuary."

"Reverend, I aim to bring your tribe together again. You stand with me on that, don't you?"

"Of course, but, please, no more violence—Did you hear? Will Thomas is back. You should call on him."

Jason arose at daybreak and rode to Quallatown, a day's journey, to Colonel Will Thomas's farm. He arrived just after suppertime.

Sarah Thomas, the colonel's wife, answered the door and showed him into the parlor. "Good to see you, Jace. May I offer you food?"

His stomach replied for him.

A few minutes later, Thomas shuffled into the dining room, wielding a cane. “Thanks for coming, old friend.”

Jason swallowed the bite of ham he was chewing. “How are you, Will? You look awful.”

Thomas sat down, balancing his cane against a chair. “Don’t bother yourself about me. I wasn’t so bad as I made out in that White Sulphur jail. Tell me, what news is there?”

Jason explained what happened in Buffalo Town.

“Yes, I know,” Thomas replied. “The whitecaps hit Raven Town, too, and other villages near the Tennessee border.”

Onacona! Jason’s concern heightened.

“They assailed my Negro sharecroppers before they let me out of that stinking jail. Sarah and I rode out to inspect the damage. We found my best foreman swinging from a rope with a note pinned to him. *N–––––– git out*, it read.” He hung his head and slumped in his chair. “His wife packed her bags and left as soon as we laid her husband to rest. Such a sad day.”

“I’m sorry, Will.”

Thomas’s eyes met his. “We *must stop* those infernal night raiders.”

“And we need to reunite the Snowbirds.”

Thomas straightened and squared his shoulders once more. “Agreed. I’ve given this point some thought…” The colonel poured a glass of water from the table pitcher. “Excuse me, my gullet is still sore.” He sipped, all the while regarding Jason. “My adoptive Cherokee father willed his land to me before he passed. Much of it is in Cheoah Township, near my old trading post, where Buffalo and Cheoah Creeks run through. It is heavily wooded, with fertile valleys filled with lakes and streams and suitable for building new lives. If the tribe wants it, it’s theirs. And yours. My offer includes every displaced family.”

Jason’s brows spiked. “You serious? Will, this is unexpected. ”

“My father would wish that they rebuild their village there.”

Overcome with gratitude, Jason gazed out the window at dusky shadows in the fields and dared hope life would improve. “You should tell ’em yourself; it would mean much more to them. You’re a Snowbird chief. Come to services at the Old Mother on Sunday? Many tribal members will attend.”

"I will. You'll stay with us tonight, yes? I'll have Sarah prepare your room."

Jason left Quallatown the next morning, optimistic for the first time since he arrived. While eager to share his good news, a pressing urgency seethed beneath the surface. He spurred Ghost homeward. Near the turnoff to his father's cabin, he spied a familiar trail and steered him off the main road and into the forest up a steep incline.

He rode his stallion along the inner route to the crest of his favorite mountain, dismounted, and led him the last half-mile across rutted out dry brooks and over tree roots. The sun hung low as he neared his special place overlooking the Nantahala Gorge. He fed his horse a carrot from a ready stash in his saddlebag, patted his side, then left him to nibble grass.

A massive boulder marked his secret praying rock, and at its edge, he inhaled the sweet clean air. *I'd almost forgotten how beautiful it is.*

He removed his shirt, bearing himself to the universe. Willing the tension to leave his body, he extended his arms, tilted his eyes to the heavens, and began his ritual.

"Your love is strong today, O Lord." He commanded his troubled soul to rejoice. "Blessed be thy name! Bless our people with Your Grace!"

He sang the Cherokee prayer the village elders taught him as a boy. "O Great Spirit, help me speak the truth, listen to others with an open mind, and remember the peace found in silence."

Jason knelt at the edge of the world and thanked God for bringing him home. "Lord, not long since, I thought You left me. I beg You, hear me now. Help me take care of my family. Help me save the Snowbirds—they're my family, too." His voice became a trembling whimper as emotion swelled within his soul. "Forgive me my mistakes and comfort me in my effort to right the wrongs I did to others. To Nancy, to young Ira, and many more. Show me the way forward, *please*. You are my only hope."

He drew a stuttering breath and fell to his knees. "I am with you, Snowbirds!" he shouted, again, and again. His echoes reverberated off the mountains. "Lord, help me. Help us."

Big, salty drops squeezed from beneath his closed eyelids. His sobs intensified until at last, his heart opened and grief held from the war merged with that of the previous few days. All of it rushed forth at once. He collapsed, pounding the rock under him with his fist, as loud, heartrending wails of despair emerged from deep within. He sobbed until the torment drained from inside him and he lay, spent.

Jason opened his eyes, sensing the passage of time. Overhead, the setting sun accented a blue velvet sky with red and orange clouds. The evening star winked at him, just visible in the twilight. He sat up, put on his shirt, and used its sleeve to scrub lingering tear streaks from his cheeks. In the crevasse below, a pair of hawks drifted in lazy circles against a backdrop of low-lying mist. Weary but feeling serene and one with God, he was ready to face the world again.

Stronger now, he filled his lungs with pure mountain air. He thought of his partners in the counterfeiting ring; the debt and fear that drove him to become part of it; and remembered Joel Lovin's words, *I helped you feed your family. I know you'll help others in need.* An idea fixed in his mind. Still, good sense warned him: *Pshaw, you're crazy as a loon if you think... Don't do it, it'll never work. And it's illegal.* The thought caught him up short and he laughed at himself. *What have you done lately that* isn't *illegal?*

"Dang it, I gotta try."

He scrambled up the bluff. At the top, Ghost nickered in greeting.

Jason scanned the crest near an ancient dogwood tree, its trunk bent from the wind's relentless embrace. Soon he found what he sought—a cairn so small he overlooked it on his first pass in the dim light. He removed the stones and scraped the rocky soil at the bottom with his bare fingers until a metal box revealed itself. He pulled it from the rubble and lifted the lid. Cautiously he glanced around him, then removed the leather pouch he placed there before the war changed his life. A smile tugged at his lips as he lifted the sack from the box.

Inside lay a small fortune in counterfeit Federal bills, twenty dollar gold pieces, genuine tender, and Mexican silver he had saved in the months prior to joining the Legion. He grabbed a handful of coins, letting them slip through his fingers into the bag. He extracted a corded stack of fifties and flipped his thumb over the money while the wind fluttered its cool tendrils over their edges. "This play money may not be legal but, God help me, it's more'n anybody else got around here. I'm gonna use it to put a roof over everyone's head. No one will freeze this winter, if I have anything to do with it." Reverently, he laid the bundle within the pouch once more, drew the strings tight and tied it to the calico sash he still wore at his waist. He reburied the box deep in its earthen vault, patted the ground, and restacked the cairn, allowing his hands to linger on the topmost stone. *This will be our salvation.*

25

Libby observed from the rear of the crowded church sanctuary with Hawes at her side. She had heard rumblings for half the week of something big happening at the Old Mother Church, and it involved Jason Hyde. Whatever it may be, she and Hawes would be on hand to witness it.

The morning chill had burned off, and ladies fanned themselves inside the warm chapel. In the front pew, Colonel Will Thomas and his wife, Sarah, sat beside Jason and his family. Babies and small children slept in their mothers' arms as Reverend Old Tassel delivered his sermon. Some men nodded off while boys squirmed in their seats, restless to get outside. In a chair near the old reverend's pulpit, a young white minister observed them all.

The reverend broke into a broad grin. "Brethren, a distinguished guest is with us today. It is my pleasure to introduce Colonel Will Thomas. The colonel would like to share happy news with you." Old Tassel took a seat next to his colleague.

Aided by his cane, Thomas shuffled to the base of the minister's platform. He faced the congregation of Snowbird Cherokees and highlanders and cleared his throat. "Good people," he began, "I am aware of the troubles befallen upon our villagers and tribe and I am sorry for it. Our friend, Jason Hyde, came to me asking for my help in this matter. Now, as a chief of the Snowbird tribe, I am honored to serve you."

Hawes leaned close to Libby's ear. "How'd they get a white man for a chief?"

"I dunno, but I'll bet there's a story behind it."

"Therefore, I humbly extend acreage near Cheoah Township in the Buffalo Creek area. This land belonged to Yonaguska, my Cherokee father, and your chief in days past, before he bequeathed it to me. It is beautiful, thick with trees, filled with life-sustaining lakes and streams. Good for hunting, fishing, and raising your families. It would be my father's wish that you here today, and all tribal members displaced by the night raiders, build new homes there. Please accept this gift on behalf of both of us."

The astonished congregation sat silent for a moment, then exploded into discordant voices. Squalling babies added to the excitement. No one slept now.

"Praise the Lord—Hallelujah!" Some rose and extended their hands to the ceiling.

"Some of us whites lost our homesteads that night, Colonel," a voice in the crowd responded. "Who's looking out for us?"

Thomas stood straighter. "My offer is for *all* who lost homes. In addition, I recommend expanding Fort Montgomery's commercial area at the same time. Only a mile from Cheoah, it won't be long until they merge to accommodate the growth."

"We should rebuild in Buffalo Town!" a dissenter hollered. "Why leave?"

"Because the place ain't nothing but charred rubble," came the speedy retort. "It's not the home we left behind when we went off to war. I say we move." This declaration met with a hubbub of agreement from many.

Libby nudged Hawes in the side with her elbow. "This'll be fun."

"Shush," Hawes whispered.

"That's right. Let our old village go home to Mother Nature. She will renew it and fill it with beauty once more. Today it is a place filled with sad memories," another shouted.

They continued to argue the merits of moving.

"What's stopping 'em whitecappers from torching us again?" a voice from the back called out. "Ain't nobody thinking on that. Or did y'all forget?"

"There's nothing to prevent them from returning," Thomas replied. "We must deal with them, with the same malice they brought upon you."

"Hold on there, Colonel!" The reverend leapt to his feet, knocking over his chair. "The war is over and I don't aim on starting another one here. I will not allow talk of violence inside God's house. It's not Christian. Jesus said, *Turn the other cheek*."

"What about an *eye for an eye*, like the Old Testament says?" someone bellowed.

"Chief Thomas is right," cried another.

"No!" the young parson boomed. The room fell silent. He stood and walked to the front of the podium. "The esteemed gentleman before you is mistaken." He raised his arms high, palms open to the gathering. "In the Book of Matthew, Chapter five, verse forty-four, Jee-sus says, *love* thine enemies."

Without hesitation, he launched into his first sermon to the congregation, a fire-and-brimstone homily, each sentence more incensed than the last.

"Jee-sus says to bless them that curseth you-uh. *Yes*. Do not shake your fist at them, do not curse them, *bless* them-uh."

The assembly stilled and emitted not so much as a sniffle. Colonel Thomas stepped aside, and leaning on his cane, he observed with utmost interest.

Libby raised up on her tiptoes, doing her best to suppress a smile, though an excited "eep" forced its way from her mouth. Hawes shushed her.

"Our Savior tells us, do *good* to them that hate you. That's right! He wants us to pray for them which persecute you." He strolled across the platform. "And *why* does He want you to love thine enemies?" He poked a long bony digit at a different parishioner with each question. "To bless them? To do good unto them? To pray for them?"

The preacher arched his back, shook his hands and head. *"Why, indeed?"* he bellowed. He ambled to the other side, one hand to his brow and the other on his hip, seemingly in profound thought. Every eye in the church followed him.

"It's simple, folks. Clear as the light of the Lord-uh." He swept his pointer finger across the crowd. "Jee-sus wants you to pray for your enemies—demands you do good unto them—for one *ver-r-ry* great reason-uh."

He strode to the pulpit with long strides. All heads moved with his short trek, his boots on the wood floor of the ministers' platform the only sound in the sanctuary. He sipped a cup of water while scanning the gathering with spirited eyes.

"Jee-sus," he began again, "tells us to pray for our enemies so that you, and you—and you, fine sir." His tone elevated with each *you* while he air-punched his index finger at one church member and then another, ending with a jab in Jason's direction. "So that you *all-uh…*" His hand swept over the heads of the congregation. "May become children-uh…" He drew a breath. "Of your Fa-ther-uh…" He thrust his fist skyward, finger extended, and cried out the last word with such zeal that the window glass rattled. "In Hea-vennn-uh." He stretched out the last phrase as long as his lungs would allow.

Libby tapped her fingertips together in a soundless clap.

The rest of the stunned parishioners gawked at their new minister until the cry of a baby broke their stupor. The performance over, they took up their noisy discussion once more.

Reverend Old Tassel fixed his eyes upon Preacher Edwards, who appeared well-pleased with himself. "I say to you again, good people," Old Tassel bellowed to his flock, "I will not tolerate rowdy babel in the Lord's house." Rapid fist-thumps to the pulpit produced marginal results. "Take this mess out of my church!"

Old Tassel's eyes widened when no one responded. He removed one shoe and banged its hard leather heel on the lectern.

Libby chanced a quick glance at Hawes to check his reaction to the spectacle before them. Her partner stood, smirking, with his arms folded over his chest.

The shoe-smack worked. The yammer ceased, and the surprised flock gave Old Tassel their rapt attention. Cheeks pink with frustration, he shook his finger at the front door of the church. "This service is over!"

"What in God's name did we just witness?" Hawes mumbled.

Libby tilted her chin. "Whatever it was, this outing was well worth the trip."

"I never heard a livelier sermon." Jason hooked his thumbs on the waistband of his Sunday pants and gave the dirt under his feet a light stomp. A small cloud of dust stirred and settled on his freshly-brushed boot.

He glanced around at the others close by. In the fresh air, the men and older boys gathered under a shade tree. Women stood in clusters, gossiping and ready to voice an opinion when warranted. Amongst them, Nancy cast her eyes about. Next to her, Sarah kept a hand on her mother's arm. Nearby, young children played a game of tag. Jason's sons jostled and elbowed each other, enjoying every moment of the day's proceedings.

Jason Hyde stood in the center of them all. "Colonel Thomas is right. We gotta deal with those whitecaps and do it while we rebuild our homes. We always worked together before. We'll do it again." He panned the crowd. *O Lord, tell me what to say.*

The gathering parted, allowing Will Thomas to move through them. He positioned himself next to Jason and gestured for him to continue speaking.

"Listen everybody, we gotta adjust to changing times," Jason began, his voice raised. "Remember our history. Snowbirds enjoyed peace these many years since the Removal. The white settlers amongst us, my family included, benefited from it. Out of respect for your ancestors as you rebuild lives, you must hold to long-standing values and traditions." Jason smacked one hand into the palm of his other. "Regardless of where you plant your feet. I vote we leave dark memories behind. Cling to what is good inside your hearts and begin anew on the land the colonel offered you."

"Jace is right," Green Longfeather replied. "Listen to what he says. I cast my vote for rebuilding at Buffalo Creek."

"I second it," another added.

They agreed, and disagreed, until they reached a noisy majority consensus.

"You people have gladdened my father and me today," Thomas said. "Folks, Fort Montgomery, and the Cheoah Township must expand to serve our collective needs. The elders and I will meet with their leaders soon. Remember, I represented your interests in the state legislature for many years. I intend to do so again and will do my best to get Cheoah and Fort Montgomery recognized. Once that happens, the town fathers can apply for funding."

"You mean the government'll pay us?" a voice in the crowd said.

"It's not as simple as that," Thomas replied. "There's a mountain of bureaucratic paperwork involved. However, opportunity awaits."

"Will they give us cash to build our homes?" another voice called out.

Thomas hesitated.

"You ain't said nothing about 'em whitecaps, Chief," someone yelled.

"He's right, Will," Jason said. "We gotta flush 'em out."

Thomas rested his eyes on Jason with a look befitting a proud papa and clapped Jason's shoulder. "I know just the man for the job—*you.*" Thomas spoke louder. "I nominate Jason Hyde to lead a posse to stamp out those cussers. He's the best tracker around. If anybody can find these evil-doers, he can. Is there a second to the nomination?"

A resounding, "Second!" erupted. Jason lifted his brows high.

"A show of hands?" Everyone reached a hand skyward. "Done. Jace, appoint a crew. I'll leave it to you to decide on a strategy."

"Don't I get a say in this?" All eyes fell on Jason. He wavered, recalling his pride at being promoted to lieutenant. He remembered the night he sneaked inside the gates of Washington City on a mission for the stalwart General Early. He thought of Nancy's reaction. No doubt, she would be against it.

"Well, will you do it?" Thomas asked.

Jason shoved his hands deep into his pockets and dared to glance at the crowd before him. "I–I reckon so." He cast a sidelong look at Nancy, who stood apart from the huddle, chatting with Will Thomas's wife, seemingly unaware of what just took place.

Will Thomas clapped him on the back. "Done! Congratulations, Jace, you're in charge."

As the throng dispersed, Libby moved closer to Jason to better hear his words, careful to keep out of his line of vision.

Birdy Blevins caught her eye and confronted her. "Hi'dy, Miz Hawes. Good to see you at church today."

"Hello, Miz Blevins," Libby replied, hugging herself.

"What'd you make of Preacher Edwards' sermon?" Birdy clutched her elbow with a firm grip.

Joel Lovin stepped up to Jason, his expression grim, and clasped his hand. Libby strained her ears to catch drifts of their conversation.

"You're a good man to take this on, Jace. Let me be the first to join you."

"Miz Hawes, are you listening to me? You ever hear anything like that sermon in your life?"

"Uh, sure, Miz Blevins, Preacher Edwards." Annoyed, Libby pursed her lips; she had just missed something Jason said.

"... a shame about your brother, James." Jason pressed his lips together. "Murdered by Home Guard over a saddle."

"Pointless waste of a good man." Lovin shook his head.

"Joel, listen, I been meaning to, er,—I'm so sorry about Ira." Jason reached into his pocket and pressed something into Lovin's hand. "Take this. It was his watch. He found it on the battlefield. You're his only kin; he would have wanted you to have it. Ira loved you."

Libby's jaw dropped.

Lovin's eyes glistened as he grasped Jason's shoulder. "Nothing you coulda done different..."

"Miz Hawes?" Birdy asked, shaking Libby's arm.

"... Murphy woods. Evie and I will cherish this. We loved Ira like a son."

The murdered soldier was Ira Lovin? Libby restrained herself from gaping at Joel Lovin. *That means—Joel Lovin is my uncle! It can't be true!*

"Miz Hawes?" Birdy's voice raised an octave.

Joel drew closer to Jason's ear. Libby wrenched her elbow from Birdy's grasp and leaned in, straining to hear the words spoken between them.

"Tomorrow night. Miz Penley's Boarding House, nine o'clock. Be there."

Libby staggered to the far side of the crowd, balanced against the trunk of a tulip tree, and dabbed her eyes with her handkerchief. She preferred that Hawes not see her unnerved, and she especially didn't want him to see her cry. She took a moment, then staggered to the oak tree where he waited.

At her approach, he crushed the stub of his cheroot under his boot and stroked his black mustache. "Learn anything?"

She glanced up at him. “More than you might think.” Her voice shook, though she tried hard to control it.

“Don’t waste your time, Thorne. Hyde’s of little importance. My trip to Warm Springs revealed that much. Hey, you look peaked. Let’s get out of here.” Hawes guided her away from the churchgoers. To those they passed, he tipped his hat while Libby offered a lady-like nod and blinked back tears.

“One thing’s certain,” he added in a low tone, “with homes to build, the counterfeiters’ll be sticking around. We got the goods on most of the ring members, but we don’t know where they meet or how they collect the script. At the same time, we’re in an awkward position. Our cover could get blown.”

“Why would our cover be at risk? We sell Bibles, as far as anyone cares.”

“We been here too long. Traveling salesmen don’t stick around.”

Defiance welling, Libby would go nowhere, not now. “Fort Montgomery is the best place to monitor their movements, and you know it. We’re close, Hawes. I can feel it. A few weeks more and we’ll have ’em.”

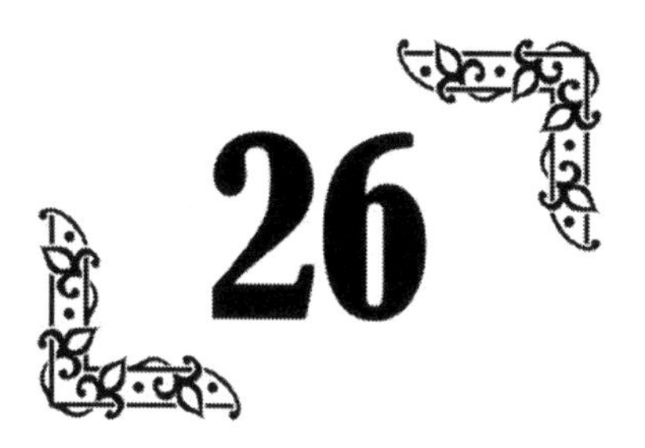

26

Jason had spent the morning poking around Olly Oliver's dirty cabin and nearby hunting grounds. Not finding him, he spurred Ghost west toward Raven Town. A long ride, with the settlement's entry gate anchored in Tennessee, he wished he could pick up the village and turn it around.

Raven Creek bubbled and gurgled down the mountainside, flowing into the Little Tennessee River, its ice-cold mountain water clean and sweet. Dismounting, he knelt on the shore and cupped his hands, scooping spring water to his mouth.

Next to him Ghost ceased to drink, whickered, and swung his head, looking behind him. Sensing trouble, Jason rose to his feet, peered left and right and into the woodland around the stream. One hand on his pistol, he spun around and drew his gun, ready for an ambush.

The raucous shrill of war cries sang out. A band of boys, faces marked with warriors' paint, leapt from the limbs of trees, from behind rocks, and out of the tall wheat grass wielding fishing spears, carved bone clubs, and swinging bolas. They encircled him.

Jason raised his hands.

"Who are you? Whadda you want?" The oldest appeared to be around fifteen and seemed to be their leader.

"My name is Jason Hyde," he replied in Tsalagi. "I'm Onacona's friend. We served together in the war. I aim to pay him a visit, if that's all right with y'all."

The boys shifted their eyes, one to the other. "Prove you are who you say!" the leader barked.

"Forget that. Tie him up!" one whooped.

The others voiced approval of the idea, except for one. A young teen eyed Jason hard. "You say you know my *doda.* Tell me his first name."

"Joseph. Joseph Onacona. You must be Yona."

The boy lowered his bola-swinging arm. "My *doda* was a general in the army," he said in English. "Tell me your rank."

"And a fine general, he was, too. I was only a lieutenant."

The boy let his bola drop to the ground.

"What're you fellas doing out here?" Jason asked.

"At ease, men," their leader commanded. The others lowered their weapons and relaxed. "We're guarding our village. Darn it, why ain't you a bushwhacker?" He jabbed his spear into the soft earth.

Jason grinned. "Lucky for me I'm not. You'd have me hog-tied."

One of the younger boys lifted a cow horn to his lips and blew a quick series of blasts, that to an untrained ear, would sound like nothing more than a cow's lowing. The boy followed them with a bird call.

"Now they know we're coming," Yona explained. "They'll be waiting for us."

Jason mounted Ghost, then pulled Yona up behind him. They ambled across Raven Creek and into Onacona's village with the young cortege. The scent of scorched wood met his nostrils as they approached. The wall encompassing the town, having collapsed after burning, was being rebuilt, its remains stacked nearby. He recognized men from the Thomas Legion among the laborers; they ceased working long enough to acknowledge his presence.

A welcome committee comprised of the tribal holy man, elders, and curious onlookers converged upon him. Excited children and dogs, chattering and barking, ran to greet them while the women scurried about. Wood smoke and the aroma of cooking pots filled the air.

The village was a mix of simple one-story log homes and wattle and daub structures with thatched roofs, many partially burned. The winter quarters escaped damage. A council house stood in the center of town, surrounded by dwellings, gardens, arbors, smoke houses, cook sheds, and a long house. A water tower supported by stilts stood to one side. It reminded Jason of Buffalo Town without white highlanders' cabins.

Onacona, his expression serious, approached with an air of authority from the thick of the melee. A woman and two girls walked beside him, presumably his wife and daughters. Onacona's eyes sparkled when he saw Jason. Yona hopped down from Ghost's back and ran to his father. Jason dismounted and met his friend half way.

"I am pleased to see you, Jason Hyde. Welcome to my home. As you see, it needs repair." He extended his hand.

"You're looking well, my friend. You've been on my mind since the day of our homecoming. It's not been easy for either of us. This is your family?"

"My wife, Noya, and my daughters. You met Yona." He smiled down at his boy. An elder joined them. "My father-in-law, Dan Laughing Crow. He is our tribal leader."

"Welcome, Jason Hyde," Laughing Crow said. "Onacona has told me much about you."

"I will take Lieutenant Hyde's horse to the paddock," Yona said, reaching for Ghost's reins.

"Thank you, Son. Jace, come with me. Noya will bring us food and drink."

An hour later, Jason and Onacona were up to date. While distressed to learn of the deaths of several elders in the Raven Town raid, details of their rescue by Taylor's Raiders impressed Jason.

"Dan Taylor's a good friend of mine. I don't know how he escaped conscription but, for your sakes, I'm glad he did." Jason grew serious. "Onacona, there's something I need to talk to you about. I told you what happened to my daughter."

"Yes, that is terrible news."

"No doubt, the same man who led the raid on your village also attacked mine. I'm putting together a posse. I'd like you to join me in catching this murderous animal."

Before his friend could reply, Noya stepped forward. "No, Joseph. You just came home from a war. I forbid you to take part in another one. The Great Spirit kept you safe these past years, but do not tempt fate. I almost lost my father and my uncle in the raid. I could not bear to lose you."

"Noya, I must help stop this evil." He turned back to Jason. "Of course, I will—"

"Joseph!" Noya's sharp voice cut the air. "Remember, our baby—" She brushed her belly and gave Onacona a warning glance and left the room.

"The chief has spoken, my friend," Jason said. "I'll miss having you with us. My appointment displeased my wife, too, but I have an important reason for wanting this man caught. Her name is Mary." He took a bite of the savory deer meat stew Noya served them and nodded approval. "Now that we're alone, there's another topic I'd like to discuss with you. I got an idea about how to help the Snowbirds replace their homes…" He relayed his plans.

"I think you lost your mind," Onacona said. "You cannot raise a town with counterfeit money. It would be unlucky. Besides, it is wrong. How many times must I remind you?"

"We got natural rcsources. We can cut lumber to build the walls and we can thatch the roofs, but we gotta buy finishings. Window glass, hinges, door knobs and locks, sinks, stoves. We need them before winter sets in. Nobody's got cash for that. I made a promise I would leave no one out in the cold."

"You shouldn't make promises you can't keep. Who did you promise?"

"God."

"Then may God forgive you for that."

27

Libby rocked in the shadows of the Penley's Boarding House balcony, her shawl draped about her shoulders in the mountain-cool night. Lightning bugs winked in the deserted dark of Main Street below her. Tears wet her cheeks as thoughts drifted through her mind of a time long ago—when a girl, about Mary Hyde's age, held a babe in her arms and knew a mother's love for her child. The infant, a boy, slept as his mother stroked his soft shock of strawberry-blond hair and caressed his pale skin. Too soon, the midwife whisked the child away from her forever.

The clip-clop of horse hooves drew her attention. Leaning forward in her chair allowed an unrestricted view of the main street below. The rider dismounted and tethered his horse to the front hitching post. Light from the door glass illuminated his face as he approached the steps. Excited, she brushed tears from her cheeks and glanced at the watch pinned to her bodice: Nine o'clock.

Guest number one, Jacob Rose.

He disappeared under the balcony and she heard his footsteps on the porch. The entry bell tinkled and the door closed with hardly a sound.

Two more riders appeared from the opposite direction, their faces obscured by darkness. They angled down the narrow street to the barn at the rear.

Brimming with curiosity, Libby sneaked into the hall. Quiet conversation filtered up from below, so she hurried to the top of the steps, hid from sight, and peeked into the lobby. Three men lingered near the reception desk, their voices unmistakable. She recognized them despite lowered lanterns and shadows cast across their faces: Jacob Rose, Adam Cable, Joel Lovin.

A sinewy umbra, the all-business rap of leather soles, and the rattle of keys on a ring preceded Louisa Penley's entrance from the kitchen. She carried a tray of refreshments. Greeting them, she led them down a curtained hallway close to the welcome desk. Somewhere at the end, the sound of another portal opened and closed, followed by the muffled click of a lock.

With a silvery tinkle of the entry bell, a late arrival entered the lobby—Jason Hyde.

Libby's heart thudded in her ears. Acting on impulse, she moved to the top step and descended, not taking her eyes off the visitor. Jason watched her, unmoving. At the bottom, she sauntered past him without breaking eye contact. "Good evening, sir. Lovely night for a stroll." At the exit, she paused and regarded him over her shoulder.

Befuddlement written across his face, Jason tipped his hat.

The brisk tick of the landlady's shoes signaled her return, prompting Libby to leave—but she was not fast enough to avoid talking to her.

"Going out, Miz Hawes?" The displeasure in Louisa's voice was clear.

"Yes, Miz Penley, I thought I would. I just said to your guest, what a pleasant night it is."

"Unescorted? Don't tarry, madam. The hour is late. It's not safe to venture out alone. Evil men lurk about these days. Too many 'round here can attest to that." Her eyes darted to Jason and back to Libby.

Libby did not miss Jason's almost imperceptible chin twitch. "Thank you for the warning. I'll be fine."

She quietly closed the door behind her. "Got 'em!" she mouthed and danced down the boardwalk. "They meet right under our noses! Wait'll I tell Hawes."

Jason sat with the other three men at a small wooden table laid with a bottle of whiskey, glasses, and a plate of sandwiches. They each helped themselves to food and drink, exchanged pleasantries, and news of the day.

"Gentlemen, we meet again," Joel Lovin said, opening the meeting. "It's been a long time. Shall we begin by welcoming Jace and Adam back into the fold?"

With general business brought up to date, Jason took over. "I got a couple of things to address. Tonight a resident saw me come in, maybe saw all of us. Louisa called her Miz Hawes—her husband is a Bible salesman."

"I know 'em," Cable said. "My wife is real chummy with Miz Hawes."

"Mine, too," Joel added. "Hear tell, your Nancy don't much care for her but it ain't for lack of trying on Miz Hawes's part."

Jason glanced in Jacob Rose's direction; Rose shrugged.

"We gotta stop meeting here, starting now," Jason said. "Better we move around to different places." He thought of the boys who accosted him near Raven Town. "We'll do it the Cherokee way, with lookouts and a tracking system so we know who's coming and going."

The men frowned.

"You been in the fight too long, Jace. It's made you skittish," Joel remarked.

"Trust me, my instincts are never wrong. Say the word. I'll handle the details."

"I think you're overreacting. However, I know your judgment is good. What do you fellas think?"

"If you're willing to do the work, we'll go along, right Jake?" Cable replied.

Rose grunted.

"So be it," Jason said. "Now, I've got new business to discuss. Boys, we're all doing well enough these days. We got our bills paid, food on our tables, our families clothed. Most of us here got a place to call home."

"Heard about your house being burnt," Rose said. "Crying shame."

"Along with all of Buffalo," Jason snapped. "Which brings me to a proposition. I believe it's time for us to give back." Blank stares met his eyes. "You heard me. Our neighbors are suffering mightily."

"What *are* you going on about?" Cable asked, bewildered.

"I'm proposing we start up a building and loan."

"You wanna lend folks money. Like a bank?" Joel snorted. "Maybe you forgot, our currency ain't real."

"Exactly like a bank. When a customer asks a bank for money to buy a farm or build a barn, they pass out their own notes, printed in back rooms. Nothing but shinplasters in the truest sense, endorsed by the government. They hand it out and want recompense *with interest* from the poor sods. Nothing's stopping us from doing the same thing, but our loans will have lenient payback terms. I wanna push it as far as we can so these folks can rebuild their homes, their town, and their lives."

Joel's drumming fingers accented leaden silence.

"A cannonball musta cracked your skull." Cable shook his head, heavy brows knitted. "Too risky. It'll draw undue attention to our operation."

"I'll make it work, boys." Confident, Jason continued. "After what took place in Buffalo Town, and other villages around here, we got an obligation to help 'em. It's the right thing to do."

"There ain't nothing right about what we're doing, and you know it," Cable muttered.

"All the more reason to do one thing that *is* right."

"You looking for a ticket to salvation? Law ain't gonna be lenient if they catch up to us," Jacob Rose groused.

"This isn't about me, or us. It's about our friends and neighbors. They need help and we're in a position to give it to 'em like nobody else around."

"Why don't we just fix up the entire town while we're at it?" Rose sneered.

Three sets of eyes deadpanned him.

"Why not?" Joel jumped in. "Hey, I'm serious. Who's gonna squawk when they gotta roof over their head and a no interest loan? What'll the Feds do, arrest everybody? Destroy the town?" His statement swept over them. "But they won't. They pledged to rebuild."

"And then, we'll be living like damn Yankees." Rose thumped his fist on the table.

"Forget that. We can't afford it," Cable said. "We gotta pay for our notes."

"You'll get it back," Jason replied. "Everybody's gotta buy what they can't make. Store-bought goods from outside will bring legal tender—which they get in change at purchase—in loan payments. We'll rake in a boodle. As for paying us back or not, y'all know folks here give what they got, like in kind—be it favors, money, or meanness. I'll pitch in capital for startup costs. Anything y'all chip in will earn you a bigger stake in our company."

Cable and Rose hemmed and hawed.

"Jace's gotta peach of an idea here, boys," Joel said, sealing the deal. "We oughta listen to him. He's been right before."

"When do we start?" Cable huffed.

Jason suppressed a smile. "Right away. I'm thinking we set up shop at the Old Mother. Everybody meets there to discuss building plans. I move we put Jake in charge of setup—are you with us?" He settled his gaze on Rose.

Rose scowled. "Yeah, I guess."

"We gonna charge interest on the payback, right?" Cable complained.

"Half a percent good?" Jason asked.

Cable grumbled a bit more, then nodded.

"I'll get Reverend Old Tassel's permission to set up a table at the Old Mother next to the building plans. Joel, you and Jacob talk to Burchfield. Arrange for our deliveries to double. Once this gets going, we may need to punch it up triple."

"My brother operates a small printing press," Rose said. "I'll ask him to print up announcements. What're we gonna call our little venture?"

Jason leaned back in his chair and grinned at his new business partners. "Revival Loan Association. Any objections?"

The ensuing weeks and months occupied much of Jason's time. He arranged for the partners to meet in Joel Lovin's study, in Adam Cable's barn, and other clandestine locations. They mapped out the details for their company. At the same time, he appointed a posse comprising men he knew well: Dan Taylor, Green Longfeather, Munson Crisp, Joel Lovin, and a half-dozen others. Though grateful for those who volunteered, he would miss Onacona's presence. He devised a plan of action. The hunt for the whitecaps was on.

Though satisfied with his progress, one thing still ate at him…

28

Late Summer 1865

Jason's daddy took his younger grandchildren fishing while Sarah busied herself with chores. Jason prepared for a trip to the Old Mother Church and hitched the mule to the ramshackle buckboard, then looked for Nancy.

He found her on the cabin's back porch. A honeysuckle vine meandered across one corner, filling the morning air with its sweet scent. Under it, Nancy kept time in her rocker while humming "Amazing Grace." She had her eyes affixed to bees swarming round a blooming tulip tree and cradled a mug filled with steaming liquid in her hands. Her dark brown locks, streaked with gray though she was thirty-four years old, hung loose. She wore a pair of Jason's old coveralls, pants cuffed to fit her shorter legs, and a white sleeveless shift tucked inside the garment's shapeless form. Jason smiled and wondered if she picked up the habit of wearing pants from Sarah.

"Hear the bees up there, Sarah?" Nancy said. "Their song sounds just like *Amazing Grace*."

"You're doing a mighty fine job of humming it," Jason replied.

The moment he spoke, Nancy grimaced and increased her rhythm.

"Nance, I been looking all over for you. You going with me to the meeting this morning? We're finishing the plans for our house. I'd think you'd wanna tell 'em how big to make your kitchen."

She stared straight ahead, rocking hard.

"We're gonna have modern fixin's, like plumbing," he said, trying to excite her interest. "Imagine, all you gotta do is raise the spigot handle and siphoned creek water spills out into the sink, just like at the pump. No more breaking ice in the wintertime and carrying filled buckets inside. I'm getting you a coal-burning cast iron stove like one I saw in Virginia. A shiny, new one with built-in ovens. Doesn't that sound grand?"

Color rose in her sunburned cheeks, tinting them a deep shade of crimson that emphasized the rifle-butt gash across her forehead. The sight stabbed Jason with a painful reminder of what she had gone through.

"Why won't you talk to me?" he pleaded. "Please, tell me what I did. I'll make it up to you."

She stilled her chair and glowered at him. "You can't turn back time," she spat out. "You *deserted* me and the young'uns while you traipsed all over tarnation with your war buddies."

"That's not so!"

Nancy stood and flung her enamel coffee mug at him, splashing hot liquid on Jason's feet and legs. He sucked air against the sting.

"Nancy, I missed all you all so much. My heart ached for you every day."

She rushed at him, then inclined her face to his. "You weren't here for the bushwhacker raids. You weren't here when we half froze to death in the cold months. Last winter, with snow so deep we couldn't get out, the young'uns got the fever and Lucy almost died. I didn't know if we'd make it through without you or if we'd ever see you again. Where were you when 'em cappers burnt our house? When they shot your daddy? When they raped my Mary?—In jail, that's where! Now you wanna make it up to me? You can't!"

"I–I'm sorry," Jason stammered. He stepped away from her, perplexed. She moved toward him. He backed off again, stumbled off the porch, and landed hard on the ground a foot below.

"Now you're running around with your pals looking for more trouble with them capper scoundrels. Ain't they done us enough damage already?"

"Wouldn'ta changed a thing if I was here that night. Most likely, they woulda gunned down Daddy and me, both."

"I wish—!" Nancy's face contorted with rage.

"Don't you understand? I'm doing my best to find the whitecaps so we can bring them to justice for what they did to us and everybody else."

"I understand this—*You abandoned us!*" she screeched. The sound echoed through the timbers. She grabbed two handfuls of her hair and pulled. Wads ripped from her scalp.

She stared at the tufts, then dropped them to the floor. She leapt onto the dusty turf, forcing the chickens to scatter, and stormed into the woods.

"Nance?" Jason said in a small voice. He stared at her departing back, then scrambled to his feet. "Dang, I've never seen her so mad."

"Let her cool off," Sarah said. "She'll be back."

Startled, Jason swiveled toward the sound of her voice. "How long you been there?" She stood in the doorway, munching on a paw paw fruit.

"Long enough. Daddy, I want you to know that none of the rest of us feels like Mama does. Mary and I tell Janie and Lucy all the time how you went out in the world to save us. We dreamed of the day you'd come home. The boys think you're a hero. We all do. Except Mama."

"What's happened to her, Sarah? She's not the same as when I left for the war."

Sarah shrugged. "It's the headaches. She's had 'em for a while. They're worse since she got rifle-butted."

Jason kicked a wad of hair out of the way and stepped onto the porch. He faced his daughter. "I'd give anything to have your mama back like before. You know that, don't you?"

"Sure, Daddy, we all would. Remember when that stranger came to the house looking for you? You mentioned it the day you got back."

"Of course."

"Mama never told you about him, did she?"

Jason prepared himself for the answer.

"A conscripter, come to enlist you into the same war you ran off to. If he'd a found you, she coulda been mad at him instead of you."

Jason stared at Sarah, unsure of how to react. *A conscripter! The law was never after me, like Joel said. Could be, they still aren't.* "I mighta been in a different army, not fighting side by side with my brothers. Lotta things might be different. I might be dead. But I'm here now, and honey, I'm gonna catch those devils who did this to us."

"Catch 'em and put 'em six feet under. They ruined our lives." With an angry thrust, Sarah tossed the last bit of paw paw off the porch and wiped her hands on her coveralls. "Take me with you. I'd love a kitchen with running water and a fancy oven. I do all the cooking." She turned to go back inside, then stopped and faced him. "Let's visit Mary on the way. She might remember more about that night."

Jason secured the mule to the wagon and tethered Ghost to the back. He and Sarah climbed in. He jerked the reins and set the mule plodding along the rutted mountain pathway, the wagon's rattle and squeak signaling their approach to every creature around.

He turned them off the trail onto the main road and saw a man walking a quarter mile ahead of them, rifle in one hand, a handful of pelts in the other. They drew closer, and Jason recognized him—Olly Oliver.

Jason led the mule to the side of the road and handed the reins to Sarah. "Stay put. If there's any shooting, duck into the forest, y'hear?"

"What's going on?"

"Do as I say." He grabbed his Springfield musketoon from under the bench, jumped from the wagon and loosened Ghost's tether. Swinging onto his back, Jason gave his flank a small kick and urged him onward at a full gallop.

Oliver swung around, dropped his pelts, and drew up his rifle to take aim.

A signal from Jason's knees pulled Ghost up hard beside the trapper. Pebbles and dust flew in the still summer air, as Jason aimed his weapon between Oliver's eyes.

"Drop it," Jason growled.

The man flung his rifle away. Cowed, he looked up at him through strings of greasy hair and raised his hands high. "I didn't do nothing, I swan."

"Olly Oliver, I been looking for you."

"Well, you found me." Oliver snapped his head upright.

"Hear tell, you had something to do with the whitecap raid on Buffalo a few weeks back—and the one on my home. Supposing you tell me about it." He adjusted his aim and looked Olly in the eye.

"Got nothing to do with that. A bunch of 'em boys was on the road that day coming back from the war. Wanted to be part of the celebrating so's I was on my way into town. Now lower your rifle and I'll tell you what I saw at your place. 'At's what you want, ain't it?"

Jason uncocked his weapon and lowered it.

Olly stuffed his hands into his coverall pockets and kicked a stone in the dusty road with the toe of his boot.

"Keep 'em where I can see 'em, Oliver. Start talking."

"Okay, okay." He crossed his arms over his chest. "Afore I got to Buffalo Town, I smelt smoke. They was a powerful squalling coming from up your way. I knew something weren't right so I headed my ol' mule up Hyde Road. Your homestead was all aflame. A gang of about eight or nine men on horseback shooting up the place. Some carried torches—set everything to fire. I quick rode into the trees so's they wouldn't see me. I watched the going's on from there."

"What'd you see?"

"Miz Nancy, laying in the front yard, bleeding from her head. Your pap, face down in the dirt." Oliver's hand movements mirrored the layout of Jason's property. "Lots of blood all around him. Both of 'em looked to be pretty bad off."

"What did the attackers look like? Could you make out faces?"

"None a'tall. They had flour sacks on their heads pulled down to their shoulders. Eye-holes cut outta the coverings so's they could see."

"Why'd you call 'em a gang?"

"'Cause they all wore the same red shirts with these white patches pinned to 'em. Some kinda drawn symbols on 'em. A triangle, some lettering."

"What happened next?"

"Well, they was making a ruckus and calling to one of 'em holed up inside a little shack off to one side—"

"Not a shack. A smokehouse," Jason interjected, irritated. *My next smokehouse won't look like a shack.*

"One man got down off his horse and kicked in the door. He acted mighty pissed. *Damn it, Win!* he said." Oliver hesitated, furtively glancing up at Jason.

"Win what? Didn't you get more'n that?"

Oliver winced and shoved his hands in his pockets again. "First one, he said, *Selfish som'bitch. Shoulda passed her 'round so's we could all have at 'er.*"

Jason roared and raised his rifle to smack Oliver with it. "How dare you repeat something like that! I oughta kill you."

Olly squeezed his eyes shut and dropped to his knees. He raised his hands, defensively shielding his head. "Hear me out. I'm telling you what happened—Then another one, he hollered, *Hyde ain't hereabouts, neither. Let's get the hell on the road.*"

Jason froze. He spit a gob of saliva off to the side to get the sour taste out of his mouth. It didn't work. "Who is Win?"

Oliver moved into a crouch but hovered near the ground, shivering. "Dunno."

Jason glared at him, reflecting the hatred he felt for the vile little trapper. "Keep talking."

Oliver cowered, half-standing. "Ain't no more to tell. I couldn't do nothing or they'd shoot me. After they rode out, I went to check on Miz Nancy and your pap. Out cold, both of 'em, but breathing. Next, I ran over to the shack." He gave Jason the side-eye. "Er, smokehouse. Miss Mary—t'was awful what he done to 'er—but she was alive, too, thanks Jesus." He got to his feet, sniffed, and rubbed his nose. "Jace, no pap should see a sight like that."

"Keep it to yourself, damn you."

Olly shifted his weight. "All right, all right. I covered her up and put her on my horse. Carried her straight to Doc Martha's so's she could patch 'er up.

"They's buncha others already in the waiting room who got beat up or tuck a bullet. Somebody went for a midwife to help out but she sure coulda used more'n that. Felt right sorry for 'er."

"What about my wife and my daddy?"

"I told some of 'em 'bout Miz Nancy and Mr. John Aaron lying in your yard and needing help. Two Feathers and me, we rode to your place and fetched 'em, and carried 'em both to the doc's." Olly raised his eyes and met Jason's. "S'all I know. I hate this happened to y'all."

"I'm sure." Jason sensed more to the story. Oliver knew too many details. However, he wouldn't get much more from him, for now. "Go on, get outta here."

Oliver grabbed his pelts and rifle and hurried off-road into the trees, running into the woodlands as fast as his bandy legs would carry him.

"Hey, Olly," Jason shouted after him. "What color shirt did you wear that night?"

"Don't recall!"

One thing's certain, they're after me. The knot in Jason's stomach wrenched.

Jason and Sarah pulled into Martha Taylor's yard and hitched the wagon to the post next to another visitor. Before he could knock, the door opened.

"Jace, Miss Sarah!" Dan swung the door wide, welcoming them into Martha's parlor.

"Morning, Mr. Taylor," Sarah replied with a quick dip of her chin. She marched into the cozy room with a purposeful stride. "Is Doc Taylor around? Daddy and I came to see Mary."

"She's with her now."

"You stove up, Dan?" Jason asked, strolling in behind his daughter. He removed his hat and hung it on the finial of a ladder-back chair.

"I just stopped in to say hi'dy to my cuz and pick up something for my wife's dyspepsia. Y'all going to the planning meeting?"

"Yep."

"I'll meet you there later." Dan stepped into the morning sunshine.

Martha exited the sick room carrying an enamel pan filled with water and a roll of bandages. "I thought I heard voices. Good to see you, Jace. You too, Sarah."

"Yes, ma'am. What're you washing her wounds with?" Sarah asked.

"I steeped water with calendula and yarrow. Would you like to visit with Mary?"

"Morning, Martha," Jason said. "Go on, Sarah, honey. Spend some time with your sister. I'll wait for you here." Sarah wasted no time and went into Mary's room.

"Make yourself comfy," Martha said to him. "I'll fix us some coffee." She hurried off into her kitchen.

He sat in the easy chair and stretched out his legs. A tea table stood between it and a small upholstered lady chair. "There's something I wanna ask you."

"Sure, what is it?" Martha yelled from the kitchen.

"Nancy's acting strange. Like I told you before, she's been huffy ever since I got back, but she's getting worse. This morning she threw a conniption fit and ran off into the woods. I didn't go after her. Figured I better leave her be."

"She'll get better. Be patient."

"What if she don't? Then what do I do?"

Martha peered around the kitchen door. "Don't fret. I gave her laudanum for her headaches. Maybe she needs more."

"I don't want her taking that stuff. I saw fit soldiers undone after they got hooked on laudanum. Docs give it to 'em for pain and soon it's all they think about." Jason rubbed his chin. "Her bump on the noggin might be something deeper. Sarah told me she's been having headaches for a while."

Martha reappeared, carrying a tray with a china pot and three cups on saucers. She set them on the tea table, then settled into the smaller chair. "Nancy's had a hard run of it. You can't know how difficult it's been for folks here. A bout of scarlet fever went around. *Twice.* A lot of children and elderly died of it last winter. Many who survived that starved to death." She poured the hot liquid. "Sugar?"

He raised a hand. "Black for me, thanks."

Martha took a sip and set her cup on her saucer. Frowning, she looked Jason level in the eye. "Now the war's over, our money is worthless. Did you know a barrel of flour costs two hundred and fifty dollars? Who can afford that?"

"It's been a misery for everybody." Annoyed, Jason's jaw twitched.

"No major fighting here in the hills doesn't mean we got off easy."

He set down his cup. "Don't go giving me speeches, Doc." He stood and gazed down at her. "I just wanna help my wife."

Martha frowned. "I only wanted to impress upon you how hard it's been. For Nancy—for all of us. To be honest, I don't have an answer."

The door to Mary's sick room opened and Sarah emerged. Her face fell as soon as she saw them. "What's going on?"

Martha stood and smoothed her skirts. "Your daddy and I were chatting about some serious matters. Nothing for you to worry about, dear. Please, come sit with me. Coffee?"

She gave them a hard look. "Mary asked to see you, Daddy."

He crossed the room in a few eager strides and let himself into the sickroom. Mary sat in a comfortable chair near her bed, dressed in a bodice and skirt. A basket filled with knitting was on the floor nearby and a short stack of books lay on a side table. The morning sun filtered through the branches of a tree outside the window, lighting her face with its soft glow.

He smiled at the tranquil scene. "How you feeling?"

She stood and teetered to his side, then hugged him. "The doc's been taking perfect care of me."

"You'll come home soon, then. Everybody misses you."

"We need to talk about that." Mary eased back into her chair while Jason planted himself on a corner of her bed. "I'm not going home."

"What do you mean?"

"I'm seventeen years old. Most young ladies my age marry and start a family. But the boys been off fighting, and dying. There's a surplus of marriageable girls." Mary lowered her eyes. "No decent boy would want me for a wife. Not now."

"Don't talk that a-way. Come home. Live with your family."

She shook her head. "I need a change. Living with Mama and my sisters would be a daily reminder of—" She flinched. "That horrible night. I can't do it."

"What will you do?" His voice cracked.

"For now, I'm staying here with Doc."

"And after?"

She shrugged.

He blinked hard. "Is Martha all right with that arrangement?"

Mary turned her gaze to the outdoors. "Mmm. I'll help her treat the sick while I ponder the future." She played with the cuff of her sleeve. "I thought I'd take on some students." She glanced at him. "And teach, like you."

Jason swallowed his regret. "Your mama won't be happy, but I think staying with the doc is just what you need. I reckon you'll be a mighty good help to her."

A bird singing on a redbud branch lifted Jason's mood, but Mary's expression turned serious. "I remembered something that might help you find that—" she hesitated, "that awful man."

"I'm listening."

She gazed out the window. "First heard his voice one day in the village." Her words came soft and slow. "Deep and quiet. Heard it again, when shopping down in Murphy. I think he followed me."

Jason felt sick to his stomach.

"Both times, he talked to me from just behind my shoulder, where I couldn't see him. He'd gone by the time I turned around."

"What did he say?"

"A Bible quote. *The sins of the father shall be visited upon the sons*. After that, I didn't go to town alone." Mary glanced at her shaking hands. "I was afraid."

His chest tightened. Loathe to pressure her, he needed to keep her talking. "Do you remember anything else?"

"Yes. Once, I caught his shadow when he stood next to a stand of goods with the sun coming in the shop window behind him. I grabbed Janie and Lucy and left. I know it was the same man who attacked me—Same voice, same build. Tall, bulky. Strong." She blinked fast, then looked into her father's eyes. "Find him, Daddy. Make him pay for what he did."

"I will, Fairybell, I will." He stood and his legs quivered like a leaf in an autumn breeze. He clutched the cast iron footboard to steady himself.

"Bet you a nickel he followed Mama and said those same words to her. She's been real wrought up of late. Sometimes it's embarrassing."

He stared. "How long has this been going on?"

"Months."

"You notice anything else?"

"Well, yes. She gathers mushrooms, dries 'em, makes 'em into a drink, together with mistletoe." She tapped nervous fingers against her knees. "I tried her *special brew* once last winter. It tasted bitter and made me woozy. She got wrathy when she saw me drinking it."

He decided to change the subject. "You heard of anybody named Win?"

Mary's hands balled into fists. "I–I think so, that night. Is that his name?" She avoided Jason's eyes. "Th–the one who hurt me?"

"Might be. Keep trying to remember. Every little thing is important." He kissed Mary on the cheek and turned to leave.

"Daddy?" Her voice was soft, her eyes dark and intense. "One more thing. The man walks with a limp."

Jason calmed his jangled nerves, then returned to Martha's parlor. "Nancy's been drinking mushrooms and mistletoe."

Martha looked perplexed. "You mean, as a tea? Certain mushroom varieties will calm her nerves—My word, I wish I'd known before I prescribed laudenum."

"Sarah, did *you* know?" he asked.

"I told you about her special brew. Mama's taken to harvesting mushrooms of late; I don't know what kind. She makes a tea from them and mixes it with mistletoe that Will gets for her. Drinks it all the time." She gazed wide-eyed at him, her brow creased.

"Who told her to take mistletoe?" Martha asked.

"Cornwoman," Sarah replied. "Last winter she doctored us when we got the fever and croup. Mama had it, too."

"What's it for, Doc?" Jason asked. "Will it hurt her?"

"I'd want to examine her and the mushrooms before passing judgment. Mistletoe may help what ails her. Ama Cornwoman knows what she's doing."

He placed an arm around Sarah's shoulders and gave them a squeeze. "Mama'll be fine, honey. Let's go to the meeting." He picked up his hat. "No more laudanum, got that, Doc? By the way, Mary tells me she's staying with you for a time."

Martha's eyebrows hitched. "Oh? But of course, she'll be a big help. Question is, are you okay with that?"

"For now. With all of us crammed into Daddy's cabin and Nancy having a time of it, Mary's better off with you. I'm beholden to you for all you've done for her." He gave Sarah a fatherly pat. "Let's go."

Outside, the south wind turned the backs of the leaves skyward while gray thunderheads churned overhead. Jason checked Ghost's tether, climbed onto the bench seat next to Sarah, and shook the reins. The old mule jerked his head and complained with an irritable bray. An ominous rumble signaled an approaching storm.

"You look worried, Daddy," Sarah said.

"I'll miss Mary."

"She's going to be a teacher, like she wanted. Can I ask you something?"

"Sure, honey."

"You said we're getting an indoor waterspout and a fancy stove. How is it we can build such a fine house? The church ladies are talking."

A rumble of thunder accented her question. "I been saving, except what I sent home." A twinge of guilt tugged at him for lying.

"Maybe you ought a explain that to some of the townsfolk, you know, to quiet their rattling tongues."

"No concern of theirs." A thunderclap added an exclamation point.

Sarah initiated a new line of questioning after the rumble dissipated. "Did you talk with Mary about that night?"

"I did. You brought it up; suppose you tell me what you found out."

"She won't talk about the gory details."

"You don't wanna hear 'em, child. Nor do I."

"She said she'd know him if she saw him. Her attacker's burnt into her memory like a cattle brand. "

Lightning slashed the sky, followed by a deafening crash. Ghost, tied to the back, whinnied and yanked at his tether.

Jason cast an eye skyward. "Easy there, boy!" he called to his nervous steed and shook the mule's reins. "Hey-a!—Reckon that's true. We been looking for 'em but they been working other towns."

A zig-zag brightened the heavens. A blue snap hit the ground, filling the air with its electric charge, and an ear-splitting thundercrack rippled through the air waves. The flash highlighted the Old Mother just ahead. Sarah cringed, grabbed an oiled leather wrap from under the bench and threw it around her. The first fierce raindrops spattered on the brim of Jason's hat.

A second firebolt hit a tree near the road and set it ablaze. Ghost squealed and yanked harder on his tether. Fear gleamed in the mule's white-rimmed eyes, and it brayed and leapt into a near gallop, heading for shelter in the churchyard. Sarah gripped the bench brace and peered from under her wrap.

"Daddy, will Mary be safe at Doc Taylor's?"

"I hope so, honey. I sure hope so."

Jason tied up the wagon and sprinted across the muddy yard into the church where Sarah waited for him in the small vestibule beyond the front doors. She shook raindrops from her wet cloak and hung it to dry. Jason stomped his feet and slapped his hat against his leg, removing as much of the wetness as he could.

A rabble of excited voices lured them into the sanctuary. People gathered at the planning tables along the far border of the sanctuary, as expected, but the clamor around a single table exceeded anything else.

They greeted friends as they strolled past the line of housing plans. At the last station, the busiest one, sat Adam Cable and Jacob Rose. A printed sign secured to the front of it read, *Revival Loan Association.*

Jason grinned. “How’s it going?”

“Couldn’t be better,” Cable replied. Though gruff as always, he winked before returning to complete a transaction. Next to him, Rose recorded details in a large ledger.

While Sarah designed the kitchen, Jason reviewed the plans for their home, and ensured that building would proceed post-haste.

As they prepared to leave, Tom Cooper pulled Jason aside. “Say Jace, hear tell, you’re the brains behind this new bank. Who’s backing you?”

“We wanna help folks rebuild their lives, Coop. Seems a good way to start.”

“But who’s fronting the cash? Nobody got money these days.”

“You know as well as I do, somebody’s always flush. Don’t you fret about our backers; that’s our job.”

"Hi'dy, Jace, Miss Sarah." Birdy Blevins butted into the conversation. "How's Miz Nancy?"

Cooper dipped his head, murmured, "Excuse me, ladies," and departed.

"Poor soul," Birdy continued, "everybody seen what them headaches do to her. Now this." She lowered her voice and leaned closer. "Get the medicine woman to make sure she ain't got a curse laid on her."

Sarah scoffed, "Pshaw, Miz Blevins, Mama's not cursed."

"Cornwoman'll fix her," Birdy said. "Injun medicine's better'n Martha Taylor's or Doc Hooper's, anyhow."

"Thank you for your advice," Jason replied. "Miz Hyde's gonna be just fine."

Birdy squinted at him. "Scuttlebutt says you pinched greenbacks from the Federals to build your house. That true?"

"Oh, *really*," Sarah hissed under her breath.

Jason scrutinized Birdy Blevins for a long moment. "Do I look like a thief to you, ma'am?"

Birdy backed off. "I ain't judging you. Think I care if'n you stole from the Yanks?"

Sarah lobbed an *I told you so* look at him, then leveled a glare of disdain at the woman.

"You'd do well to keep your meddlesome mind under your bonnet, Miz Blevins." Jason tipped his hat and ambled toward the exit.

A deep blue sky framed the landscape in the storm's aftermath. A light breeze blew fleeting vapor sails across a golden sun, emblazoning wet leaves with bejeweled sparkles.

On the steps outside the church, Dan pulled Jason aside. "I gotta talk to you."

"Sarah, you go on. I'll be there in a minute." She tiptoed through the mud to the wagon, leaping over puddles. "What is it, Dan?"

"Got new information regarding the night raiders." Dan kept his voice down. "I talked to 'bout everybody in town and they're all sure about one thing. The whitecaps wore red or red-checkered shirts with white badges pinned to the front. They're after somebody in particular."

Lips pressed into a thin line, Jason kicked a stone with the toe of his boot. "They're looking for me."

Dan's eyes widened. "You—why?"

"Vendetta. Something to do with the war, I guess."

"Damn," Dan said, too loud. Jason glared at him. "Anyways, Tuck Stamper got a close look at one of 'em symbols right before the bastard knocked him halfway to tomorrow—a red diamond on a white circle. Inside, a cross outlined in black."

"He's positive?"

"Yep. He read the gang's name scrawled around the edge: Brothers of the White Cross. What do you make of it?"

Jason folded his arms over his chest. "Brothers of the White Cross. Nothing holy about 'em, that's for certain."

Jason pulled in front of his father's cabin, late afternoon sun gilding the treetops. His father stepped outside, grim faced, followed by Will and Johnny. "What's up?"

"Somebody been spying on us," Johnny blurted.

"We don't know that for a fact, Son," Jason's daddy said.

Sarah gasped, hopped down from the bench seat and rushed inside. "Mama, Janie, Lucy!"

Jason jumped from the wagon and dashed after her, stopping at the door. "Everybody all right?"

"Just a scare," his father replied.

"Johnny, put up the animals." The boy grumbled about being left out. "Then get yourself back here quick." Jason peered inside the cabin. "Your mama there, Sarah?"

"Yes, Daddy," she answered from the depths of the interior gloom. He made out the anxious faces of his youngest daughters sitting at the family table, but not much else.

Satisfied of their safety, he addressed his father and oldest son. "Now, you two sit yourselves down and tell me what happened." The three of them pulled porch rockers into a cluster. "Daddy, suppose you start."

"This afternoon, Will and I was cleaning fish out yonder. Young'uns were inside. Nancy came hurrying outta the woods 'round back. I could see her just a little from where I sat. Bald spot on her head, like somebody done grabbed her by her hair. She looked scared.

I asked, *You okay?* but she ran through the back door without speaking."

"That's right," Will said, eyes filled with fear. "Mama looked real strange. I headed to the back. The bushes rustled near where she came from. I thought, maybe a black bear. They come rooting about now. That's when I saw him." He gulped.

"Who, Son?" Jason said, his voice low and serious.

Will squinted at the forest. "A man—big and dirty-looking, in a checkered shirt. A stringy carrot-top for hair.

"Red shirt?"

He nodded. "Like they wore that night in Buffalo. He looked straight at me, Daddy. Pointed and said something about sins of the father." Will flattened his lips. "He grinned and ran off. Creepy! What did he mean, *sins of the father*?"

Johnny swung around the corner post and onto the porch. "Yeah, what Will said. I saw everything from inside." All eyes shifted to him while he dragged a rocker into the cluster and plopped himself into it. "Once, when I was sneaking about in the forest, he came outta the scrub. He'd kilt a possum and carried it by the tail. My guess, he's holed up out there, watching us."

Jason blanched at the thought. "You notice how he walked?"

"Had a stiff leg," Will replied. "After he spoke them words, he lumbered off like he wasn't afraid of nothing."

"He got around real good for a gimper," Johnny added.

The ambush in the Murphy woods where Ira Lovin lost his life played out as vivid as if it happened yesterday. The sinking feeling in Jason's gut devolved into nausea while the screech of summer cicadas closed in upon him and he fought the rage in his head.

Jason flicked his eyes toward his father. "Daddy?"

"I seen him, too. Made the hair on my neck stand up. Red-shirted fella, heading into the woods. The man's a gimp, for sure." He glanced into the forest, then looked at Will. "So big, he might well be mistaken for a bear. Jace, I swear, the same filthy maggot set fire to your barn." He touched his bullet wound. "Can't forget his outline against the flames—" He shifted in his chair. "What does he want with us?" he asked under his breath.

Jason recalled the bushes stirring that morning when Nancy rushed into the forest. *He listened to every word!* Unable to contain himself any longer, he leapt from his seat, his roar echoing against the trees. He picked up the rocker and threw it into the yard, breaking one leg and dislodging an arm from its peg.

He ran into the house. “Nancy, where are you?”

“Shh, you’ll scare the little ones,” Sarah whispered. He skidded to a halt. His youngest daughters huddled beside Sarah at the table. Sarah’s face in the yellow light of the single oil lantern reflected Jason’s worry, yet she maintained the calm that was her greatest strength. “Mama’s over there.” She jerked her head toward a dim corner.

He detected Nancy’s form on the floor, knees pulled in tight, her arms wrapped around them. She rocked back and forth in a slow rhythm while a loose floorboard under her haunches creaked with each backward movement. The whites of her frightened eyes glowed in the half-light, as did the bare spot on her scalp.

Jason knelt between his little girls. “How you two doing?” They gazed at him, close-lipped, their big eyes, frightened. He stroked their hair, then enveloped each fragile shoulder and pulled them into a hug.

“Why you yelling?” The fear in Janie’s small voice tugged at Jason’s heart. “It scares me.”

“Me, too,” Lucy echoed.

“I’m sorry, little ’uns. I’ll try not to shout so much. Now, don’t you bother your sweet heads, you hear? Everything’s gonna be fine.” He kissed them, tip-toed to the corner where his wife sat, lurching to and froe, and squatted in front of her.

“Nancy,” he said in a quiet voice, “I’m awful sorry about all this—and I mean all of it. The boys and Daddy told me a man followed you in the forest. Is that right?”

She flashed a glance in his direction, then away.

“Did he hurt you?”

She squeezed her eyes shut against her tears, then shook her head.

“That man hurt our Mary and shot Daddy. If I’m right, he’s the same one who’s been shadowing you of late.” She twitched. “Yeah, I know about that. He’s dangerous, but I’m getting close to catching him. When I do, I’ll make for damn sure he never comes near us again. Ever. Nancy, you gotta help me help you. I love you. I love the family we made together. I’m doing my best to make us safe again. Do you understand?”

Nancy stopped still. Her face softened and for a split-second, he saw a glimpse of the woman he'd known all his life. She looked as though she was trying to speak, but no words came forth.

"May I hold you? Please? It might help. I won't hurt you."

Without waiting for a reply, Jason sat down, slipped an arm behind her, and pulled her to him. He hummed a favorite tune he once sang to his children to put them to sleep at night, while rocking gently, cradling her in his arms.

Nancy reached for his hand, her grip that of a woman permeated with dread. She cried into his shoulder. "Why is that man haunting us?" she whispered.

"Shh." He stroked her hair. "I'll sort this out. You gotta trust me."

In time, Nancy's tears subsided. Jason felt her weight grow heavy against his body and knew she'd fallen asleep. He looked up—his entire family had gathered 'round them.

"Will, you and Johnny get me some blankets. We'll make Mama a pallet; she can sleep here tonight. Then let's eat. It's been a long day."

"I'm plum tuckered out," his daddy said. "We gonna sleep hard tonight, right young'uns?"

Jason knew he'd not sleep a wink. Someone had to stay alert in case that demon of a human being reappeared to set another fire. A glance at his father told him he'd have company.

31

Cornwoman inspected her late-season herbs while she waited outside her door for an unannounced visitor. Before long, she saw him ride out of the tree line to her cabin, and her heart warmed at the sight of him.

"Afternoon, Ama Cornwoman." Her guest dismounted and removed his hat. "I need your advice."

"I always have time for you, Jason Hyde. Welcome. You survived the war. I am glad." She led him inside. "Come in."

He stepped into her living quarters and surveyed the room. "Same as I remember."

His interest caused her to observe it herself: it had not changed. Drying herbs still hung from rafters while tincture bottles and apothecary jars fought for space along shelves over the sink. The old leather-bound volumes, worn from frequent use. In the middle of the room, a swing-armed cauldron in the fireplace contained a freshly made stew; its aroma mingled with the other herbal scents. A pair of wooden benches graced either side of the hearth. Today, the mirror faced the wall: Spirits of the fallen filled the woods, their souls reflected in the glass. Turning it around allowed them to cross into the next world.

Cornwoman picked up a long-stemmed pipe from a shelf, opened a small box, and tamped a dried herb that elevated her senses into its bowl. "The war changed you. Your river of life sprung many branches since I last saw you. Some green and fertile. Others are foul and need damming."

Jason flicked his eyes at her, then away, and shifted his weight.

She waved him to the benches. "I tended your young'uns last winter when they were sick with fever. How are they?"

He lowered himself onto the nearest one. "They're well enough, but my wife and eldest daughter need your help—Nancy got hit in the head and she's in a lot of pain. I worry it's more than a bump on the noggin. Mary, my daughter, she's hurt real bad."

Cornwoman lit her pipe and puffed. A cloud of smoke circled, adding its earthy aroma to the room's herbal mixtures. "I like to pace while I listen. Please, go on."

"I don't know if you heard, but a gang of raiders burnt our village. It happened right before I got back from the war."

"Yes, a tragedy." She encouraged the pipe smoke to undulate to the ceiling timbers.

"They went after my homestead, too, sacked it, and rifle-butted Nancy. The doc said it's a concussion."

She halted mid-stride. "You mean Martha Taylor? Good healer, that one."

"There's more to it than that. My young'uns told me their mama's been having headaches for a long while. More so, now I'm home. You are an accomplished medicine woman. Can you treat her?"

Recalling Nancy's words—*He walked out on us*—she searched Jason's face. He was sincere. His troubles were not born of a lack of love for his family; she sensed that much.

She laid down her pipe and lowered her eyelids, then spread her arms wide to the spirits and recited a chant designed to open her mind. At its end, she said, "The doc is right, your wife has a concussion. She hurts bad but her injury will heal. I prescribed mistletoe tea last winter for her headaches. Does she still drink it?"

Jason dipped his head. "She mixes it with dried mushrooms."

"Do not fret. It calms her and will not hurt her." Cornwoman sat down next to him. "You were wise to come to me. I feel Nancy's worriment. She is angry and scared."

"Mad at me?"

"You, and the world around her. She is afraid of the changes coming. I will call on her tomorrow. Since I spoke with you first, I know what to bring. Now, about Mary."

Jason clenched his fists. "One of the night raiders defiled her."

She gasped. "*Tla!* Oh, I am sorry. She is a nice girl. Where is she now?"

"Staying with Doc Martha."

"Ah, good." Cornwoman nodded. "What can I do for her?"

"Mary's spirit needs healing as much as her body. Will you help her?"

"I will try. What else can you tell me?"

Jason told her what he knew about the raid, the outlaw who raped his daughter, and about Martha's subsequent care of her. While she listened, a heavy sadness swept over her and she moaned from a stabbing ache that overwhelmed her body, and most of all, her heart. She whimpered, then cried out, holding her belly. She cupped her face in her hands while tears wet her cheeks.

He reached out to her. "You all right?"

She pulled away. "No touch!"

"I'm sorry if this hurt you."

"Hurts Mary more. When my aching subsides, so will hers." She leaned back in her seat and grew still, whispering prayers under her breath. Minutes passed, along with her discomfort.

She looked at him, her expression serene. "Want some stew?"

"No, thanks. I have to go soon."

Sometime later, they finished their visit.

"Thank you, Ama, I'm glad I talked with you."

"If ever you need advice, I am here. You are special to me, Jason. I remember, you were the first babe I birthed when I was training to become a medicine woman." She smiled. "So tiny and perfect. It is a moment I will always remember—And look at you now. A grown man, with a growing family. A learned man and a soldier. Your heart is good—" She saw greenbacks, stained black by corruption. They rained from the sky, massing at his feet. "Take care you do not fall to the dark side."

Jason squirmed in his seat, and stood to depart. "See you tomorrow, then."

She followed him to her door. He stepped into the fresh air, unhitched his horse, and swung into the saddle.

Aramarinda rounded the corner of the cabin, carrying the bounty from her hunt. Cornwoman watched the young woman stop in her tracks and gape at the visitor, her green eyes filled with surprise and fascination. Suddenly shy, she backed away a few steps.

"Jason Hyde, Aramarinda Hooper. She lives with me now."

His face revealed recognition and he tipped his hat. "What a pretty name. Nice to meet you, Miss Aramarinda. I believe we've met before. You saved my life at Slickrock Creek."

Aramarinda blushed and dropped her catch onto a barrel next to the door. She bolted into the cabin.

Cornwoman felt his attraction to the girl. An energy awakened between them, and it troubled her. However, there was more. She sensed a message attached to his last words.

"Slickrock Creek—You seek a band of murderers and thieves."

Jason's attention snapped to Cornwoman.

"I see the symbol of a white cross. Dangerous men carry it. There is blood—Your people, my people, and others. Their leader uses your family to get to you. His cruel pleasure brings grief to many. More will suffer. Find his followers and you will stamp him out."

"But why is he after *me?*"

"Remember the bad blood between you and you will know."

"What's his name? Where is he?"

Cornwoman shut her eyes; visions floated behind their lids. "A black bird flies with the wind. It is a bad omen. The man you seek lurks amongst the trees. He feeds on fire and fear. Be careful. There lies evil."

32

Autumn 1865

The tribal members and white mountaineers labored together: logrolling, barn raising, farming, and hunting. The influx of ready money from Revival Loan Association, allowed residents to complete many homes before the snows arrived.

Hawes and Thorne looked on in frustration. They learned that, besides local transgressions, the counterfeiters had ties to rings across the South. The two of them could never bring these men to justice. They sent regular updates to Pinkerton asking for help, but their pleas fell on deaf ears.

"Gahhh!" Libby wadded the telegram and threw it with all her might. It bounced off the wall of the Murphy telegraph office and landed in the trash receptacle below it.

The transmitting handler hitched an eyebrow, then went back to his work.

"I'd like to see you do that twice in a row." Hawes yawped.

Libby glared at him, stormed from the lobby, and marched down the boardwalk. Hawes tipped his hat to the worker and followed her out. He climbed into their wagon, caught up to her down the street, and reined in beside her.

"No need to be huffy, Thorne. Get in." Libby folded her arms across her chest. "I'm not gonna ask you again. Do it now or you'll sleep in Murphy tonight."

She marched forward a few paces, spun around, then traipsed back to their vehicle. "All we do is wait. Watch and wait. We got what we came for. Why don't they give us what we need to finish the job?" She climbed onto the bench seat. "This is making me crazy."

Hawes jounced the reins and started for home. "It ain't easy for me, neither. You got a lot to learn about the detective business. Finding bad guys is the fun part, and you've proven yourself good at that. Waiting is hard when you're undercover. We don't know what's going on outside of what they tell us. Pinkerton wants this to be one giant sting operation. Maybe he's stalling till the other agents do what we already done. Be patient."

Libby waved him away. "Bah! Those criminals in Fort Montgomery build a town with phony money under our very noses—a town, mind you—and there's nothing we can do about it? I don't believe it. Do something, or I'll round 'em up and haul 'em off to jail myself."

He guffawed. "You're one stubborn woman, Miz Thorne. You ain't much good at taking orders, neither. To think a husband put up with the likes of you." He pretended amazement.

Libby crossed her arms and glared at the passing scenery. "Mr. Thorne said the same thing."

"Finally, a straight answer. That's more than we get from Pinkerton."

Near the Qualla Boundary
Winter 1866

At Thomas's homestead, Jason dismounted and tied Ghost to the hitching post. Worried fingers searched for the note in his jacket pocket to make certain it was still there: Colonel Thomas's summons requested his visit within two days' time, yet did not explain his intended motive. That concerned him.

From a tree branch overhead, a robin's merry song encouraged him, *Cheer up, Cheer up, Will is your friend.* He hurried up the porch steps and rapped on the door. A young Cherokee girl opened it.

"Come in, Lieutenant. The colonel is expecting you. I will take your coat."

He shook the ice from his greatcoat and handed it to her, along with his scarf. She led him to the colonel's study, where he sat in a high-backed wing chair. Near him, a fire blazed in the fireplace.

Thomas coughed once, but did not stand to greet him. "Jace, what a surprise."

"You sent for me." He showed him the note.

"Ah yes, so I did, so I did. Forgive me, I am forgetful of late. Please sit. Would you like coffee?"

"That'd be nice, thank you. I'm half frozen. What's this about?"

"A pot of coffee and two cups, please, Bessie, and make sure it's hot." He tapped the ends of his fingers together, and appeared to search for the reason he summoned him. His eyes lit and he grunted. "You close to catching the miscreants who sacked Buffalo Town?"

"Ahhh." Jason sat back in his armchair and crossed one leg over the other, mimicking Thomas's posture. "It's coming. We're on his tail."

"Got a name?"

"Win."

Thomas raised a brow. "Win. That's all you got? Jace, it's been—how many months?"

"Getting folks housed took precedence."

Thomas nodded. "Where is this Win?"

"Holed up for the winter near Cheoah Valley. When I catch him, I'm gonna nab his band at the same time."

Bessie returned with a tray laid with coffee, matching white porcelain cups and saucers hand-painted with miniature yellow roses, and cream and sugar. She set it on the sideboard and poured, bringing each man his cup.

"Thank you," Will said. He took a sip, then cleared his throat. "Last year's cough lingers. A warm drink helps. You may go, Bessie. Close the door behind you, please." He turned his full attention to Jason. "So, you're closing in. What do you plan to do when you arrest Win and his gang?"

"In the old days, according to Cherokee law, they would get the death sentence. The council would decide how and where to execute 'em."

"Now we must follow North Carolina code for a fair trial. The council elders support me on this." Thomas sat forward in his chair and wagged a finger at Jason. "I want our town recognized by the state. Abiding by its laws will gain favor with the Raleigh government. You know how I feel about men taking justice into their own hands. No lynching or scalping."

"No scalping? In White Sulphur you threatened to scalp every one of Bartlett's men."

"An empty threat. I also commanded you not to allow it."

"True enough. I'll do my best, but it won't be easy. Folks are hopping mad. Fact is, we haven't built our jailhouse yet. We got nowhere to lock 'em up."

"A jail just became a priority, understand? Once you catch those no-accounts, take 'em alive. After you jail 'em, notify the state prison in Salisbury. They'll try them, good and proper. Then *they'll* hang 'em."

"Like Cherokee law."

"Exactly." Thomas drummed his fingers on his knees, thoughtful. "I know you won't disappoint me."

Early Spring 1866

During the long winter months, Jason's mind often drifted to Cornwoman's last words to him: *A black bird flies with the wind. The man you seek feeds on fire and fear.* What did they mean to his search for the beast who raped Mary and destroyed his home? His anxiety built on the question as each day dragged into the next.

After the spring thaw, with the Hyde homestead completed, Jason and his friends moved on to building the jail. The council house would follow. Once the mountain roads became passable, he and his men resumed their pursuit of the Brothers of the White Cross, and a man called Win. The gang's unflagging rampage through the Cheoah Valley perpetuated, but so far, they had evaded him and his posse.

His mood lightened as the mountains lit with spring's verdant flush. Today, the Hyde family made ready to move to their new home.

"Johnny, bring Trix around and hitch her to the front of the wagon," Jason said. "You can ride Ghost."

"Woo-hoo!" he shouted, and sprinted to the barn.

Will helped Jason heave the last boxes onto the back next to a few open-slat crates filled with cackling chickens. Jason's father stretched a rope across the entire lot, securing everything in place against the potholes and ruts ahead.

"We about ready?" Nancy asked.

"Almost," Jason responded.

She marched into the cabin and reappeared wearing a bonnet, her cape draped about her, the handle of a large handbag fashioned from a blanket looped over one arm. She climbed onto the bench seat, placing her purse on her lap. "Come on, young'un's, we're going home."

Sarah helped Janie and Lucy settle behind the driver's seat and then sat herself beside them. Bedrolls, boxes, foodstuffs, crates, and two rockers that his father gave them filled the rear. Will tied a pack containing his few possessions in back of his horse's saddle. Johnny did the same to Ghost. Jason's father stood on the porch of his cabin and watched.

Nancy counted heads, then scowled. "Mary oughta be part of this." Besides her objections to taking up the hunt for the Brotherhood, she seethed at Jason for allowing their daughter to live with Doc Martha. Though her headaches had eased, her ire at this point would take longer to heal.

"Forgot something!" Will shouted. "Go on ahead. I'll catch up."

"I'll hang back, too," Johnny added.

"Don't be long, boys," Jason replied.

He guided the wagon down the trail and onto the main road to Cheoah Township. The old buckboard bounced and swayed. The younger girls played pat-a-cake and Sarah sang nursery rhymes to them when they tired of games. A crisp breeze swept the air with the invigorating scent of evergreens. Their branches sighed, and brushed the blue sky with wispy white mares' tails.

"Look, ducks from the fishing hole," Janie said, pointing skyward.

"How can you tell it's the same ones?" Nancy asked.

"Cause the drake is black, like the one where we fish. See?"

"Mean d-ake," Lucy chirped. "He chase me."

Sarah laughed. "If you'd keep away from his babies, he'd leave you alone. Look how fast this breeze is carrying 'em."

Jason tilted his chin. Overhead, a jet-black duck led his flock in a V formation. The others pursued him in the stiff breeze while Jason listened to Lucy's singsong.

"Mean d-ake, wind d-ake, mean d-ake, wind d-ake."

Like a posse after a night raider? The thought grabbed him as he pondered Cornwoman's riddle: *Black bird, black duck. A drake.*

"Mean drake, mean drake, fly away wind drake," Lucy and Janie sang together.

Fly away wind drake? "That's it! Bless your hearts, you answered a riddle."

"What riddle?" Sarah asked.

"The biggest—wind drake. Windrake, it's a man's name."

"Oh, I know Mr. Windrake," Janie said, smoothing her doll's yarn hair. "Only he's not mean. He's nice."

Jason pulled up on the reins and twisted his body to stare at her. "How do you know this man, child?"

"We play in the woods. He used to bring me rock candy before the store burnt down."

Jason gaped at her, horrified.

"Ah Law," Nancy hissed, then screeched and in a swift move, reached for Janie. He clutched at his wife's shoulders and held her back.

Trix whinnied and jostled them in reaction to the disturbance.

"Janie, honey, tell us about Windrake. How long y'all been friends?" Jason asked.

She gazed between Jason and Nancy, confusion written across her childish face. "I dunno. We got a secret place. Under a tree a ways behind Granddaddy's cabin. He leaves me presents there. We played at the old house, too. Mr. Windrake got a boo-boo leg, but he says it don't hurt much."

"What games do you play?" Nancy's voice trembled.

"Hide and seek. One he calls mum–mumble-ty-peg." She stumbled over the name.

Jason and Nancy exchanged alarmed glances—a boy's game, mumblety-peg involved knives.

"But one time he was ugly to me. Me and Mary went to the store. Mr. Windrake was there, too. I asked would he bring me lemon drops instead of rock candy, and he told me to shoo. I hid in back of the pickle barrel. He whispered in Mary's ear and she made a funny face. After that, she wanted to leave, real quick—She scared me."

"What else happened, Janie?" Jason asked.

"The next day, Mr. Windrake, he brang me a whole bag of lemon drops. And this." She pulled an object out of her skirt pocket and showed it off. "A whirligig."

"Give me that!" Nancy snatched the toy from Janie's hand and threw it in the road, then seized the girl by the shoulders and shook her. "Bad girl, why didn't you tell me about this man?"

Janie squealed, then let loose a torrent of frightened tears as Will and Johnny rounded the bend behind their family's wagon. They pulled their horses to a stop and observed the fracas from a distance.

"Let go of her." Jason wrestled the girl from her mother's grasp. Janie squalled and cried harder.

Nancy struggled against his grip, reeling backward over the side. "Let me go!" Trix whickered and pranced in place while the wagon jostled and rocked. Before she tumbled out Jason yanked her upright and sat her down hard on the bench.

Lucy wailed.

Johnny shook his head in disgust. Having seen enough, Will nodded toward the woods and they left.

Sarah wrapped her arms around Janie. "Leave her alone, Mama!"

"Daddy," Lucy cried through her tears. She pointed to the empty road behind them.

"What did I do wrong?" Janie asked between sobs.

"Why does it have to be like this?" Sarah griped.

"D–Daddy—" Lucy's whimpers evolved into hiccups. "Will and Jo–hic–Johnny—"

Jason's inner turmoil reached its breaking point. "Quiet, all of you! Don't anybody say another word." He glared at them until they settled down.

Sarah made a face and pulled Lucy onto her lap. "Shh," she said, stroking her between the shoulder blades. One arm hugging Lucy, the other cuddling Janie, she hummed a tune.

Jason snapped Trix's reins, and the wagon rattled forward while, next to him, Nancy sat rigid for the balance of the trip, fists clenched, glowering at the pathway ahead.

Jason halted Trix facing their new cabin. "Welcome home, y'all."

His family gaped at the sight before them. The two-story chink-log dwelling, sitting on three-foot pillars, and twice the size of their old farmhouse, featured chimneys on each end. The porch stretched across the front. A shed stood to one side with stacked kindling while a coal-filled bin, ready to fire up the new stove, sat near the rear. A chicken coop and a sturdy stone smokehouse were close to the kitchen. Nearby, a barn for horses and goats completed the homestead.

"Oh, Daddy," Sarah said, breathless. "Can we go inside?"

"Of course. Have a look-see. The boys and I'll unload—when they get here." His eyes searched their traveled path. He didn't see them, and shook his head.

Nancy flashed him a glance mixed with so many emotions that he couldn't fathom what she felt. She climbed down, walked across the yard and up the steps. Crossing the porch, she threw open the door, peered at the interior, then sniffed. "Smells of new-cut wood. Guess I better change that to cooking." She and their daughters trooped inside, single file, their gaits all business.

Jason scratched his head. "I can read anybody, but my own wife is a mystery." He hopped off the wagon bench and began unloading while keeping an eye out for his sons.

"Where's our food?" Sarah called out from the door. "Our pots and pans?" She looked around. "Where are Will and Johnny?"

Her father pointed at several boxes he'd placed on the steps. "Your supplies. Take 'em inside. Tell your mama I'm going after your brothers. And not to worry. We'll be back by supper time." He unhitched Trix, fastened a saddle on her, and headed for Dan Taylor's farm. He would need his friend's help.

Afternoon sprinkles became a steady drizzle.

"Finding your boys in the rain will be hunting for a needle in a haystack," Dan said.

"We'll find 'em as long as it doesn't erase their tracks."

Around four o'clock, near a trail in the forest, they saw a man skinning a muskrat next to a creek bank. A foul stench hovered in the air despite the cleansing shower. Jason unsheathed his musketoon and cocked it.

"Hey, you there!" Dan called.

The man leapt to his feet and spun to face them.

"Well, I declare—Olly Oliver," Jason said. He uncocked his weapon and lowered it slightly.

The trapper glared up at them, blinking through raindrops.

"We're looking for my boys. Seen 'em?"

Olly scratched his belly. "Durn, these woods're busy today. What'd they look like?" Jason described his boys and their horses. "Yeah, I seen 'em."

"Which way'd they go?"

"Followed the trail up the mountain." He pointed. "What they doing out here?"

"Tracking your pal, Win, I reckon," Jason said.

Oliver's pasty skin blanched whiter under its dull pallor. He backed off a couple of steps, brushing raindrops from his silt-streaked face. "I done said I dunno nobody by that name."

"Dang, you gotta be a no-account poker player cause you can't lie to save your life."

"I told you everything." He spat a wad of brown chewing tobacco.

Dan dismounted and aimed his pistol at the grungy man. "I smell the lies coming off you, trapper. Smells like piss. We oughta hog-tie you and carry you into town. More'n few would consider it a privilege to squeeze the facts outta you." He stepped closer.

"Leave him be, Dan," Jason said.

The scrappy little man gulped and raised his hands higher. "All right, maybe I know the fella, but I–I got nothing to do with him. N-not no more," he stammered.

"Okay, spill it," Jason demanded. He nodded at Dan and he uncocked his weapon.

"Ain't much to tell. Him and his brother come up here during the war. Fell in with a gang of bushwhackers, they did. Injuns kilt the brother and made Win a gimper."

The struggle at Slickrock Creek played out in Jason's mind. *They musta been amongst the bushwhackers. Could his brother have been the big one who almost drowned me?—One of 'em boys got away, but Windrake's not the name that young pissant called out. What was it?*

Amid the pitter-pat of wet drops on leaves, a trembling Olly Oliver spilled his guts. "I ran into him a while back. He talked me into joining up with his gang. Brothers of the White Cross. Win said they was after stray coloreds. They find their way up here sometimes, you know. Didn't figure on 'em going after Injuns, too." Oliver licked his lips, beady eyes darting from one man to the other. "I got nothing against Injuns. Or your family, neither, Jace.

"They pulled some sick sh—well, I split with 'em." He sniffled and wiped his nose with his sleeve. "Like I told ya, I got nothing to do with any of it. That's the truth, I swan."

"No, no—You were there the night y'all burnt my place down."

"I weren't, I tell you."

"You already said so, moron." Jason studied him through narrowed eyes. "You know too much not to have been. Guess Dan's right, we gotta string you up by your feet till the truth oozes outta you." Jason swung his leg over his saddle as if to dismount. Dan moved in on Oliver again.

Olly squawked and hugged the nearest tree. Dan pulled him off the tree and wrenched his arms behind him. "Okay, okay, you got me. But I weren't no part of what happened to Miz Hyde or Miss Mary 'cepting to help get 'em to the doc's. Ask her, she'll vouch for me."

"Now you're singing the gospel," Jason smirked. He motioned for Dan to back off. Dan edged away from the weaselly little man. "You seen Win around here lately?"

Oliver tossed him a dirty look and pulled at the collar of his filthy wet undershirt. "He passes through here regular. I keep outta his way and don't let him see me." He thought for a second. "Not today, though. Today I saw a different rider."

"Tell me about this other rider," Jason barked.

"Like I said, these woods been busy. The two boys come through first. Not long 'fore y'all showed up, come another behind 'em, bigger than your older boy, but not by much."

Perplexed, Jason didn't know what to make of the second rider. "You recollect this Win fella's last name?"

"Never knew it."

Jason grunted. "You coulda said that the first time and saved yourself some bother." He put his musketoon away.

Oliver ran grimy hands through his rain-soaked hair and toed the mud with his shabby boot. "Jace, I gotta tell you, what I saw that night at your place been weighing on me mightily. What he did to that gal of yours, it ain't right. I'm real sorry 'bout all of it." He stared at the ground. "Win's gonna come after me if he catches wind I talked to you."

"He ain't gonna do nothing if we got anything to do with it." He motioned to Dan. "Come on, time's a-wasting."

Olly peered up at them through greasy strings of hair. “Hope you catch that bast’id.”

Jason and Dan followed the boys’ trail until the downpour forced them to stop. They found one of the shallow caves that pocked the area, and huddled together under its entrance ledge. In a low tone, Jason told Dan about the Slickrock Creek debacle three years ago. “You ever come across a fella fitting his description?”

“Nope. Well, maybe. The raiders that hit Raven Town last summer, their leader was a big’n. Hard to forget.”

You don’t recall hearing his name?”

Dan shook his head.

Jason squinted into the fading light. “The som’bitch is out there, Dan. He’s out there—and so are my boys. Their trail will wash away, but it’s a safe bet they’re headed to Daddy’s place. I’d like to think they made it to his cabin before this downpour broke out. We’ll set out again after the rain lets up. Meantime, we got a ways to go and I need some shut-eye. You want first watch?”

Will crept out of the rain into his granddaddy's barn. Johnny followed behind him. They secured their horses in stalls and fed and watered them. Ghost whickered as they dashed for the cabin.

"Who's there?" their granddaddy barked.

"It's me," Will hissed.

"And me," his brother added in a loud whisper.

Their granddaddy let up on his shotgun trigger and they slipped out of the darkness onto the porch. "Gol durn it, you coulda got yourselves chock full of lead. Look at ya, you're dripping wet. What the devil are you doing here?"

"Everybody's fighting again, Granddaddy," Will said. "We're gonna come live with you. If Mary can stay with the doc, I reckon we can stay here."

"Ya do, do ya? I gotta think on that. Your parents know you're here?"

Will stared at the floor and shrugged. Johnny stuffed his hands in his pockets.

"So, no. Your mama's likely having a conniption over this. Your daddy'll figure it out and be here by morning, no doubt."

Will and Johnny dried off and their grandfather wrapped them in blankets. The fireplace's glowing embers warmed them as they huddled before it, rubbing feeling into their chilly hands and feet.

"You realize there could be a scoundrel snooping 'round here," their granddaddy said.

"Not could be, *is*," Will replied in a low tone. "He followed us up here."

"How do you know?"

"We heard somebody behind us and circled back," Johnny said. "We saw a rider following our tracks. I remember him bigger, but last time, I was scared."

"You sure it was him?"

"Pretty sure," Will replied.

Their granddaddy grunted. "Tonight we'll stay sharp, just in case. If'n that critter thinks he can take us all at once, he's got another think coming. I wouldn't want to face you two with your rifles aimed at me." He tossed them a thin smile. "We'll camp out down here where it's warm. Meanwhile, I'll throw a pan of beans on the fire."

After a meal and a story, John Aaron watched the boys fall asleep listening to his olden days' reminiscences and the soothing pitter-pat on the roof. Afterward, he kept vigil against unwelcome visitors, then slipped into a light doze before the rain stopped.

The mantel clock chimed 4 a.m. Smoldering cinders cast sinuous shadows throughout the room. In the gentle quiet of predawn, a dull thump emanated from the loft. John Aaron's eyes flew open.

"What was that?" Johnny whispered.

A soft scurrying came after. "Squirrel, maybe."

Beady black eyes and twitching whiskers appeared at the rim of the upper level and disappeared. Soon, a mischief of tiny field mice scuttled across the room and vanished into a knothole in the floor.

"Mice. Maybe chewed a gap in the roof thatch. Go back to sleep, Son." He laid his shotgun over his lap and closed his eyes.

Johnny heard a faint crackling and sniffed the air. "Jiminy Christmas, I smell smoke!" He scrambled to his feet.

Ill-matched footsteps pounded across the rear porch, the floor rattling under their weight. A snapping golden flicker appeared beneath the door as the pinewood stacked outside the cabin wall ignited into flames. The neat stack fell apart and burning cut logs scattered while smoke seeped through tiny fissures in the chinking.

Will bolted upright, startled from sleep. "What's happening?"

A fist punched a hole in the shuttered window, and a torch wrapped in flaming kerosene rags scudded across the floor. John Aaron cocked his shotgun and fired.

Will dove for the firebrand and lobbed it back through the broken opening. Tails of smoke drifted through the floor cracks. “It’s coming from under the house.” Coughing, he stood and rushed to his granddaddy.

“Follow me. We better get outta here quick,” John Aaron herded his grandsons to the front door.

The front window shattered and the flare of another flaming stick streaked inside and tumbled toward them while flames licked at the windowsill. John Aaron fired again, too late.

Will grabbed the burning stick, cracked the door, and tossed it as far outside as he could. The porch was ablaze, and the odor of kerosene and burning wood wafted into the room. He slammed the door shut, hacking from the smoke.

“How’re we gonna get out?” Johnny shouted.

“Gotta make a run for it. He can’t be front and back at once,” John Aaron wheezed. Sweat streamed down his face; he swiped it from his eyes with a shirt sleeve and hurried to the sink where the water bucket sat, half-filled. Slinging the dipper to the floor, he dunked three kitchen towels, then handed one to each boy. “Soak yourselves down as best you can, then wrap the wet cloth around your head and shoulders!” he shouted over the fire’s roar. “We’ll run out the front!”

Will stood next to the door while John Aaron targeted the entrance. He flung it open. Smoke and heat poured in.

“Come on!” John Aaron rushed through the doorway and across the porch, his grandsons on his heels.

An enormous figure, waiting to one side, struck him with a heavy firewood log, knocking him cold.

“Granddaddy!” the boys screeched. A mountain of a man heaved toward them, his boots thumping in an ominous, uneven concussion. Will and Johnny backed into the burning room at the sight of him.

Heart quaking in his ears, Will watched the brute squint into the smoke-filled room over a bandana pulled up to his eyes. Framed by the fire behind him, his enormous body smoked while water dripped from his clothing onto the floor. Choking, Will aimed his rifle through the haze at the hulking figure and squeezed the trigger. His bullet ricocheted off a post, sending splinters of wood flying.

The giant man crossed the area in a few quick steps, yanked Will's firearm from his hands, and tossed it out of reach. Will grabbed Johnny by the sleeve and turned to flee.

An enormous hand grabbed Will's coveralls and jerked him backward. From the man's other side, his brother's terrified yelp rang out. "Johnny, I'm here!" His attacker dragged him through licking flames. Shrieking, he swung and kicked at the intruder and slapped at sparks searing his overalls.

The hulk dropped them outside, beyond the burning porch. "Now I can see you, you little pissants." He leveled his revolver at them. "*The sins of the father shall be visited upon the sons*—Know what it means?"

Too frightened to move, Will and Johnny hugged each other.

"It means, this ain't your lucky day."

A woman in men's clothing sprinted around the corner of the cabin, and skidded to a halt behind the outlaw. She aimed her pistol at him. "Harm those boys and you're a dead man."

Will scrubbed his eyes with his fists to better see her: hardly taller than him, her red-rimmed blue eyes gleamed in the smoky firelight. A tendril of curly nut-brown hair peeked from beneath a battered army hat pulled down over her ears.

In a sudden move, the thug grabbed Johnny and spun to face her, clutching him to his chest. He pressed his pistol against the child's ear. In the same instant, Will hit the ground, and scrambled to his grandfather's side.

The woman brandished her gun. "Unhand the boy and step away from the cabin."

"Shoot me, I shoot him—I got no quarrel with you, lady, so butt out of my business."

"Oh, but you do, Windrake Ferries."

The scoundrel froze. "Who are you?"

"You don't remember me, do you?" She shot at his feet.

Off-kilter, he struggled to keep his balance while maintaining his grip on Johnny. "How do you know my name?"

"I'm taking you in for the murder of Ira Lovin—and the attempted murder of these boys."

"Who the devil is Ira Lovin?"

"My son! And yours. You murdered your own child, you ungodly heathen."

Libby's chest tightened. She had carried the painful secret inside her for so many years! How she had longed to find her rapist! As if murdering Ira were not enough, now he stood before her, about to murder two more young men.

"Lying bitch," he snarled. "I'd never kill my own kin. You mistake me for another—"

"No mistake," Libby interrupted him. "I got a witness to the killing. Besides, I'd know you anywhere; I gave you that beauty mark you used to call your right eye. In case you forgot, you raped me seventeen years ago, same as you raped Mary Hyde. And countless others, no doubt."

With a roar, Ferries flung Johnny aside and charged. Libby fired, lodging a bullet in his shoulder. Ferries grunted. Though unsteady, he kept coming. A swipe of his good arm knocked her off balance and she dropped her weapon. She grabbed a burning ember with leather-gloved hands, swung, and connected with his fresh wound. He cried out, stumbled, then broke into an oafish run, lumbering for the timbers behind the cabin. She snatched up her pistol and shot at his fleeing back, then took off after him into the murky shadows.

Jason and Dan burst through the trees at the far end of the clearing. Jason pulled on Ghost's reins, aghast at the scene before him. His father's home was engulfed in flames. Light from the burning cabin revealed the dire state of his family—his sons' faces burned, their clothing singed and muddied, his father, bloody and disoriented, all three blackened with soot.

"Everybody okay? What happened?" Jason shouted.

Will pointed. "It was him! The man who followed mama—he ran off into the woods, that way! Hurry!"

Jason and Dan spurred their horses into the forest in Ferries' pursuit. Light from the cabin fire faded as they plunged further into the timbers. They had but one lantern between them, and a dense overhead canopy concealed the breaking dawn, impeding their search. Ahead, the sound of thrashing guided them into a steep gully. Forced to walk their animals down the slope to avoid injury, the noise trail gradually lessened into silence. Broken limbs and trampled shrubs led to a dead end.

"What're we looking for?" Dan asked.

"A cave. They pock this place. He could hole up in any of a dozen hollows."

Aided by the dappled morning sun, they scoured the area on horseback. Peaceful activity amongst the forest creatures contradicted the intensity of their mission.

"We're going in circles," Dan complained. "We searched a ton of hideouts and we ain't found a sign of him."

"There's one more." Jason steered Ghost around a sweet-scented honeysuckle thicket beset by bees and up a small bluff.

Nearby, cool air emerged from the back of a thick laurel bush, the entrance to a dark opening. An old hemlock grew above the cave atop a craggy mound.

Jason dismounted. "Follow me."

They slipped behind the laurel branches and stooped under a jutting rockledge. Beneath the shelf, an opening, low and narrow. Inside, it opened, creating a perfect den. It smelled of damp earth and wood smoke.

They found cold ashes from a small campfire, discarded bones from consumed meals, dried blood, and a yellow hair ribbon. Jason's stomach clenched as he tried not to think about Janie passing time here with a murderer. He lifted the ribbon, ran it between his fingers, then stuffed it into his pocket.

Near the cave wall he noticed spiky tongues of dirty-yellow behind a rock. He upended the stone with his boot and revealed a corn-husk doll shoved into a crevice. "It's Fairybell Too, Janie's doll."

"You sure?" Dan asked.

"I made it for Mary when she was just a scrap of a girl." He picked it up. "Nancy added black yarn for the hair and some decoration. Stitched Mary's nickname onto the skirt, here." He fingered Nancy's careful, even stitches. "When she outgrew it, Mary passed it to Sarah, then she gave it to Janie. This doll is almost a family relic." Feeling nauseated, he leaned against the wall. "See what you can find farther back."

While Dan wandered deeper into the cave, Jason tried to calm his nerves. *My baby girl, here. If that beast hurt her*—The stone under his hand wobbled. He looked closer; it didn't match the surrounding rock. His fingers wriggled it loose with a little effort, and it thudded to the floor, leaving a small recess. He peered inside: a stubby pencil, a few sticks of charcoal, two knives, a doubled scrap of brown paper. He unfolded it and smoothed its deep creases.

He moved nearer to the entrance, crouched, and held it to catch the morning light. On it, a child's drawing that took time to create: A little blue-haired girl held the hands of a big fella and a woman with long black hair. Trees and birds populated their surroundings while fish hop-scotched over a stream, all of them Janie's favorite things from nature. He'd seen her draw them before. The girl's expression, sad; the man appeared to be yelling. Large drops fell from the woman's eyes. *Nancy and me?* He fingered a hole punch near the male figure, as if a pencil point broke through the paper, and flipped the sheet over. He sucked in his breath.

On the flipside a rudimentary map detailed a scrawl of local villages with sacked towns crossed out, including Buffalo, and targets still left to be hit. Most notable amongst them, Cheoah Township. *They're planning to attack us again.* A list of family names scribbled down one side showed several marked through, with *Hyde* underlined. Here, an angry jab broke through the sheet. The name *Oliver* scratched in fresh graphite appeared at the bottom. *Olly was right; the rotter is out to get him.*

Most interesting, a penciled-in X in the topmost corner. The words *Slippy Rock* leapt off the paper. Jason felt his air escape from his lungs.

"Hey Dan." His voice echoed throughout the cave. "You gotta see this."

Dan reappeared from the darkness. "Find anything?" Jason asked.

"There's another way out, plenty big. Reeks of dung. Hay's scattered about and there's an empty feed sack. Som'bitch kept his horse in here. The tunnel twists and turns. You'd never know the two of these crannies connect." Dan eyeballed the paper scrap in Jason's hands. "Whatcha got?"

"This map, stashed in that hidey hole, yonder."

Dan studied it, muttering to himself, while Jason continued to investigate the cave. He walked to the rear entry and observed the lay of the land. A rise about thirty yards away afforded an unobstructed view of his father's cabin. Smoke curls rose from the rubble. The weight of what took place descended upon him and he said a quick prayer of thanks that his sons and father had not lost their lives to the flames. Jaw twitching, he came back to the entrance mumbling through gritted teeth: "That filthy—"

From overhead, a shower of stones fell on him. A slender figure toppled off the edge of the bluff, landing in front of him with a whump. The forced landing "oof" belonged to a woman. Startled, he drew his pistol and cocked it.

Dan stepped into the space she had vacated and grimaced. "Found a snoop."

Jason yanked the hat from her head. A tumble of chestnut hair fell past her shoulders. She glared at him with angry eyes and raised her hands in surrender. "Miz Hawes!" He lowered his gun.

"You know this woman?" Dan asked.

"She's staying at Penley's Boarding House. Lady, what in tarnation possessed you to show up here, now?" He helped her to her feet.

Huffy, she dusted herself off while Dan climbed down from the bluff. "A fine how-do-you-do after I saved your boys."

"*You*?" Jason and Dan exchanged looks. "Miz Hawes—" Jason's throat tightened. "*Thank you* can't express my gratitude, ma'am. But why are you here?"

"That's my business."

Jason flicked his eyes at Dan, who still scowled at Libby. "You're looking for somebody. Did you find him?"

She grimaced. "I found him. Now, I've lost him again."

Libby retrieved her horse and left, and Jason and Dan rode to the remains of the cabin.

Jason's father sat on a stump with elbows propped on knees. Upon seeing them, he staggered to his feet. "Damnation!" He held his side and rubbed his fingers across the bump on his skull. A crusty tail of dried blood stained his cheek. He lost his balance and reeled forward. Dan caught his arm.

"Careful, Daddy," Jason grasped the other. "We oughta get you to the doc's."

"Leave me be." He glared at Jason. "Guess he got away."

"We found his hideout down yonder, but he was long gone by the time we arrived," Jason said.

"How far down yonder?"

"Far enough where he could watch our comings and goings and not be seen." Jason regarded his sons, their faces scorched red. His heart ached for the terror they experienced. "Why on earth did you boys take off?"

Will hung his head and looked at him through his lashes. "Can't stand no more of you and Mama fighting. I wanna come live with Granddaddy."

"And I ain't gonna let Will go by himself," Johnny said.

"Dammit, that beast coulda—"

"I didn't know Ferries would come back," Will blurted.

Jason gaped at him. "What'd you call him?"

"Ferries. That woman, the one who saved us." His nose wrinkled. "Seen her in town, but I can't recall her name. Anyways, she called him Windrake Ferries. She tried to arrest him but he got away."

Will's statement fell on him like an anvil. *She's the law!—We're hunting the same animal.* Suddenly, the memory of Slickrock Creek flooded his mind, clear as the day it happened. "That's it!"

"That's what?" Will asked.

"A whopping piece of the puzzle."

The cabin roof caved in with a resounding crash, leaving the fireplace as a monument to the lives lived within its walls. Sparks and cinders flew in every direction, breathing new life into the raging fire.

His father sighed. "Everything, gone up in flames."

"I'm sorry, Daddy. You aren't the only one around here with nothing much to your name."

"Course I ain't. It hurts, is all, watching memories go up in a blaze."

"Well, you got your life." Jason embraced his sons. "You all do, thank the good Lord." *And Miz Hawes.*

Hoofbeats rumbled on New Hyde Road as Jason, his two boys, and his friend Dan rode up to the family's new home. Jason's father pulled up the rear in his old wagon.

Nancy and the girls poured onto the porch to greet the returning men. Nancy held tight to Lucy and watched Jason creep from his horse, dragging from fatigue. Sarah greeted him first; he hugged her, then handed her Ghost's reins. "Take the horses to the barn, would you, honey?"

"Sure." She looked at the others. "Granddaddy! Will! Johnny! What happened? Your faces. Your clothes. You're burnt!" She spun around to her father. "Daddy?"

"I'll tell you all about it," Jason said. "We all will."

The boys climbed off their horses and shuffled toward the house.

"Wait. Boys, come here," Jason said. "Where's Janie?" She peeked out from back of her mother's skirt. He held out his arms, and she ran to him. He picked her up, and hugged his boys tight. "I'm going inside with Will and Johnny to get cleaned up."

A wave of heaviness swept over him and he rubbed his eyes. "Dan, round up our posse. Tell everybody we'll meet at Cooper's store in the square tomorrow at daybreak. If Ferries and his gang are out there, we're gonna find 'em."

Still holding Janie, he reached for Nancy. She slipped her arm around his waist and he pulled her close. "What's for dinner? I'm half-starved."

Libby tucked her hair under her hat and brushed soot and debris off her pants before entering the boarding house.

"Where have you been?" Hawes fumed. "You look like a scrappy tomboy who just lost a fight. Your gloves are burnt, your britches, ripped. You're a mess."

"I had something important to do," Libby retorted.

"You did, did you? Not as busy as me, I reckon."

Libby fixed an angry stare on him.

"While you were off galivanting, I uncovered a major puzzle piece."

She glowered. "You gonna tell me or make me guess?"

"The fake money's being transported via the Ohio River from Illinois to pick-up points along the way, through Kentucky, and beyond. Burchfield's the gang's runner, which I knew. Didn't know where he took possession of the bogus bills. Now I do."

"Good work. How d'you find out?"

"Right place, right time, and the slip of a loose tongue."

35

Jason slept under his own roof for the first time in four years. An hour before daylight, a clamor on New Hyde Road awoke him.

"Jace, come quick!" a familiar voice called from the gate.

Jason's tired muscles complained when he crawled out of bed.

"What's happening?" Nancy asked, drowsy with sleep.

"I'm about to find out. Go back to bed."

She threw off the bedcovers. "Like heck, I will. Where are my slippers?"

He pulled on yesterday's shirt and dungarees as quick as he could and clattered down the stairs. Other family members shuffled into the hallway.

Heavy footsteps clambered up the front steps and a fist banged on the door. "Jace!" the voice roared.

Jason swung open the door and found Tom Cooper pacing the porch, making broad gestures with his arms.

"Something terrible bad's happened," Tom panted. "In the green, right outside my store. God's Mercy, what a sight!"

"I'll saddle up Ghost." Jason grabbed his musketoon rifle and ammo belt off the wall. He faced his family who huddled before him, their faces awash with concern. "Sorry, I gotta go."

"Take your coat. It's cold out," Nancy said, handing him his heavy jacket. Her eyes met his and she squeezed his hand. "Be careful."

Jason's father pushed past his grandchildren, carrying his shotgun. "I'm going with you," he said, his voice gruff with sleep. "No way I'm staying behind."

"Okay. Come on, Daddy."

Will stepped forward, his rifle tucked under one arm. "I'm coming, too."

Jason raised an index finger. "No. Stay here and protect the womenfolk."

"We're always left out." Will kicked the floor.

"Yeah," Johnny whined.

"You boys had enough *fun* yesterday to last you a long while." He frowned to let them know he was serious.

Astride their horses, Jason and his father trotted from the barn to a small group of horsemen waiting near the front gate. A light spring snow floated around them as they galloped to the center of Fort Montgomery.

Gray ash sullied drifting snowflakes, a symbol of human violence contaminating nature's pure creation, while the sting of fumes in Jason's nostrils forewarned the grim scene awaiting them in Fort Montgomery. Their horses' slow cant along Main Street stirred the swirling silver-blue smoke that hung heavy beneath a purple predawn sky. To either side, several buildings smoldered. Men worked against choking wood-burn to extinguish lingering blazes. At its center, a stunning scenario greeted them. A shocked hush blanketed gawking clusters of Cherokees and mountaineers who circled the chestnut tree that graced the front of the newly framed council house, now a pile of embers. Their aggrieved faces were lit amber by their dancing lantern and torch lights. Above them all, as horrific a sight as some would ever witness.

There, a lifeless mutilated body, hands tied behind his back, noose around his neck, swayed from a branch of the old tree. At its base, a woman wailed, no doubt his wife. Friends surrounded her, their futile attempts at soothing her grief, to no avail. A note nailed to the trunk bore an abhorrent message written in what appeared to be blood: *NO TIMBER N——————*.

The weight of the moment bore into Jason's core. He forcibly dismounted, his movements sluggish, while Ghost's nervous neigh echoed the crowd's somber mood. He stroked his stallion's neck and eased through the crowd, eyeing the hanged man. "What abomination is this?"

"Talman Bearclaw, God rest his soul," a voice whispered. "You can tell it's him, he's darker'n most, except his wife, Blessed, poor woman. Bearclaw never harmed no one."

He teased his eyes from the corpse to the speaker. "Reverend Old Tassel, you shouldn't oughta see something like this. What's happened here is ungodly." While coatless, the elderly minister had remembered to don his clergy collar.

"Brother Hyde," another voice answered, "we appreciate your concern, but after four years of war, we've seen as bad before." It was Preacher Edwards.

Jason grunted, then elbowed his way into the circle. "Who amongst you saw or heard anything?"

First met with uneasy silence, at length old Jim Hammonds cleared his throat. "I did. My wife and I live close by. She woke me. We smelt smoke. I ran out back and started ringing the dinner bell."

"I knew bother was afoot when I heard it," someone else spoke up. "Nobody rings a dinner bell at four in the morning. I woke my sons and we got here lickety split."

"I could hear 'em murderers hooting and hollering," another man said. "They done set the council house ablaze. Schoolhouse, too, and Walker's store was a'burning. They took off when we showed up."

"We fired at 'em, maybe wounded one," someone in the crowd echoed. "We doused what fires as we could. Couldn't save the council house."

"Coop and some others got here by then," Hammonds said. "Terrible thing, what they done to Tal."

Preacher maneuvered into the circle, ripped down the sign, then faced the throng. "It's blasphemous, is what it is. Who's gonna help me cut him down and carry him to the church?" He surveyed the crowd, hands on his hips. "This man deserves last rites and prayer. That business falls to me," he announced in his booming voice.

"Bearclaw never once set foot inside a house of worship, Preacher," Doc Hooper responded.

"Doesn't matter. After what these devils did to him, he's getting a proper send-off to the Lord." Hammonds stepped forward. Three others followed. "Bless you, gentlemen."

Jason glanced at Cooper's store. A rabble waited for him in front, his appointed posse plus a bushel more. In the first blush of dawn, he could see their restless, eager faces. “Let’s go, Daddy.” Leading Ghost, he crossed the square with controlled strides.

“Morning fellas.” Jason scrutinized them, recognizing many as former brothers-at-arms from the Thomas Legion, battle-scarred and missing parts of themselves—a nose, an eye, or like himself, an ear. Those with empty sleeves or pants legs stayed home. Improvised war paint defined some faces while other men wore portions of their army uniforms. Altogether, they were a fierce-looking, enthusiastic lot.

“We’re with you all the way, Jace,” one man said.

“Let’s get them bastards!”

“Damn right!”

“Hold on, boys,” Jason interjected. “I know y’all are itching to go after these rotters.”

“That’s putting it lightly, Son,” his father grumbled.

Jason acknowledged him with a quick glance. “None wants ’em more’n me. ’Cepting maybe Bearclaw’s kin—Any here?”

A dark-skinned boy, a little older than Will, with Cherokee features stepped forward, eyes red, his dirty face streaked with dried tears.

“Talman Bearclaw was my daddy. I tried to stop ’em but—” He shook his head. “Too many. Couple of ’em held Mama’s and my arms and made us watch while another one cut him. “He didn’t make a peep,” the boy whispered. “Just stared ’em down. Daddy wouldn’t give ’em the pleasure of listening to his pain. Them bastards stood around my suffering daddy and—” he took a stuttering breath, “and *laughed*.”

Tom Cooper gave him a comforting pat.

“Who did this, Son?” Jason asked.

He nodded with emphasis. “His name’s Win. Heard it said more’n once.”

“What’s your name?”

“Grayson, sir, but most call me Gray.”

“You’re a brave man, Gray.” He grasped the lad’s shoulders. “We will avenge your daddy.” He eyeballed those before him. “Let me be clear—You’ll follow my orders. I understand we all want revenge. That band of thugs took something or someone from everybody. It’s time we put ’em out of business. So, listen up. Anybody riding off half-baked this morning will either get himself killed or get others hurt or killed. Mind what I tell you, or skedaddle now. Got that?”

A loud “Yes, sir!” satisfied his concerns. “Okay, then we’ll be on our way.”

Onacona arrived, accompanied by a Cherokee chief, Standing Bear, Dan Taylor, and a few other men. “What in hell happened last night?”

“See for yourself. They burnt down our council house and killed a man.”

“Who done it?”

“Windrake Ferries and his Brothers of the White Cross.” Jason cast a thin smile. “Glad you’re here, friend.”

His former comrade-at-arms gestured to the old warrior who arrived with him. “You remember my wife’s father, Chief Laughing Crow. Are these the same vermin that hit our village last summer?”

“You can bet on it.”

Dan motioned to the men riding with him. “These are some of my Raiders.”

Jason acknowledged them with a dip of his chin. “Glad to have you.” He faced his volunteers. “Mount up and follow me.” He checked his pockets for Ferries’ hand-drawn map, appreciating that it remained in place from the day before, then gave the signal to ride.

War cries pierced the early morning air and the thunder of hooves shook the ground while the enraged crowd spurred them onward. Jason and his posse galloped out of town toward the mountainous wilderness of the Nantahala Forest.

Spotty sun filtered through the forest canopy while a flat silver veil overhead kept the temperature cool. Spring fairy snow danced while giant evergreens whispered in a light breeze. Slickrock Creek gurgled and frolicked through the forest, oblivious to the human intrusion splashing through its rippling water. On the opposite bank, Jason guided the posse on horseback deeper into the woods.

"Over here!" Dan called out and pointed. "Look at all them hoofprints. Gotta be ten or twelve of 'em, easy."

Jason slipped Ferries' map from his shirt pocket and checked its primitive scribblings. "This looks like the place." They tailed them up a rough mountain trail for miles through scrubby terrain, around boulders, into and out of gullies, past waterfalls and rushing streams. At last, he motioned everyone to halt. "We're moving on foot from here," he said quietly. "Keep your voices down." The company of men dismounted.

"I need a couple volunteers to guard our horses." No offers, so he chose two wildcards. "Daddy and young Bearclaw."

"No way in hell am I holding back," his father retorted.

Gray opened his mouth to protest, but Jason held up a hand. "What did I tell you? Orders are orders. Now, keep a sharp eye out, men. If one of 'em comes by here, they'll kill you." The youth scanned every direction. Jason turned to the rest of his men and continued, "Defend yourselves if they attack, but Chief Thomas and the elders want these wretches taken alive. Remember this. Whatever happens, Ferries is mine. Onacona, come with me. The rest of you, follow us."

For another three miles, they retraced the tracks left by the early morning riders. Employing the quiet stealth of the Cherokee fox walk, they trekked deeper and always upward. A timber rattler warned them of its presence, then slithered into the brush. A mother hawk dived at them when they passed too close to her nest. Undaunted, Jason climbed higher in the wooded terrain, trailed by the posse.

Their path led them through a narrow mountain pass, barely wide enough for a pack horse. A muffled sound of alarm preceded a guttural feline yowl. Behind Jason, a cougar poised for attack on the pathway between him and his men, its yellow eyes focused on its prey.

Dan Laughing Crow padded between the boulders to the front. He drew an arrow from his quiver, fitted it in place, pulled back the bowstring, and aimed. The arrow pierced the cat's paw. It squawked, leapt onto a rock shelf, and sprang away into the forest.

"We are in its territory," the chief explained. "But now it knows who is boss."

Jason saluted him and signaled the men to move forward. Beyond the boulders and halfway around the mountain, the thinning air made the climb an arduous assignment.

A man in a red shirt darted past an opening between the rocks. Jason leapt behind a cropping and motioned for his search party to scatter. They followed the red shirt to a clearing near the top of the bald. Outside a cave, more than a dozen men sat wearing similar shirts with visible *BOWC* badges still pinned in place. Their white head coverings lay discarded in a pile close by a campfire. A makeshift spit roasted a small pig.

One fellow tended the spit while the rest gathered in relaxed clusters. Some drank whiskey while others sipped coffee. Most smoked cigarettes as they chatted amongst themselves, certain words prominent—half-breed, porch monkey, coon-squaw. Their demeanor revealed no evidence that a few hours earlier, they tortured a father in front of his family and then took his life.

One stood apart from the rest, a redheaded mountain of a man. Blood spatters covered his shirt and pants. A boot was blood-soaked. He limped across the clearing, sat down alone, and wrapped a bandage over and around his injured upper torso while watching a young fellow seated a few yards away.

"Gotta be Ferries," Jason whispered.

The hulk kept watch over a dark-skinned mixed-breed youth propped against a boulder at the edge of the camp, his hands and feet tied and a gag in his mouth. Beaten but conscious, the boy's terrified eyes darted across the scene, then settled on a noose hung from a large oak. A horse stood nearby, pawing the ground with a hoof.

"That's Mose, Gray's big brother," Munson Crisp whispered from Jason's other side.

One murderer guffawed and slapped his knee. "Whoo-wee. Did you see them half-breed faces when ol' Buck started beating that Injun?"

The gargantuan grimaced at them as he tied off his bandage, pulling an end with yellow teeth. "Let's finish this so we can eat. I'm hungry."

"You're the big bug, till your cuz gets back," another man said, grinding his cigarette stub with his boot. He got up off the rock that served as his chair.

The other whitecaps followed him. A couple wrenched Mose upright. The boy struggled against his bindings, a spate of squalls gushing from behind his gag. One captor held him still while the other untied the rope from his ankles. Once freed, the youth kicked him in the face. The thug smacked him.

A third man guided the horse under the noose. They wrestled the howling young man onto the animal's back and then looped the rope around the youth's neck.

With the gang's attention on Mose, the posse surrounded the camp.

The largest outlaw limped over to their captive and jerked him down to his level. He ripped off the gag with an impatient tug. "You got something to say, boy? Then do it now." Tossing the scrap aside, he set him upright and hobbled away.

Mose panted, chest heaving, eyes rolling. "Help!"

"Ain't nobody gonna hear ya out here, bub," Buck smirked.

At Jason's signal, his men let loose curdling war cries and rebel yells that permeated the prickly-cold air. The startled gang drew their guns and spun around.

"Hell fire!" one yelped. "Injuns!"

The posse leapt from cover and charged the raiders, firing their weapons.

Spooked, Mose's horse reared on its haunches and ran, leaving him kicking his feet and swinging in wide erratic arcs from the end of the rope.

Jason fended off an attacking hoodlum, the two of them exchanging wallops. A gang member stepped from behind a tree to Jason's rear and took aim at him.

In a flash, Jason's father leapt from his hiding place, grabbed the outlaw, and sliced the man's throat with his hunting knife. He let the would-be murderer's dead weight fall and ran to help Mose. He pressed the boy's legs upward as far as he could. "Damn it! Somebody cut the noose!"

Crisp shimmied up the tree, crawled out to the branch, and sawed the rope with his Bowie knife. The strands separated and Jason's father eased Mose down. The boy filled his lungs with air while Jason's father severed his bindings and carried him away from the melee.

Jason caught sight of Windrake Ferries limping away, headed for deeper woods, and gave chase. Sprinting through the brush, he dodged trees, splashed across an icy stream, leapt over downed logs. Catching him, they squared off, both men panting and glowering. "You're mine, you yellow-bellied pig." Jason shed his jacket.

"Yella-belly? Haw, not likely." The massive killer squinted and cocked his head. "You're that mix-breed cracker that kilt my kin, ain't ya? I can best you any day of the week."

"Try me," Jason sneered and charged. He connected his first punch squarely on Ferries' jaw.

Ferries staggered and fell on the hard ground with a surprised grunt. He rubbed the back of his head, then clambered upright, favoring his injured foot, and swung. Jason ducked and lunged. They grappled, jabbing left and right. They separated, bloody, their chests heaving.

"Come git it, ya li'l gallnipper. Hell, you fight like a girl." Ferries flexed his fingers and hunched his body.

"I'll fix your flint, you pansy-ass no-account! Just gimme a minute," Jason hacked. He charged, and they went for a second round.

Jason landed a knife-slice to the back of the murderer's neck, slamming him to his knees. A knee to his chin jolted him backward. He spread-eagled into the dirt. Blood gushed from his mouth and he gasped for air.

"Get up, maggot," Jason squawked between breaths.

Ferries staggered to his feet, dazed but refusing defeat.

"This is for my wife!" Jason threw a series of backhand punches, shouting with a passion he never knew he possessed. "And for my sons! And my father! And Janie!" He drew back his fist. "And this one is for raping Mary!" He bashed him as hard as he could. The sound of the man's nose shattering sickened him.

Ferries stumbled. "I–I nev—." Gasping and spewing blood, he faltered, unsteady. "I never done that."

"*Liar!*" Jason pulled his pistol and aimed at the fallen man, panting.

Ferries tumbled and lay unconscious.

Onacona and Standing Bear sprinted from between the timbers. Onacona grabbed Jason's arm. "That's enough. Fight's over."

"Get lost!" A cut above Jason's eye trickled a bloody stream down the side of his bruised face. He held his left hand close to his chest, knuckles reduced to raw meat.

"It's over," Standing Bear said. "The others are handcuffing 'em. One of ours is dead, another, injured."

Jason winced. "Who?"

"Redmond and Lovin," Dan Taylor answered.

Jason's gut clinched at Joel Lovin's name. "Oh God. I'll–I'll let Evie know," he mumbled.

"Lovin'll be fine," Dan explained. "Redmond took one between the shoulder blades."

Jason flattened his lips. "Then I'll let his family know. Evie won't be happy, but at least she isn't burying her husband." He turned to his victim. "This one doesn't deserve to live." He refocused his aim at Ferries.

"That ain't the way, Jace," Onacona replied.

"Can't break your own orders." Dan reached out to him. Jason shook him off. "Enough, I said!"

Jason gave him a sideways glare and limped a few paces from the beaten man, gun still aimed.

"Listen to him, Jace," Standing Bear murmured.

Jason's father burst from between the trees. "Kill him! You'd be right to do it."

Jason peered at him and then at Ferries. The fallen man half-sat up on one elbow, fear and hatred etched across his battered face. "You miserable wretch." He fired.

Ferries bellowed and collapsed onto his back. Moments later, he looked up at Jason and glowered.

Jason stood over him, smoking pistol in hand, and met his adversary's glare. "Lilly-liver. Put him with the others. Come on, Daddy." He holstered his gun and limped through the timbers to take charge of his detachment.

They emerged at the battle site. "Round 'em up, boys," Jason ordered.

"Scalp 'em!" a warrior hollered. The whitecaps squalled and struggled at their bindings.

"No!" Jason commanded. "You beat the crap out of 'em. That's enough. Chief, get their horses." He turned his attention to his father. "You disobeyed my orders. In the army I woulda arrested you for insubordination."

"This ain't the army, Son, and I ain't your dang soldier. I'm your daddy. I saved your life back there and Mose Bearclaw's, too. So, don't give me no sass."

"You better hope nothing's happened to his brother, Gray. I put you there to protect him." He lifted the skewered pig off the spit. "Take this." He handed him the skewer and gathered the white hoods, tossing one to his father. "Tote the pig in that."

Jason extinguished the campfire and Cooper approached. "Tied and tethered. The big boy, too. Ready when you are."

"Good man, Coop." Jason limped to the waiting posse and captives. "Longfeather, help Laughing Crow with their horses. Boys, y'all done real good. Let's go—but keep a close eye on these maggots."

Gray Bearclaw spotted his older brother before they reached their horses. He ran to him and threw his arms around him. "Thanks Jesus, you're alive!" On seeing the raiders, Gray's face went purple with rage. "Where's that Win fella?"

"Yonder." Dan pointed to the largest man in the group.

Gray walked up to the bloody, beaten man, scrutinized him, then glowered at Dan. "Hell-fire, this ain't that Win feller!" He went after the captive, pounding with his fists.

Dan pulled him off the man. "Stand down, sonny. What do you mean, it ain't him?"

"Listen to Dan, Son," Jason interrupted. "This man's going to the Salisbury State Prison. He's gonna hang, along with his pals here, for what he done. A hanging for a hanging."

"Gray, tell Jace again, louder." Dan whipped around and leveled a hard look at Jason.

"You can't send 'em off to Salisbury!" Tom Cooper called out. "We oughta be the ones to hang 'em." The posse members backed him up.

"Our leaders want it that way." Jason shifted his eyes to his adversary. "And ol' Win Ferries here, he's gonna swing first."

"I done tol' ya, this ain't Ferries!" Gray Bearclaw pointed to the beaten man. "Him's the one what made me watch."

"He's right," Mose croaked.

"The dirty little nose-picker ain't lying," one outlaw piped up. "Dumb buncha timber—" Onacona slammed his fist into his jaw before he could finish his slur.

"Who the hell is it, then?" Jason snapped.

"That there's Crusher Bolin," another gang member declared. "The toughest scrapper in the Carolinas. Him and Win is cousins."

"Crusher ain't no gimper, like Win. Least not till today," the first outlaw said, rubbing his jawbone. "He took a plug in the foot this morning. That monkey-faced redskin done it." He nodded in Mose's direction.

Jason stared at Bolin's bloody boot. "One of you cussers gonna tell me where he is?"

"Win ain't come up here with us," a whitecap said. "Said he had something to tend to." He spit out a mouthful of blood along with a tooth.

"Dammit!" Jason barked. "Throw these no-accounts over the horses' backs and tie 'em tight. Take 'em to the Fort Montgomery jail. Daddy, Onacona, Dan, we gotta get to town, fast. Longfeather, you're in charge till I get back."

Tuck Stamper, a lanky youth of seventeen, waited outside the jail, perched on a chair, its top rail propped against the wall of the building. He hopped up as soon as Jason reined in his horse.

"Tuck, I need your help."

"Yessir! Where're the others?"

"They'll be coming along. They got the Ferries gang with 'em. Help 'em lock up the murdering swine when they get here."

Tuck hooked his thumbs under the suspenders that held up his hand-me-down britches. "My pleasure!"

Jason dismounted and took a slip of paper and a pencil stub from his pocket, jotted instructions, and handed it to the young man. "Give this to Crisp. I need him to ride to Murphy quick as he can and send a telegram to Salisbury Prison. Just as I wrote it here. Got that?"

"Yes *sir*."

"Make sure these lowlifes stay put. And mind the lynch mobs. There's gonna be a heap of folks down here soon as word gets out." He shifted to his father. "Daddy, get home quick and check on the family. Take Dan with you. Y'all be careful. Ferries could be waiting on you."

"Sure thing. Come on, son." The two men took off.

"Onacona, we gotta get to Doc Taylor's," Jason said. "If he's not at my place, then he's going after my daughter."

They spurred their steeds onward, riding as fast as their horses would carry them.

37

Martha carried a basket of dirty laundry into her kitchen, where Mary stood at the sink washing breakfast dishes. “Thank you, dear,” Martha said.

“No bother,” Mary replied. “I like to stay busy.” She dried a plate and set it on a shelf with the others. “Want help with the laundry?”

“Not today. It’s beginning to snow. I’m just taking the sheets out. Why don’t you check on the new schoolhouse? A trip to town may do you good.”

“Grand idea.” Mary wiped a cup dry.

Martha stuffed the small container of safety matches she kept near the stove into her skirt pocket and walked out the back. She headed for the washhouse, humming *Rock of Ages*. She set down her basket, stepped inside, and reached for the oil lamp. Her other hand searched her pocket.

An arm stretched from the half-light and grabbed her around the neck. She shrieked. A dirty hand, metallic-sweet with blood, clapped over her mouth and yanked her backward. Her captor’s foot caught the corner of the door and kicked it shut. Martha struggled to free herself, then gagged, as the stench of an unwashed body, sweat, and adrenaline permeated the interior.

“Make a peep, and I’ll put your lights out,” a voice growled into her ear.

In the kitchen, Mary laid the last clean plate in place, then draped the damp dishtowel to dry. Eager for her journey, she untied her apron, hung it on a hook, and turned around. To her surprise, a blue-eyed woman faced her. Strands of curly chestnut-brown hair peeked from beneath her tattered army hat.

"Oh, my word!" Mary stepped backward, bumping into the sink. "Miz Hawes—"

"Call me Libby. Now do as I say. We're going to the washhouse. The doc needs us."

"What?" Mary gazed out the window at the small plaster-coated block building. The laundry basket sat on the ground outside the closed door. Martha was nowhere to be seen.

Libby gave her a large pistol. "Take this. It's loaded. Can you shoot straight?"

The hair on the back of Mary's neck stood up. She gulped and nodded, and clutched the weapon with both hands. Colt. Army issue. She opened the cylinder and spun it; six bullets. She shifted her eyes to the window once more, the scene unchanged.

"Follow me and keep quiet. Hurry!"

Mary nervously approached the building. She heard the growl of a familiar voice from behind the wall, to the right of the door—"Do as I tell you" She gasped, feeling suddenly dazed. *It's him!*

Libby delivered a kick to the door, slammed it open, and took a marksman's stance. She aimed her pistol with both hands. "Get out here, you filthy murdering rat!"

"You again!" Ferries barked, and dragged Martha into the open doorway, gripping one of her arms. He yanked her off balance, and with a deep-throated bellow, slammed her head against the jamb by a hank of hair and heaved her limp body at Libby.

The two women tumbled; the doc's inert body pinned Libby prone. Mary stood to one side, holding a gun on the huge red-headed form.

Ferries confronted Mary in a stand-off. She stumbled backward, pistol trembling in her grip. "You devil!"

He took a step and knocked her gun from her hands. He grabbed her by the throat. He squeezed, lifting her off the ground, and shoved her against the side of the washhouse while she clawed at his hands.

"Mary!" Jason sprinted across the yard, Onacona close behind him.

Jason clutched Ferries' shoulder with a firm hand and whipped him around. He balled his fist and swung with all his might. Pain seared his knuckles as they connected with the man's jaw.

Ferries staggered, releasing his hold on Mary, then regained his footing and prepared for attack. She crumpled onto the snow-dusted ground.

Jason head butted his mid-section. Ferries punched and jabbed. Wounds opened and their blood mixed, smeared, and stained each other's skin. Onacona threw himself into the scuffle. Together, he and Jason slammed the enormous man against the washhouse, cracking the plaster, and wrestled him to the ground.

Panting, Jason straddled the man's bulk, pinned his arms with his knees and grasped his throat, thumbs pressing on his larynx. "How does that feel, bastard?"

Onacona stepped away. "All yours, friend."

Ferries gasped for air and slapped at Jason's legs. The man slipped one arm free and reached to his lower extremities, stretching his fingers toward his boot.

"He got a gun!" Onacona lunged. He grabbed Ferries free hand, knocking Jason to one side. Jason lost his grip on Ferries' throat, and his knee slid from Ferries' other arm. The three of them grappled and grunted, skin smacking skin.

Ferries forced himself onto one knee. Cold steel flashed in his hand. He aimed at Jason.

Time transfixed within an ear-splitting blast. The acrid smell of black powder lifted into the mountain air. Ferries went limp, he buckled, and hit the dirt face down.

Mary stood a few feet away, trembling, and clutching the butt of her smoking pistol, her chest heaving with stuttering breaths. She stared at the inanimate lump lying before her.

Onacona kicked Ferries' derringer out of reach and extended a hand to Jason.

The doc sat up and gingerly touched the rising knot on her bleeding forehead.

Libby helped her to her feet before casting Jason a sidelong glance. "About time y'all showed up."

Ferries jerked, and grimacing, flipped onto his back. Mary reeled but lifted her pistol, cocked it, and threaded her index finger around the trigger. She took careful aim. The injured man shifted his head toward the sound of the hammer cock.

"Sadistic pig," she hissed. "You enjoy the pain of others. Excited about your own?" She fired into the door frame, showering him with splinters and plaster.

"Mary don't," Jason warned, between breaths.

"I'm gonna kill him, Daddy. Don't try to stop me."

Ferries gurgled and choked while a dark red stain oozed from beneath him. He pointed at Jason. "You ain't no Injun." He coughed, spit a mouthful of blood, and swallowed. "That don't change nothin'—my brother's still dead. I *will* kill you one day, you shifty-assed som'bitch." His body shuddered, his eyes rolled upward and the lids closed.

Mary lowered her weapon.

Jason removed it from her hands and passed it to Onacona. "It's over, child."

Mary flung her arms around him. "Oh, Daddy!"

A zing of pain swelled across his ribs. "Easy! Thank the Lord you're all right. Doc, you gotta remove that slug or he'll die. I swore to bring him in alive."

"*What?*" Mary yelped, stepping back from him. "You want to save this beast? After what he did to me?"

"Orders," Jason replied. "Besides, I wanna see this bastard hang for his crimes."

"*Arrgh!*" She stormed into the house and slammed the door behind her.

Martha tossed him a concerned glance.

"I'll explain it to her later," Jason said.

"Right. Let's get this man inside," Martha said. "We need a sling. Libby, grab a sheet and pillowcase from the laundry basket. You men push him onto his side."

"Hell no!" Ferries barked. "I'll walk on my own two feet." He gurgled and struggled to sit up, abandoned the effort, and flopped to his back.

Martha ripped the pillowcase and stuffed a scrap into the gunshot wound on Ferries' back. He groaned and passed out. The doc ripped an end off the sheet and repurposed it to a tourniquet. She tied it tight around the injury, then performed a quick check of her massive patient.

"He seems stable. Spread out the sheet and help me lift this stinking giant onto it."

Jason and Onacona positioned the hulk to move.

"Jace and I will take the back," Onacona said.

The two women grabbed an end of the improvised sling. "Ready?" Martha said. "Altogether, lift."

Once inside, the doc guided them to a small examination room between the kitchen and the infirmary. Together, they lifted Ferries on a table, and she cleaned his wounds.

"I'll help you," Libby said.

"Miz Hawes," Jason interrupted, "come to the parlor with me. I got a couple questions for you. Doc, I'm sure my friend will help you any way he can." The two moved to the other room.

"Sit down" Jason motioned to a group of easy chairs and sat in one.

"I'll stand."

"Up to you. Miz Hawes, you're sure a mystery. Tell me, how d'you come to be here today?" He caught her eyes and held her gaze until she looked away.

"A hunch. After y'all rode out of town this morning, I started thinking about what I'd do if I was Ferries."

"And you figured he'd go after my daughter while we all looked for him and his gang. You seem to be in the business of saving my young'uns from disaster. Amongst other things. Why do you care?"

"I came with my husband to sell Bibles. Soon after, I discovered Ferries killed Ira Lovin. He *murdered* him, didn't he?"

"Assuredly."

She turned and stared at him, a glimmer of comprehension in her eyes. "You were there—You and the Indian at the Murphy encounter are the same person."

Jason observed her with caution, not wanting to incriminate himself, but determined to learn about her relationship to Ferries. "During the war, I served in the Cherokee battalion— How do you know about Ira?" The mention of the young man's name stirred something troubling in her. He could see it in her eyes.

"Fort Montgomery is a small town. One hears things." Blinking hard, she crossed the room, her hands outstretched, and took both of his in hers. "Thank you for trying to save his life, Lieutenant Hyde. Ira was all I had in the world."

Jason stared at her. "What do you mean?"

"Years ago, down in Gaston County, that man out there did to me," she glanced in Ferries' direction, then back at Jason, "what he did to your Mary. I gave birth to a baby boy from that unholy union. I named him Ira. Got to hold him but a minute before they took him from me. After that, Mama sent me to live with my Aunt Aggie up north."

"Joel and Evie Lovin reared him," Jason murmured. "You a Lovin?"

Mrs. Hawes nodded her head, then lowered her eyes. "Never knew 'em. After my aunt died of fever, I came looking for my only kin. My Ira. Lost a second time to the war before I found him. Lost forever when Ferries murdered him." She shuddered. "I want that animal dead as much as the rest of you."

Jason sighed. "I'm so sorry. Ira was one of my students. A good, smart boy with his whole life ahead of him. I loved him, too." He looked away. "It's my fault he's gone. I beg your forgiveness for that."

"Your fault?"

"When they assigned him to my company, I took him under my wing. Protected him. Promised Joel I'd keep him safe. He wanted to ride with me that day we went to the Murphy woods. I knew the risks, yet I allowed him to come along. I enjoyed his company. He died because of my selfishness." Jason blinked hard. "I tried my best to save him when we got attacked. My best wasn't good enough. I failed his Uncle Joel. I failed you before I learnt you ever existed."

Pain lined her face as she gripped a chairback. "Was my boy handsome?"

"Yes, ma'am. He looked older than his years. A lot like you, but tall. Curly reddish hair about your color. He woulda grown into a solid, respectable man. Have a seat, ma'am. I'll fetch you a cool drink."

She drained the cup of water he handed her and set it aside. "You think Ferries will make it?"

"Doc Martha will do her best."

"He deserves to die."

"I agree," Jason said. "Just not here. He's going to prison to be tried in a court of law. Our community elders assigned me the task and I will see it done."

She gave him a long look. "They must think well of you."

"We all do," Martha interjected from the kitchen doorway. "You find that surprising? We hold Jace in high regard around here."

"Forgive me. I didn't mean to imply otherwise. I appreciate your kind words, Lieutenant. I don't fault you for Ira's death, nor should you blame yourself. My son was a casualty of war—Ferries' war against humanity. That man is the devil incarnate and I won't rest until he lies in his grave." She turned to Martha. "Now, if you want my help, Doc, I'd be glad to oblige."

The two women returned to the surgery room, prepped the supplies and went to work.

The doctor removed Mary and Libby's bullets, amongst others, from Ferries' body, cauterized his wounds, stitched him up, and applied herbal poultices and bandages against infection. Onacona supplied clean water while Libby handed Doc sterile surgical instruments. It required a group effort to move his inert bulk to the infirmary. After the patient was sedated and handcuffed to a bed, they rested.

"Y'all have been a big help," Martha said, her voice bathed in fatigue.

"Glad to do it," Libby replied. "I best be going. Say goodbye to Mary for me." She started for the exit.

"One last thing, Mrs. Hawes," Jason said in a quiet tone. "If you're a Lovin, then you're not alone in the world. Joel Lovin's your uncle; he'll help you. He's a good man. He helped me at a dark time in my life."

Libby Hawes leveled a compassion-filled gaze at him. "Everyone's been through hard times of late. War may cause a body to choose paths which he otherwise might not take."

"I dunno what you mean."

"I think you do."

Jason raised an eyebrow. "Some things—and people—aren't what they appear on the surface. Listen, I'd trust Joel Lovin with my life. I dare say, you can too." Jason paused. "I hear you're friendly with Miz Evie. Tell her what you told me. They won't leave you out in the cold."

She grasped the door knob, and her shoulders slumped. "If only that were true," she said in a small voice. "I wish I knew before I came here what I know now."

"Would it have changed anything?"

She paused at the open doorway—"No"—then closed it quietly behind her.

Jason glanced toward the kitchen.

Martha stood in the doorway observing, and answered his unspoken question. "She'll find her way. The Lord's watching over her."

A few days later, Cornwoman fetched a pail of water from Little Snowbird Creek; its brume enveloped her feet and lent an otherworldly essence to the chill morning. A weak morning sun in a rosy sky tinted nearby mountain crests while she mulled over a disturbing pre-dawn dream. *Trouble comes this way. I fear it will touch us all.* She hurried back to her cabin, where she welcomed the warmth of her fire and put the kettle to boil. The front door opened and she looked over her shoulder. Aramarinda came inside, returning from feeding their livestock: a couple of horses, a goat, and a few laying hens. Just sufficient for the two of them.

"There you are! I am expecting a visitor from town. Jason Hyde." The young woman's eyes lit up and an amber flush tinted her golden cheeks. Seeing her reaction, Cornwoman added, "You ran from him when you met him last year, remember?"

Aramarinda removed her poncho and hung it on a hook. "That was then. I'm different now."

Cornwoman could not argue with that. Over the years, she watched her young friend blossom from a Cherokee rose to a fancy many-petaled hybrid, like the gilt-edge ruby ones in Miz Cooper's yard. A hybrid in her own right, Aramarinda inherited her charms from her mother, a lovely mixed-blood girl, and was high-spirited like her father. A relative of the venerable Doc Hooper, he sowed his seed within her mother's loins and afterward, like the good Dr. Hooper, married a woman of his own kind.

"Do not set your cap for him, girl. He is fifteen years your senior and a family man. He got enough worries without you fawning over him."

Aramarinda tilted her chin in feigned dismay. "I don't know what you're on about."

"No? Then do me a favor and go hunt us some dinner."

The girl groused a moment, grabbed her bow and quiver and left.

Cornwoman frowned, remembering the spark that ignited between Jason and Aramarinda on their last encounter. It was not something she wanted to encourage.

Horse's hooves outside signaled Jason's arrival, and Cornwoman opened the door before he knocked. "I thought I would see you today."

"Ama, I need to speak with you. May I come in?"

"You are always welcome in my home."

He crossed her threshold and removed his coat, flinching with the effort.

Cornwoman winced. "Have you been in a fight? Let me look at you."

"But that's not—"

"I will not take no for an answer. Go sit over there." She pointed at a pair of benches near the fire. After checking him over, she applied a unique blend of salve to his cuts, rewrapped his bruised ribs, then handed him a small vial. "These herbs will help that cut over your eye heal quicker. It must affect your eyesight."

"As a matter of fact—thank you." He buttoned his shirt and tucked the bottle into a pocket. "Before I tell you why I'm really here, I wanna say I'm grateful for what you did for my family. Mary's much better. So's Nancy. You made a world of difference."

She smiled. "It means a lot for someone to acknowledge my skills. Warm yourself while I make tea. Do you like ginseng?" Minutes later, she set a tray with cups and a pot on the low table in front of the fire, poured the refreshment, and sat down. "Now, what brought you all this way?"

He described recent events. "Windrake Ferries is a ruthless killer. You know what he did to Mary. As if that wasn't enough, he's been fooling about with one of my other little gals, Janie. He tried to kill my sons and my daddy. A few days ago, he tortured and murdered Talman Bearclaw. He and his whitecaps lynched him in the town square."

"By the gods!" She thought of her warning of fire and fear and shuddered.

"My posse and I tailed his band to their hideout. We captured 'em, but not without a fight. Meanwhile, Ferries went after Mary again and Doc Martha."

"*Tla!*"

"Mary gave him a dose of lead." A shadow smile passed over his lips. "But he lived. We moved him to the Fort Montgomery jailhouse yesterday. He's recuperating in a cell with his gang members. We got a twenty-four-hour guard on 'em until he's fit enough to travel to the state prison. They'll await trial there."

Relieved, Cornwoman relaxed against the bench. "Well now, a piece of good news! I expected we would discuss a serious matter."

He bobbed his head. "Serious to me. I'm worried he'll get off. It makes scant sense, but the thought's eating at me. You got the gift of Sight. I want you to tell me the future."

Cornwoman's dreams niggled at the back of her mind. She felt her ancestors stirring in the ether and watched their shapes dance in the flames of the sacred fire—an omen. "I will cast the bones."

The table before them held an ancient wooden plate with markings painted on it and a black pouch. Crafted by her great-great-grandfather, a tribal high priest, it had passed through her family's generations. She slid it to the center, shook the pouch contents—a smattering of small bones—into one hand, then cupped her other palm over it while asking the spirits for guidance. Rattling them, she felt their magic come alive against her skin. She spread her fingers, and they clattered across the plate's shapes and symbols. She studied their placements for the next few minutes, muttering to herself.

Aramarinda returned with a string of brook trout, interrupting their session. Her legs appeared long and slender in close-fitting moleskin breeches that complimented her muslin tunic. Her locks hung loose about her shoulders, lustrous in the firelight, and scented with lavender oil. It appeared as if she had pinched a blush into her cheeks before entering the cabin. Obviously, she had not heeded Cornwoman's words regarding Jason.

"My traps were full," Aramarinda said. "We can eat for days." She smiled and fluffed her hair. "Lieutenant Hyde, what a pleasant surprise. Join us for dinner?"

He sprang to his feet. "Hi'dy, Miss. You–you look, ah," he stuttered, "quite fit."

She eyed him closely. "My stars, but somebody gave you a good wallop!"

"Ama fixed me up."

"Then you'll be good as gold in no time." A kittenish smile illuminated her face. She laid her catch in the sink, poured spring water over them, and then breezed into the bedroom.

"I've overstayed my welcome," Jason said. "I don't want to impose on your meal."

"Not at all." Cornwoman moved to the door and opened it wide. "But if you must go, then you must."

"But, my fortune—what did you see?"

She hesitated. "Do not worry. All will be well." She sensed her ancestors rail against her words.

He cocked his head, lips pressed together. "You sure?"

"Thank you for coming."

He made ready to leave. Aramarinda joined them, wearing a dress, her hair twisted into a hasty knot. She pouted. "Going so soon? I hoped you might eat with us."

Cornwoman glared.

Aramarinda ignored her. She approached Jason's horse and stroked its muzzle. "He's a fine animal. What's his name?"

"There's none finer. His name is Ghost." He patted his stallion's flank.

Aramarinda closed the distance between them and smiled up at him. "Maybe we could ride together sometime."

"Aramarinda!" Cornwoman scolded.

Jason's eyebrows hitched, yet he stared into the girl's face as if mesmerized. "Aramarinda." Her name slipped off his tongue like a song, its vowels molding his lips for a kiss. He seemed suddenly shy. "I'd like that."

Cornwoman wondered, *Had he whispered it to himself, over and again, never believing he would stand this close to her?*

He tipped his hat, mounted up, and trotted toward the trail.

Aramarinda leaned against the cabin's doorframe, observing his departure, arms folded under her breasts. Jason slowed Ghost's canter, twisted in his saddle, and looked behind him. Cornwoman saw his eyes connect with Aramarinda's and hold her gaze. In a simple movement filled with a woman's yearnings, her young friend fluttered her fingers in goodbye.

Saddened by this turn of events, Cornwoman could do nothing more than shake her head. She knew well Aramarinda's incorrigible nature, and was aware of Jason's present emotional vulnerability. *No good will come of this, no good a'tall.*

39

Penley's Boarding House
April 1866

Hawes advised Pinkertons of his breakthrough in the case and requested permission to pursue the counterfeit money trail to Ohio. For weeks Libby had watched him for weeks act antsy as a boy before Christmas while he awaited their reply. He rode daily to the Murphy telegraph office.

Now, rapid heavy footfalls in the boarding house hallway announced his return. He charged into the sitting room and slammed the door shut.

Startled, Libby looked up from her newspaper. His angry scowl surprised her. "What's eating you?"

He reached inside his jacket pocket, extracted a telegram, and flung it. It spun to the floor. "Read it. It's from the main office. I'm too bowed up to say the words out loud."

She blinked at him, perplexed, and retrieved it:

PINKERTONS OFF CASE—STOP—UNITED STATES TREASURY DEPARTMENT TO TAKE CHARGE—STOP—FIELD AGENTS RETURN TO CHICAGO IMMEDIATELY

She refolded the cable and dropped onto the divan, stunned.

"I spent two years of my life in this godforsaken wilderness," Hawes grumbled. "Finally, I crack the case—and this is my reward!" He spit his words. "Pinkerton wanted his agents to nab all the rings at once. I *told* him there were too many for the few of us he had in place. The poor sod wouldn't listen. Now the new administration is ripping the rug out from under our feet. Damn it all!" He paced the room, his anger electric.

"I don't understand. The Treasury Department doesn't have detectives."

"Right. Good luck to 'em. They'll need it!" He stormed into the hallway. "Start packing, Thorne. We'll clear out tomorrow after breakfast."

Morning dawned misty and gray, with the promise of showers. People filled the town square; nobody wanted to miss the spectacle. Today, Jason Hyde's posse would escort the Brothers of the White Cross to Buncombe County Prison in Asheville. Inside the jailhouse, Jason and a few of his best men prepared for the journey.

He heard the blacksmith halt the adapted prison cart in front, then leaned against the doorjamb, watching an admiring crowd mill about, thumping the carriage sides and testing the strength of its bars. "Ain't she a beauty." "Good job!"

"Bring out the prisoners!" The onlookers' cries grew louder as others rallied with them.

Will Thomas rounded the corner in a black phaeton buggy and parked behind the prisoner transport. He whistled softly at the sight before him, then climbed down and inspected it. "That's as nice a jailbird cage as I've seen."

Jason approached him. "Colonel, good of you to come. They'll be leaving soon."

"Wouldn't miss it, Lieutenant. You put Fort Montgomery on the map with your arrest of the Brotherhood. But why are you taking them to Asheville? Salisbury Prison's more fitting for the likes of them boys."

"Government's accused the Salisbury warden of murdering Union soldiers during the war. They arrested him and closed the prison."

"What?" Will exclaimed.

"Buncombe County's the closest place to hold 'em. You know how it is. Yanks do things different from us. This Reconstruction business got everything topsy-turvy."

"Humph. Well, one thing is certain. There's no growth without chaos. Speaking of chaos, Jace. We need a competent lawman around here."

His words punched Jason's gut. Hands stuffed in his pockets, he fingered the counterfeit bills buried deep inside. Local law enforcement was the last thing he wanted.

"You showed leadership in catching these killers. I'd like you to consider becoming our first sheriff."

Jason stared at the colonel in disbelief.

"Think on it, Jace. Somebody's gonna do the job. You oughta be him."

At a loss for words, he turned to his men. "Haul out the prisoners."

Soon after the outlaws and their escorts left town, a gentle rain began to fall. Libby stood outside Penley's Boarding House and took a lengthy last look. "I want to remember everything just as it is."

Coy Hawes plopped their bags into the wagon bed. "Ain't nothing in this muck-ridden hellhole worth remembering. So quit your stalling, *Thorne-in-my-side*."

"Says you! These mountains are beyond beautiful. There are none of Chicago's horrible slaughterhouses here—no factories spewing coal ash and stench."

"Get in. We gotta long way to go."

Teary-eyed, Libby cooperated, and they left an hour after the departed convoy. She watched the town recede, holding vigil until they rounded a bend and it vanished altogether. Sullen as they bounced and swayed over the muddy road, the unrelenting drizzle intensified her dispirited mood.

"Pull over," Libby muttered several miles into the trip. Hawes didn't respond. "Blast it!" she squawked. "Pull over! I'm getting out."

"You'll do nothing of the sort. Settle yourself."

A wet stream cascaded off the brim of her old army hat as she jumped from the moving vehicle into a mud puddle, splashing slush across her leather overcoat.

Hawes reined the mule with a hard jerk. "What the hell?"

"This is as far as I go." Chilled fingers fumbled past her coat flap and dug deep into her skirt pocket. She handed him an envelope. "Give this to Mr. Pinkerton. It's my resignation. Sorry, Hawes."

"You're acting like a child. Just because they yanked us off this case don't mean there won't be others. You're a dang capable detective. Don't quit now."

"It's not that. I'm glad we're off it. I came to know these folks. They're good people. They're helping each other get by in the worst of times."

He wagged his head, slinging raindrops from his Stetson. "I told you, never ever become personally involved. Beginner's mistake."

"Yes, it is personal. That's why I'm staying."

"Listen," he said, "there's something I oughta tell you. Maybe it'll change your mind—We ain't going to Chicago. You and I are taking a detour to the Ohio River. I got too much invested in this not to follow that bogus money trail to its source."

She squinted up at him. "And you're telling *me* not to get involved? Practice what you preach, Bible salesman. Now you listen. I came here to find my son, Ira. An evil man murdered him before we ever arrived. You witnessed it, in Murphy."

"Murphy—That was your boy? Thorne, I'm sorry."

"I aim to bring that devil to justice whether or not I'm a Pinkerton agent."

"They hauled him and his gang off to prison this morning. Your job's done here. Come with me."

"When he's six feet under, I'll rest easy. Not till then. However, there's more to it than that." She bit her lip. "Never mind. Thank Mr. Pinkerton for giving me a rare opportunity." She grabbed her duffel bag and her rifle from beneath the bench, and began the long, wet trek back to town.

Hawes cursed under his breath. "Hold up. If you're bent on staying, then keep the wagon and mule."

"Don't be daft."

"I can make better time without it. I'll take Blackie." He paused. "I ought not to say this—but I'll miss you, Thorne-in-my-side."

The windows of the old stone and clapboard farmhouse were dark. Pencils of smoke trailed from the chimneys. *She must be here.* Soaked to the skin despite her overcoat, Libby hopped from the cart and knocked on the door of the now-familiar Lovin home. She set her bag on the porch floor and rapped again, harder. At last, footsteps approached.

"Land sakes, Libby Hawes!" Evie Lovin said. She opened her door wider. "Come in, dear, come in. I was working in the kitchen. Sorry, can't hear a thing back there. You're shivering, child. Get yourself in here by the fire before you catch your death."

Overcome with emotion, she allowed Evie to help her out of her wet coat.

Evie grabbed a woolen throw from the divan, wrapped it around Libby's trembling shoulders, and herded her to the fireplace. She placed a fresh log on the fire and stoked the flames. Libby wobbled, and Evie clasped onto her elbow. "What is it, child?"

Libby knew Evie Lovin's reaction to the truth would determine her fate. Her anxious blue eyes searched the older woman's worried face while her heart begged acceptance. "I g–got something to say." She gulped. "My name isn't Hawes…"

Six Months Later

Sooty debris and smell of burnt wood long gone, the memory of Talman Bearclaw's horrific murder would live on. It compelled Jason's journey to Asheville. Summoned to testify at the Brotherhood trial, he fidgeted. Hitched near the completed Fort Montgomery court house, he checked Ghost's saddle and tightened the strap of his knapsack for the third time that morning. Jason's father and a pregnant Nancy waited in their wagon, ready to accompany him.

Tom Cooper and his friend, Wendell Reese, rode into the square and halted their horses close by. Joel Lovin arrived a moment later. "We're going with you," Joel said.

"Y'all don't have to do that."

Cooper lowered his voice. "If an Indian thrashes a white man for stealing his horse, they hang the Indian. White man keeps the horse and goes free. You know the laws—Bushwhackers, night raiders, you name it, they do what they like in Indian territory. Jace, you gotta gang of beat up outlaws to explain. A couple shot, with one recuperating from a bullet to the back, another dead. That puts the Cherokees in your posse in jeopardy. And you, as their leader."

"But Thomas put me in charge. He's white, and so am I. He'll back me up."

"Jace, Will Thomas is in a hospital in Raleigh."

Jason pressed his lips into a worried line while he scanned the growing numbers of tribal members and highlanders riding into town. "I didn't know."

"In his absence," Joel said, "Reese, Coop, and me, we're witnesses on your behalf since we took part in the roundup. Listen Jace, they could jail you right alongside our prisoners. In a crazy world, they could let them outlaws go on account of you leading the posse. Look around you, see all these folks? We're on your side—and we're coming with you."

"The colonel asked me to give you these." Cooper slipped two unsealed envelopes from his pocket and handed them to Jason. One read, *Mr. Levi Rubin, Esquire*, and listed an Asheville address. The other bore Jason's name in the colonel's graceful cursive.

"He hired a lawyer?"

Jason browsed the contents of each envelope. Rubin's missive attested to Jason's time in the Legion, and Thomas's appointment of him as the search party leader assigned to capture the marauding Brotherhood. The other comprised instructions regarding what to do upon reaching Asheville. He read each letter, replaced them in their respective envelopes, and tucked them into his vest pocket as Dan and Onacona arrived.

"It's about time. Come on, let's go."

On a hillock above town, a well-placed boulder marked the memorial site of the revered Snowbird chief, Junaluska. There, Aramarinda and Cornwoman, in ritual garb, observed the proceedings below. They turned away from the scene and went to work.

Cornwoman placed seven stones around the boulder, one for each of the tribal clans: Wolf, Deer, Wild Potato, Bird, Paint, Long Hair, and Blue. They arranged a small pyre atop each rock, including the chief's and lit them. They tossed herbs, tobacco, and saltpeter into the flames. They sang prayers of protection, and circled the fires in an ancient dance, their colorful fringed garments whipping in the breeze. Waving eagle feathers clustered into a fan, they encouraged threads of silvery smoke toward the people gathered below.

Beneath pink and coral streaked skies and towering autumn-tinted mountains, the caravan embarked on their journey west to Asheville. Cornwoman held her arms wide to them. "Good people of Cheoah Valley!" she called out. The mantle of protection is on your shoulders. May the blessings of the spirits be with you!"

Aramarinda stood at her side and brushed loose strands of hair from her face. Her eyes followed one individual amongst the clattering throng below. Feeling the flutter of life within her belly, she caressed it lovingly, then mouthed her own silent prayer: *Be safe, my love. May the Great Spirit soon bring you home to us.*

BOOK III

Deliverance
1867-1873

Asheville, North Carolina
March 1867

Jason watched the proceedings from his seat in the crowded gallery of a small courtroom in the Buncombe County Courthouse. Nancy, his father, and others surrounded him while the rest of his friends and supporters looked on from the upper arcade. The tension amongst them was second only to the underlying level of excitement, amplified by the sheer number of warm bodies packed shoulder to shoulder into the room.

In front of the gallery were two attorneys' tables. Against the wall, the raised platform of the judge's bench, enclosed by a balustered half-wall. At its left, a witness box, similar but floor level, with two rows of jurors' chairs beyond. The defendant's enclosure stood along the far side of the room.

The lawyers entered, their expressions disgruntled. Twelve Asheville jurymen, pallid carbon copies of one another, followed them. Handcuffed gang members of the Brothers of the White Cross, accompanied by a jailer, shuffled across the room and crowded into the defendant's box. Crusher Bolin limped in last on crutches. The ragtag assortment appeared somewhat respectable with their hair combed and wearing clean shirts.

Joel leaned in to Jason. "Where's Ferries?"

"Maybe he's being tried separate."

"Wonder what a court run by Yankees will be like," Reese said.

Tom Cooper shook his head. "Who knows. This Reconstruction business does nothing but take bad and make it worse."

"Shush," Jason's father said, "it's about to start."

The bailiff called the room to order. "All rise. The Court of the First Judicial Circuit, Criminal Division, is now in session, the Honorable Judge Thomas Dubose presiding."

A buzz filled the air when the judge entered.

"A colored judge!" Nancy whispered. "I never heard of such!"

"Everyone but the jury may sit," Judge Dubose boomed, and took his seat behind the bench. The rumbling in the gallery failed to curtail. He rapped his gavel on the sounding block. "Quiet! I will find in contempt anyone in this courtroom who says another word out of turn and fine them twenty dollars." The thrum stilled. "That's better. Swear in the jury."

With the jury sworn in and seated, Dubose opened a portfolio and scanned a sheath of papers. "Clerk, please call today's case."

"*May it please the court,*" he read aloud, "*the case of Buffalo Town, North Carolina, plaintiffs, versus the Brothers of the White Cross, defendants, is on the docket. Defendants stand accused of aggravated assault, murder, accessory to rape, and destruction of private property, including, but not limited to, an entire mountain village.*"

"Mr. Davis, how do the defendants plead?" Dubose asked.

Davis stood. "We plead not guilty, Your Honor."

The judge scanned the motley collection of men in the defendants' box. "Mr. Rubin?"

Levi Rubin, attorney for the plaintiffs, took the floor. "Gentlemen of the jury, today I will illustrate for you two of the most violent days in the history of North Carolina." He enumerated the crimes committed, elaborating on each. "The defendants, a band of outlaws known as whitecaps, night raiders, Red Shirts, and the Brothers of the White Cross, perpetrated heinous offenses upon the good citizens of Buffalo Town. For brevity, we will hereon refer to this gang as the Brotherhood."

Harlan Davis, counsel for the defense, followed him. "Gentlemen," he began in a thin nasal whine, "just look at the beleaguered men and boys before you. These falsely accused victims of sore injustice. These upright citizens of valor…" His complaint went on and on. "You will come to believe, as I do," he swept his arm in a wide arc that included the gang members, "these men are not criminals."

Jason's ire rose at the man's words and he gripped Nancy's hand.

Rubin called his witnesses: Tom Cooper, Joel Lovin, Martha Taylor, and more. Wendell Reese gave testimony regarding the lynching of Talman Bearclaw and testified as to his role in the arrest of the Brotherhood. Olly Oliver and Mose Bearclaw were sure to provide the most controversial and damning testimonies of all.

Olly took his place in the witness box. He had bathed and slicked his hair flat with pomade, and wore an outdated suit. "Yup, I rode with 'em that night."

Thunder erupted in the court. Judge Dubose settled disapproving eyes on Oliver while he hammered his gavel. Oliver hung his head.

"The Injuns, they was celebrating the soldiers coming home, like Mr. Wendell done said. Most all the town was there. Win, our leader, he passed out hoods. We put 'em on—and burnt that town to the ground." He peered up at Rubin. "I made a mistake, and I'm mighty sorrowful for it."

"Mr. Oliver, would you describe those hoods for us?" Rubin asked.

Olly glared at the defendants. "They was white flour sacks with holes cut out for the eyes."

"Does this look like one of the hoods?" Rubin handed Olly a head covering Jason collected from the fight with the Brotherhood.

Olly fingered it with an expression of disgust. "Yes, sir."

Rubin passed it to the judge, detailing its origination. "Please record this into evidence."

Next, Olly recounted the mayhem: burning shops and homes. Attacking men, women, children, and elderly. Firing into the fleeing crowd.

"After we sacked the town, Win led us about a mile down the road to the Hyde homestead. They snuck up on 'em and set the house afire. Win burnt the barn and stole the horses." Olly stared at his hands. "I saw him with Mary, Hyde's oldest daughter. He dragged her to the smokehouse and shut the two of 'em inside whilst his men were busy torching the homestead. I heard her screams."

"Where were you during this raid?"

"In the woods, hiding. I'd had a belly-full of these doings."

Next, attorney Davis took his turn at questioning Olly. "Mr. Oliver, is it true that the prosecution asked you to accuse these innocent men in exchange for your freedom?"

Olly's eyes flashed. "No, sir! I'm co-operating cause I never kilt no one, and that's a fact. Seen all their faces, though, and know what they done that night. 'Em boys over there." He pointed a boney, shaking finger. "I swan, they are the Brothers of the White Cross. They wore that name on their shirts while they burnt and kilt and did all manner of terrible things. Mostly for the fun of it."

Mose Bearclaw shambled to the witness stand next. The pitiful sight of him alone brought tears to the eyes of many.

"Mose, please explain what took place at your home that terrible night last spring," Rubin said.

"Well, sir," he opened in a soft voice. "A crackling noise woke me. They was a big cross in the front yard, all aflame. Those men over there stood betwixt it and us. Couldn't see their faces right then cause of their head coverings. I saw 'em real good when they took 'em off. They all wore red shirts. The one on crutches over there," his eyes shimmered with hatred for Crusher Bolin, "I shot him in the foot when he hit my mama."

"Son," Rubin said gently, "tell us what happened to you later that morning."

The boy's awful tale descended into gruesomeness as he detailed the ensuing horror. Ladies dabbed at their eyes with handkerchiefs while the men grimaced.

"They cut my daddy, and beat him, then lynched him. Somebody knocked me out cold. It was daylight when I woke. I was on the ground somewhere in the woods." He recounted his own near-lynching, the fight that broke out around him, and his rescue.

"Mose, can you identify the men who tortured and murdered your daddy, and attempted to murder you?"

"Yes, sir, they're standing over there." Mose pointed at the Brotherhood with a shaking hand. "As God is my witness, these men kilt my daddy—and tried to kill me."

"Thank you, Mose, you're a brave young man. No further questions, Your Honor."

"Would the defense like to question this young gentleman?" Dubose asked. Davis shook his head. "You may step down, Master Bearclaw. Thank you for your testimony."

"Have you more witnesses, Mr. Rubin?" Judge Dubose asked.

"One, Your Honor, Lieutenant Jason Hyde. First, I offer into evidence a letter I received from the chief of the Snowbird Cherokee tribe, Colonel William H. Thomas. It is a character reference for Lieutenant Hyde." He handed the letter to the judge, who read it aloud to the court.

"Colonel Thomas speaks well of you, Lieutenant," Judge Dubose said. He added it to his stack of case papers. "Swear him in."

Jason clutched the arms of his chair and gazed into the gallery, seeking the supportive faces of his friends and relations.

"Lieutenant Hyde," Rubin began, "please summarize the events that took place in the month of May last year. Beginning with the attack on East Buffalo, to the day you arrested the Brotherhood gang members."

"Yessir. For me, it started the day I came home from the war, May eleventh—"

A hush fell over the courtroom while he related his side of the events, from finding his home burned, family members brutalized, and his town destroyed, to the capture of the Brothers of the White Cross.

"No more questions, Your Honor," Rubin announced.

"Mr. Davis, do you wish to cross-examine this witness?"

"I thought you'd never ask, Your Honor." Davis strolled to the witness stand, rubbing the palms of his hands together. "Lieutenant Hyde, you fought in the Confederate war against the United States government, did you not?"

"I took part. We in the South have varied reasons for being mad at the Washington government."

"Did you or your men ever scalp white soldiers?" Uneasy murmurs spread across the gallery.

"No, sir. Scalping is against the law. I do not break laws I swear to uphold."

"You do not break laws you swear to uphold, you say." Hands clasped behind him, the lawyer paced back and forth, back and forth.

"During the struggle between your men and my clients, one of your men murdered one of theirs. Two others suffered serious injury from bullet wounds. All of them beaten, some evidence of their injuries still apparent." Davis pointed out Crusher Bolin's crutches. "Is this *upholding the law*?"

"They were about to hang Mose Bearclaw. My posse and I rescued him. The gang tortured and hanged Mose's daddy, Talman Bearclaw, earlier that morning. We were duty bound to arrest 'em and take 'em in for their crimes. They did not readily comply."

"Do you know the penalty for an Indian assaulting a white man?"

"Are you referring to me? Cherokees were my neighbors and friends growing up. I fought with them during the war. That does not make me an Indian, sir. I'm white."

"When you ordered your Cherokee friends and neighbors to attack the Brotherhood, they followed your command—and broke the law. You're as guilty as they are, regardless of your heritage."

"Lieutenant Hyde is not on trial here," the judge interjected.

"I'd like to respond, Your Honor," Jason said. "I commanded my posse to act as they did, myself following orders from the Snowbird chief, who is also white, and my former commander in the Thomas Legion. Furthermore, the incident you refer to was not assault."

Davis ceased his maundering ramble and faced Jason. "Who attacked whom in those woods?—And why should this court believe you?"

Davis called his witnesses—indignant fathers, sobbing wives, proud mothers. Parson Greene, a pinch-faced reverend from Topton, defended his oldest son, Harold. "Harold is a Christian son of Jesus. He would never commit these crimes! Besides, he was at church both nights in question."

Next, he announced Fedosia McNeill, a heavy-set woman who pointed out her son, Buck. "Buck and his uncle Joe was out of town both times. He's innocent of these charges, I tell ya. A mama knows her child."

Every defendant had an alibi.

"Any more witnesses, Mr. Davis?"

"Just one, Your Honor. May it please the court, I call Crusher Bolin to the stand."

Bolin hobbled to the witness stand amid a general hubbub.

"Mr. Bolin, please tell the court what you and your companions were doing the morning of your arrest."

"My friends and me, we been hunting since 'fore daylight. We worked us up a appetite, so we caught a wild pig. We was setting around roasting our dinner, jawing, and minding our own business when these ruffians, Injuns, and others that done said things ag'in us today, they jumped us outta nowhere. Their leader," he pointed a finger at Jason, "he beat the tar outta me. Meant to kill me, too. I never did nothing to him. Never seen him 'fore that day."

"It's obvious to anyone with a pair of eyes that you sustained debilitating injuries in this attack," Davis said. "Are you telling the court that y'all are *not* the murderous fiends the Lieutenant and his posse sought? Do you suggest, Mr. Bolin, that this is a situation of mistaken identity?"

"That's right, I been mistook for somebody else. It's what I been saying."

Davis tossed a sly smile in Rubin's direction. "Some of Mr. Rubin's clients mention a man amongst you named, ah," he glanced at his notes, "*Fargus*. Do you know anyone who goes by that name?"

"I don't know any Ferries. I dare say, none of t'others do neither."

Crusher's slip prompted a stern glance from his attorney.

"Mr. Rubin's witnesses identified the lot of you as members of a gang called the Brothers of the White Cross."

"They's lying."

Davis turned to the jury. "Well then, it would appear this is indeed a case of mistaken identity. Our plaintiffs are the guilty parties—of assault, battery, attempted murder, and one count of murder in the first degree." He slapped his thigh in delight. "I rest my case."

"Your clients are on trial here, Mr. Davis, not the plaintiffs," Dubose said.

Rubin's fruitless questioning of Davis's witnesses went nowhere, each dodging his questions or outright deceitful.

"Have either of you more witnesses to call?" Judge Dubose's tone bordered on reproach. Both attorneys declined. "Counselors, you may present your closing arguments."

Mr. Rubin gave a blistering recap, citing eye-witness accounts. "According to the defense witnesses, none of the accused were anywhere near Buffalo Town or Fort Montgomery on the night of the first attack or the night of Talman Bearclaw's murder. We heard convenient alibis. In church, out of town, indisposed, or otherwise engaged. One perpetrator even attempted to play upon your sympathies, claiming to be a victim himself. Members of the jury, a quandary lies before us. Some in this courtroom are not telling the truth and—dare I contend?—perjured themselves."

Davis ambled from behind his desk, thumbs hooked under his suspenders. "Gentlemen, all afternoon you listened to Mr. Rubin's so-called eyewitnesses give dubious testimony—amongst them, a traumatized boy and a pitiful animal skinner. I ask that you disregard their statements.

"Mr. Rubin presented into evidence one of the hoods that concealed the faces of those who attacked the good people of Buffalo Town and Fort Montgomery. As you saw, it would indeed hide a man's face. One cannot verify what one cannot see. I have no doubt, the fine young men on trial before us did *not* commit these heinous crimes. So as not to further sully the reputations of the prosecution's witnesses, I reiterate, this is an instance of mistaken identity."

By the time Davis came to the end of his plea, afternoon shadows loomed throughout the courtroom.

Dubose addressed the jurymen. "Gentlemen of the jury, you may retire to determine your verdict." The twelve men filed out to sequestered quarters as solemnly as they had entered hours earlier. "The court will recess. Bailiff, remove the defendants to holding."

As soon as the door closed behind the judge, the court erupted in excited chatter.

"Let's get some air," Jason's father said.

Jason headed for the courtyard with his companions. *Where is Ferries? Can't be he got away again.*

"Davis is aiming for a mistrial," Tom Cooper said. "He can't prove his clients' innocence because they're guilty as sin. His only option is to discredit us."

"Davis ain't no better'n the boys he's defending," Jason's father remarked. "Goes to show you, no amount of educating will fix what's in a man's heart."

The bailiff called the courtroom together near sundown. After the refreshing cool of the outside air, the room felt stuffy and close. The gallery members settled into their seats. It soon became apparent that the jury and defendants would not return with them.

"All rise," the bailiff announced over the murmur of voices. Everyone stood, all eyes on Judge Dubose as he took his position behind the bench.

"Ladies and gentlemen, our jury remains hard at work," the judge declared. "Deliberations will resume tomorrow morning at eight o'clock and will continue until they arrive at a unanimous decision. I thank you for your patience. Court adjourned." A slam of his gavel dismissed them.

A collective groan echoed throughout the chamber. Above the din of gathering coats and donning hats, tempers flared, and they hurled verbal accusations right and left across the aisle.

"Lieutenant Hyde!" Jason's name thundered above the hubbub and he followed the sound to its source.

"Lieutenant Hyde," Judge Dubose roared, "please see me in my chambers." The judge exited the courtroom, black robes rippling behind him.

Bent over a small fireplace, Thomas Dubose stoked the fire and placed the fireiron in its holder. His robe hung on a nearby coat tree. Dressed in a green three-piece wool suit, he appeared less formidable, but commanded respect. The moment he saw Jason, the judge crossed the room and lowered himself into a padded leather armchair on the far side of a large, carved desk. He gestured to the guest chair in front of it. "Please sit, Lieutenant."

Jason offered a tentative smile. "Guess you got some questions for me. I got one for you, too."

"One thing at a time." He shuffled through papers in a binder labeled *Buffalo Town versus Brothers of the White Cross*, then removed Will Thomas's letter and laid it on the desk in front of him. "I advise you to keep the details of our conversation quiet until after the trial. Say nothing to no one, not even your wife. Do you understand?"

"Yessir," Jason replied.

Dubose removed his wire-rimmed glasses and polished the lenses with the edge of his sleeve.

"Do you believe in Divine Providence, sir? I do. I'm a lawyer for the Freedmen's Bureau in Washington, where I fight for the civil rights of Negros less fortunate than myself. The Buncombe County military government requested a bureau agent in Asheville because of ongoing violence in this part of the state. The barbaric nature of the defendants in your case characterizes why we're needed here. I applied for the job.

"Judge Bierce, who would have heard today's arguments, took ill. Had he sat on that bench today, presiding over a case brought by mountain highlanders and indigenous natives against upstanding white citizens, *Buffalo Town versus Brothers of the White Cross* would never have seen justice. They assigned me to the case in his place at the last minute—your Divine Providence. However, while you and your people will have a fighting chance in my courtroom, prejudice may ultimately weigh against you."

Judge DuBose donned his glasses and scrutinized Jason. "Lieutenant Hyde, a Tennessee war hero—one Nathan Bedford Forrest—is organizing factions of misguided hate mongers like the Brotherhood into a powerful force. These men may be the first evidence of his efforts in western North Carolina."

Dubose pointed a finger at Jason. "Mr. Davis correctly stated the tenets concerning the rights of white men outweighing those of an indigenous native. State law would never convict a white man of the crime attributed to your Native posse members. Criminal guilt wrought by their heritage and what authorities say is the color of their skin—a point that resonates with me." The judge leaned back in his chair and threaded his fingers across the green and gold damask of his vest.

"Had you been a white sheriff chasing down outlaws, you would be within your right to use force to apprehend them. But—they are Indians and you are not a duly elected sheriff. If you and your people lose the case, the defense could press charges against *you*."

Jason squirmed in his armchair, hands wrapped tight around the carved lion heads that formed the ends of its arms. "Judge, I followed orders from my superior."

"He is equally at fault."

Dubose studied Jason with resolute eyes before rising to his feet. Three steps placed him at an oak cabinet between the two windows in his office, where he withdrew a pair of small crystal tumblers and a bottle of scotch from behind its glass-paneled doors.

Outside the window, a lamplighter made his way down the sidewalk. Touching his long pole to the streetlamp wicks, light brightened the darkening street beyond the judge's chambers, and cast a glow upon people milling about, unaware of an indoor observer a few yards away. They looked cold.

Dubose poured two fingers of the amber liquid into each glass, then followed Jason's gaze. "Your kin out there?" He placed a whiskey in front of Jason and returned to his seat.

"My daddy and my good friend, Joel, are right up front. My wife's the pregnant lady over yonder talking to that busybody Birdy Blevins. The rest, friends and neighbors."

A youth broke from the crowd. Face twisted in anger, he mouthed words and shoved Wendell Reese. Reese shoved back. In a flash, a tussle evolved. Others attempted to pull them apart, and the scuffle escalated into a free-for-all. Fedosia McNeill intervened and dragged the youth away by his ear, a privilege reserved for a mother. Asheville military police confronted the fracas and, almost as soon as the brawl began, it ended.

"A sign of the times, Lieutenant." Dubose raised his glass in a toast. "To justice." Dubose took a sip and set down his glass.

Jason mimicked his gesture, fighting to keep his hand from shaking. The amber liquid rolled down his throat, smooth and warm, igniting a pleasant glow throughout his belly. He wanted to relax, but apprehension prevented it. To his relief, he saw kindness in the judge's eyes.

"Colonel William H. Thomas was your commanding officer," Dubose said. "I've heard of him. He fought for the wrong side, of course, but many respected him as a legislator in the former North Carolina government. I've seen his name recently in documents lobbying for incorporation of your little township of Fort Montgomery."

Jason sat up straight. "I didn't know he was working on it. We'll make a point of thanking him."

"A win for this case would further that goal." Dubose tapped Thomas's document with his index finger. "Here, he writes a commendatory report of you and your efforts to bring these no-good lowlifes to justice. He also states you helped to hold the fabric of the town together after those scoundrels destroyed it."

Embarrassed by the praise, Jason's cheeks heated. "I couldn't let the tribe fall apart." Jason gazed at the judge with steady eyes. "I just did what I thought was right, Your Honor."

"To significant accomplishments." Dubose saluted Jason, then tossed back the last sip. "This country needs men of character—like you." He set down his glass with a sharp thunk.

"Now, you have a question. Why was Windrake Ferries not in court today?" Jason dipped his chin in the affirmative. "It's complicated. In short, Windrake Ferries is not a North Carolina resident."

"Your Honor, sir, Ferries has lived in this state a long while. I first ran into him four years ago in the mountains near my home."

"There is no record of his residency. Ferries' last known address is a small town in South Carolina, near to Gaston County. As such, we must notify his home state of his arrest. South Carolina authorities arrested Ferries for crimes committed there before he escaped and fled."

Jason grunted. "We got no shortage of outlaws up our way."

"So true. By law, in a case with prior charges, we must allow the prisoner to be tried in their home court. His extradition order came through this morning. I had no choice but to let him go. In lawful custody, of course."

Jason thumped the arm of his chair with his fist. "*This morning?* I don't blasted believe it." He glared at the carpet, then looked at the judge. "What crimes?"

"Theft, child desertion, and abandonment," Dubose answered.

"Not rape, not murder. Not much compared to what he did here."

"Agreed. However, the family bringing the charges down in South Carolina is powerful."

Jason left Dubose's chambers with a crushing headache. *I shoulda let Mary kill Ferries that day. Or shot him myself at Slickrock Creek. What's that saying about hindsight?*

42

"Ferries will be tried at a later date," Jason replied when asked about his conversation with the judge. He hoped he was right. The next morning, after an unsettled night at their campsite on the edge of town, he and his companions gathered once again in the Buncombe County courtroom.

"We'd better get our conviction today," Dan grumbled. Onacona nodded agreement.

Grumpy and tired, Jason was in no mood to indulge in idle chatter. "Convincing twelve men to agree on anything isn't a simple task."

"The longer it takes to reach a verdict, more likely the chances of a mistrial," Tom Cooper said.

"If that happens, God help our little town," Reese mumbled.

Heat mounted in the cramped room. Tension tightened the faces of the Cheoah Valley residents while, across the aisle, the Brotherhood families appeared equally strained. They waited, for the second day in a row.

At last, Davis strolled across the courtroom to his desk, cocky and self-assured, while Rubin took his place behind his own small table. Hands cuffed, the defendants filed in. In the gallery, conversations curtailed mid-sentence.

The jury followed them, faces taut with the pressure of their deliberation. Jason tried to read them, but couldn't come to any firm conclusion. The bailiff called the dead-quiet courtroom to order. "All rise."

Judge Dubose entered and sat down. "The court may sit. Members of the jury, have you reached an agreement?"

The foreman, an edgy middle-aged man, slowly stood. "We have, Your Honor." He handed a folded paper to the bailiff, who delivered it to Dubose. His movements measured, the judge unfolded it, read it, refolded, and redelivered it, his expression impassive.

"Defendants and counsel for the defense, please stand. Jurymen, in the case of Buffalo Town, North Carolina versus the Brothers of the White Cross, what say you?"

Jason stared hard at the prisoners, each drawn face looking straight ahead. *Will this be their end? Or will they go free to seek revenge?*

"We the jury—" Jason pressed his eyes shut and listened to the paper rattle in the foreman's hands. The foreman paused for a breath. "We the jury find the defendants guilty as charged."

The courtroom exploded into a babel of jeers and hoorahs.

Music to Jason's ears, the symphony of the phrase repeated—*Guilty as charged*—muffling every other sound. He slumped in his seat with a sigh of relief. *We won* resonated in his mind while the consonants and vowels that formed their meaning vibrated within each cell.

Cries of anguish amidst clamors of joy brought him to his senses. Jason's family and friends, laughing and crying, hugged one another. Those nearby clapped him on the back. Everyone wanted to shake his, Mose Bearclaw's, even Olly Oliver's hands.

The judge banged his gavel repeatedly and roared at the court until the crowd quieted. "Gentlemen of the jury, thank you for your service," Judge Dubose said in a steady tone. "You may go." The jurymen filed from the chamber, their expressions both relieved and anxious.

"Do you prisoners care to speak before I sentence you?" Dubose asked.

"I got something to say!" Buck McNeill shouted, shoving to the front of the defendants' box. "We got a God-given right to these lands. We ain't done nothing nobody else wouldn'ta done. The way things is now, we white folks gotta fend for ourselves. You gotta pardon us, Judge. We're innocent."

His fellow defendants shouted in support while Davis nodded in Buck's direction and showed him a fist of approval.

The judge hammered for silence. "You boys think you deserve pardons, do you?"

"Yes, sir," Buck replied. "Maybe you ain't got much experience judging in the South, being a nig–" He stumbled. "A Negro. So, I'm letting you know, white boys get pardoned. That's how we do."

"I see." Dubose looked hard and long at the Brother over his glasses rims. "Thank you for enlightening me, Mr. McNeill." The judge shuffled his papers into their binder and neatened his desk top while the courtroom waited, every eye on him. He scanned the room, settling on the defendants.

"I have made my decision. Brothers of the White Cross, the hateful nature of the crimes you committed—from destroying a town, murder, mutilation of a fellow human, accessory to the rape of a young woman—leaves me no choice. I condemn the lot of you to hang by the neck until dead." A stunned gasp sucked the air out of the courtroom. "At eight o'clock tomorrow morning, the warden will carry out your punishment. Until then, I remand you to your holding cells.

"Ladies and gentlemen of this court, take note. These men broke the law. They took the lives of innocent men, women, and children, and will pay for their actions with their lives. Today, justice has prevailed."

Attorney Harlan Davis jumped up. "Hold on there, Judge! Er-er-er—This is discrimination! I appeal the sentence."

"You have insufficient grounds, sir. Case closed." Judge Dubose slammed his gavel one last time and stepped from his bench.

Rubin stood and clapped his hands in a slow, emphatic rhythm. Cheoah Valley onlookers followed his lead.

Pandemonium ensued. Defendants' wives howled with grief. Mothers wailed. Enraged fathers bellowed. Tensions escalated from yowling to pushing and shoving as both sides of the aisles clashed. Caught in the middle, Jason clutched Nancy's elbow and steered her toward the chamber doors.

A crack of pistol fire silenced the storm.

The blast rang in Jason's ears, and he cried out as a blow jolted him backward. He tumbled into the crowd.

"I got him, Buck! I got him!" a voice shouted.

Jason focused on a small derringer, a weapon easily concealed inside a boot or under an arm, and made to fire at close range. From his vantage point on the floor, his attention moved to the shooter—the boy who scuffled with Wendell Reese the previous afternoon. Hands grabbed at him from every side, and jerked him to and froe.

"Bailiff, get help!" Dubose thundered.

"You won't die for nothing, brother," the boy shrieked. "This damn Injun lover is a goner."

A figure blocked Jason's view and a familiar voice hollered, "Gimme that, ya li'l—"

The boy fired again. Olly Oliver collapsed across Jason's legs.

"Everybody stand back!" the police sergeant shouted. His team surrounded the shooter and disarmed him. Police formed a barrier between the victims and the angry crowd.

Nancy knelt beside Jason and smoothed hair from his face. "Get a doctor!"

"I'm here," Martha replied, her voice calm amid chaos. She nudged through the throng and knelt over Olly's inert form. She frowned and shook her head, then examined Jason. A warm smile softened her worried expression. "Merely a flesh wound."

Looking through his pain, his heart filled with gratitude. The Battle of Piedmont, Virginia—the last time he sustained an injury—floated through his mind. Onacona was there, and Nate LeFevre. So much had happened since. He clutched Martha's hand. "Thanks, Doc."

She squeezed his fingers. "Don't talk. Here's Nancy." She placed Nancy's hand in his.

He gazed into his wife's worried eyes. "I love you," he said, his speech garbled. She seemed not to comprehend his words.

A police officer found gurneys. His comrades placed Olly's body on one—a jacket covering his upper half—and Jason on the other.

"Doc Venable's infirmary is two blocks north. Follow me," Martha said to the officers. "Coop, you run ahead. Let Venable know we're coming. Explain what happened and tell him to prepare for surgery. We must get started as soon as possible. Every second counts."

"It's like the war ain't even over," Jason's father mumbled.

"May never be," Onacona replied.

Jason felt suspended above everything and everyone. Distant voices spoke of him as though he were not present. *Hey, I'm here!* He drifted from the familiar into pitch black darkness. Voices ceased, replaced by pounding and snuffling. The dark horse of his nightmares galloped ever nearer, ever nearer. *Is this the end?* It passed over him and he slipped farther into the void. A new terror took shape. There, a wolf with fur the color of a winter blizzard stood in inky darkness, panting, its amber eyes fixed on Jason.

Jason opened his eyes to the cool blue of first light streaming through a break in the curtain panels. Although a screen partly blocked his view, Jason could see one end of a bed-lined infirmary room. His father slept in a chair at the foot of his bed; Nancy's rounded form snoozed in the bed next to his. Two sleeping patients occupied the last beds in the row. His eyes searched for Oliver.

Martha strode into the room with Dr. Venable. "Good morning," she whispered. "How do you feel?"

"Olly? Nancy? The baby?"

"I'm sorry, Jace, Oliver didn't make it. Nancy and your baby are well."

"Dear God, he died to save me." He covered his eyes with his hand.

"Lieutenant Hyde, I'm Dr. Horace Venable. I did the best I could for your friend. We cabled his family."

"Olly had kinfolk?"

"Two sisters. You didn't know? You were lucky. That bullet just missed your lung. I removed it. We'll check the injury now."

Martha cut away the bindings, and the doctor inspected Jason's wound. "You'll be fit in no time," Dr. Venable said.

"I can't miss the hanging," Jason said.

"It's early yet," Martha replied. "Eat breakfast and freshen up first."

"Our patient's going nowhere," Venable interrupted.

"I'll take responsibility, Horace. This hanging is important."

The doctor gave her a stern look. "Promise you'll bring him straight back here afterward."

"Yes, Doctor," Martha and Jason answered together.

"And if she don't, I will," Nancy murmured in a sleepy voice.

43

Delicate snowflakes drifted in a clear blue sky, contrasting with the somber intent that loomed. Jason and his companions entered the courtyard behind the Asheville prison and claimed space near the scaffold. Surrounded by Nancy, his father, and Martha Taylor, he scanned the scene from his wheelchair and sniffed the crystalline air, thankful to be alive. A blight on the beautiful morning, the gallows stood tall and gray in the middle of the yard, formidable against the rising sun. Three new hemp ropes tied into nooses hung from its crossbeam and swayed in a light breeze, a beacon of what lay ahead.

Jason's friends arrived, astonished and pleased to find him there.

"Jace!" Joel exclaimed. He shunted his way through the gathering crowd, with Dan at his heels.

Martha raised a cautionary hand. "Keep your distance, folks." Her tone, firm but kind. "You can talk to him later."

"Crying shame about Oliver," Jason's father said. "But if he hadn't tackled that no-account who shot you, you'd be a dead man, instead of him."

"You never know who your saviors will be," Jason mumbled. Gratitude and grief jockeyed inside him. "Wish I'd gone easier on him."

A hundred or more onlookers clustered around the scaffold, encircling it. They huddled in tight groups until the area overflowed. Asheville curiosity seekers filled any space between opposing factions. Morbid excitement pulsed throughout the grounds, raw and human, sliced by cold, hard dread and the smell of whiskey.

Jason's heartbeat quickened when the warden appeared, trailed by jailers escorting the handcuffed members of the Brothers of the White Cross. Police guided them up the steps to the platform and forced them into three lines facing the rabble below. In the third row, Buck McNeill wept. Beside him, a defiant Crusher Bolin glared at the throng.

A local pastor joined them on the scaffold floor. Calling the rowdy horde to order, he delivered a short homily. "Amen, Brother," some wailed. A jumble of voices harmonized in reciting the Twenty-third Psalm. Between the amens and the pastor's sermon, a din of forced worship arose.

Fedosia McNeill clutched a soggy white handkerchief. "Love you, Buck." Her red-rimmed eyes affirmed her suffering; one son at the gallows and the other in jail for murder.

On the green in front of the prison, the clock tower chimed eight o'clock. The hour for the spectacle had arrived. Three at a time, the warden, presiding as executioner, lined the prisoners behind the ropes. Bible in hand, the preacher asked each one, "Son, do you wish to repent for your sins?" One by one, the condemned men declared, "Jesus, take me into your forgiving arms."

The hangman bound their legs. He placed a black canvas hood over each man's head. Jason gripped his wheelchair handles while he watched their fabric suck in and out with each anguished breath, his own breathing keeping pace with theirs. With quiet ceremony, the hangman slipped a noose around each condemned neck.

A group of men sauntered into the courtyard and stood to the rear of the crowd. By ones and twos, they extended angry fists skyward, shouting, "One true family! Pride and sovereignty!"

Jostling amongst the onlookers evoked insults and provoked shoving until one policeman fired his weapon into the air. The crowd quieted. In one corner, a journalist scratched frenzied notes onto a small pad.

The hangman signaled to the pastor to step away from the trap doors. Prison guards under the gallows platform knocked aside the supporting planks, and the traps fell open, dropping the prisoners.

Like a rubber ball attached to strings, they jolted up again and the crowd let out a primal yawp of excitement. Fifteen minutes later, the presiding doctor declared the bodies dead and ordered them removed from the yard.

Trap doors were reset. Deputies prodded the next three reluctant night raiders forward. The preacher repeated his ritual, and the executioner repeated his. Legs tied, sacks over heads, nooses in place.

Last up, Crusher Bolin.

“Son, will you repent for your sins?” the pastor asked.

“Hell, no! I’m innocent!”

The minister stepped backward and crossed himself.

Crusher’s accusing eyes sought Jason within the throng and found him. Unblinking, Jason stared back.

“No hood. I want them Injuns to remember my face!” Bolin shouted. At the rear of the yard, his supporters bellowed.

“They gonna remember you, all right.” The hangman pulled the hood to Bolin’s shoulders and strung the noose over his head. Bolin’s death mask dragged inward with each angry gulp.

The hangman clapped his hands twice, and the trap opened. Too tall for the drop, Crusher’s feet hit the ground. He struggled, toes touching dirt, his body careening from side to side. He writhed and choked for ten excruciating minutes. At last, he ceased to move.

“Dead,” the doctor announced.

A pulsating cheer rebounded off the walls. Consumed by overwhelming relief, Jason covered his face with his hand and wept.

44

Yorkville, South Carolina
March 1867

Windrake Ferries leered out a window of the Yorkville County courtroom at an overcast March morning framed by budding tree branches. Raindrops tickled the windowpanes and formed tails down the leaded glass. Shackles cut into his ankles, and his bad leg ached.

I gotta get outta here! An involuntary shiver crept down his spine.

The bailiff announced the Honorable Ambrose Bratton and the judge breezed into the courtroom, robes rippling, and took his seat. The bailiff directed the plaintiff, a young blonde woman, to stand to Ferries' right.

A head taller than her, Ferries' eyes roamed from her straw-colored hair to her creamy white nape, then settled on two apple-mounds pressed upward by her corset against the blue ditsy print of her otherwise-demure bodice. He imagined squeezing them. *I could make this sow squeal extra loud.*

The little boy holding tight to her hand looked up at him, his somber expression unwavering.

Huh, sow's got a piglet. Beneath neat, strawberry-colored hair, the child's keen pale eyes bored into his own. Ferries stifled a smile. *Looks like my brother at that age. Cleaner'n Ben or me ever was.*

A gavel crack brought his attention to the judge scowling in front of him. "I asked you a question, Mr. Ferries," Judge Bratton said. "Do you, or do you not, recognize this woman whose family is bringing charges against you?"

The woman confronted the prisoner, brown-eyed rage burning within a girlish face. A life far removed, redolent of a dream, flashed through him. A tryst between billowy white sheets on a lazy summer day. Flirtatious giggles. Wet kisses. Soft whispers. Moaning and humping in a hayloft.

"That there is Miss Luella Henry."

"Correct. Her father, Mr. Emmett Henry, who employed you as a foreman, filed the following complaint. After wooing Miss Luella, you then stole cash and a horse, and disappeared, leaving her with child. Mr. Ferries, this court charges you with theft, fornication, abandonment, sullying the good name of a white woman, and crimes committed apart from your employ at the Henry farm, most notably robbing the First Bank of Yorkville, *twice*, and swindling the good citizens of York County."

"Lies, Judge, all lies. And I dunno nothing about no baby."

Luella closed the distance between them and slapped Windrake, hard.

He grinned. "Hey, Luella. Nice to see you, too."

"You plead not guilty. So noted. You've been on the loose four years. Now we have you, it's up to this court to mete justice in this case. Will you retain representation?"

"Like a lawyer? No. Can't afford one."

"Let it be noted, the court shall appoint a solicitor to represent you. Mr. Ferries, we remand you to your cell." Bratton cracked the gavel.

Amid noisy shackle clanking, he turned to Luella. "This is bull—."

"Far from it. Would you like to meet your son?"

"My son." A vague memory crawled across his brain: *A fathered child. A murdered son. His name? Ira.* He shoved the recollection into a corner of his consciousness and locked the door. "That boy really mine?"

"Strapping little fella, isn't he?" She smiled down at her son and smoothed a cowlick in place with a loving hand. "Looks just like you. Benji, say hello to Mr. Windrake."

"Pleased to meet you, sir." The tyke held out his palm.

A glimmer of paternal instinct stirred. "You gave him Ben's name. I thought you hated my brother."

She grimaced. “I named him after *my* brothers, Benjamin and Caldwell. Unhappy coincidence, that.”

“All the same, it’s what I woulda picked.” Bending low, he gingerly took Benji’s hand.

“He won’t break, Win. Give him a real handshake.”

He glanced at her with a crooked half-smile, then clasped the boy’s tiny hand with both his large mitts. “Master Benjamin Henry, pleasure to know you.”

“It’s Ferries, Win. His name is Benjamin Ferries.”

A week later, Judge Bratton handed down his decree. “Windrake Ferries, this court finds you guilty as charged. I hereby sentence you to six years’ hard labor in the York County Penitentiary.”

Ferries recoiled at the final gavel strike. “Six years? I ain’t—hey, let go!” Four officers wrested him from the room while he struggled against his restraints.

Later that afternoon, from inside the paddy wagon, he scrutinized his new home: a former plantation turned labor camp. The Penitentiary featured a foreboding, new-built brick edifice with impenetrable walls and little obvious hope for escape. Crenellation along the top of the outer barrier bore resemblance to a fortress, while a guard tower in the center overlooked the grounds from every direction. The warden’s residence—the original mansion—sat on a rise a quarter mile away.

Prison guards stripped him naked, drenched him with icy water, and declared it a bath. He couldn’t stop shivering, and his baggy convict rags did little to warm him. “Be still dammit, before I cut your ear off,” a guard sheering his hair growled. Jeers greeted his entrance as his jailers dragged him to a dark, dank, basement-level corridor lined with barred, eight-foot-by-eight-foot cells packed with former slaves. At the end loomed a malodorous closet, a cage smaller than the rest. Ferries stumbled inside and collapsed on the floor. The slam of the iron door rang in his ears and he cringed at the immutable clunk of the tumbler falling into place inside the lock. He lay still for a moment, taking stock. To his right, a narrow cot outfitted with one thin blanket. On the left, a dirty, dented mush bowl and a reeking enamel piss pot. His lip curled involuntarily. *If this ain’t hell, I dunno what is.*

From sunup until after sundown, six days a week, Ferries broke stones in the adjacent rock quarry while chained ankle to ankle to former slaves. Damp fifteen-hour days turned to sweltering heat in the summer. Unlike changeable seasons, the work remained invariable—grueling and thankless.

Two Years Later

A guard led Luella to Windrake's lockup on a Sunday. "Hey, Win," she said through her handkerchief. "My word, the stench in here is godawful."

"A nose gets used to stink." He gripped the iron shafts of his confinement. "Get me outta here. I'm begging you. They got me living and working with animals, like I was no better'n 'em."

"I'll see what I can do. Meanwhile, I intend to reform you."

"Reform me? Birthing musta turned your head around backwards."

"You've got good in you. I aim to bring it out."

He slammed his fist against the bars. "You can't do nothing for me, woman!"

"Careful. The walls have eyes." She reached into her cloth bag and held up two Bibles. "Mama didn't live long, but before she passed, she taught me to love the Lord. Trust me, it's the most important lesson you'll ever learn." She handed one Bible to Windrake. He flung it across his cell. "Embrace faith and you might go to Heaven."

"This is a living hell. Why you gotta make it worse?"

"The hell is inside you. Repent your sins and hell will find a new home." She glowered. "Ask His forgiveness for *our* sin—I did. The Lord forgave me and saw fit to bless me with a beautiful baby boy."

"And ruined your reputation for life."

"*You* did that."

"I wanna see my son."

"*Our* son." She paced in front of Ferries' cage, and stole a quick glance at him, her dark eyes flashing. "I'll allow it. Benji needs a daddy's influence. I figure you can do him little harm in here. These are my conditions: obey the warden's rules and he'll grant you visitation rights in the yard. You also must bathe and keep your hair clean. Do as I ask and I'll get you moved."

Ferries squinted. "You guarantee it?"

"Judge Bratton is my uncle. If I wanted you out of here, I'd get you sprung. It happens, you're right where I want you." She flipped through the pages of her Bible. "Now, open to Psalm 5."

Days later, guards moved Windrake to an old building used for overflow and assigned him to a third-floor compartment. A tiny window on the opposite side of the corridor allowed a modicum of natural light and fresh air into the area while the prison stench seeped out, making living conditions bearable. His sole companion on the block lived at the far end, a big German fellow who kept to himself. Breaking rocks in the quarry fields shifted to washing and folding in the laundry. To Windrake, it felt like a holiday.

Weather permitting, once a month Luella brought Benji and a picnic lunch, and the three sat in a corner of the inner yard as a family. Afterward, she read them Bible stories. Windrake played with Benji and told him tales of his own creation.

"Your uncle, *Mad Dog Ben Ferries*, was the scrappin'est, most meanest cusser around and the greatest Injun fighter ever. One time, when me and Mad Dog Ben was ridin' together—"

The remaining years of his imprisonment were apportioned into clusters of long weary days, fruitless plans for escape, and happy moments with Ben. The youngster filled him with pride. Big-boned, stubborn, and quick tempered, he scrapped with older boys, often besting them. "A chip off the ol' Ferries block," Windrake boasted to anyone who would listen. Laundry detail gave him time to gamble with the inmates during brief social hours, but it also led to trouble.

"Ya cheated, ya lousy gimper!" a fellow prisoner accused during a poker game.

In a flash, Windrake flipped his stool and knocked the chips and winnings—cigarettes, gum, and small change—from the makeshift table to the floor. He grappled with the offender, secured his neck in a choke hold, and held tight. He savored the euphoric feeling of power as his victim's life drained from his body. It was like opium to an addict. The kill earned him respect from the other inmates. The jailers never discovered the identity of the murderer.

Throughout his incarceration his passion for revenge on Jason Hyde festered, a cancer growing within his soul. *I'm gonna make Hyde suffer like he done me. That sweet young'un he had; mmm, should be ripe for plucking by the time I get outta here. That older girl, that black-eyed beauty—What was her name?—Mary. Yeah, Mary.* Thoughts of her wheeled in his head and aroused him at night. *I'll be back, Hyde, and hell's coming with me!*

Spring 1873

White sweet bay blossoms showered Windrake and Luella with their lemony-scented petals as they watched their son play a short distance away under a tree on a warm afternoon.

"You're getting outta here next week, Win."

"Think I don't know that? I been counting the days since you put me in this hell hole."

"Old news, Win. Listen up, I got something to say." She faced him, her lips set in a grim line. "After this, I never wanna lay eyes on you again. Today will be the last time you see Benji, so make the most of it."

Windrake's eyes went cold. His glare slowly shifted from Luella to Benji and back. "Luella, for six wretched years you made me suffer with your verse-spewing. If I stay, I will surely kill you—For our boy's sake, I'm leaving."

"That's the first smart thing I've heard you say!"

Benji jogged over to his parents. "Come on, Daddy! Injuns got Mad Dog surrounded. He needs our help—did you say you're leaving?"

"I am."

"When you coming back?" he asked.

Windrake extended his arms and Benji snuggled into them.

"I dunno, Son. One day." He glanced at Luella. She gave him the evil eye and stormed off. "You recall how I told you about me and Uncle Ben and all my brothers fighting Injuns up in the mountains?"

Benji bobbed his head.

"They were our family, yours and mine. They're gone now. It's up to me to make sure they ain't forgotten." He lowered his voice. "Can you keep a secret?"

Benji bobbed his head again.

"Just between you and me, right?" Benji nodded again, vigorously. "There's revenge needs exacting up in Injun country."

"Mama says forgiveness is the best revenge."

"Uhn-uh. Wanna know what the best revenge is, Ben Ferries?"

Benji gazed at his daddy, eyes wide.

"The best revenge is *revenge.* Jason Hyde—remember that name, boy. He kilt Mad Dog—"

"They'll be looking for you up there, Win. That's where you're headed, isn't it—the mountains?" Luella leered down at him, then quickly packed her basket.

A bell rang at the end of the social hour. Luella picked up her picnic basket and guided Benji toward the visitors' exit. Windrake followed them. At the door, he bent awkwardly and hugged Benji tight.

"Bye, Boy. Mind your mama. She'll raise you right." His chest heaved with unexpected emotion.

Benji squirmed to be released. "Sure, Daddy." He waved goodbye, turned, and trailed his mother.

A week later Windrake Ferries stuffed his few belongings into the small pigskin bag Luella bought him: a comb, tooth polish, a few sheets of paper and a dull pencil, a tintype of Benji. He had five dollars he won in craps games, and letters of introduction scribbled by prison mates, endorsements into a club of like-minded men, an outgrowth of his own Brothers of the White Cross.

He passed through the prison gates. Shielding his eyes against the glare, he inhaled the aromas of hayfields and cow dung, scents that would forever remind him of freedom. After six years, freedom smelled good. *Ain't nobody gonna know me with a hood over my head, least of all Hyde. Time's come for a reckoning for him and his kin, the Ferries way.*

Windrake Ferries turned northward, bound for Snowbird Mountain.

45

Fort Montgomery, North Carolina
Autumn 1872

Cornwoman paid Tom Cooper for the bag of grain, brushed gray strands of hair from her face, then hoisted the awkward bundle onto her shoulder. She stumbled backward a step.

Cooper steadied her. "Let me give you a hand."

"I got it. My wagon is just outside." Her load balanced, she trundled to her old buckboard and tumbled her sack into its bed.

Across the street, Jason Hyde stepped from inside the Revival office and ambled toward the jailhouse. Now middle-aged, he cut a fine figure of a man, with silver temples accenting his black hair clasped in a tail at the nape of his neck. His shiny sheriff's star glinted in the sunlight.

Blinded by its flash, a vision overtook the medicine woman. Darkness engulfed Jason. Lost, he stumbled along a high-walled corridor, looking over his shoulder as if pursued. A row of men in tall hats lined the walls, their faces dispassionate. They observed his maneuvering, then checked their watches.

"You should've let Tom help you!" Martha Taylor exclaimed as she exited King and Cooper's General Store.

The vision dissipated. "I do not need help."

The doc smiled. "Ornery as ever, aren't you?

"I done for myself all my life and reckon I will keep doing till I plumb give out. What brings you to town?"

"My mail order package from Montgomery Ward came in. They stock anything you might want at better prices than either Tom Cooper or his competition down the way. I'll bring you the catalog, if you like."

Cornwoman shook her head, then gestured toward Martha's parcel. "Medicine for your clinic?"

"That, a couple bars of Pears soap," she glanced around, "and a little pot of blush," she said quieter. "I'm of an age now where a lady can use a bit of extra color." She fingered the brown paper. "Wrapped up tight, nobody's the wiser."

Three town commissioners exited McFee's Tavern at the end of the street, passed the two women as they chatted, and tipped their hats. "Afternoon, ladies." A whiff of whiskey accompanied their greeting.

Cornwoman nodded hello, then turned to Martha. "Our little village has grown. I never thought we would need a Board of Commissioners, or a sheriff." She tilted her chin toward the jailhouse.

"Both are essential," Martha said. "The Ku Klux tries to drive out anybody who's not to their liking. Folks don't challenge 'em because they're afraid."

"Or cause they agree with 'em," Cornwoman interjected.

"That, too. They put the Brothers of the White Cross to shame."

Two brawling men tumbled through the tavern doors, then resumed pounding each other. Jason and Dan Taylor sprinted from the jail in their direction.

"Jason's got his hands full, all right," Cornwoman mused.

"You going to Doc Hooper's funeral tomorrow?" Martha asked. Cornwoman pursed her lips. "Join me, won't you? I'll be on the hillock overlooking the cemetery."

The scents of early fall raised Cornwoman's spirits as she viewed the graveside proceedings from a hill at the Joel Crisp farm in nearby Stecoah Valley. Overhead, a never-ending blue bird-colored sky framed the mountains beyond. Below, the First Baptist Church held as a monument to the devout while its congregation, along with most of Fort Montgomery and Cheoah Valley, converged in the graveyard to bury a pillar of the community, old Doc Hooper. Never had one man brought forth so many to say goodbye.

Dr. Enos Hooper fathered two families, one white by his legal wife, Margaret, and the other Cherokee by his companion, Polly Monroe. Today, his children, grandchildren, and great grandchildren clustered on either side of his grave to pay their last respects.

Cornwoman could not see the expressions on his wives' faces but imagined they paid less attention to their departed husband's casket than to each other.

I wonder, if he's looking down on them now, is he amused by his cruel joke?

She returned her attention to the crowd and noticed Aramarinda Hooper near the front—Doc had been her uncle. At the deceased's feet, Nancy Hyde jockeyed for space with her brood —Sarah and Will, in their twenties, teens Johnny and Lucy, and six-year-old Nannie. The youngest, Newt, held his mother's hand and gazed at the coffin, his round black eyes filled with wonder. Two children were missing. Four years earlier, Mary wed a clergyman and moved to Tennessee, her one hope for happiness after her tragic encounter with Windrake Ferries. And Janie, who succumbed to fever last winter, was also missing. Her mother insisted on Doc Hooper's ministrations, but after a period of prolonged leeching, the poor girl died anyway.

At Doc's head, the pastor stood ready. Everyone else jostled for space.

"Where's Jace?" Martha asked.

"Working, I imagine. A sheriff's always on duty, as we saw yesterday."

Jason soon pushed his way through the packed-in viewers. Today, his butterscotch-colored pants complimented a stylish jacket, its yoke adorned by his winking tin star. Stopping next to Aramarinda, he scanned the flock.

Martha tugged on Cornwoman's sleeve. "Did you see that?"

"See what?"

"Jace. I'm certain Aramarinda passed him a note."

Cornwoman saw it, but hoped the doc wouldn't. *I should never underestimate the trained eyes of a healer.*

"She slipped something into his pocket. What do you think it means?" her friend urged.

"Probably nothing."

Nancy waved, and he advanced toward her, sliding between people, many of whom wanted a quick word with him. He reached her side, and the preacher began his eulogy.

"Is she still living with you?" Martha whispered.

"Aramarinda? No, she moved out ages ago to a small cabin in Little Snowbird, near me."

"See her much?"

"She brings me food, especially in winter months, and I help her with—things."

"Is it safe these days for a young woman to live alone?"

Cornwoman threw Martha the side-eye. "You and I live alone." Her tone was sharper than she intended. "Aramarinda can take care of herself."

Martha raised her eyebrows at Cornwoman's curt reply and waited for her to elaborate.

Midway through the eulogy, Aramarinda left the huddle, wandered to the church, and stopped behind a magnificent elm whose branches almost brushed the ground. From her vantage point, she watched from afar. The sermon completed, pallbearers lowered the coffin into the grave. Enos Hooper's wives, each eyeing the other, tossed a symbolic handful of earth onto the casket lid before gravediggers covered it with dirt. Aramarinda prayed she would not one day share their position so publicly.

The throng dispersed and she monitored Jason's movements. He hoisted Newt with one arm, Nannie with the other, and followed Nancy to their spring wagon. He placed the youngsters inside, then helped his wife into the front seat and said a few parting words. After he set his family on their way, she scrutinized his expression as he removed the letter from his pocket and gave it a quick read. Looking up, he searched for its writer.

Hugging herself, Aramarinda leaned against the old elm trunk, dropped her lids over dancing eyes, and smiled.

Meanwhile, Martha and Cornwoman strolled to the hill's summit where they had secured their transportation. The doc continued her probing chit-chat.

"Do you mean, Aramarinda's not alone?"

"I'll tell you, healer to healer, but you must swear to keep this information confidential."

"Of course."

"A few years back, in '68, as I recall, a man pounded on my door in the middle of the night. He had a woman with him in premature labor. He himself was in a sore state of panic. The next day she delivered a girl-child, but almost died. The baby, poor soul, lived only two days."

Martha appeared puzzled. "That's sad. Who were they?"

Cornwoman glanced at her sideways but kept mum.

"So, Aramarinda—The father already had a family, I take it."

"Digging won't help."

"Who did the little one favor?"

"All newborn babies gotta face like a walnut."

"Ama Cornwoman!" Martha laughed, then climbed into her buggy.

"The next year, she birthed a second baby. This delivery went much better. Another girl."

"Same father?"

Cornwoman almost smiled. "She gave both babies the same name, Joshene. An adorable little creature. I wonder who's taking care of her now?"

Later that afternoon, Jason dismounted Ghost and hitched him to the post beside two other horses in front of the ramshackle roadside cabin near the Tennessee border. A windowless structure with its thatched roof in need of repair, the entrance featured a tin overhang supported by a pair of age-warped posts, while an add-on with a stovepipe angled off the back. The sweet scent of moonshine hung in the air and mingled with boiled ham and butter beans. *Poole's Feed Store* read a battered sign over the door. *'N Road House* scrawled on a wood scrap had been tacked to the end. Across the road, opposite the store, an ancient hay barn leaned to one side. Near it stood a corral and three small, new-built structures.

Bales of hay sat stacked on the tin-roofed porch. A girl of about fifteen, with mousy blonde hair, bone-thin and barefoot, lounged on a hay bale, her skirt hiked to her knees. She strummed an old banjo nestled in her lap, stopped, and removed the pipe from her lips. "Hi'dy, Sheriff. Fine day, ain't it?"

Jason tipped his hat. "Cover yourself, Verna Mae. Bare legs aren't lady-like."

"Lady-like!" Her annoying barrage of giggles followed him inside the store.

The dim light within revealed a riot of farm related items: grain sacks, muzzle bags, harnesses, and coiled rope. Drying corn husks and peppers hung from the rafters. Three tables with chairs occupied the center of this disarray. An open doorway led to a kitchen that smelled of cooking. Feed, hay, mold, food, and 'shine created a heady combination, though not unpleasant. Across one side of the room, a bar sported a large spigoted barrel at one end and shelves to the rear where a few spotty glasses rested. Ransom Poole, surly and middle-aged, manned the counter.

"Afternoon, Sheriff. Got business up Tallassee Pike?"

Before he could reply, a second woman shambled through a rear entrance, flouncing her skirt. She shut the door with a swing of her ample hips. Older than Verna Mae, she was plump, sturdy, and rough-hewn from plowing fields. A wealth of unkempt black hair, tied into a loose knot on top of her head, offset tanned, coarse features. Seeing Jason, she proffered a lewd gap-toothed grin, and allowed her chemise to slip from her shoulder, exposing full-bosomed cleavage.

"Eula, stop your prancing and move your duff!" Poole yelled. "Fetch the sheriff here some vittles."

She wiped her nose with her hand and shuffled to the kitchen.

A stranger sauntered in behind her, buttoning his pants. Seeing Jason, his step quickened, and he avoided the sheriff's eyes. He tossed a few coins on the bar. "A tip for Miss Eula," he muttered. "She earned it." He promptly left.

A man at the counter slugged his whiskey, clapped the glass upside down, and departed without looking up.

"Dang, you just chased off all my customers," Poole complained.

"How about that. We gotta have us a chat."

"'Bout what?"

"Unpaid taxes, and, from the looks of it, 'shining."

"Aw, come now, Jace," the proprietor whined. "What I got on hand is but a sampling of my personal stock. No law against allowing my customers to wet their whistle while they shop. A fella gets thirsty."

"Depends on what your customers are shopping for while they're pouring your homemade hooch down their gullets. If they're dunking their dippers in Miss Eula's well, then we got a problem. Running a bawdy house is illegal."

"Ain't no problem here. Listen, how's about we sit down, peaceable-like. I'll give you what taxes I owe on my feed business. But I ain't selling no 'shine, I swan, and ain't nobody dunking, or dipping, or whatever you said. Chrissake, she's my brother's daughter."

Eula returned with a steaming plate of ham and beans and set it on a table. She strutted to the bar, leaned against it next to Jason, and looked him over. "Anything else I can do for ya, Sheriff?" She smelled like a plowed field and sweat.

He peered at her, then shifted his eyes to Poole. "You're kidding me, right?"

"Dammit, girl, get outta here! Wait out front with Verna Mae."

She sashayed to the door and bumped her hip into an arriving customer. An empty jug dangled from his index finger.

The newcomer eyed the sheriff. "Never mind, Rans, I'll come back later." He about-faced and smacked Eula on the bottom. "Next time, sugar."

"Hey, Lester," she cooed. "I need help lifting something in the hay barn." She flicked her skirt.

Jason grinned. "Better quit while you're ahead. Eula's digging your grave deep."

"Aw, Jace. A man's gotta make a living."

"If your daddy was alive, he'd be mad as a March hare if he knew what you done to his business. Your family's always been respectable."

"Times a'changed. Cash money puts food on the table, clothes on my back. Decency don't. Ask any carpetbagger. Listen, we been friends a long time. You'll look t'other way for me, won't ya? I'm looking to the future here. You see the new buildings out yonder? I aim to make this place a bonafide tourist stop." He jogged to the waiting plate. "Hey, your vittles is going cold. Let's me and you sit down and discuss it. Grab yourself a bite to eat, no charge." He fidgeted with the place setting and refolded the napkin.

"Not hungry. I know it's hard to get by around here. I'll go easy on you. But not for free."

Poole's face clouded. "What're you getting at?"

"Give me the taxes you owe on the feed store today."

"No problem."

"Keep your whores off the porch where passersby can see 'em."

"They ain't whores, but I'll tell 'em not to sit out there."

"Move that still of yours. You're stinking up the air."

A broad, brown-toothed leer lined his face. "Anything you say, Jace."

"And you pay me a liquor fee—every month."

His grin melted. "What?"

"I'm supposed to collect seventy cents a gallon in taxes on whiskey sales. Gimme forty cents a gallon and I don't report your sideline here. The government won't know you exist."

"*What?*" Poole sneered. "You learnt to work the system real fast, didn't you?"

"Your whoring business—I want ten percent off the top of your draw."

Ransom Poole's jaw dropped. "The hell you say! That's highway robbery!"

The sheriff pointed to the road. "See that out there? It's a highway. Take the deal or I'm taking you in. Right here. Right now."

That evening, Jason watched from the bedroom doorway of Aramarinda's two-room cabin as she pinched her cheeks and applied mulberry stain to her lips. After pinning a nosegay of violets into her hair, she twirled and struck a girlish pose, then stepped back to gaze at her image in a tiny wall mirror over her washstand.

He smiled. Her youthful manner delighted him. Despite feeling guilty for cheating on his wife, time spent with Aramarinda took his mind off mundane occurrences and life's worries. She was the one person in the world to whom he could tell everything. Not that he did, or would, but if he had, unlike Nancy, he trusted she would accept him without judgment.

She captivated him the moment he saw her in the Nantahala Forest, many years ago—no more than a lovely young sprite. She panicked when their eyes met and scampered into the woods. Their next encounters fared little better. Having since matured into a woman, full of life and loveliness, she lit his world on fire. To say that he loved her hardly expressed the depth of his feelings.

He approached her, embraced her from behind, and brushed her neck with his lips.

She leaned into him and pulled him closer. Turning to face him, she linked her arms around his neck and kissed him. “You’re late.”

“Daddy, Daddy, I made this for you.” Joshene bounced into the room and danced at his side, waving a piece of paper depicting crossed arrows painted by her three-year-old hand.

Fort Montgomery
March 1873

Dear Daddy, *2 March 1873*

Hope you and Mama and everyone at home is fit. We settled into the new church parsonage and the congregation of Maury County Presbyterian Church welcomed me into their fold.

Our beloved Laura is almost three and into everything! She chatters non-stop, winning her way into everyone's hearts. I think she gets it from you, Daddy. Truly, she favors her Grandpa Hyde more with each passing day. Our little girl is a blessing and I thank the Lord for His precious gift. I thought I could never conceive after what that awful Ferries man did to me.

On a sad note, Mother Ammons succumbed to pneumonia in February. John, however, has a robust constitution and his health remains good. Though we want to visit you soon, it may be September before my dear husband will have time off from his duties.

Until then, remember that I love you, Daddy. Give my love to Mama, Sarah, Will, Johnny, Lucy, Nannie, and Newt. I grieve Janie's passing but I take comfort in knowing that after suffering so long with fever, she is with Jesus. I miss you all and think of you often.

Your Loving Daughter,

Mary

Jason folded her letter and slipped it into his shirt pocket. He stoked the fire in the potbelly stove and warmed his hands.

Dan Taylor hurried into the jailhouse. "Jace, get over to Rough right away. There's gonna be trouble. Miz Libby and her Temperance ladies are on their way there to agitate. Remember what happened last week when they pulled their stunt here in town?"

Jason reached for his hat. "I do. Turned into a shouting match. Darvis Pouncey, that new barkeep down at McFee's Tavern, he stepped in to settle folks till I got there."

Rough, a settlement along West Buffalo Creek, near Little Snowbird, boasted a general store, a livery, a grist mill, a dance hall, and a saloon. It lived up to its name almost daily and saw trouble enough without Libby Thorne getting into the mix.

"Thanks for the heads up. If she's thinking on repeating there what she did here, somebody's bound to be hurt. See if Hugh Dockery's around. As Libby's fiancé, I'd think he'd wanna know about this. Check the tavern. He's likely hobnobbing with his future voting public. I want you both riding with me."

Libby and her lady friends arrived in Rough just before the dinner hour. On a typical day, men lolled along the streets while a few citizens attend to business. By noontime, aimless customers packed the saloon, which grew busier throughout the afternoon. Libby's ladies' organization had a lot to accomplish in Rough.

She parked the wagon in front of the general store and the Graham County Temperance League members climbed down. They all wore white ribbons across their bosoms that read, *It's Up to You!*

Two ladies carried an armload each of sobriety pamphlets which they handed to the crowd. The slogan across the front declared:

Lips That Touch Whiskey Shall Not Touch Ours

The rest of Libby's group passed homemade placards amongst themselves and marched to the tavern. "We want temperance! Say no to liquor!"

Light spring snowflakes drifted on air currents as bystanders gathered and soon, hecklers lined the walkway. Besotted saloon patrons filed out the establishment's door, carrying about them the bouquet of beer, whiskey, and their noonday dinner about them. Men jeered, some threw bits of their meal at them, others chunked wadded up fliers at them.

"If you was my wife, I'd teach ya some respect," a man bellowed, popping his balled fist.

"Piss on you!" another sneered. He unbuttoned his dungarees, and encouraged by howls and whistles from his pals, urinated in the protesters' general direction.

Libby and her friends met the men's challenge, shouting back. Another man chucked an empty bottle at the ladies. Stones, fried chicken, and handfuls of mashed potato followed it.

A little girl scampered onto the boardwalk from inside the market and stood watching the ruckus.

"Get that child outta here!" Libby yelled. A woman—presumably the child's mother—dashed through the store's front door, scooped the girl into her arms, and scurried back inside. A chicken leg hit Libby's shoulder and she spun around to face the hecklers. "What yellow-bellied banty throws fried chicken at women?" She shook her fist at them. "It'll take more than grease stains to stop us!"

Jason, Dan, and Hugh Dockery trotted over the bridge into Rough, halted their horses in the middle of the blustering crowd, and dismounted. The tenor of the rabble changed the instant their feet touched the ground.

"Sheriff Hyde!" Harvey Walldrup wailed, weaving and poking a finger in his direction. "I oughta kill you, you damn son of a bitch! Cause of you, the bank took my land!"

"Serving liens is my job, Harve. You can't say I didn't warn you."

"Bull—!" Walldrup bellowed.

"Settle down. Lemme get the Temperance League outta here, and then we'll discuss your farm."

Hugh Dockery marched over to Libby, grabbed her by the arm and hustled her into the relative privacy of the market.

Libby struggled to remove his grip. "Hugh, you're hurting me!"

"Whatever possessed you to come to Rough? These drunkards mighta hurt you. This temperance business is nothing but a bother."

"I'm not afraid of boozehounds." She patted the derringer hidden in her jacket.

Dockery grimaced. "Even worse. I want you and your ladies to go home. *Now*. No more scenes. Come on, I'll walk you to your wagon."

"Stop treating me like a child." She shook his hand off her arm and started for the door.

Aramarinda pushed past her, holding tightly to Joshene, and dashed outside.

"Are you all right?" Aramarinda scanned the crowded street; no one appeared to be watching them.

"Daddy!" Joshene extended her chubby hands.

He took her from Aramarinda and kissed her. "Minda, what are you doing here? And you brought our daughter—It's not safe!"

"It's not as bad as you think."

"Hogwash. I know what this town is like. Shop in Fort Montgomery."

"I don't shop there cause I could run into Nancy," she quietly said. "Neither of us wants that. She would recognize you in your daughter."

"Dammit, Minda. This has gone on for what, five years? That's five years too long. I love you and I love Josie and I don't mind who knows it. I'm tired of hiding."

Aramarinda glanced at the townsfolk and reduced her voice to a whisper. "I love you, too, Jace. More than anything, but we must be careful. Back in the day, Uncle Enos, and others, got away with it, but—"

"We're not doing a thing that's not encouraged by the government. Besides, folks around here don't care. They love me."

Aramarinda tightened her lips. "What a poor excuse! Think about your family."

Washington, Department of the Treasury, Secret Service Division
April 1873

Coy Hawes had a spring in his step on a cheery morning in the nation's capital city. Bright green buds of newly planted shade trees lined its avenues and its streets bustled with the sounds of vendors hawking their wares and horse-drawn carriages clattering across cobblestones.

He entered the United States Treasury Department and the cool marble hallways echoed the hushed patter of busy feet. Guilt-framed portraits of solemn statesmen and staid politicians looked down from the walls on him as he passed. He passed along its corridors. Doors opened, doors closed, ever gentle in their entry and exit. No one paid him much mind. Why should they, when behind each door, agency employees would manage the financial import of a nation?

Coy reached the second floor, set down his heavy black leather valise, preened his bushy mustache, and straightened his tie. He took a moment to brace himself, and stared at the sign on the door in front of him, *Colonel Hiram C. Whitley, Chief of United States Secret Service.*

Coy dreamt of this day. He had worked hard to prepare for it, banking on the chance that displaying the scope and detail of his clandestine work would catapult him to the next chapter of his detective career—and put an end to the Southeastern counterfeiting rings, for good.

Whitley's secretary ushered him into the colonel's office. Coy had waited for hours but would have waited hours more, if necessary. At last, he sat face to face with Colonel Whitley.

"Sorry to keep you waiting," Whitley glanced at Coy's business card, "Mr. Hawes. You're with Pinkerton's?"

"Thank you for seeing me without an appointment, Chief. I'll come right to the point. I have information about counterfeiting rings in several states that will allow the Service to put them away for good."

The chief leaned forward in his chair, eyes narrowed. "Is that so?"

"I was with Pinkerton's almost from its start in 1850."

"And no longer?" He flicked Coy's calling card to the side.

"Forgive me, my card is dated. I investigated the North Carolina counterfeiting rings during the war until the government took up the case. At that point, I continued on my own, and spent the past six years undercover in Ohio, Indiana, Kentucky, and Tennessee. I have compiled rather impressive documentation on the gangs involved. Here." He patted his briefcase, pausing for effect.

Coy declined to tell the chief that he first went to Chicago and presented Pinkerton with enough evidence to convict the entire Burchfield ring. The man had brushed him off, and Coy handed in his badge.

He shared with Whitley the information he had collected while passing through Ohio on his way home.

"You conducted your own private investigation?"

"Yes, sir. It paid off. Let me show you—"

"Cheeky. We train our agents to act with military rigor. One follows orders or faces severe discipline."

"Indeed, sir, I understand the value of discipline."

Whitley regarded him for a moment. "I don't mind saying our forces infiltrated the Ku Klux throughout the South—and arrested five hundred clan members. Two hundred more surrendered. Only the northernmost region of South Carolina and western North Carolina have proved to be impenetrable. Can your investigative prowess hold a candle to that?"

"No doubt. At the risk of sounding presumptuous, I can help you crack that Carolina nut. I know my way around the mountain wilderness. Granted a few moments of your time, I will show you samples of my fact-finding, including detailed dossiers." Coy unlocked the brass clips on his leather case.

Whitley licked his lips like a cat presented with a bowl of fresh milk.

His secretary knocked twice and popped his head in the door. "Sir, your next appointment is here."

"I can't see them now, Mosby. Please extend my apologies and explain that I have been detained. Clear my agenda for the rest of the afternoon."

Fort Montgomery's continued growth meant more strangers wandering the streets. Wary, Jason increased security and varied their meeting places. He posted a patrolman inside and out, arming the field guard with an old army telescope and a Cherokee blowing horn—a hollow cow horn used to alert the others of intruders. They kept gathering locations secret until the day before.

In a storeroom at Rose's granary, Jason eyed two newcomers while he waited for Joel Lovin to call the meeting of the Graham County Counterfeiters to order.

"Attention, everybody," Joel announced. "We agreed last we met that we would expand the number of guards. Tonight, I'd like to introduce you to our newest members.

"First, I'll run through our roster and identify each member's role. Please stand when I say your name. Officers, Adam Cable. Jacob Rose. Jason Hyde. Louisa Penley, cashier. J.C. Howok, inside guard. Julius Bradshaw, outside guard. I, of course, am Joel Lovin, officer and headman." He turned to the newcomers. "We welcome our two newest members, who will also be guards. Darvis Pouncey will backup Howok as an inside guard, Henry Ditman will cover Bradshaw…"

At the officer's meeting the week before, Jason argued against allowing Pouncey into their fold. "What do we know about him, Joel? Nothing, except he's from Kentucky." He unfolded his copy of the *Weekly Pioneer* newspaper and jabbed a finger at the headline:

GOVERNMENT AGENTS NAB COUNTERFEITERS IN KENTUCKY RAID

"See that? The South's crawling with agents looking for konlackers like us. Pouncey could be one of 'em."

"Relax," Cable fussed. "They'll never crack our ring up here in the mountains. You done too good a job keeping us a secret."

"Bar tending at McFee's puts him in a good position to keep tabs on suspicious travelers," Joel added. "We need a fella like him watching our backs."

They voted Jason down. Pouncey was in.

48

Fort Montgomery
July 1873

At the stroke of twelve from the tower clock, Dan Taylor strode through the jailhouse door after investigating reports of a highway robber along the county's south border. Jason folded his newspaper and laid it aside. "Learn anything?"

"No robber, but I spotted local bootleggers on the Topton-Murphy road."

"Like who?"

"Like Tuck Stamper." He poured coffee into a mug.

"Tuck? Didn't figure on him being in that line of business. Musta taken over his daddy's still after he died. Bootlegging's a nasty racket, not fitting for a youngster his age."

Cornwoman entered the room, interrupting their conversation.

"Ama." Jason stood. "This is a surprise. Please, sit."

Dan offered her his chair.

"I must talk to you, Jason." She turned sharp eyes on Dan.

"We're just finishing up. Dan, I'll set Tuck straight. You go on back out there and arrest any bootleggers coming back this way. Leave 'em be on their way out."

"Why wait?"

"They got no coin going out. Whatever we take, we split, fifty-fifty. Remember that." He waited for his deputy to exit, then leaned forward in his chair. "Is Aramarinda all right? Is Joshene hurt?"

Cornwoman settled in her seat and observed him for a long moment. “They are well. What is this about keeping what you steal?”

He relaxed. “It’s not stealing if they come by it illegally. Splitting it gives Dan incentive.”

“It is stealing. Like your other ill-got money.”

Jason squinted. “What d’ya mean by that?”

“You know what I mean.” She shook her head. “I had high hopes for you. Now I worry. My dreams tell me of dark times coming.”

“Pshaw, dreams are nothing but dreams.” Nighttime visions continued to plague *him*. The horseman of his nightmares persisted; and now a wolf accompanied him. He admitted none of it.

“I know when a dream is just a dream,” Cornwoman’s eyes bore into him. “These foretell of something more. This morning, an iron door awoke me. Bam!” She slapped her hands together. Jason flinched. “But—the wolf worries me most.”

Stamper’s moonshine still, a shabby, slipshod operation in deep woods near Panther Creek, had been in operation for two generations. It was a cinch Tuck was nearby, though Jason couldn’t see him.

“Tuck! Tuck, lower your gun,” he called from behind an oak.

“I ain’t coming out, Sheriff. You gotta take me by force.”

“Aw, come on, don’t get bowed up. Let’s have us a sit-down.” Jason moved closer to the sound of the boy’s voice. “Your daddy and I were friends a long time. I’ve known you all your life.” He slipped closer. “We can work this out, Tuck.”

“You mean that?” Tuck stepped into the open, rifle aimed.

Jason moved from behind his tree, arms raised. “Of course. Lower your weapon. Let’s talk.”

Looking sheepish, Tuck complied. Jason walked him to his still and sat him on a crate, then pulled up a second one for himself.

Tuck laid his rifle down and offered Jason a sip of fresh homebrew. “Try it. I put honey in it from my hives.” He admired the amber liquid in his mason jar.

Jason waved it off. “I see you took over your daddy’s business.”

“A still ain’t got much overhead, and I got no other options.”

"Well, I'll tell you, it's not a crime to make 'shine. Selling it is. Unless you pay the government their share of the profits."

"I ain't selling." Tuck tossed back a mouthful of corn liquor and inspected the ground around his bare feet.

"Dan spotted you on the Topton road yesterday toting jugs of hooch outta the county. Can't have that, Son. You're liable to get hurt." Elbows on his knees, Jason chewed on a straw. "Got a proposition for you. It'll help with your daddy's funeral costs and then some."

Tuck raised his head and looked at him. "Like what?"

"Come work for me. I'll make you Special Deputy."

The young man's eyes lit up. "You ain't gonna arrest me?"

"Not unless you keep on with your 'shining business."

"Can I make my brew *and* come work for you?"

"Sure. Just don't sell it."

Tuck grinned and pumped Jason's hand with a vigor that expressed his excitement more than words ever could. "Special Deputy. Got a right nice ring to it. When do I start?"

Libby paced the kitchen, tapping a rolled copy of *The Revolution* newspaper against her free palm while her Aunt Evie plucked a chicken. Suffrage pamphlets from the American Equal Rights Association in New York City sat in a crate in the corner, next to another filled with temperance flyers. Though her Temperance League membership had grown, their ongoing efforts for an ordinance prohibiting liquor sales continued to be ignored.

"With the right to vote, women can bring about change," she fumed, and whacked the rolled newspaper on the kitchen table as she passed it.

"That'll be the day," Evie flipped the chicken and tugged at feathers on its other side.

With the exception of her aunt and Caroline Cable, Libby's other Temperance League members had expressed mixed feelings about the idea of voting. "We must never give up. I'll address the Old Mother's congregation after church on Sunday. You and Caroline can pass out booklets."

At church, her women's suffrage appeal met ridicule from the men and skepticism from many of the women. The Cherokees were derisive. "We can't vote no how. How 'bout agitatin' for our citizenship?"

Afterward, Libby complained to her fiancé as they walked to his buggy.

"What did you expect?" Hugh Dockery said. "Frankly, Libby, I disagree with this suffrage business. Wives should be content raising children and making a pleasant home for their families. What do they need with complex matters of politics?"

"The decisions you men make affect us. Women ought to have an equal say."

"Darling Libby, you will change once we marry. What you need is a home to care for and a few young'uns running around. I'll see to that." He stroked her arms; she shook him off. "A woman's mind is a delicate thing, incapable of handling complicated matters."

She balled her fists. "You must think little of me. Men squander their pay on drink and brawl in the streets. They go home drunk and hit their wives and children. Men start wars and destroy society. Y'all have made a mess of things. We women can effect change with a say in government."

Hugh backed away. "You forget your place, madam! I care for you, but your Temperance League is an annoyance. And this, this wild idea about women taking over the world is downright ridiculous."

"Forget my place? Poppycock! I'm talking about equality, not taking over." She jutted her chin. "Women are equal to men in every way. Better in some."

A flush crawled up Hugh's neck. "Your agitating is a silly waste of time. It endangers you and others. On top of that, your antics embarrass me. I'm campaigning for a seat on the Board of Commissioners next term and your behavior hurts my chances. But, of course, *you* wouldn't understand."

Open-mouthed, Libby gaped at him. "I'm an embarrassment? I could hurt your chances? Who *are* you? I feel I don't know you a'tall."

"I'm learning more about you every day!" He gazed down his nose at her. "Let me tell you something as your prospective husband. I need a wife to serve me dinner when I come home, keep my house clean, raise my children proper. I do not want a wife who goes around stirring up trouble. If that is not agreeable to you, we may need to reconsider our engagement. Think it over, my dear, but ponder my words. You'd be throwing away a future any woman would want."

"Is that so!" She jerked his engagement ring from her finger and handed it to him. "Take it. The ladies waiting in that lo-o-o-ng line you see there," she swung her arm at the emptiness behind her, "may choose to share in your glorious future. But not me."

Two weeks later, heartbroken but undaunted, she outfitted her temperance wagon with a second sign, *Votes For Women*. Soon after, she headed to town with Evie Lovin, Caroline Cable, and a host of other temperance supporters. They met with the Commissioners once more and presented their case, along with a petition calling for a shutdown of moonshine stills proliferating the area. One hundred women and quite a few men had signed it.

The commission rejected their proposal.

August 1873

Libby awoke to the smell of wood smoke and a crackling and popping more familiar to crisp October nights. She donned robe and slippers and joined Evie and Joel Lovin in the doorway of their home.

"What's happening?" Stunned, she gaped at the sight before her.

Fifty white-robed, hooded figures—some mounted on horseback, most on foot—loitered in the front yard. A fiery cross blazed behind them. At Libby's appearance, they began a chant, the depth and thrum of their collective voices rattling her bones. She slipped an arm around Evie to hide her fear. Her aunt pulled her closer, each holding tight to the other, quiet as mice.

Joel had opened the door with rifle in hand. He lowered it, propped it against the frame, and raised his now-empty hands in surrender, lifting Evie's free hand with his. "We don't want any trouble!" he called out.

The Klan leader commanded silence. The rhythmic pulse of voices ceased. In the dearth of man-made thunder, the hiss of the burning cross stood as a sinister beacon against the blackness of night.

"Miz Thorne," the Ku Kluxer began, "as knights of chivalry, we prefer not to harm ladies. But—you disrupt our society. We will not tolerate disrupters. Conform to our ways or leave our community. But know this. If you persist in your attempts to sully our womenfolk's pure minds with radical notions, we will punish you as we see fit. Cease your meddling or pay the consequences."

The robed men shouted obscenities, their words confused, unintelligible. In the mix, a singular voice carried forth. "…barefoot and pregnant. Enough poking your pert little nose where it don't belong!"

"Hugh!" Libby screeched. "*You* did this, you no good vermin. Hugh Dockery, I'd never vote for you!" A hood bobbled. Her barb hit home, whether or not she had a vote to withhold. "I'd never marry you now! Come on, Evie, Uncle Joel. We've heard enough."

She swung about, then stopped, chilled to the bone by a vulgar acoustic which stood out amongst the baritones, a voice recalled from years before. Its fierce bass notes thundered in an earthy growl that provoked gooseflesh as much as did the words it uttered. "You're next, Mary Elizabeth Lovin Thorne."

Libby slammed the door shut and locked it. "Windrake Ferries!"

The Next Day

Dear Daddy, *14 August 1873*

Good news, Laura and I expect to arrive in two weeks' time. I so look forward to seeing you and hugging every one of you a hundred times over. It's been too long!

Love to you all.

Your affectionate daughter,

Mary

Jason noted the date; her letter had taken ten days to arrive. "She could be here any day!" On top of the world, Jason placed Mary's letter in his pocket to share with Nancy that evening. He leaned back in his armchair and enjoyed the quiet morning.

Life couldn't be better. Child-rearing kept Nancy busy. She and the kids were healthy—eight of them, including granddaughter Laura. Aramarinda enthralled him; Joshene, his daughter with her, delighted him.

That makes nine. Lord have mercy! No worry, ready cash from 'shiners, bootleggers, and side accounts allows a comfy life. And plenty to lay aside.

At work, order mostly prevailed, except for that annoying highway robber, still on the loose. He insisted on alternating meeting places for their counterfeiting operation, and between Cable's barn, Lovin's home, Rose's granary, and Penley's Boarding House, the rotation had proved an effective decoy to lurking snoops.

The Harvest Festival's coming soon. It's always fun. Now, my grown-up baby girl is coming to visit. Yes, life is grand. He smiled.

Libby Thorne interrupted his reverie. "He's back." She stood in front of his desk hugging herself, her expression grim. "You gotta stop him."

"G'morning, Miz Libby. Stop who?"

"Windrake Ferries. The Ku Klux called on us last night and he was with 'em. Him and Hugh Dockery, too."

Jason sat up straight, his smile forgotten. "Ferries? Are you sure?"

Her nod washed away every last bit of Jason's good mood.

September 1873

In the wee morning hours, Jason awoke panting. The same dream repeated itself, night after night: running, running, chased by a wolf, ever closer to catching him, it seemed, with each repetition.

Nancy rolled over, faced him, and half sat up. "What's the matter?"

"That dream again."

"What dream?" Her tone suggested little interest in hearing it.

He told her anyway. "Strange men in tall hats. A big, white wolf's after me. Huge! The Cherokees got a story about a ghost-wolf. It feels so real, like it's part of me. Makes no sense—Are you listening?"

"Ghost-wolf. You're a ghost of the husband I once knew. Go back to sleep." She curled on her side, and within a minute, her even breathing signaled slumber.

Mary arrived on Sunday with Laura at her side. "My goodness, it's good to be here! Mama, you look well. Prosperity becomes you."

Her mother's face clouded as she smoothed the skirt of her new dress. "Pshaw, child. We get by. How long you here for?"

"A month, if that's all right. John's coming in a couple of weeks." She climbed down from the wagon and gathered her daughter in her arms. Her family flocked around them admiring their toddler niece.

"Stay as long as you like!" Nancy exclaimed. "It's so good to see you. And here's my grandbaby. My, my, look at you! Honey, you won't remember me. I'm Grammy Hyde."

Suddenly shy, Laura hid her face against Mary. "We traveled a considerable distance, Mama. She's tired."

An old hound dog, roused by the commotion, popped up in the wagon wagging his tail, and begged to join in the fun.

"You brought your dog?" Her mother grimaced.

The excited youngsters bubbled and, as soon as his four paws touched the ground, Newt and Nannie fawned over him while Laura hugged his neck.

"That's Beaucephus. He's John's," Mary explained. "When we took off, Beau insisted on following and Laura squalled until I let him come with us. They're very attached to each other."

"You couldn'ta tied him up before you left?"

"And listened to the child fuss our entire visit? She's stubborn, Mama."

"Spoilt, is what she is." Her mother glowered at the animal, then clucked her granddaughter under the chin. "No matter, Grammy's gonna spoil you even more." Laura batted at her hand. "Once she gets used to me. Come in, come in. You and the baby can sleep in the back bedroom. Beaucephus will stay outside. Johnny, bring Mary's things."

At dinner, everyone wanted to hear about Mary's life in Maury County and about John's parish.

"Nobody in our family's ever been anything but Baptist!" Her mother voiced her displeasure regarding his appointment as minister to Maury County Cumberland Presbyterian Church.

Mary changed the subject. "Daddy, what's it like to be sheriff? Is it exciting?"

"It's okay." Her father fed Beaucephus bits of food under the table, Nancy's intent to keep the dog outside quickly forgotten. "The good reverend didn't let you travel alone with a baby, did he?"

"Oh no, John arranged for the deacon to ride with us to Maryville, Tennessee. He got out there, then I drove to the toll booth. We stayed the night at Poole's Roadhouse."

His brow furrowed. "What toll booth?"

"The one at the state line, at Mr. Poole's place. He gave us free room and board when he learnt we were your kin."

"Nice of him. How was it?"

"Food coulda been better. Verna Mae played banjo and sang during supper. She's quite the entertainer."

Her father cocked an eyebrow. "You meet Eula?"

Mary pushed her food around her plate with her fork. "Eula. Poor girl, she didn't have on enough clothes to wad a shotgun." Mary slyly smiled. "I told Mr. Poole he must pay her more so she may afford proper attire."

Jason grunted. "What did he say to that?"

"He said, *Yes, ma'am, I'll see to it.*" Mary knew full well what was going on but would never speak of it with small children present.

"The place busy?"

She nodded. "The bar, especially. We were lucky to get a room."

Her father scratched Beau behind the ears and made a mental note to call on Ransom Poole. The pooch reciprocated with lavish tongue-slurps. "Who's a good boy? We oughta get us a dog."

At the other end of the table, Nancy scowled.

The annual Harvest Festival, suspended during the war, returned at folks' insistence on reviving the Snowbird tradition. Held in Stecoah at Buckannon farm, the fair celebrated the end of fall harvest and combined both ethnicities, Cherokee and white. It held special significance for Jason and Aramarinda; their courtship began at one.

The late fall afternoon percolated with excitement, drums, and traditional Cherokee songs, and steeped with mixed aromas of turkey and deer meat pies, roasted corn, stew, and frybread topped with cinnamon sugar. Jason parked their buckboard under a tree near the outskirts of the festival, amongst the other wagons. His children hopped to the ground and danced with enthusiasm, eager to visit their favorite attractions.

Beaucephus, determined to accompany Laura, proved a liability. They left him secured to a wagon wheel, where he huddled next to it, howling. Jason plucked a few counterfeit dollars from his money pouch and handed them to Nancy. "Money for food and entertainment. Ya'll have fun." After saying his goodbyes, he excused himself. He had a job to do.

Monitoring the carnival presented expected challenges. However, he never imagined Windrake Ferries might lurk around every corner. He remained on high alert, clutching his pistol as he patrolled the grounds, unaware of the festivities and laughter. He jumped when a warm hand brushed against his.

"Hi'dy, stranger. My, but you're antsy. Where's the family?"

Aramarinda sidled up next to him.

He forced a smile. "I'm glad you're here. Nancy and Mary took Laura, Nannie, and Newt to the puppet show. Daddy and the others, they're scattered about. Where's Josie?"

"With Cornwoman. Come, I want you to see the quilt I made. It won second place."

He tugged on her arm. "Lemme kiss you, first."

Aramarinda shook her head. "Jace, careful!"

"I'm being careful." He pulled her behind a hedgerow and embraced her.

From a distance, Cornwoman watched Jason and Aramarinda duck behind the hedges and pursed her lips. "I thought I saw your mama up ahead, Josie, but it is not her. Come on, archery is this way. You like bows and arrows. See, just there." She pointed at a large sign. "Mama will be along soon. Maybe Daddy will come with her."

Cornwoman stood at the fringe of the archery field and observed the crowd. She noticed several outsiders who did not fit in. A medicine man, clean shaven with neat clothing and shiny boots. He doggedly observed the festivalgoers. A hawkish fellow selling pots and pans from an enclosed cart paid less attention to peddling his wares than to the goings on around him. A raggedy man limped on a crutch, favoring the wrong side of his body: his bad leg, fake; his dirty clothes, not what mountain folk wear. She counted seven strangers total. Most odd, while they watched the stream of revelers, they eyed each other. *Who are they? Who are they looking for?*

Jason stepped through a break in the shrubbery, then helped Aramarinda after him. Giggling, she brushed stray leaves from his hair, then let her fingers trail down his cheek.

In the background, Beau's howls resumed, then evolved into furious barking.

"What on earth is that?" Aramarinda asked.

"Mary's dog, Beau, came with her from Tennessee. He followed us here. He's tied to our wagon."

"I think he's trying to tell you something."

"He just misses Laura. Let's go see Josie and Cornwoman." They strolled across the lawn to the archery competition.

"Daddy!" Josie chortled when they approached. She ran to his waiting arms.

He picked her up and spun her around. "There's my beautiful gal."

"Jason," Cornwoman earnestly said, "I gotta talk to you. Something is not right."

"You can say that again!" Nancy snapped, appearing out of nowhere. She scrutinized Joshene, then gazed long at Aramarinda. Under her intense glare, Aramarinda took a wary step backward. Trembling, Nancy fixed her fiery attention on Jason.

He averted his eyes, unable to look at his wife, then flattened his lips.

"Your daughter looks just like you, you cheatin' bastard," Nancy raved. "Years ago, you wouldn'ta done this to us." She waved a hand. "Thank the Lord, your children ain't here to see *this*." She gave him a healthy shove with both hands. Josie, still in his arms, squealed. Nancy stormed into the crowd, biting her knuckles.

Beau's ferocious alarm ceased.

"You knew this would happen," Cornwoman said in a quiet tone. "I warned you. Deal with it later. There are folks here you should know about…"

Cornwoman relayed her observations, but was interrupted by Tuck Stamper bursting through the gathering, breathless. "Been looking all over for ya, Jace. Get to your wagon, quick! If I was you, I'd keep your young'uns away."

"Take 'em home. *Now.*" Jason handed Josie to her mother and sprinted to the parking area.

Jason squeezed through the disquieted crowd. Anguished cries at the center told him his family had already arrived. He broke through the onlookers, and was stunned at the sight before him: his granddaughter in a state of frenzied squalling, his daughters, sobbing, sons and father solemn, wife, stone-faced. Everyone's attention focused on their wagon—Beaucephus, his throat a gaping slit, roped to a crude cross.

Jason ripped a scribbled note from the cross. *Shiruf Hyde, yur next.* "Ferries!"

"No-o-o!" Mary shrieked.

He drew his gun and spun in a full circle, seeking him behind a shrub, near a carriage, or beside a horse. The murdering wretch seemed to be everywhere and nowhere.

Jason pulled Mary close, and held her tight. She clung to him, quivering.

"Your fault!" Nancy ranted. "It's all your fault!"

The drive home felt endless. They arrived and entered with sullen faces and heavy hearts. Nancy threw blankets and an old pillow at Jason. “I don’t care where you sleep from now on but know this, Jason Hyde, it won’t be with me.”

After midnight, he awoke on the parlor divan with a startled jerk: the wolf from his dream had pounced. Panicky, he gulped a breath of air.

He felt the weight of the world on his chest. Another burden weighed on his abdomen and bored into his thighs. Musty wet canine with a hint of old forest filled his nostrils. *Am I still dreaming?* In response to his query, a sour smell washed over his face and a thread of warm drool glopped onto his cheek.

Woolly minded, he raised a hand to thick, rough fur. He pressed on the animal’s flank and muscled a shove. “Down, Beau.” It didn’t budge.

Jason opened one eye, then the other. Abject terror replaced sleepy annoyance. A white timber wolf perched above him, its gaze piercing yet inquisitive.

The visitor leapt, its spring a gut-punch. Jason bolted upright, and his eyes swept the room. In the peaceful silence, the silvery light of a harvest moon showed nothing out of order.

“Just a dream,” he muttered, unconvinced. Under his night shirt, red welts were rising, together with two paw-shaped bruises. Shivering, he stumbled to the kitchen and felt along the top of the pie safe for the whiskey. He tossed back a slug, then followed it with another, and crawled back into his makeshift bed. He spent the rest of the night in fitful sleep.

The next morning, Nancy avoided him. Nobody in his household had much to say except Laura, who was inconsolable. Edgy, he left for the jailhouse without a *goodbye*.

It felt good to put distance between himself and the uncomfortable situation but he was happy to see Sarah step through the door of the jailhouse a short time later. "G'morning, honey. You look nice in a skirt. Special occasion?"

"It's Mary's. She came with me but stayed in the carriage." She pointed a thumb over her shoulder. "Mama says I should dress more ladylike. What's the point, britches are more practical. Not giving up my boots, though. They're broken in." She poked a well-worn Jeff Davis brogan from beneath her hem.

"Aren't those Johnny's?"

"Not anymore." She hesitated, brows weaving, "Daddy, I hope whatever happened between you and Mama will blow over. This reminds me of when she was sick after the war."

Jason shook his head. "It's different this time. Your mama's right, this is my fault."

"What about that rotter who killed Beau?"

"My fault, too. The wretch is after me."

She gasped. "Oh, Daddy, be careful!"

"You, too, honey. Where you off to?"

"Doc Martha's, to get something for Mary's nerves. She's shaky after last night."

"I don't like it. Why didn't you bring Will? It's not safe, y'all riding alone through the woods."

"We'll be fine."

"I'll go with you."

"Better not. Mary needs time to herself."

"Well, if you won't let me ride along, I'll at least walk you to the buggy." They ambled outside into the autumn sunlight. "You gals armed?"

"Of course."

"Good. Remember to stay alert on the road. Doc'll fix you up right, Fairybell. I'll see y'all at supper."

"Supper with the folks. That should be fun," Mary said in a dull voice.

"Oh really, Sis," Sarah's eyes shifted, then widened. "Where'd that dog come from?

Mary looked past her. "What dog?"

"You don't see it? Jiminy Christmas, it's big enough to be a wolf."

Jason swung around. A few yards behind him sat last night's visitor. "Shoo, git!" He waved it away. The animal trotted down the walkway, and disappeared around the corner.

At the outskirts of town, Sarah drove the rig onto a little-used shortcut through the forest. The fall morning featured bursts of scarlet, russet, and brilliant gold glinting amongst the evergreens. She reveled in its beauty and relaxed, then made an attempt at light conversation. "I'm looking forward to seeing Pastor John again. Sis, you got yourself a good man."

"*Pastor John.* Sounds funny to hear you say it. How about you? Any lucky beaus come a'calling?"

"Nope. Don't want any. Look in my purse." Sarah's eyes twinkled.

Mary removed the dime novel from inside Sarah's cloth bag. "*Buffalo Bill, the King of Border Men* by Ned Buntline."

"I'm headed to the frontier, Mary. I can ride and shoot better than most anybody, boy or girl."

"It's dangerous!"

"I can take care of myself." Sarah raised her chin high.

"You'd leave home?"

"You did. I wanna see the world. Like you, I can always come back to visit."

"My situation was different." Mary flashed her a side-eye.

"Everybody's situation is *different.*"

They approached a narrow bridge over a creek where crystal-clear water sparkled in the sun as it tumbled over glistening stones in its rush to one of the abundant waterfalls. They clattered over the brief span of the stream.

A movement caught Sarah's eye. From the other side of the expanse, a brawny, ginger-haired figure lunged headlong toward their horse and seized its harness. He threw himself against the animal's chest and it stumbled amidst anxious whinnies.

Mary grabbed the double-barrel shotgun. "Let go or I'll shoot!" The mare reared, flinging the man into the air. "Ferries!" Mary screeched. She pulled the trigger, her aim wild.

Their horse bucked, and the buggy hoisted onto two wheels. Sarah gripped the dash rail and held tight. Launched from the seat, Mary hit the bridgeboards, her weapon flying from her hands. She rolled, slid off the edge, and sprawled on the rocky shore below. Her shotgun struck the boards, and the second barrel discharged. It caromed end to end after Mary, and pitched into the creek.

Ferries lurched to Sarah's side and grabbed her skirt; a section of fabric ripped from the waistband. Terrified and crying for help, she booted him in the face with all her might. He let go of her dress. She lashed out with the horsewhip, catching him across the chest.

"Cussed bitch!" he growled. "I'll show you who's boss."

The frightened horse squealed and danced as their struggle continued. The carriage jounced, inching ever closer to the side of the bridge. A rear wheel slipped off the platform, and the buggy tilted. Sarah clutched the arm rail to keep from being hurled from her vehicle.

He persisted and attempted to drag her out by her ankle. She hung on and braced her free foot against the inside while she kicked hard with the other.

His hand went limp and he toppled to the ground with a thud.

Trembling, she peered over the carriage side. Ferries lay crumpled, a gash on his head. Mary, bruised and bleeding, stood over him, clutching a large rock. He moaned and stirred. She slammed him in the temple and he lay still.

"You okay?" Mary asked.

Sarah managed a cursory nod.

Far-off hoofbeats grew louder with each passing moment. Moments later, Dan Taylor, their father, and others arrived.

Their father leapt from Ghost's back. "We heard shots!"

"It's *him.*" Mary clung to him. "He attacked Sarah."

Stifling tears, Sarah tucked her skirt under its waistband with shaking hands and repositioned her bonnet.

Her father helped her down. "You hurt?"

She shook her head and clutched his other side while they watched the men hogtie Ferries and right their buggy.

"Take him in and throw him in our slammer."

51

Jason tied Ghost to the rear of the carriage and drove his daughters to Doc Martha's place. A heaviness settled over Mary and she confined her conversation to a quiet please and thank you while Doc tended to her cuts and bruises.

Martha lent Sarah a pair of canvas trousers to replace her torn skirt. Jason observed his daughter's rattled nerves, but was filled with pride as she threw shadow kicks to her attacker's face and, contrary to her sister's silence, recounted their harrowing ordeal. With no other patients to attend, Martha sat next to Jason, savored a cup of tea, and listened.

"Hush up, Sister!" Mary spat. "How many times must we relive it?"

"As many times as it takes!" Sarah snapped. Her voice quivered. "I'd give that fusty lump a good work over, if I could." She threw a last kick, punched the air, then buried her face in her hands.

Jason got to his feet. "See you at the lockup, Doc. Thanks for everything." He nodded to his daughters. "Come along, ladies, let's go home."

Cornwoman barged through the door. "You girls all right?" She turned to Jason. "Sheriff, you go on back to town. You got things to do. I will take 'em home and make sure Martha gets to the jail. You want her to look over your new prisoner, yes?"

"Y–yes, I do," he stammered. "He caught a nasty blow—"

"Then we agree. See you later." Cornwoman hustled him out.

Ferries slept throughout the doc's examination. Martha closed the iron door to his lockup, rotated the key in the lock, and handed Jason the keyring. "He'll live, for now. See that rash on his hands, his patchy hair? That's syphilis."

"Good Lord! If he'd—"

"You sending him to Asheville?

"We'll try him here. The Board'll find him guilty, of course. It falls to me to execute him." He envisioned the Asheville hanging and a silent shudder ran down his spine.

Hours later, Ferries awoke woozy and complained of a headache. He sat on his cot and cursed Mary, Sarah, Jason, Fort Montgomery, and everyone in between.

Jason set a chair against the wall outside Ferries' cell and sat down. "About time you woke up. Welcome to my calaboose. Once again, you sample Fort Montgomery hospitality."

The outlaw cussed him and demanded he leave.

"Temper, temper. I'm not going anywhere till you and I chat." Ferries glared at him. "How long you been in these parts?"

"None of your damn business."

"Tell you what *is* my business—the rape and assault of my daughters."

"Your daughter. Hell-fire and damnation, that mule-kicking bitch of yours is rabid. Why ain't she locked up?" He spit a glob of red-tinged saliva from his bitten tongue at Jason's boots.

Jason shifted his feet and sat forward. "Amusing. There are old murder charges hanging on you from nine years hence. About time you paid for your crimes—like your gang did."

"I never kilt *nobody*!"

"I know for a fact you did. You murdered Ira Lovin. The boy's people want justice—Oh, yeah, almost forgot, you're his *daddy*. Seems you murdered your own son."

Ferries held his glare. "Liar! I'd never kill my own. You mighta caught me today, Sheriff, but I'll get free. I always do. When I do, I'm coming after 'em gals of yours. First, I'll give that kicking bitch what she deserves. I'll take my time with the black-haired beauty she got for a sister. I spent six long years thinking on being with her again—"

Jason shattered his chair against his prisoner's cell bars and fixed a deep glare on Ferries. "By the way, Doc examined you while you were out. You know you got the pox? Bad blood. The syph."

"Another pernicious lie!"

"Nope." Jason stormed to his office.

The outlaw mocked his every step, laughter trailing into the front room, where Tuck Stamper waited to start his shift.

"That him back there?" The young deputy gulped.

"It's him, all right. I need some air. I'm going to supper at Miz Penley's." Steaming, he set hat to head and marched up the road to Penley's Boarding House.

At the boarding house, Jason took the steps two at a time, pausing at the top to listen to the thunder of approaching wagons and hooves. He never noticed the white canine at his side entered the establishment behind him.

Boarders and guests enjoyed their evening meal in Penley's dining room while Jason pushed his food around his plate. Louisa Penley's ham, turnip greens, beets, and cornbread held no appeal. *That bastard deserves to die. But if he doesn't get a fair trial, it'll look bad for the town. The press'll rake me over the coals. I may even lose my job.*

Hearing a disturbance outside, a few diners wandered to the front exit. "Hey, there's a rabble at the jail!" a guest called out. Within moments, only Jason remained in the dining room.

Aware of being watched, he looked up. The wolf glowered at him from the corner with relentless amber eyes.

"Sheriff?" A straggler stood at Jason's side, oblivious of the unwelcome creature not three feet from him. "Oughtn't you have a look-see at what's going on?"

"Leave me be!" *Am I the only one besides Sarah who sees this beast? How can it be? And why her?*

A throaty growl captured his attention. The animal caught his eye, then shifted its gaze to the parlor and back.

Is it hungry? He tossed it a slice of meat; it lay on the floor untouched.

"Sheriff! Pick it up," Louisa Penley scolded.

Ignoring her, he lapsed into a staring match with his furry tormenter. It snarled, baring its teeth.

"What's gotten into you?" Louisa scooped the ham into a napkin, scrubbed red-eye gravy off the floorboards, and marched to the kitchen.

The wolf never flinched.

Now alone, except for the ghostly visitant, Jason hesitated, then stood.

It charged.

Jason stumbled over his chair, pulling the cloth off the table with him. Plates half-filled with food clattered to the floor as the canine sprinted past him. Jason scrambled to his feet and hastened after it to the parlor.

Not finding the beast, he ran out the door and elbowed his way through gathered diners. Oblivious, they gazed en masse at an empty street while the dust settled around them. He looked for the creature and spotted it on the road ahead. The moment their eyes met, it sprinted toward his office and he bolted after it.

Tuck Stamper, bruised and favoring his right arm, met Jason halfway. "Don't know how he did it but Ferries busted out! Mob showed up. They took out after him but he got a head start."

"Which way'd they go?" Jason scanned the street both ways.

"Heard him take off that a'way." He pointed. "Making for Three Notch Road, I reckon. They aim to hang him if they catch him. You better hurry."

"Get Dan. He's at home. Tell him to meet me there. Fetch the doc. Make sure she brings her medical bag. Leave a message at the Commissioners' office and tell 'em what went on."

"Sheriff, it was the Commissioners who come after him. Them and a bunch of others."

"*Dammit!*" Jason mounted Ghost and prepared to leave.

"Wait—that som'bitch took my horse!" Tuck exclaimed.

"Borrow another one!" He spurred his stallion to action, galloping toward Three Notch.

The thrill of the hunt rushed through Ferries' veins. Breaking out of his cell had been too easy, and he understood why. The moment he

exited the jail, that gangly woman on horseback just ahead lured him, and he gave chase.

Anticipation sped up his breathing and culminated in a pleasant hardness between his thighs. Just ahead, at the split of three old Cherokee trails that gave the pathway its name, his quarry slowed her horse and appeared to hesitate, seeming unsure of which path to take. "I gotcha now, you little bitch."

The rider removed her hat, and swiveled her horse toward him, revealing her face. Her dark eyes met his with a defiant gleam, devoid of fear.

Above him, a high-pitched shrill filled the air. A shrieking woman dropped from the tree branch above, swinging from a rope and wearing worn Jeff Davis boots. Their hard leather soles blocked his line of sight, but he recognized them—and the owner of the shoes—as soon as they connected with his chin. On impact, his neck snapped, accompanied by a loud crack inside his head.

"Ben!" he cried before his brain went numb. Piercing pain needled down his vertebrae. Pitching backward off his saddle, Windrake Ferries hit the ground with a scudding thud and lay still.

A lynch mob, comprising the Board of Commissioners and others, gathered in surly silence at the feet of Ferries' inanimate body. His broken neck rested at an odd angle while sightless eyes, already clouded by death, gazed into the distance. Prior to stringing him up, his executioner had removed a center strip of the outlaw's patchy carrot-colored hair and scalp, leaving behind a blood-spotted white stripe, front to back, like that of a skunk.

Jason pulled Ghost to a halt. "You men were duty-bound to try this man in a fair court! Which one of you bastards scalped him?"

"It wasn't us, Sheriff, I swear," the board president growled. "Somebody got to him first. No loss, though. He's guilty of any crime you wanna mention. Rape, murder, arson, assault, thievery. You oughta want him dead more'n anybody."

"Forget what I want. There will be hell to pay when the newspapers grab aholt of this. Get outta here. Go home!"

One by one, the would-be lynchers departed, quiet at the back of death, leaving Jason and his nemesis alone together for the last time.

Jason stared at Ferries' purpled face in the gathering twilight. In death, he seemed smaller.

A twitch of regret sneaked into his psyche, and he shoved it away. *He burnt my home, gunned down my daddy, bludgeoned Nancy. Raped Mary, assaulted Sarah. Attempted to murder Johnny and Will. He murdered Ira Lovin—You can rest, Ira. It's over—Dammit, he deserved to die! Just not like this.* A trickle of remorse coursed through his body. *I failed again, didn't I? I shirked my sworn duty.* He considered his obligation to perform Ferries' execution. *It woulda been an ungodly spectacle.* "Thank the Lord for small favors," he said to no one.

Bone-weary, he slumped at the base of the hanging tree and listened to the lazy crick-crock of the lynching rope's slow-motion grind against the limb above. His thoughts drifted to the past, to a simple life when he lived close to the land. Familiar memories swelled his heart. *I used to teach school, over yonder. Back then, I was a just man.* He pondered the poverty wrought by the war, the petty thefts he committed to feed his household, and the guilt they inspired. He thought, with a twinge of shame, about the clandestine sense of freedom passing counterfeit money gave him.

I shoulda quit once I paid my debts. I didn't, even knowing it hurt people, knowing that one day there would be consequences to pay. Now I can't stop. I'm unfaithful to my wife. That's wrong. Still, Nancy accused me of abandoning her and our family. I don't see it like that. If only she coulda seen her way to forgiveness, things mighta been different between us. Maybe I wouldn't a strayed. Aramarinda's image formed in his mind. *Then again*—He considered the advantages he took in his role as sheriff, of the law, and of others. *If I hadn't a done it, somebody else woulda. That's how life is.*

Damnation, Jace, who do you think you're kidding?

For the first time in what-felt-like forever, he longed to be on top of his mountain, sitting on his prayer rock. Instead of here, with Ferries' lifeless body. He glanced at the man's remains, rotating in an unhurried arc. "I wonder, did the wretch have any family?"

A low, guttural moan caught his attention and he willed himself to look toward it. The wolf lounged a few feet away, tame as any dog, its intense golden orbs observing him in the coppery late afternoon haze.

A sudden panic seized him. He yanked his pistol from his holster and pointed it at the animal. "Go away! Git, or I'll shoot you."

Unalarmed, it rested its chin on its forepaws.

He tried to fathom the phenomenon of this ghost imposing its presence on him. *It is a ghost, isn't it? The diners at Penley's didn't notice it. Louisa Penley almost stepped on it. Sarah saw it, but not Mary. What does it mean?*

"What do you want from me?"

Swept with the feeling that somehow this creature dwelt within him, he felt killing it would be akin to killing a part of himself. He uncocked his gun and lowered it.

"I *was* a good man. You know that don't you?" *I'm explaining myself to a haint. Am I going mad*? "You're playing tricks on my mind. Stop it. Stop it, right now, you—wolf." He glanced toward the sound of approaching horses.

In a blink, the wolf disappeared. The Indian grass where it crouched, not even disturbed.

52

One Week Later

Reporters publicized the story of Windrake Ferries' lynching in newspapers across the Carolinas—*The Asheville Weekly Review, The Greensboro Press, The Highland Gazette*, and more. They painted a picture of Graham County as a lawless wilderness and condemned Sheriff Hyde for allowing mob rule.

"They hardly mention his crimes. Damned death-hunters." Disgusted, Jason tossed the newspaper in the trash and refilled his unwashed coffee mug, a housekeeping chore that went undone now that he made his home at the jail.

Mary's wagon pulled up in front. She pranced inside, Laura on her hip, accompanied by Will. "G'morning," she curtly said. "Didn't wanna leave without saying goodbye." She settled on the edge of the guest chair and refused to look him in the eyes.

"Doggy." The toddler pointed to Jason's daily companion, the white wolf, sitting in the corner.

"Beau's in Heaven." Mary jogged her on her knee to quiet her.

Will perched on Jason's desk. "I'm riding along. Promise I'll take care of 'em."

"Good. Thank you for coming, Mary-Fairybell." Jason's attempt to recall their former closeness fell flat. Mary wouldn't look at him. "I'm sorry you're cutting your visit short."

"Me too. At least that horrible man will never bother us again." Her chin held high, a shadow smile flitted across her face. "Tell me, what's going on between you and Mama? I wanna hear your side of it."

"I shoulda warned you, things at home been shaky."

Mary's eye-flash provoked Jason's guilt.

"I–I tried, I did, but I couldn't be the husband she wanted me to be. We married young, more'n twenty-five years ago. We grew up together—bonded in our youth. The war came along. Nothing's the same, you know that. But Nancy wanted everything to be like it was, including me. I couldn't—I've always loved her and still do. Just different now."

Mary bobbed her head. "Mama blames the war for the trouble between y'all nigh as she blames you. But it doesn't explain much."

"Yes, everything, and *everybody's*, different now, but that's no good excuse. I confess, I've strayed far from the straight path. I got a lot to atone for." He fidgeted with a pencil, staring at nothing. "It pains me when I think about it."

"Who's the woman Mama's running on about?" Will asked.

"Oh." A hint of heated shame crept up his neck. "You mean Aramarinda Hooper."

Mary gasped. "Enos Hooper's niece? She's not much older than me."

The taste of metal dried his tongue and he bit back an angry retort. "Age doesn't matter. First time I saw her, she was but a shy girl. She grew into a fine woman. I fell in love."

"So, this is not a passing fancy." Disapproval clouded Will's face.

"Aramarinda and Joshene are not amongst my regrets."

Mary's reproachful gaze met his. "Who is Joshene?"

"My daughter with her. She means as much to me as you, Will, and every one of my young'uns with your mama. Think how precious Laura is to you and you'll understand."

"You have children with this woman?" Mary yelped. Laura snapped her chin upward at her mother's outcry, then screwed her face into a whine. "Well, I *never*!" She sprang to her feet, and in a swift movement, boosted Laura onto her hip. The child squawked. "This is the last straw. Goodbye Daddy, I won't soon be coming back." She leveled an anguished scowl at him and marched to her wagon.

On his way home from school, eleven-year-old Ben Ferries—he insisted on Ben now, having outgrown his baby name, Benji—shuffled along the path to the Yorkville, South Carolina farmhouse where he lived with his mother and uncle. He fingered the Lutz marble in his pocket that he stole from a classmate earlier that afternoon. The smaller boy put up a fight to keep his prized possession, but Ben fought him and nabbed it for himself.

"Daddy'd be real proud," he said aloud.

Ben missed his father. He often recalled their afternoons together in the prison yard, and his tales of Mad Dog Ben Ferries. He remembered the advice he gave him. *The best revenge is revenge.* It played in his mind, like a repeating tune on his Uncle Caldwell's pianola.

The boy skipped into the kitchen and slung his books by the book strap onto the bench next to the door. "I'm home, Mama."

His mother sat hunched over the small breakfast table, elbows on the surface, forehead propped on her hands. Pages of the weekly newspaper lay scattered on the floor beside her. She straightened and extended her arms to him. Her eyes sparkled and her cheeks glowed. She seemed happier than usual. "Come here, Benji."

"Don't call me that!" He reached for the front page. Its headline blared:

YORKVILLE MAN, WINDRAKE FERRIES, SCALPED AND LYNCHED BY NORTH CAROLINA MOB

The words hit Ben with the force of a cannon, their image forever emblazoned in his mind. His heart plummeted to his toes. His back to his mother, he read the details, not fully comprehending, but he grasped enough: *They hung my daddy! Happened in Graham County, North Carolina, a mountain town fulla them no-good hill folk and Injuns that killed his friends.* In the second paragraph, he found the name of the man *held accountable*, whatever that meant, for his death: Sheriff Jason Hyde.

That's the one Daddy said killed Uncle Ben. Now him and his Injuns killed Daddy, too.

His father's words became clear: *revenge is the best revenge.* And revenge Ben Ferries vowed to get, no matter how long he had to wait. *Jason Hyde murdered my daddy.* Rage seeped into his veins, a poisonous seed passed from father to son, destined to invade the boy's every cell, where it would grow and thrive.

Lovin Residence, Fort Montgomery
October 1873

Joel Lovin called the impromptu officers' meeting to order. "Two days ago, a fella passed one of our bogus silver pieces at McFee's Tavern in payment for a whiskey. Pouncey noticed and questioned him. His name is Horace Pendergrass. Says he's from Operations and wants to meet. Burchfield never heard of him but wants us to be hospitable and learn more about him."

"I don't like it!" Jason ranted.

"Aw, come on," Jacob Rose protested.

"Jace's right to be suspicious," Adam Cable countered.

"Being sheriff done made you jumpy," Joel said. "Burchfield said—"

"More strangers lurk about town every day," Jason interrupted. "This Pendergrass is just the latest. We can't be too careful."

"I'm still the leader of this group," Joel snapped. "We'll meet him at Penley's, ask for proof of his identity, and feel him out."

The next day, the Graham County Counterfeiting Ring met in Penley's back room during the dinner hour, to take advantage of the clientele's preoccupation with the noonday meal. Pouncey introduced the visitor. Pendergrass greeted them, then sat near Joel and laid his briefcase on the desk.

"How do we know you're bonafide?" Joel asked, eyeing his bag.

"This should settle any doubts." Pendergrass passed him a membership card for the *Numismatic Association, Ohio Office*, with his moniker engraved on the front, together with two letters of introduction. The first was from Tom Ballard, an infamous figure in the counterfeiting business.

"You're friends with Tom Ballard?" Joel said. He handed the card to Jason, who studied it, his brows knit. "Impressive. Ballard's the best there is."

"I heard he moved to Canada," Cable said.

"He comes and goes," Pendergrass replied. "Ballard's reliable. Knows his trade."

"What's your interest here?" Joel pressed. "Must be important. The journey from the Ohio River Valley to the mountains of western North Carolina is arduous."

"Rest easy, sir, I am an emissary of good will. Operations sent me to check on our best *clubs*. You've been active for some time without interference from, er, bothersome factions." He slid his valise to Joel. "We congratulate you and wish you continued success."

Joel clicked the latches and raised the lid. The smell of fresh ink from newly minted bills filled the air. "We didn't order this."

"It's a gift from us to you for a job well done."

Joel frowned and nudged the case to Jason. "You've got a good eye." He opened the second letter. "This is from Burchfield."

Jason stopped thumbing through the bundles of fake money and leveled his eyes on Pendergrass while his partners exchanged glances. He slammed the briefcase shut and shunted it to Joel. "This crap wouldn't fool a coot."

Joel sneaked a hard look at Jason, then stood up. "Mr. Pendergrass, you must take us for fools. Did you think I wouldn't check with Burchfield before meeting with you? I dunno what your game is, but no way in hell are you who you say you are."

Jason slapped the table. "I knew it!"

"Sirs, you are mistaken!" The visitor's voice spiked an octave.

Jason reached for his handcuffs. "I got special accommodations for you at the jail."

Horace Pendergrass snatched his case and bolted.

"Grab him!" Jason ordered.

His partners sprang from their seats and tackled Pendergrass at the exit. Jason snapped shackles on his wrists amid the imposter's falsetto protestations. Joel threw open the door—Louisa Penley, caught eavesdropping, backed up against the opposite wall of the hallway.

"Right again, Jace," Joel muttered as Jason hustled Pendergrass past him.

"I just hope he's our only mistake."

Onacona met Jason in the street as he led his charge to jail. "Tuck told me where to find you. Come with me after you finish with this cracker. It's important."

A block away, on the balcony of McFee's Tavern, Coy Hawes sipped a beer, his feet resting on an empty chair seat. He gazed uptown at the group departing Penley's Boarding House: Lovin, Cable, Rose. *Where's Hyde?*

He sat up straight and cursed when he witnessed the sheriff leading his prisoner to the jailhouse. "Damn amateurs. I told 'em it wouldn't work." He wiped foam from his thick black mustache with a napkin and pulled a small journal from his jacket pocket. The man's knotted fingers gripped his pencil and scrawled, *16 October 1873. Meeting botched. Operation Graham County compromised. Must act now.*

"Yesterday I spotted a group of riders—about thirty, give or take—crossing the state line," Onacona said. He unwrapped his horse's reins from the hitching post outside the jailhouse. "They barreled through Poole's tollway. Refused to pay that crook one red cent." He smirked. "Serves him right."

"Where they headed?" Jason asked.

"Tracked 'em to the crossroads. At that point, half headed to Bryson City. Other half went to Yellow Creek. Follow me, I will show you."

Onacona escorted Jason to Lake Santeetlah, northeast of town. They dismounted at a deserted campsite south of Yellow Creek. Trampled grass and boot tracks around the ashes of a large campfire confirmed a party of men indeed stayed the night.

"You get a good look at 'em?" Jason asked.

"Government folk."

"How do you know?"

"Their clothes, their boots. Sounded like Yanks. All of 'em wore peculiar hats. Pale, with high crowns. They talked about you and your pals."

Jason's stomach knotted. *The dreams.*

"I recognized the leader."

"Who is it?"

"That Bible salesman from some years back. He came to our village. He's older but his face hair ain't changed—What was his name?"

Jason's breath caught in his chest. "Coy Hawes."

Libby noticed Jason's tension when he walked through the Lovins' door. She showed him to Joel's office, then listened to their conversation in the hallway.

"Hawes is back?" Joel barked. "This is bad, Jace. I'm calling an emergency session at Revival tomorrow, just the four of us. We'll figure out our next move. I'll notify Burchfield after we make a plan."

"Right," Jason said. "I'll tell Rose; you alert Cable." He turned on his heels and left.

Libby waited until she was sure Jason had gone, then confronted her uncle. "Uncle Joel, I've known about you and that counterfeiting ring for a long time. What you've been doing is wrong, but I turned a blind eye. You're in big trouble, now Hawes is back. He aims to take you in."

Joel gave her a steely look. "Libby, you eavesdropped? I'm surprised at you!"

"I'm glad I did! I must help you, if I can—I'm going with you tomorrow."

54

Cornwoman sensed trouble, and as the day progressed, the feeling grew stronger. Concerned, she relaxed on her bench in front of the fire, she meditated while smoking her pipe. Soon, she had her answer: Take a celestial journey to consult the spirits.

That afternoon, following the rituals developed by her forebears, she purified her body in Little Snowbird Creek, brushed aromatic oil through her hair, and braided it. She put on her white buckskin dress, fringed and decorated with flowing blue and yellow streamers, slipped on green-beaded moccasins, and painted her face with red symbols of protection.

Removing the formal feathered headdress from its storage trunk, she tried it on in front of her little wall mirror and admired the burst of wild turkey feathers sewn to the broad leather band. It had withstood well the hundred years since its creation. In the chest, under the headpiece, lay the ceremonial mantle—a heavy cloak made from the skin of a rare yellow-furred bear. She removed it with care and shook it out. Its rows of pebbles and shells woven into its fur clattered. The garment, handed down from her ancestors, held power she had yet to tap. *Will this be the time?* She set the cloak aside.

After sunset, amid dark rumblings overhead, she prepared a bonfire behind her cabin, kindled with embers from the sacred tribal fire that always burned within her home. Next, she brewed a pot of sacred tea, a recipe for divine insight passed through generations of elder healers.

She wrapped the mantle about her shoulders, donned the headdress, and lit a fresh smudge stick. She paraded around the bonfire and fanned the burning sage into the air with an eagle feather reserved for important occasions. After saying a prayer to open spiritual channels, she swallowed the drink and smashed the empty cup on the flaming logs, a final gesture.

Cornwoman was ready to release her soul to the universe.

She stepped to an ancient spirit dance learned as a child, whirling and hopping around the fire. She sang age-old Cherokee chants taught to her by her great-grandmother. Ghosts of time-honored warriors and healers celebrated with her, encouraging her spirit to join the cosmos. The essence of her being released, and she flew into the heavens.

The souls of her forebears appeared as a multitude of fireflies and clustered 'round her in the black of night, lifting her higher and higher into the ether. She journeyed beyond vermillion-red Mars and the radiant agate-slice of Jupiter, his many moons dancing around him like children. Saturn dazzled with her icy rings. A shower of stars spilled across the sky, shooting past her as she soared, their brilliant beauty fleeting in infinite inky darkness.

The golden giant Orion appeared on the tail of a comet, his belt glittering. A shimmering aurora lit the universe in his honor.

She extended her arms to him. "Mighty Hunter, patron to a favored son, I salute you. I need your help. Jason Hyde, a once virtuous man, has lost his way. The Fates have arrived and I fear his destiny is near. Tell me, how can I protect him?"

Orion set an arrow into his bow and aimed far beyond the North Star. It rained shards of fire as it streaked along its course, creating an illumined river. "*Greetings, esteemed Ama Cornwoman.*" The Hunter's voice resonated as a cosmic thunderclap. "*Jason's actions determined his path. However, your medicine is powerful. The answer you seek lies within you. Listen to your heart and trust its message. Go forth with confidence. Allow your tongue to speak our Creator's words as they form upon it. I will be there if you need me.*"

Cornwoman's journey was complete, and her *uwoduhi adanvto*—soul energy—plummeted to earth amidst a rush of splendorous light. Lying before the dancing campfire flames, she gazed at the stars, replaying her journey in her mind. Her eyelids grew heavy and once again, Jason's dreams played before her: Running hurry-scurry, he stumbled through a dream-maze, a hunted man…

Cornwoman opened her eyes to daylight and sat up next to the smoldering embers of her fire. "*Ha!*" She knew what she must do.

Peering skyward, she saw sunlight nearing the tree tops, and frowned. "The hour is late." She quickly smoothed her dress, rumpled from sleeping in it, straightened her headdress, and draped her ritual mantle over her shoulders. Without bothering with breakfast, she drove her old wagon to Aramarinda's cabin.

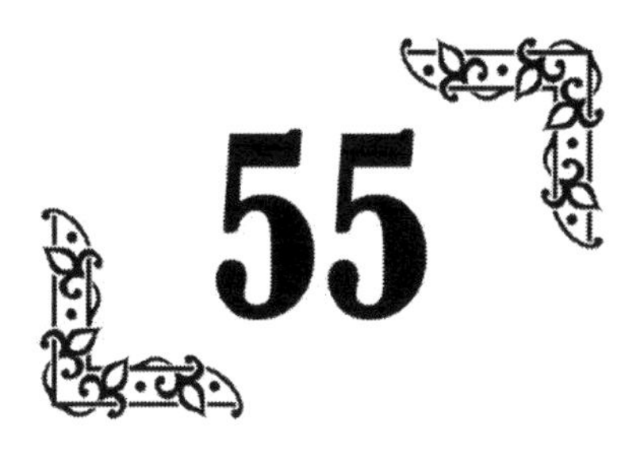

55

Jason buckled on his holster, and poured himself a mug of coffee, brows knit with concern. Revival Loan Association had a dilemma. The local market was flush with money, counterfeit or real—everyone who wanted money had it. Though the price of goods had inflated, the loan business lagged.

Tourists and carpetbaggers imported a significant portion of the Graham County Counterfeiting Ring's monthly take, with the rest gleaned from bootlegging sales, but not in sufficient quantities to prevent occasional cash flow deficits. The economic balance was off. Worse, they were almost broke.

What can we do?

"Mornin', boss." Tuck strutted through the entrance, with Dan not far behind.

"G'morning. Help yourselves to coffee." He did his best to sound casual as he laid out tasks for them. "Dan, I want you to patrol the highway to Bryson City and Yellow Creek."

"What am I watching for?"

"Anything odd. You see something, let me know."

Dan sipped his coffee, a puzzled frown clouding his face.

"Tuck, keep an eye on things. I've got a meeting at Revival. If you need me, come get me."

An autumn sky framed the surrounding mountains above the storefronts of the bustling town, while a distant haze over their peaks cautioned an afternoon shower.

The hands on the tower clock tapped a minute closer to twelve noon. Cornwoman arrived with Aramarinda at her side, the pebbles woven into her bearskin cloak rattling as loud as her wagon. She parked in front of King and Cooper's General Store and scoured the area: At either end, Main Street parted into a hodgepodge of pathways. Some led into the mountains, others swept downhill into Cheoah Valley, a haphazard tangle of civilization. She widened her eyes. *It's the maze!*

Down the street from Penley's Boarding House, she saw Libby loitering near the Revival office. She clutched what seemed to be a weighty object inside her skirt folds. Outside Walker's Mercantile, a few local men played a game of checkers while a row of strangers wearing identical buff-colored hats rocked nearby on the covered porch. The store's large window mirrored their images.

One, two, three, four. The clock struck the hours in sonorous methodical cadence. The cookware monger Cornwoman had seen at the Harvest Festival rounded the corner in his rattletrap cart and parked near the center of town. From the other direction, the driver of the snake-oil wagon, also from the Festival, pulled up outside McFee's Tavern, at the far end, across from the Revival Loan office.

Five, six, seven, eight. She observed the visitors outside Walker's store check their watches. One scratched a note into a pocket-sized journal. They seemed out of place, yet familiar. Reflected sunlight on the glass behind them momentarily blinded her, and when it did, her dreams transposed against the spotless window, and she knew—her nocturnal visions had foretold their arrival.

Nine, ten, eleven, twelve.

The cookware salesman approached Libby with a frying pan.

"Go away! I don't need any blasted pans." Her angry words carried above the even chimes of the clocktower as the hawker harassed her. She whipped her revolver from her skirt folds and aimed at him. "Back off!"

He swiftly knocked the weapon from her grip, tossed the pan to the side, and grabbed her, then dragged her, screeching and flailing, to his transport. He shoved her inside, and locked the door.

Cornwoman and Aramarinda exchanged wary glances.

Several Fort Montgomery neighbors came running. Tuck Stamper bolted from the jailhouse, hurrying to Libby's aid.

"Hey, waddya you doing?" A checkers player confronted the pushy peddler, and a fracas ensued.

The strangers roused to action. Three men bounded from their rockers and sprinted to the kerfuffle. One grabbed the checkers player and held him; the others assisted the peddler with Tuck. Amid clattering cookware, they shoved both the young deputy and the good citizen inside the conveyance with Libby. Her other would-be rescuers fled. Two men crossed the road to Penley's Boarding House, while another strolled to the jail.

The snake-oil salesman moved his cart near the panhandler's vehicle, climbed down, and threw open the back.

A rumble of hooves grew closer. In a dust cloud, a rabble of men, badges gleaming on their shirt fronts, thundered into town. Leading them, a man with a bushy black mustache and wearing a high-crowned buff-colored hat—Coy Hawes.

Local folks on the street ran for cover.

Hawes reined his horse to a stop and looked around. McFee's Tavern doors flew open. Its patrons spilled out and scattered. Darvis Pouncey marched out holding a gun to the backs of ring members, Julius Bradshaw and Henry Ditman, their arms held high above their heads. Hawes flicked his eyes at Pouncey and nodded before a commotion up the street diverted his attention.

The two strangers who had entered Penley's Boarding House escorted Louisa Penley onto the boarding house porch. They now sported shiny badges on their shirts, identifying them as federal agents. She almost lost her balance, then regained her composure.

"Don't touch me!" she huffed. "I dunno who you're looking for! Find 'em yourself."

Across the street at the jail, Horace Pendergrass appeared in the doorway. He grin-squinted into the noonday light, adjusted his wire-rimmed glasses, and hot-footed it to fall into step with his liberator, who also wore a badge. Together they ambled up the street with the other federal agents, Louisa in tow, and joined the group rallying ’round the pan wagon.

Hawes heard banging from inside the wagon. A familiar voice shouted, “Let us out of here!” He guffawed and dismounted his horse, then strolled to the source of the racket and slapped the side.

“Would that be Miz Thorne-in-my-side? Whatcha doing, outfittin’ your kitchen?”

“Hawes! Get me outta here, you devil.”

“In good time, Miz Thorne. Do you, by chance, know where I can find Jason Hyde?”

“No. Now open the dang door.”

Hawes turned on his heels and strode back to his men. “Where are they?”

“You said they’d be at Penley’s,” one of the agents barked.

“Well, they’re here somewhere. Search every building in this cussed burg, if you have to.”

Dan galloped into town and halted next to Cornwoman’s wagon. “What’s going on?”

“They arrested Miz Penley and a couple of others. Now they are looking for Jason. You can do nothing here, Daniel. Go let Miz Nancy know he is in trouble.”

After the deputy departed for the Hyde residence, Cornwoman gathered the reins and, with a hey-ah to the mule, repositioned her vehicle closer to the action.

Inside Revival Loan, Jason’s nightmare unfolded before him. Outside, in full view, his handcuffed partners presented a harbinger of what lay ahead. The Graham County Counterfeiting Ring had seen its day. “They’ve come for us.”

“It can’t be,” Jacob Rose insisted.

“Can and is.” Jason gulped air and willed his racing heart to slow down.

“We got about eight hundred in cash,” Joel said. “We’ll divide it between us, separate, and lie low for a while.”

“Before we skedaddle, let’s take out as many of ’em as we can,” Cable growled.

"You crazy? We won't last five minutes against trained shooters." Rose opened the safe and scooped out the bills. He made four equal stacks and pocketed one. "Your cuts are here. Do what you want, I'm gone." He scurried to the back exit.

"Don't be stupid!" Joel snapped. "They're waiting for us out back."

"You suggest we stay here until they break down the door?" Rose retorted.

"No. Help me block it."

While the others shoved a heavy table against the front exit and piled chairs on top, Jason barricaded the rear. The fortification in place, Cable grabbed his pistol and shot through the entry door's opaque glass.

They dropped to the floor amidst a barrage of return fire.

"Now look what you did!" Jason barked from all fours. "Listen, Will Thomas told me more'n once about this town's Cheoah Trading Post days. Long before the Removal in '38, the Snowbirds built many of the original stores with hidden exits. The day the militia came to take 'em prisoner, Will created a distraction and his Cherokee friends escaped to safety. This place is pretty old. Grab a lantern and follow me." He crawled to the cellar door.

"Y'all go. I'll cover you," Cable said. He exchanged volleys with the Secret Service detail.

Jason led the other men to the basement, lanterns in hand. At the bottom of the stairs, Joel brushed cobwebs out of his face. Stacks of ancient crates lay scattered about, long forgotten. A tall filing cabinet leaned against one wall.

"Nobody's been down here in donkey's years." Jason ran his hands over the cool walls and stopped at the cabinet. "Joel, help me move this." Their effort revealed a low doorway. Jason tugged the rusty hand-cut nails securing the old latch. They squeaked, and slipped from half-rotted wood trim. He swung the door open. Joel held a light while the others peered inside.

The cool smell of earthy loam quieted Jason's nerves.

Steep stone steps led from the small opening into darkness blacker than pitch. Moving with care, Joel descended, lantern in hand. "It's a hallway. Looks sound. I'm game."

Cable clattered down the treads from the first floor, holding a bloodied arm. Behind him, heavy pounding spurred a sense of urgency.

"You're shot?" Jason said.

"A scratch. Nothing more."

"We better get. No other choice," Rose groused.

Jason ushered Cable and Rose into the cavern. He hesitated. *Do I have a choice?*

He watched the wolf descend the stairs from above. At the bottom, they locked eyes.

Do the right thing, echoed through his mind.

"Come on, Jace!" Joel shouted from below. "We're waiting on you."

"Go on, I'll catch up."

Upstairs, the clamor threatened.

Do the right thing! rang louder, more urgent this time.

"Suit yourself," Rose called, his voice muffled by distance. Lantern-glow and footsteps melted into the cavernous blackness.

"It's the end of the road, wolf. Maybe not for them, down there, but for me, it is." Despondent, he followed the animal up the steps. His shoulders sagging, he scuffled to the front of the building.

A man peered through the entrance. "I see one of 'em!"

"Don't shoot, I'm coming out!" Jason hollered the words again, louder.

"Jace, what're you doing?" Joel's voice rang out from behind him.

"Turning myself in."

Joel's footfalls hurried toward him. Reaching Jason's side, he grasped his arm. "I'm going with you. We had a good run, didn't we, my friend?"

"Here they come!" Rifles and pistols readied.

The two men crossed the threshold, their hands and chins held high, and stood still. Trembling from fingertips to toes, heart racing, Jason shut his eyes.

"We surrender!" he declared.

56

"Hold your fire!" Hawes commanded.

Hands dragged Joel from his side, and Jason's world transformed. An iron grip seized his arms, jerked them behind his back, and snapped handcuffs on his wrists.

Steely-eyed Secret Service agents, a stony, immovable force, stood before him; beyond them stood a throng of onlookers and curiosity seekers. Many were friends he grew up with; others, folks he knew from church. Dan Taylor, Tom Cooper, Wendell Reese, and more. Their combined expressions reflected sympathy and concern, mistrust, gloom, judgment, outrage.

He searched for Onacona amongst them, relieved he did not see him.

This is a bad dream. I'll wake up soon.

The breeze shifted. Dazed, he lifted his eyes and sniffed the air. *Rain's coming.*

His family arrived on their buckboard, sullen disbelief etched into their faces. Nancy parked their wagon near Cornwoman's, glowered at Aramarinda, then clambered down from the bench.

Bradshaw and Ditman stood aside, handcuffed next to Louisa Penley, all of them appearing at once anxious, frightened, and angry. What sounded like Libby Thorne and Tuck emanated from the peddler's cart he'd seen about town—*Locked up, why?*—Horace Pendergrass lounged against it, gabbing with its driver and the traitorous bartender, Darvis Pouncey.

Pouncey, our first mistake. "You weasel!" Jason balled his fists and charged. A vice-grip held him in place.

The barkeep broke into a churlish grin.

Coy Hawes fixed himself before Jason with a smirk lining his face. "Jason Hyde, High Sheriff of Graham County, by authority of the United States Treasury Department, you are under arrest for distributing counterfeit. You bastard, I've long been waiting to say those words." He backhanded him and shoved him to his knees.

At the back of the throng, Aramarinda yelped, scrambled out of the wagon, and plunged through the crowd.

Reeling, Jason licked fresh blood from his lip, its sweet metallic flavor startling his tastebuds. His shame intensified.

Thunder rumbled over the mountains in dramatic punctuation.

Nancy broke from the crush of bystanders and lunged at Hawes, fury unleashed. She swung her fist at his midsection, her slug rewarded with a surprised eruption of air from his gaping mouth.

"Keep your stinking hands off my husband. I never liked you, you—Bible salesman."

Jason opened his lips to speak.

"Not one word!" Nancy snapped. "I got no pity for you, Jason Hyde." She shook an angry finger at him. "After all you put us through, you deserve what's coming to you, you two-timing, no-account swine."

A tickling rain, fine as feathers, pecked at his head from a darkened sky, its mist on his eyelashes, fleeting hope.

"I know you don't believe me, but I do love you," Jason said. "I love you all. Sarah, Johnny, Lucy, Nannie, Newt. I did it for you. For Mary and Will, and Janie, too. To give you a better life. What they're accusing me of, I did. It was wrong. I'll pay for my mistakes.

"My intentions were good. I wanted to help our town. And then I couldn't stop. I betrayed your trust. Please forgive me. I'm sorry."

"You're *sorry*?" Nancy shrieked. "What about me? What about the trouble you brung on your family? Sorry don't cut it, Jace. Some hurt you can't undo."

"Oh, Daddy," Sarah wailed, and collapsed into heartfelt sobs.

"Listen, y'all," Birdy Blevins declared, "we didn't have nothing after the war ended. Remember those days? Jace and 'em pulled us up by the bootstraps. Him and his friends put roofs over our heads. Even now, they lend us a hand when we're down. If it weren't for Jace Hyde, and all the rest, most of us crackers would be without a bean to our name. These men deserve our thanks."

"Hush your mouth, Birdy Blevins!" Nancy snarled. "He deserves to go to jail. They all do. Counterfeiting's akin to thieving and lying in the same breath." She glared at Jason. "You betcha you was wrong! And you, the sheriff. What a fine example you set. *Bah*! I hope you rot in prison."

Her tears mingled with mizzling pitter-pat from above. She swiped at the raindrops streaming into her eyes and spun around, bumping full on into Aramarinda. "Som'*bitch*!" she squawked, and propelled into the crowd.

Aramarinda staggered across the clearing, sank to her knees, and with the hem of her cloak, dabbed at the rust-colored rivulets on Jason's bloodied face. She cupped his cheeks in her hands. "Listen to me. Whatever you need, I'll do it. I cherish you. Josie does, too. We'll be here, waiting for you."

"Minda…" Jason's words stuck in his throat. His tender gaze conveyed his love.

Hawes yanked him to his feet. "Time to go. I'm letting your wife off easy. Seems she got plenty reason to be pissed." He leered at Aramarinda. "Missy, you get on back where you came from."

Jason peered once more at his offspring's pained faces staring from beneath oil-cloth coverings. His heart, marred by regret, ached for their sorrow. Though stained by his actions, and tarnished by disgrace, his love for them was impossible to deny.

Cable and Rose, scowling, handcuffed, and prodded forward by four agents, stumbled into place with the others.

"Looky who we found sneaking out the back way," one agent scoffed. He untied two sacks from his gun belt and tossed them to his boss. "Took these off 'em."

Hawes caught them and looked inside. "My stars, if it ain't a coupla money bags." His sneer spread wider before he turned to his men. "Release our detainees from the peddler wagon."

"Well, big man, you nabbed us. Where you taking us?" Jason muttered.

"For now, Bryson City jail. After that, we'll transport you and the Burchfield gang to Asheville. They'll try you and sentence you— You're going to prison for a long, long time, former High Sheriff of Graham County." He snorted, his puffery bordering on contempt.

Libby, now free, marched up to Hawes. "You don't give up, do you? I thought you hated this place."

"I got one reason for being here." He motioned to his prisoners. "Tell me you didn't know about this."

She shrugged. "My uncle doesn't confide in me."

"Your uncle?"

"Joel Lovin. Didn't you know?"

Veins of light stroked the heavens in rapid succession.

Hawes pulled a face. "So, that's why you bowed off the case. Well, nothing's keeping you here. Come back north, Miz Thorne. There's opportunities for sharp ladies like yourself."

She folded her arms. "I love this land. These are good people. Guess you wouldn't understand." She cocked her head. "I belong here—don't fit anywhere else."

Hawes growled. "These *good people* here, they broke the laws of this country. They're gonna pay their due." He jerked Jason's arm. "Come on, Hyde. Your new home is waiting."

Chords of thunder underscored his words. The wind, sweeping from west and north, whipped the gathering, prompting a few faint-hearted souls to scamper for cover. Most did not budge an inch.

"My home? My home is with my people," Jason replied. "You didn't change a thing today, Mr. Government-man, though you may think you did. These folks will be here long after you leave. They, like the Snowbird Mountains, will remain. Nothin' gonna bring 'em down. Them *or* me."

The sky opened. Sideways rain and lunging currents barreled about the tree branches and unloosed the sign over Walker's Mercantile. It crashed to the ground and pitch-poled end over end before settling into the mud.

The crowd parted and Cornwoman strode into the clearing. With each determined step, her ceremonial robe shimmied and rattled in concert with the watery din, while her feathered headpiece bobbed, its long, wind-whipped fringe undulating like Medusa's snakes. The medicine woman's formidable spirit matched heaven's ire.

"Let go of that man," she commanded.

Her black eyes dashed any intention Hawes may have had of noncompliance. Mute, he released his grip on Jason and took a step backward.

Cornwoman's intense scrutiny bore deep into Jason's psyche.

He wanted to look away. He could not.

She lay a gentle hand over his heart. Her palm emanated raw power, its radiant warmth spread from her five digits and shrouded him. Uplifted, his soul swelled with hope and opened to the possibility of renewal.

"Be aware, Jason Hyde," she said, her voice soft but firm, "what comes next is of your own making. My son, you are a man of many faces, moving down a hundred separate paths, pieces of yourself lost to life's misfortunes. Use the time ahead to find yourself. Beg forgiveness of the Creator. If your heart is true, He will grant you redemption."

Jason wrenched his gaze from hers, for a moment engrossed in the multitude of single raindrops. He became one with their descent, feeling his own life crash and dissolve into the muck.

This can't be real, yet it is so. Real as death on a battlefield. Real as holding a newborn babe in one's arms. I am done for. Death and rebirth are all that's left. He sighed. *Can I become the man I was? Can the Lord turn back time?* "Ama—" He raised his eyes.

Gone.

In her place, his companion, the wolf, commanded his attention, its piercing eyes striking against the gloom. For once, he welcomed its presence. *I'll miss you.*

No, you won't, it responded. *I* am *you.*

The animal crouched and took two long strides. A blinding flash struck the ground with a deafening crack. In that moment, Jason recognized the beast for what it was: this noble creature, this white wolf, pure in spirit, loyal, and strong, embodied the better part of himself.

It lunged.

The wolf and Jason became one.

57

Buncombe County Courthouse, Asheville, North Carolina
November 1873

How much do they know? Jason wondered.

He discovered the prosecuting attorneys knew everything he wished to hide. Day after day, he endured the scrutiny of his most private affairs. From counterfeiting, to clandestine deals with bootleggers, to law-bending attempts to help his friends slide through tough times. Journalists representing newspapers across the South, and as far away as New York City, scribbled double-time. Charcoal sticks screaked against paper pads as courtroom artists rendered his likeness. The case against him deepened while criticism for his spurious actions over the course of a dozen years grew more intense. Daily, a hundred pairs of hate-filled eyes would draw and quarter him, filet his innards, then skewer him upon shafts of public judgment, their condemnation worse than any prison sentence. His one salvation, Aramarinda's faithful, enduring presence at the back of the courtroom, her unwavering trust and steadfast affection for him written across her face.

At the end of the longest week of his life, while he awaited the court's ruling, a guard shoved a small package toward him through the iron bars of his holding cell. "From the young lady. She comes ever' day and begs to see ya. Ain't supposed to, but I told her if she could write, I'd let her pass ya a note. Here, take it."

Inside the coarse brown paper, he found a Bible. Between its pages, the small carved wooden cross Aramarinda wore about her neck, and a message:

Dearest Jason,

Keep this holy cross, a token of my love for the Lord, as evidence of my devotion to you. I hope you find the answers you seek and peace for your soul within the pages of His Book. May His words guide you through your present darkness.

Come back to us soon.

Love Always,

Aramarinda

Jason Hyde's fall from grace was twelve years coming. It began with an honest man's despair in the face of poverty. An invitation to satisfy his every dream. The thrill of unexpected good fortune, a stranger's charity for a favor borne of trust.

His descent to ruin hit bottom in the state pen, in Albany, New York. The court convicted him of passing and dealing in counterfeit, fined him $1,000—an enormous sum—and sentenced him to two years' hard labor.

Cornwoman's cabin, Snowbird Mountain
October 1874

While Hawes made his arrests, Secret Service agents busted counterfeiting rings in South Carolina and Georgia, from Alabama to Texas, and Virginia to Missouri. Working together, the government closed the door on the entire operation.

After the excitement, life seemed quiet and slow. Cornwoman followed the trial in newspaper reports, and shook her head sadly as Jason's secrets were made public. He had been hand-in-glove with robbers and bootleggers while he was sheriff, and accepted bribes as a substitute for payment of debts. He and his pals even formed an illegal bank. It seemed to her his shameful behavior had no limit. She often contemplated the events leading to Jason's dishonor. Did Chance, Orion's Destiny, or Divine Will lead him to misguided judgments? Whatever the reason, she knew his way home would be long.

To everyone's surprise, a year to the day after the lawmen hauled Jason away, he and Joel Lovin rode into town as free men, pardoned by President U.S. Grant.

Soon after their return, she invited her prodigal son to share a pipeful of tobacco.

"Jason, you look well. Come, sit."

He removed his jacket and settled himself on her bench.

"How did you get out so fast?"

He flashed a quick smile. "I wrote to Zeb Vance."

"The North Carolina governor?"

"One and same."

"But?"

"He owed me. Seems Governor Vance wrote to President Grant, and here I am. Been a lotta changes here. I left Fort Montgomery only a year ago—now, it's called Robbinsville."

Cornwoman chuckled. "Nothing to do with you, though you called plenty of attention to us, for better and for worse." She paused. "What is it like up there?"

"Come walk with me and I'll tell you."

Cornwoman thought she knew every inch of these mountains, but never saw the view from the top of that one. The climb took hours. At last they settled under an ancient dogwood tree on a rockledge overlooking the Nantahala Forest. Before them, golden shafts pierced a lavender mist and drenched evergreen and russet peaks and valleys in its glory, as if the Great Creator Himself held a brush to Heaven and Earth.

Breathing hard, she sat on a cairn, her knees too old to sit cross-legged. After tamping tobacco into her pipe, she lit it, shielding the flame from the wind. "Now, let's talk."

Jason's expression was solemn. "We passed through big cities on our way north—Richmond, Philadelphia, New York. Ama, the hustle and bustle up there boggles the mind! The Albany prison looks like a storybook castle on the outside, with trees and grass, and winding paths around it. They taught us a trade. I learnt to make shoes. Living here is harder."

She threw him a blistering glance.

"Don't misunderstand me. A prison is a prison. I won't go back. A fella can't put a price on freedom. I met Tom Ballard, the famous counterfeiter. He said he heard about us."

"You speak lightly of a grave affair. What are you not telling me?"

"You know me too well." He let out a long, slow breath. "Soon after arriving, I fell into darkness. It happened during the war, but this was worse, far worse. One afternoon, I sat in the exercise yard, consumed with misery. A light snow fell around me, but I hardly noticed. I had lost everything. My family. My friends. Even Joel seemed distant. I wanted to die." He looked up. "In my darkest hour, Aramarinda came to me."

"Yes. She journeyed north to see you."

He nodded once and lowered his eyelids. "I sat in the yard facing the same dreary wall that filled my consciousness every day. She sat next to me, but no words passed between us. She took my hand, her skin against mine felt like heaven. Soft and warm, her touch tender. She smelled of herbs and a fresh breeze." Jason sighed. "I remember it well. We continued silent for a time. My tears spilt over my brims. Ran down my cheeks. My shame became unbearable and I threw myself at her feet, clutched her ankles, and wept.

"She jumped up, trembling, but in her eyes, I saw a light. The light of happiness, of understanding. The light of infinite love. She reached out to me." Jason brushed a stray tear from his eye. "I struggled to stand. We clung to each other, two lonely souls bonded as one. At that moment, I felt the dawn of renewal, and knew my future with her would be a complete resurrection. Ama, I was risen.

"That night in my cell, I pulled that Gospel she gave me in Asheville from under my pillow. I hadn't cracked it once before then."

Cornwoman sensed peace surround him. "Did you ask your Creator for mercy?"

Jason looked at her. "I thought about where I'd been and what lay ahead. Sometimes I was sure destiny had cursed me. I prayed a lot. And yes, I asked mercy for my wrongs, especially to those I hurt. The Good Lord forgave me."

"The Creator knows what is in your heart. Tell me what you learnt."

"Well now." He rested his elbows on his knees. "My education began with the war. Laying aside the horror, it opened my eyes. To loving one's brother, to the meaning of humanity, what it means to be honorable. Those long nights in jail, I studied on all three. Love, humanity, and honor.

"My first loves, I locked inside a box. A hawk's tail feather. Bits of colored stones. Love letters from Nancy." His expression became serious. "But genuine love is alive. It craves the Lord's light. Ebbs and flows like the tide.

"When my family was starving, I did everything I could for them. On the battlefield, I risked my life for my buddies. Right or wrong, my love for all of 'em outweighed my fear. I knew God then."

They watched a hawk windsurf on a breeze.

"By *humanity*, do you mean human kindness?"

"Kind heartedness, compassion, both," Jason said. "In the war I experienced little of it, but when it showed itself, I felt His presence." A smile hinted, then disappeared. "Honor, now that's something else."

"We Cherokees consider honor to be a mark of a civilized man."

"I agree. Honor slid from my fingers the day I stooped to running counterfeit. I had two options. Smarten up, or die a miserable excuse for a man. Aramarinda's constant faith in me led to my rebirth."

Jason faced the mountains, his arms wide. "Sometimes home is not a place but a truth you feel in your heart. Out there, that's my true home. It represents all that is decent and beautiful." He inhaled the chill eventide. "God is everywhere. It took jail, the love of a woman, and a ghost to show me He lived in my heart all the time."

Cornwoman's rapt attention had allowed her pipe to go out. She struck a match and cupped her palm around the bowl. A few sharp breaths, and the tobacco's peppery flavor filtered to her tastebuds. She smiled the smile a mother gives her son when he learns a hard lesson. "Ghost? I wondered if you would bring up the wolf."

"You saw it, too?"

"Of course. The wolf is a worthy creature, one of the Creator's best designs. It represented that best piece of you—virtue—about to separate from your soul. You almost lost it."

The glint of understanding shined in Jason's eyes. "Wanna know what haunts me still? Who killed Windrake Ferries?"

"*Ha!* I almost forgot. Gotta letter for you." She reached into her tunic and handed him an envelope addressed to *Daddy*. It felt bulky, as if it contained more than paper. "Mary asked me to give this to you when I saw you next."

"She came back?"

"After she learnt of your arrest, she came to stay with her mama a while. In time, she called on me."

"I see." Sadness deepened the creases of his face. He broke open the seal and tipped the envelope. An unmistakable, carroty thatch of hair and dried scalp slid into his palm. "This belonged to Ferries." Slack jawed, he stared at it, then read her note:

> *Dear Daddy,*
>
> *If you are reading this, you did your time. I pray you have seen your way back to the path of goodness. I pray also that He forgives my sin of complicit murder. All the same, no regrets. No man deserved death more than Ferries. Cornwoman can explain everything.*
>
> *Your Loving Daughter,*
>
> *Mary*

"*Complicit murder?* Impossible!"

"We are discussing Windrake Ferries." Cornwoman watched his expression as Mary's confession sank in. "Our plan was simple, really."

"Your plan. With my daughters?"

"And Doc. That afternoon, after Ferries attacked Mary and Sarah, you jailed him. Later, Martha inspected his wounds, remember?"

"When Doc arrived, he was stirring. I stood guard, worried he'd hurt her."

"You need not have concerned yourself. She slipped him a potion to put him under a couple hours more. We needed time to set up our trickery."

"But I saw her lock the door when she finished."

"She did not set the bolt."

Jason frowned. "Why not?"

"To control his getaway. After Ferries woke up, we figured it would not take long for him to discover the unbolted lock. Meantime, Mary waited outside, mounted, and ready for a chase."

"No!"

"When he came outta the jail, she guided him to Three Notch Road. There, Sarah, Martha, and me, we watched for them at a place with sturdy limbs hanging low from the overhead canopy."

"The lynching tree. The path is hardly wide enough for two wagons to pass."

Cornwoman pictured it in her mind, as if it happened yesterday. "Sarah shimmied to a stout limb hanging over the road and tied a sturdy swinging rope. We heard 'em coming. Martha called to Sarah from her hiding place, *you ready?*

"*Never more so*, Sarah answered. I watched her give her rope a healthy yank."

"Sarah up a tree," Jason interjected. "That girl will never grow up."

"Mary rode our way lickety-split. I feared for her. Feared for all of us. I braced myself and unsheathed my knife, ready to use it, need be.

"Ferries tailed not far behind. Mary slowed at the trail forks and angled 'round to look at him. His attention on her, Sarah leapt, swooping from overhead. Her boot heels caught his chin. His neck snapped and he shot backward off his horse. *Whump!*" She smacked her palms together. "He landed hard. Dead. Your daughters rubbed him out."

"Dang. Mary, Sarah. Doc," his eyes swung to meet Cornwoman's, "and you. Of all the harebrained, tomfool ideas. He coulda killed 'em! All of you!"

"Not if they kilt him first. There is order to the world though it is sometimes hard to find."

"Who scalped him?"

"Mary earned a trophy. I lent her my knife. For safe measure, we lynched him. Took all of us to hoist him up. Heavy varmint."

"My daughters got more gumption than I do." Jason's concern morphed into astonishment and evolved into a full belly laugh that echoed across the canyon. Finally, having made peace with the past, he gazed into the twilight.

"Something else is on my mind."

"What is it, my son?"

"That box I told you about earlier. It's buried in a special place." His eyes rested on the medicine woman. "You're sitting on it. But I didn't tell you everything."

Her hand brushed the smooth stones beneath her. "What do you mean?"

"I never trusted that safe at Revival. I laid by a fortune in legit banknotes and silver. It's just waiting for some fool to find it. Maybe a fool like me, who thinks he can change people's lives."

"You made change where it counted. Saved lives after Buffalo burnt. Helped fix up the town. Because of you bringing that Hawes fella down here, federals rounded up more Ku Kluxer's, including Hugh Dockery. After that, Miz Libby went on up to Washington and found her true place. Miz Evie told me Hawes got her on a fancy committee working for ladies' suffrage. You did good."

"Maybe." He flattened his lips. Tender affection smoothed his creased brow a moment later. "But I can say this, for a fact: now, my love for Aramarinda runs deeper and stronger than ever before. God made that possible."

Jason's redemption would not come lightly. Nancy's health declined into an illness she vowed he brought about. Filled with bitterness, she suffered two long years after his release from prison, turned their children against him, and made his life difficult any way she could.

After her death, the day the customary mourning period expired, Jason Hyde married Aramarinda Hooper. Six weeks later, Cornwoman delivered their second child, a beautiful baby girl. They named her Etta.

Characters

Jason Hyde	Farmer, schoolteacher, CSA Lieutenant, counterfeiter
Nancy Hyde	Jason's wife
Mary, Sarah, Will, Johnny,	Hyde children (by birth order)
	Janie, Lucy, Newt, Nannie
John Aaron Hyde	Jason's father
Cornwoman	Medicine woman, Snowbird Cherokee tribe
Joel Lovin	Counterfeiter, posse member
Evie Lovin	Joel Lovin's wife
Ira Lovin	Lovin's nephew
Adam Cable	Counterfeiter
Jacob Rose	Counterfeiter
Louisa Penley	Counterfeiter, Penley's Boarding House owner
Onacona	CSA soldier, Cherokee brave, posse member
Dan Taylor	Leader of Taylor's Raiders, Jason's friend
Tom Cooper	Store owner, posse member
Olly Oliver	Trapper
Martha Taylor	Medical practitioner
Colonel Will Thomas	Cherokee Chief, leader of Thomas's Legion of Cherokee Indians and Highlanders
Pvt. Green Longfeather	CSA soldier, Cherokee brave, posse member
Pvt. Standing Bear	CSA soldier, Cherokee brave, posse member
Libby Thorne	Pinkerton's detective
Coy Hawes	Pinkerton's detective, Secret Service agent
Aramarinda Hooper	Jason's love interest
Windrake Ferries	Outlaw, Jason's nemesis
Lt. Colonel Wm Walker, CSA	Commander, Thomas Legion
Lt. Colonel Love, CSA	Commander, Thomas Legion
Lt. Colonel McKamy, CSA	Commander, Thomas Legion, Battle of Piedmont, VA, 1864
General Jubal Early, CSA	Commanding officer, Raid on Washington, D.C. 1864
Allan Pinkerton	Pinkerton's Detective Agency
President Abraham Lincoln	United States President
Lieutenant Colonel Smith, CSA	Commander, Warm Springs, NC
General James Martin, CSA	Commander, White Sulphur Springs, NC
Colonel Bartlett, USA	Surrender at White Sulphur Springs, NC
Nate LeFevre	Smuggler and Bagatelle Plantation owner
Hetty LeFevre	Nate's wife
Judge Dubose	Judge
Levi Ruben	Prosecuting Attorney
Harlan Davis	Defense Attorney

About the Author

C. S. Devereaux's love for the history of ordinary people grew out of listening to her grandmothers tell about their lives. An artist-turned-writer, she studied people throughout her life. She has published essays in *The Sun* magazine, short stories in the *Chattanooga Writers' Guild Anthologies*, and has a short story in the *Realms of the Fantastic* fantasy anthology from Jumpmaster Press. Her previous novels include memoirs, *Another Adventure*, and *Idelle*. C. S. Devereaux lives in Chattanooga, Tennessee with her husband Tom, Zoe-cat, and Ninja-dog. Learn more at www.csdevereaux.com.